ONE
Summer
AT THE BEACH

NATALIE ANDERSON **MELISSA McLONE** **EMILY FORBES**

ONE
Summer
COLLECTION

June 2016

July 2016

July 2016

August 2016

August 2016

September 2016

ONE Summer AT THE BEACH

NATALIE
ANDERSON

MELISSA
McLONE

EMILY
FORBES

MILLS & BOON

First Published in Great Britain 2016
By Mills & Boon, an imprint of HarperCollins*Publishers*
1 London Bridge Street, London, SE1 9GF

ONE SUMMER AT THE BEACH © 2016 Harlequin Books S.A.

Pleasured by the Secret Millionaire © 2008 Natalie Anderson
Not-So-Perfect Princess © 2011 Melissa Martinez McClone
Wedding at Pelican Beach © 2007 Emily Forbes

ISBN: 978-0-263-92235-6

09-0916

Our policy is to use papers that are natural, renewable and recyclable products and made from wood grown in sustainable forests.
The logging and manufacturing processes conform to the legal environmental regulations of the country of origin.

Printed and bound in Spain
by CPI, Barcelona

PLEASURED BY THE SECRET MILLIONAIRE

NATALIE ANDERSON

Natalie Anderson adores a happy ending—which is why she always reads the back of a book first. Just to be sure. So you can be sure you've got a happy ending in your hands right now—because she promises nothing less. Along with happy endings she loves peppermint-filled dark chocolate, pineapple juice and extremely long showers. Not to mention spending hours teasing her imaginary friends with dating dilemmas. She tends to torment them before eventually relenting and offering—you guessed it—a happy ending. She lives in Christchurch, New Zealand, with her gorgeous husband and four fabulous children.

If, like her, you love a happy ending, be sure to come and say hi on facebook.com/authornataliea, follow @authornataliea on Twitter, or visit her website/blog, www.natalie-anderson.com.

CHAPTER ONE

SYDNEY: sun, surf and shopping. All that was missing was the sex.

Sienna smiled as she crossed the beach, the soles of her feet tingling on the hot sand. Beautiful bodies decorated the shore and she cruised through them, winding her way back up to the footpath. Oh, yeah. If she ever went to a doctor again this would be the only prescription she'd pay attention to. One week of pure holiday—preparation time before her big adventure. Her first week where no one knew about her health or her history—the fresh beginning she'd been hanging out half her life for.

She paused to let a couple stroll by in front of her. Tried not to envy the way the woman oh-so-casually wore her teeny tiny triangles of material—aka her bikini. Crimson-red with shoe-string straps, it revealed more than it concealed and she had both the body and boldness to wear it. Sienna didn't have either. She didn't want the looks, the ill-concealed curiosity or pity. She didn't want the speculation full stop. Hence her throat-high top—even though it did cling and her miniskirt was more on the mini than the skirt side. And sure she'd spotted the odd sideways glance her way from a couple of men. As usual she'd shied away from them. She could never show her cleavage the way that woman did. Irritation increased her pace and she lectured her wavering confidence—must improve assertiveness quotient! How was she ever going to tick her way through her list of 'must achieve' activities if she couldn't even hold a stranger's gaze for more than a split second? How was that 'living in the moment'—her new motto?

Suddenly touched by melancholy she crossed the street, moving away from the beach and into the pub, club and café scene. She needed to buck up—wasn't it her New Year's resolution to live life to the max? Take no prisoners? Maybe she'd go dancing with the girls she'd met at the hostel the previous night. Full of adventure and fun, they'd be able to teach her a few tricks. At least she could hang on for the ride and watch. But that was what she was sick of—being the one on the sidelines, unable to participate because she wasn't allowed. Well, now she was allowed. And there was no one here to tell her she couldn't, wouldn't or shouldn't. But nor was there anyone to tell her she could, would or should either. She wished Lucy were here, her crazy friend who had all the gumption and the heart as well. The person who'd shown her some fun in spite of the restrictions all those years. But she'd had to come away alone—needing to prove to herself that she could do it. Because then she'd truly believe it and could insist others recognise it too.

She glanced at her watch. A bit after three p.m., the lunch crowd had moved on and everyone was back at work—except the tourists, travellers and holiday-makers like her. The restaurant and club a couple of blocks down from the hostel had its doors wide open—circulating air on the steamy Sydney day when the humidity was high and the thunderstorm approaching. She hoped it would happen soon; she wasn't used to the hard-to-breathe air.

Then she heard it. Boom, boom, hiss, boom, boom, hiss—the unmistakable strike of stick on drum and cymbal. It stopped and then started again. Then she heard the twang of a rough chord on an electric guitar followed by a disembodied male voice. 'One, one. Two, t-t-t-two.'

Sound check.

Suddenly she felt right at home, right at ease, and her legs just walked her in there—right into the open bar that was closed for business. To where the band was onstage and the rehearsal was happening. Four guys were up there, dressed in shorts and tees and the lead singer had the skinny boy star look and mandatory crazy hair. She slipped in the back, enjoying the breeze from the fans, watched the drummer with envy, her fingers itching.

'I'm sorry, you can't stay here. The bar's not open yet.'

Reluctantly she dragged her gaze from the drum kit to the man who'd walked up beside her. She blinked. Once. Again. Then rapidly a couple more times to try to make her silly eyes focus. My God. So men like that really did exist? The kind that would have every woman in the vicinity immediately doing their pelvic floor exercises because they knew, absolutely knew, that keeping up with him in the bedroom would require some spectacular performance.

Sienna's whole body tensed—especially her pelvic floor.

Steely grey eyes with a smidgen of green regarded her. They were surrounded by dark lashes and topped with strongly curved dark brows. Great combination. But it was his mouth that had her flexing—the fullest, most sensual lips she'd ever seen on a man.

She blinked again and broke the contact. Looked down and in that speck of time took in his exhilarating appearance once more. He wore designer board shorts with artless ease and a close-fitting cotton tee shirt. His dark hair was clipped short and his sandals were of soft-looking leather. Details burnt into her brain in rapid-fire succession. But it was his hands she lingered on as they rested on his arms folded across his chest. Large palms and long fingers—he'd have no trouble reaching a couple of octaves on the piano. Nails so neat you'd think they'd been professionally manicured.

He must be gay.

She saw his glance slip over her as he paused too. Saw the hint of censure cloud into something else. The green light grew. The go-ahead signal. Attraction.

Not gay.

She snuck in a breath and remembered what she'd been going to ask. 'You mind if I watch a while?' Her voice seemed to have lost all power. It was some pathetic trickle of its usual timbre and the way he was looking at her, she'd lose all ability to speak or think at all. Man, he was hot.

He kept staring at her and she stared back, intrigued to see the green in his eyes intensify. His stance, with his arms banded across his chest, showed off the breadth of his shoulders and emphasised his masculine triangular shape. His shirt pulled at the seams slightly, struggling to contain the breadth of the bone and muscle beneath. Finally he opened his mouth to answer but the singer got in first.

'It's OK, Rhys. She can stay. Can you bring in the other amp?' The singer seemed to have forgotten about the microphone and shouted—the result so loud Sienna jumped. So did Mr Handsome Stranger.

Rhys. He jerked his head to the stage, looking as if he'd just remembered where he was. She saw a glance flicker between all the men, had no problem interpreting it. That was OK. She'd been in and around bands long enough to know what they thought. Groupie? Not today. Well, certainly not for any of the musicians. But Rhys their roadie? My God. She'd never seen a roadie like that before.

She watched as he walked behind the bar to wherever to get the missing equipment.

The singer smiled at her. 'Come sit and watch for a while if you want.'

She managed to work her dry mouth into some sort of smile and walked to a table near the front—one that gave a good view through to the back of the bar. She sat, stretched her legs out and let the air circulate around her, resting her body from the heat of the sun. She could cool down here for a moment and let the rhythm of the drum soothe her disgruntled soul.

Two minutes later Rhys came back in carrying a large black case. He strode past her to put it on the stage. Gave the singer a mock salute and returned to the bar. She honed in on his every movement. So much for cooling off—just looking at him made her sweat.

Across the tables, he stood level with her, looming in the corner of her eye. She tried to concentrate on the musicians but couldn't help her sidelong observance of Mr Utterly Attractive. He wasn't even trying to hide the fact he was looking at her. He stood with his back against the bar, arms across his chest again, and coolly watched her watching the band.

She forced herself to focus on the music. Succeeded for a time—well, her eyes at any rate. Her brain was still assessing his magnificent features. She caught movement to the side and no way could she not look. He'd turned to reach across the bar behind him. She watched, forgetting the musicians entirely as he stretched his body out. Under that tee was a flat wall of muscle. A perfect physical specimen.

Sienna, like most people, could appreciate beauty. And his was breathtaking.

He turned back, bottle of water in his hand, and speared her gaze. With a wry turn of his lips he subtly lifted the bottle in her direction, a tiny silent toast, and then sipped.

Finding herself mirroring his swallowing action, and finding her throat rawly dry, she registered her own incredible thirst. Not necessarily for water. What it would be to lick away the drops from his lips. To have him turn into her and take her mouth, giving her exactly what she needed right now. She shivered, her heat almost a fever. She remembered herself and refocused. The slight smile, the tiny tug at the corner of his mouth put her on guard. There was knowledge in his eyes. Sinful awareness. She realised he'd had a direct view into her head and seen exactly what she'd been thinking. From his expression, he didn't think the idea was too bad either.

She turned back to the band and this time really put the blinkers on. Not going to look his way at all. Unbelievable. Her insides churned. She wanted him. He was exactly what she'd been looking for and never expected to find. A man who'd take the sexiest-man-alive title unchallenged. A man who, with just a look, told her she was beautiful.

Despondency dampened her burgeoning excitement. That look would change the minute he saw her—really saw her. Attraction would fade to pity—and fear. Sienna hated seeing fear in the eyes of a lover. It didn't exactly make her feel desirable. It didn't make her feel normal and for once, just once, she wanted normal. And that put her crazy fantasy in mind once more. Number one on her list of life experiences. She'd penned it in her journal only this morning on the beach. Front page, fifteenth volume. And she meant it this time—she was going to fulfil at least one New Year's resolution. Could she attempt it? Could she really get away with it?

She pushed a breath out as her fingers toyed with the high neck of her tee shirt. She hadn't a chance. No way could she ever manage it. Lovers tended to get naked. Sienna didn't want naked—not her at any rate—because then the fun would end and the pity party would start.

She glared at the sticks hitting the drum. Watched the relentless strike on the skin, wanting a hypnotic effect. Failed. She flicked a glance back to the bar, unable to stop her need to at least look at him one last time.

An acute and way over the top amount of disappointment flooded her when she saw he wasn't there. He'd gone.

End of fantasy.

Her thumbs itched. Hell, everything itched. She stared at the stage, the energy in her bursting to get out. She knew the sure way to make herself feel better—to beat out the blues as she had many a time. She stood and walked right up to the edge of the stage. The singer stopped and the band cut the music.

'I'm sorry. I know this is a really strange thing to ask and it's fine to say no, but would you mind if I had a turn on the drums?' Her heart raced and she looked to the drummer as she asked the final part.

'You play the drums?'

'Sure. But I'm on holiday and I haven't been near a set for a while and I'd really like to.' She flashed a smile. Hoped they wouldn't think she was some desperate groupie. Really, all she wanted was to play the drums.

'We could do with a break. Go right ahead.'

Pleasure washed through her. 'Thank you.' She took the steep step up onto the stage and headed to the back. The drummer handed her the sticks with a smile. She felt the weight of them in her hands and then set them on the snare.

She pulled her hair up off the back of her neck and twisted it into a knot on the top of her head, regretting the loss of her fifty-thousandth scrunchie. She spun the seat a few turns to lower it a little. Flexed her wrists and then rotated her hands round a couple of times. Picked up the sticks, pulled back her shoulders and sat. She tilted her head from side to side in her little pre-drumming warm-up routine. Her foot tapped and mentally she worked through the rhythm, slipping easily into the zone and feeling her body come alive. Her smile spread slow and wide across her closed mouth. *This* was exactly what she'd needed. Then she moved, hands, feet, whole body— moving separately but together to create one hell of a noise.

Rhys Maitland stood at the far end of the bar and clamped his jaw shut to stop it falling to the floor. He held his arms tight across his body as if to hold back the sudden rush of adrenalin—make that attraction. He'd been in unchartered territory since that strawberry-blonde had walked into the bar and stared right into him with those huge blue eyes of hers. His brain hadn't been working properly since. Instead he'd been filled with one thought only. Getting her naked. Yep, screaming lust central. Thing was, he had a feeling that same thing might have happened to her. She kept glancing at him, and that was definitely a good sign. Either that or he was wearing his lunch on his chin—the attention she paid to his mouth. He'd taken a sip of water to cool his internal heat, but the need to move had grown too strong and he'd slipped out the bar and back round so he could watch her from behind, so he wouldn't be sent into cardiac arrest—her eyes were more powerful weaponry than anything he'd ever encountered.

So now he stood, a picture of studied relaxation, staring at the elfin honey onstage. She looked small behind the drum kit but he knew from when he'd stood beside her that she was actually quite tall. Very slim, almost ethereal, and yet there she was thrashing the life out of those drums in a way that had him, and every other male on the premises, immobile and in awe. Her hair had been piled up on her head but as she moved it started to come down—first a couple of wisps and then the whole mass tumbled about her shoulders and down her back as she rocked on her seat in time to the beat. Heaven have mercy. Her face gently flushed with the exertion. And try as hard as he could he couldn't tear his gaze from her.

He sensed the stillness in the bar. Knew all the others were equally transfixed. Felt the flare of territorial male. She'd looked at him. And in that moment, they'd swapped something. Recognition—not of him, of his name, or who he was, but awareness of something elemental.

Like desire. Evident from the moment she'd walked in with her long, long, slim legs set off by a very cute little skirt. Her sandals were just a hint of leather straps over her feet. She was like any other babe on the beach and yet somehow totally different. She lacked the usual overtly confident quality. She'd come in, but with quiet reticence. Then her big eyes, bluer than any ocean or outback sky, had sized him up. Beneath the hesitation he'd seen a flash of bold awareness—a contradiction that had him uncharacteristically uncertain of how to progress. But, man, he wanted to progress. The unshakeable fog of ennui that had hung over him these last few weeks blown away in that one second.

Tim sidled up to him at the bar. 'Have you ever seen anything like that?'

Rhys shook his head, not trusting his voice.

'That is the hottest thing I've seen on two legs. Unbelievable.' Even Tim knew to shut up after that and enjoy the view.

After a few minutes—they could have all happily watched for hours—she stopped. Sat still on the stool for a moment, head bowed. Rhys could see her panting.

She stood and handed the sticks back to Greg, the drummer. 'Thanks, I needed that.'

'Any time.' Greg almost fell over the kit to take the sticks, his complete attention on her and not the obstacles in the way.

Tim walked up to the stage, looked up to where she stood now at the front of it. 'I'm Tim. You have to come and watch tonight. As payment, you know.'

'Sure.' She smiled and jumped down from the stage. Rhys clenched his fists even tighter at the view of her legs in action. 'I really appreciate that, guys. I feel a lot better now.'

She must have known they were all watching, tongues practically hanging out of their mouths like rabid dogs. But she walked casually as if she hadn't a care in the world, as if no one was looking, not least five full-grown, deeply red-blooded men.

She felt a lot better? Rhys' blood was pumping through his body to a far faster beat than she'd been playing on the drums. More alive than he'd been in months—yep, he felt better too. And he knew what would make him feel marvellous.

It had been so long.

He tracked her progress down the room. She was looking down and ahead of her, seemingly forgetting the band onstage behind her. Coolly ignoring the four sets of eyes trained on her back. Then she turned her head just as she passed where he was 'resting' against the bar.

Five tables stood between them as she walked down the centre aisle, but they could have been millimetres apart, such was the clarity with which he could see her eyes, almost feel their laser-like intensity. She didn't smile as she looked him over—one killer inspection. He didn't smile either, didn't move a muscle in fact—couldn't.

Unspoken communication. Unstoppable contact. That screaming lust again. Every sinew and muscle in his body tightened to the point of pain, his body wanting him to take action—to reach out and grab. At three in the afternoon with a bunch of his best mates watching?

Then she looked away and walked out of the bar. Rhys jerked his attention back to the band. Finally remembered to breathe.

'Hot damn, that was some chick,' Tim called over to Rhys. 'Gave you the look.'

Rhys stood locked in position against the bar and managed another shrug. Yep. The look. He was still in recovery. Her eyes were haunting. Those brilliant blues had burned right through him and that message had passed again. Magnetic. Rhys was no stranger to 'the look'—the one a woman flicked a man to say she'd noticed him and was interested. That maybe he and she were a possibility.

Maybe a possibility?

She was a dead certainty. Right now he wanted her as he'd never before wanted a woman. Instant, inescapable, intense. His body was still coiled. He wanted to reach for her, wrap her around him and make her his. Restraining that urge made him ache.

Per capita Sydney had an excess of beautiful, glamorous women and Rhys was on familiar terms with several of them. But suddenly a slip of a girl in a casual tee and quick-dry skirt had nearly rendered him catatonic with need.

'The minute she finds out who you are, she's yours,' Tim said, sizing up the situation.

Rhys frowned. Wrong. She hadn't known who he was. And he didn't want her to find out. Didn't want to see that suggestion of raw physical attraction in her face replaced with attraction to something else—like dollar signs. He wanted to explore the desire without the hindrance and hang-ups that came of history and prejudice and preconceptions.

She was foreign. Had the vowel sounds of a New Zealander. Was wearing the garb of a girl who had nothing but a pack on her back. Kiwi girl on holiday. He was out of his native habitat too—in a part of the city he rarely came to. It was almost like being in a foreign country, one where he, blessedly, wasn't known. Thus far their interaction was pretty much a blank slate. He didn't need it to be filled in. What he wanted was physical—his body sought a connection with hers and had from the second he saw her. She'd felt the pull too and he sure as hell wasn't leaving this bar again until she walked back in.

CHAPTER TWO

SIENNA dressed with more than usual care and way more than usual excitement. If ever there was a man to help her achieve number one on her list, he was that man. She'd gone back to the hostel and lain in wait for Julia and Brooke, the two South Africans she'd met on arrival last night. No sooner had she mentioned the words 'band' and 'bar' than they'd agreed to go with her. Sienna was pleased. Total party girls those two—and they'd ensure she had a good time no matter what might or might not happen with the gorgeous guy. And that was the purpose of this overseas jaunt, wasn't it? To have fun. Be normal. Seize the day.

Sienna emerged last from the bathroom, clutching her top to her. 'Can you tie these ribbons for me?'

Julia wolf-whistled. 'That is some top!'

It was. She'd only brought it with her on the spur-of-the-moment last-minute mad decision. It rolled up really small and she'd stuffed it at the bottom of her pack, never really dreaming she'd put it on. Midnight-blue satin with a matching sequin trim. The material clung from her neck to her abdomen. Three sets of long ribbons trailed. One for her neck, one for her chest and one for her stomach. Julia artfully wound them round for her. The fabric covered her from neck to belly at the front but left her back bare—other than the ribbon ties.

She twisted her head, trying to see how Julia was getting on, while ensuring the fabric was held tight to her skin. 'Quadruple knot them.'

'Are you sure? You'll need scissors to get out of it.'

'I'm sure.' That was the whole point. It was sexy and revealing but no way could anyone get underneath to discover what was below. The ribbon across her lower abdomen stopped a hand sliding up, the ribbon at the neck stopped fingers sliding south. Perfect.

She teamed it with a short black A-line skirt and high-heeled sandals. Her legs were her best feature and she intended to make the most of them. If dreams were going to come true, then she had to help them out a bit. She massaged moisturiser down the length of them. Then discreetly adjusted the strap of her underwear—a teeny, tiny lace-fronted G-string. Knickers like she never usually wore. But she was re-inventing herself. And tonight she'd be as in-your-face frisky as she could get. Ribbons reached halfway down her skirt. She was covered far more than the bikini woman on the beach but was as naked as she'd ever been.

'That's a vamp outfit.' Julia stood back and surveyed her before sharply turning to her pack which had its contents spilling over the dorm floor. 'I gotta find me something to compete with that. Time to get ready and glamorise.'

As Julia's ample breasts provided more than enough competition, Sienna wasn't letting the comment go to her head. She'd never be page-three pin-up but with her legs emphasised, and her back drawing attention from her front, she might do OK.

Brooke's voice came distantly through the top she was

squeezing into. 'Is the lead singer cute? You want the singer, right?'

'The singer is all yours. In fact the entire band is all yours.'

Brooke's head popped through the neck of her top. 'So who is it you're after? The bartender?'

Was it so obvious she was after someone? 'No.' She came clean. 'The band has a guy helping out.'

'You're going for the roadie?' Brooke shrieked.

'God, don't tell me he's the technical guy? Not the sound and lighting geek?'

Julia sounded appalled.

Sienna giggled. 'I'm not sure what he does. He was helping with their equipment.'

The others sent her pitying looks. 'OK, if you're sure. We'll leave him to you.'

They sat on the beds, stared into tiny compact mirrors and worked hair and make-up. Sienna twisted her hair up. Put on her mascara and gloss with a slightly heavier hand than usual and wished the hostel allowed drink in the bedrooms.

This was ridiculous. She was getting worked up—and dollied up—over nothing. He probably wouldn't even be there. She almost succumbed to the urge to cancel there and then. Time for a mental slap on the cheek. This didn't matter. She was in a foreign city, free to do as she pleased. If he was there, then she'd have a great time; if he wasn't, she'd still have a great time.

Uh-huh.

She really wanted to see him again—wanted to replay the moment she'd sizzled like a drop of water in a pan of hot oil. Just another look would be enough.

Uh-huh.

'Right, girls, let's go have ourselves a blast.' Julia gave a foxy twirl.

Sienna couldn't stop the giggles bursting out. She was such an idiot. But seeing as she was dressed to kill, she might as well go and make the most of it. She could just dance at least—as she used to with her best friend Lucy. Go and dance and have a laugh.

As they linked arms and strode down the street, Sienna soaked up some of the confidence the others oozed.

She didn't arrive until well into the second set. Rhys was at the bar, half hidden but in a place that gave him a clear view of the door—so he'd see her the minute she got there. She was with two other women. They looked like fellow tourists—tanned, relaxed, riveting. The other two were staring at the stage, she was looking around the audience. He stepped back into the shadows as her gaze swept over the bar. He wanted to observe for a while. Still deciding how or even if he would make a move. He glanced at Tim. Saw he'd seen their arrival because he winked at them. Immediately he looked straight to where Rhys stood, flashing him a huge grin.

The band wrapped up the set a song early and headed straight to her—all four of them. But it was Tim, as always, who got there first, and who less than subtly cast a glance of pure appreciation over the other two. Rhys watched for a while, wanting to see if she spent that killer look on any of the others. He saw her smile, saw her introduce her friends, but then she seemed to quieten, let the girlfriends do the talking and the flirting as they headed to the table in the back corner reserved for the band. He saw her glance around before sitting. She was looking for someone. It had better be him.

Tim came up to the bar. Ordered a tray of tequila shots, his usual *modus operandi,* then came to where Rhys stood.

'Doc, Doc, Doc. Why are you hiding out here? There's a lady at that table all wrapped up with your name on her.'

Rhys frowned. He didn't want his name out anywhere. Just for once.

'Rhys, you can't go doing the hardworking serious doctor thing all your life. You have to cut loose and have some fun some time. Hell, they've ordered you to take time off. Have a holiday, for heaven's sake. *There* is your holiday.' He jerked his head back towards the table.

Rhys managed a tight grin. They had. Made him take a fortnight. Said he was accruing too many days—a liability on the budget. They didn't want to owe him three months or more. So he'd been forced to take a break. He didn't much like breaks—they meant he had too much time to sit and think. He preferred to keep busy.

'Come on, dude. When was the last time you had a one-nighter?'

It was all right for Tim. His every action wasn't watched and subsequently detailed in the gossip pages of the local rag. If Rhys was seen within five feet of a woman it was reported the next day as a new relationship—possible wedding bells every time. The exaggeration and speculation was exhausting. The prying of paparazzi keen to rustle up a story out of nothing invaded what he'd hoped could be an ordinary existence. But Rhys knew when it came to money, especially his kind of money, people didn't scruple to sell their souls.

Mandy had done just that. Sold herself, and him, to the highest bidder. She'd taken everything he held close and hung it out for the world to see. And she hadn't even got it right. He'd asked her out on a whim. She'd been working in a café near the hospital; he'd been in there after a long shift. Her effervescence had been so attractive to his tired self. It had been a fun hour, chatting over coffee. The hour became a date, then a string of dates. He didn't figure 'til later she'd known all along who he was. That the most she understood was the wealth and status his name entailed. Too late he realised he knew nothing of the real Mandy, that nothing they had shared was real, that there was no depth beneath the bubbly exterior. He'd broken it off and then really learned how money had been her biggest motivator.

He wouldn't be fool enough to trust like that again. Not someone he didn't know. So he didn't do one-night stands. He didn't want to read all about it in the paper the next day over breakfast. Instead he did the discreet dating thing with women from his own social circle. Glamorous, beautiful for sure, but also safe, circumspect and so boring.

Tonight he could do with some anonymity—be able to have some fun and not worry about where the details might surface. He supposed he shouldn't care, should shrug it off and enjoy the reputation. But he wanted his life to be more meaningful. He refused to be the rich, spoiled playboy spending his days using his money and name to score. And he refused to be used himself.

Life, Rhys knew, was precious.

Unfortunately, that seemed to make him all the more attractive to the gutter press. And with Mandy's betrayal, telling all to anyone who'd pay enough, he'd been painted as some wounded saint—the earnest ER doctor working to escape the inanity of privileged life and the tragedy of past lessons. And that he wasn't either.

He looked back over to where the drummer girl sat at the table. Watched as she sat, smiling, her head tilted to the side as she listened to whatever it was that her friend was saying. She nodded, her smile flashing wider as she giggled. He could see the sparkle in her eyes even from this distance. Any sobering memory of Mandy's sell-out fled from his head as he focused on the stranger's golden hair and pale-skinned shoulders. His abs tightened. He sure didn't have saintly urges when it came to her. Maybe, just for once, he could do the frivolity thing. His desire for her was strong enough to tip the balance. Maybe there was a way around his issue of identity.

'She's not from here, is she?'

'Kiwi, I think. Her mates are from South Africa. Met up in the hostel they're staying at.'

Rhys stared at her some more. Felt those urges bite. Figured she was only going to be in town a night or two—what would she care if his name wasn't quite the right one? More than ever he didn't want to be himself any more. He was tired of living with his recollections and his regret. Temptation won. 'OK. I'm Rhys—she knows that, right? But she doesn't know anything else. So let's say I'm Rhys…Rhys Monroe.'

Tim stared at him, his smile slow and full of wicked disbelief. 'And what do you do for a living, Mr Monroe?'

Rhys frowned. 'Dunno. What do you think?'

'Better be something you're really crap at. The bigger the lie, the more likely they are to believe it.'

'And you know this how?'

'Rhys.' Tim looked affronted. 'I'm a professional.' He smiled at the waitress as she put the slices of lemon and dish of salt on the tray. 'Let's make you a builder.'

'A what?'

'Builder. Carpenter. You know, chippie.'

'That's ridiculous. I haven't a practical bone in my body.'

'Precisely.'

Rhys gave a grunt of laughter.

'And no way are you that Maitland guy, heir to all those millions.'

Rhys shook his head. 'Never heard of him.'

Tim picked up the tray of shot glasses. 'Well, come on, Monroe, let's get lying.'

'I'll be over in a second. Just got to finalise my persona.'

Tim winked, and, grinning broadly, headed back to the table. Rhys watched, covered by the crowd, as Tim set the tray down in front of them and handed out the shot glasses. She took one. He saw her nostrils flare as she took a sniff. Not so keen. But she did it. So did the others. Tim immediately started handing everyone a second round. She declined that one. He saw the way she pulled in her cheeks, looked over the table, glanced to the bar. Rhys smiled to himself, and summoned the waitress.

Julia and Brooke were barracking for a third shot. Sienna laughed at them. Heart sliding south as she did. Already knowing she was headed for yet another night on the sidelines. The taste of the tequila was bitterly burning her up. She couldn't handle strong alcohol, would prefer a little wine. Something light—for the lightweight she was.

No sign of the roadie. She tried to tell herself she didn't mind. Looked around the bar. Loads of men, loads. All looking good, gathering in groups. But the view was tainted. That kick of attraction had been so fierce and so foreign and she'd stupidly pinned more on it than there was. Now looking around, she couldn't help the feeling the joint was a bit of a meat market—and she didn't have the goods to set up shop.

Tim had managed to find himself a seat between the two South African beauties. Leaning back on it, talking, he soon had them laughing. The others in the band sat on chairs around them, letting Tim hold court but interjecting with witticisms of their own that had the girls shrieking even more. No doubt about it, they were a polished act and Sienna knew her place was firmly in the audience. She'd leave the participation bit to Julia and Brooke.

An arm appeared over her shoulder. 'Thought you might prefer this.' A glass was placed in front of her. Cool, clear water.

'Then you might like this.' Another glass was set alongside the first. Pale wine, just the sight of it a balm on her still-screaming taste buds.

He pulled up a chair and sat down beside her, back a little, away from the others. Dressed in black jeans and a black shirt. She could see his forearms. Lightly tanned. Muscular. Capable. He gave her a barely there grin. His face had intensity all over it—accentuated by the shadow on his jaw.

'Thank you.' She lifted the water and took a deep sip, needing it more than ever.

He watched. Before she could put the glass back on the table he took it from her. Eyes not breaking their hold, he lifted it to his sensuous, sensitive mouth and drank deeply.

'You mind sharing?' he asked belatedly.

Sienna snaked in some air. 'Not at all.'

Julia's eyebrows had disappeared under her fringe. Brooke was hammily fanning herself.

Tim dropped forward on his seat, clunking the legs down. 'Glad you could finally join us, Rhys. Let me introduce you. Julia, Brooke, this is Rhys. And I think you met Sienna earlier.'

A look passed between the two men. An even less subtle look passed between Brooke and Julia. Sienna ignored the lot of them, quickly reaching for the wine.

'Rhys is an old school friend of mine who's in town for a few days. Thought I'd get him to help us out.'

'Shouldn't you be up on that stage singing your little heart out, Tim?' Rhys interrupted.

Tim smiled a sly smile, picked up his bottle and headed back to the stage where the other band members were already strapping on instruments and quickly checking their pitch.

Julia and Brooke stared after him, then turned back and stared at Rhys, then Sienna.

'We're going to dance,' Brooke declared, grabbing Julia by the hand and leaping to her feet, eyes flashing.

'Some sound and lighting geek,' Sienna heard Julia mutter as she passed her.

'Mmm hmm.' Sienna bought some time by having another sip of wine.

Julia and Brooke hit the dance floor and headed right up the front, taking Tim's tambourine from him and starting dancing in a way that more men than just those in the band enjoyed.

Sienna watched them for a moment, loving their enthusiasm. But the strong, silent presence beside her was all she could really focus on. She turned to study him as he quietly regarded her. One thing she did know how to do was talk to people. Or, rather, how to get people to talk to her. She'd been cast in the role of confidante for so many years. The one sitting, while others achieved; she'd be the ear when they needed a rest or reviving. Ironic that she, who couldn't participate, could motivate and could listen.

'You in town for long, Rhys?'

'Just a few days. I'm a builder. From Melbourne.' He took another drink from their shared water.

OK. Keen to get the basics out. She tried to get him to elaborate a little. 'A builder?'

His attention was fixed on the band. 'Sure.'

'You don't look like a builder.'

He glanced at her then. Wry amusement in his face. 'I didn't think I'd need my tool belt tonight.'

She grinned and gave up on the small talk. He clearly wasn't one to waste words. And the most she was conscious of was her Goliath-sized awareness of him—it didn't leave much room for conversational effort.

Surprisingly he took on the task. 'What about you? What do you do?'

'Not much at the moment.'

'On holiday?'

She nodded.

'From where?'

'Life in general.' She laughed at her own pretension. Expanded so he wouldn't think she was an idiot. 'I'm in Sydney for a week before embarking on my big adventure.'

'Your OE?'

The great Overseas Experience. Obligatory for most Kiwis in their early twenties. Maybe it was something to do with being stuck in a tiny country on the edge of the earth. For a year or two or more they'd pack their packs and traipse around the world. She nodded. It had taken her a little longer to get organised, but finally she was on her way.

'Europe?'

'South America initially.' There were a couple of things on her life's must-do list that she wanted to finally cross off. Peru was right up there.

'So where is home?'

She shrugged. 'I'm not sure yet.' It wasn't where she'd come from. She loved it. She loved the people but she needed space to set her life in its new direction. 'What about you?'

'I've a couple of weeks off. Just spending it hanging out in Sydney.'

'Catching up with old friends?'

'Right now I'm more interested in making new ones.'

Silence fell again. His eyes held hers as he took another sip—this time of her wine. She wished he wouldn't. She really did because all she then saw was that beautiful mouth with its perfect cupid bow. Since when did she feel jealous of a glass? But how would it feel to be pressed against his lips, to have his tongue lick her rim?

She felt heat rise in her cheeks. The way she was thinking! And the worst of it was she was certain he knew. Possibly even thinking the same. Because his attention was fixed on her when she took the glass from him and sipped.

He waited until she'd placed her glass back on the table before leaning closer to her, speaking with the world's most tempting voice.

'You know what I think, Sienna?'

'What?'

'I think you should dance with me.'

A flicker of excitement ran from the nape of her neck all the way down her spine, through her legs and to her toes. She wriggled them in her sandals. 'OK.'

They stood. Julia and Brooke were somewhere up the front, playing up to Tim's 'glam lead singer' act. Sienna stopped in the middle of the crowd, wanting to disappear into it. Not wanting to feel any more self-conscious than she already was. Fully aware that Tim and the other band members were probably watching. That Brooke and Julia would be giving the thumbs-up behind Rhys' back. She didn't want the distraction or the discomfort.

Within three seconds she wouldn't have cared if there were a film crew beside her broadcasting the action live to twenty million viewers. She'd totally lost awareness of all others, of their surroundings. She lost all sense of everything except Rhys. The thrill rippled through her—her awareness of him almost a tangible entity. They took advantage of the crowd on the floor to stand close. He smiled and she found herself smiling back, just like that. So easy. The music wasn't too heavy, he moved, she followed. Fingers brushed. She nearly jumped, the electricity practically sparking. She glanced at her hand. Quickly looked to gauge his reaction—had he felt that current? He was watching her face, then looked to her hand. With slow deliberation he reached out and took it in his, his grip firming at her tremble.

If she felt this on edge with just one small touch, how on earth would anything more feel? All she knew was that she wanted that more—with a biting need, almost desperation. Desire both ferocious and foreign.

Neither of them was smiling any more. They moved closer as the floor became more crowded. He didn't take his eyes off her. Shadows fought with emerald light. His hold on her hand tightened.

'I know this is really forward. And I know I don't really know you. And feel free to say no, but…'

'But what?'

He looked straight into her eyes with a wry turn-up of his mouth. 'I'm going to kiss you.'

Sienna stopped moving. Stood stock-still in the middle of the dance floor while a hundred others grooved close around her. Her initial reaction was relief—that she hadn't been dreaming, that the attraction wasn't all one-sided. The relief soon gave way to electric excitement. She provoked it further, confidence surging through her. 'Well, that's good, because I intend to kiss you right back.'

He'd stopped dancing too. Abandoned the pretence of caring about the music. Green eyes, not slate, burned into her. 'That's good.'

He stepped nearer. Her body screamed for the touch of his. But it was still out of range—the millimetres feeling like miles. Yet there was almost reluctance between them. A tacit agreement to draw it out, to savour the moment that they'd both been seeking since first seeing each other. She sensed it in him, the deliberate decision to take time to truly appreciate each moment.

Anticipation immobilised her. As much as she wanted to move, it was he who would have to take that final step.

He did. His hand came up, traced her cheek and jaw with a light finger. She quelled the tremor inside. Her lips were tingling. She just had to lick them, had to.

'No,' he muttered. 'Let me.'

He bent to her. Very gently touched the tip of his tongue to the full centre of her lower lip.

Sensation engulfed her. This was crazy. But the fire ripping through her was real.

His hands, gentle, went to frame her chin.

'Better?'

'No.' She tried to hide the shaking, not wanting to admit to the extremity of her reaction.

'Still thirsty?'

Desperately so. She managed a minute nod. Her chin tilted up to meet him, her neck arched to its full length.

His hand slid around it so his fingers tangled into her hair at the back. How she wanted that mouth—that beautiful mouth…

He touched her again. Brushed his lips over hers a couple of times. Such soft teasing that tore at her self-control. She reached up and mirrored his action, threading her fingers into the thick hair at the back of his head, pulling him down to her.

They stood completely still in the mass of movement. Unable even to sway in time, concentrating wholly on each other, on the fragile softness that would shatter if their passion was unleashed. This wasn't the place for it to be unleashed. Yet she knew it was impossible to hold back.

A moment of fantasy melded with reality. Just this once.

He lowered his head as she lifted her chin. They met at the middle, lips catching and clinging. Mouths opening so tongues could taste—deep and delicious.

He kissed his way down the length of her neck, and back up to her ear. 'You are quite the most beautiful thing.' He pulled back to look at her, his gaze heavy and gleaming.

She ensured her lips curved upwards but dropped her lashes so he wouldn't see the pain she knew her eyes would have reflected. Beautiful? Not entirely.

She tugged on his hair, directing him back to her mouth. Wanting the words to end and only the feeling to remain. Not wanting compliments or pretty phrases or promises to falsely gild this moment. Because that was all it was—one moment, but one of absolute bliss. The kind of moment she'd wanted all her adult life and one she wanted to extend. She wanted to make the most of the magic in the night. She melted into him in a way she'd never do at home. But she wasn't at home. She wasn't with anyone she knew.

The sexiest man she'd ever laid eyes on was holding her and kissing her as if she was the sexiest thing *he'd* ever seen. There was no one who knew to tell him otherwise. She'd keep up this pretence as long as she possibly could.

Their bodies collided as passion rose. Initial restraint fast fading as they recognised their needs matched.

More.

At the first touch of his fingers on her bare back, her body shook—the electric charge bolting through her system again. He jerked his head back, his startled green eyes reading hers.

She registered the same aftershock in them. He opened his mouth to speak but she stretched forward, reaching right up on tiptoe to prevent him. Not wanting to name it, just wanting to experience it.

Again.

His fingers traversed, burning fire as they went. The need to have them touch her all over nearly crippled her. Instead she spread fingers and palms across his shoulders. Wanting to experience the feel of him as much as the way he made her feel.

So this was what Cinderella must have felt like. To have met her Prince Charming, to be dancing, but knowing it was a fantasy that couldn't last past the midnight hour.

Make the most of it.

Time constraint made her bolder. She basked in his openly hungry gaze. He wanted her and she wanted nothing but that mouth roving over every inch of her.

No. Not every inch. She forced the miserable thought back, stepped closer into his embrace. Determined to take what she wanted while she could. And he met her, sensed her availability without censure, simply giving her what she asked for and more.

She'd never been so forward in all her life. And she loved it. It wasn't really the kind of kiss that should be in public at all. She was locked in his arms, length to length they pressed together hard. Both feeling the desperate need to seep into each other's bodies. To somehow transcend the clothing, the fabric between them and to merge into one.

What had begun as a slow, sensuous dance flavoured with restraint had now become frankly hot and heavy and not nearly enough. His hands traced over her back, fingers that had fluttered over her soft skin now stroked with increasing insistence. His palms pressed her towards him—closer but still not as close as she wanted. She ached, a real physical pain deep inside that only he could soothe—by being deep inside her.

His hand came to rest on her bottom, curved over it with pressure, pulling her tight into him. Locking them pelvis to pelvis. The feel of his erection against her was the most exquisite torture. Half of her trembled, the other half imbued with a surge of strength that had her moving in a way to torment him too. Hunting out the response her basic instinct demanded she receive—him driven to take.

His grip grew stronger, his kisses more frantic—trailing across her face, down her neck. Her eyes closed. Her breath came short and fast—faster and faster until she was panting, almost pleading.

His jaw brushed rough against her over-sensitised skin as he raised his head with sudden and unexpected force. 'We shouldn't be here any more.' His voice was low and husky and his hands tightened, keeping her close. 'I think we need to be alone.'

Green eyes searched hers. She knew they were seeking out doubt. But she had no intention of stepping away. For the first time in her life she ignored her worry and just went with the want.

'Somewhere close.' Miraculously her voice worked.

'You're sure?'

Again the intensity together with a sensitivity she hadn't expected. And faint hesitancy just as there had been when they had first hit the dance floor. Desire most certainly, but something else as well. Some other thought, small but inescapable, that had him pausing. But as he pulled on her arm it seemed that he, like she, had no choice.

She gave him the only possible answer. 'As sure as you are.'

CHAPTER THREE

THE door closed behind them, muting the noise of bottles, beat and bar. Sienna was in some oversized pantry. Half-dazed, she took in the shelves where giant jars of sun-dried tomatoes vied for space next to sacks of rice and tins of whatever. Rhys had taken her by the hand and led her off the dance floor. Known exactly where he was headed. She'd simply followed, unquestioning. He closed the door behind him. Bolted it. Swung her so her back was to the door, the lock just by her arm. He nodded to it.

'You can leave any time.'

'I don't want to.'

She saw his tension as he braced against the door but holding his body away from her. She looked along the length of his arms, pinning her in. She could see the strength in them. Not overdeveloped, bulging biceps, but defined, long muscles that were, frankly, beautiful. She sensed he was pushing against the door as a way to keep himself in check. She didn't want him to hold back. No restraint, she wanted everything. Wanted him to want her in the deeply physical way she wanted him, and she wanted to feel it, experience it. All.

It was her turn to seize the moment. Daring, she reached

out quickly before habit returned and she hesitated. She unfastened the top button of his shirt. She heard the catch of his breath. A tiny smile tugged the corners of her mouth. This could be an awful lot of fun. And she'd gone too long without fun. Well, not tonight.

Her fingers shook only a little as she worked the buttons with surprising ease. Until both halves of the shirt hung apart and she was able to see his taut bronzed torso. The initial attack of butterflies in her tummy was fast replaced by a serious tightening. Transverse, internal and external obliques—all those abdominal muscles tensed at the sight of raw male in perfect prime.

She must have a fairy godmother to grant her this wish. She forced her gaze from his torso to his face. She could see the way he'd clamped his jaw shut as he watched her admiring him.

Their eyes met. She saw the serious look in his again. The reality of what she was considering hit her.

She spoke. 'I don't usually…'

'Neither do I.'

Somehow she knew that was true. 'I just want to…'

'Me too.'

Touch.

She reached a hand out sideways and flipped the light switch. Blackness covered them—sudden and total. She couldn't even make out his outline. But she could hear him. Could sense his nearness.

'Sienna?'

'Indulge me.' She smiled—excited by his audible tension, amused by her actions. She even sounded like a seductress. She slipped her panties down, kicking them off and to the floor. Now she felt like one. A sense of exhilaration flooded her. Freedom. In the dark, where there was only touch and scent and sensation, she could be as wicked and wild as she wanted.

'How should I indulge you?' The tension was still there, and a trace of husky desire.

'Touch me.'

He stepped closer. She heard the movement of his feet. With the loss of vision her other senses seemed more acute.

His voice lowered but she still heard every word as clear as the beat of the drum. 'Where should I touch you?'

'Anywhere you want.' Everywhere. She didn't mind. In the dark like this, anything could happen.

He was close. Very close but still not touching and she wanted that beyond belief.

She smelt the wine they'd drunk. Then caught a hint of a scent new to her but thoroughly delightful—Rhys. Aroused.

But still he held back.

Her breasts ached. She longed to feel him caress them— to both soothe and set on fire. As for his mouth, the kind of luscious lips that overly wealthy housewives paid thousands for. The perfect Cupid's bow. She wanted that *everywhere*. Where was he? Panic gripped her—he hadn't changed his mind?

Then he spoke, that low sound of temptation personified. 'I can't quite decide where to touch and whether to use my hands or mouth.'

'How about both? Everywhere.'

She heard his puff of amusement and his low murmur. 'Sienna the Siren.'

At last he touched her, his hands settling on her waist as his lips sought hers. Back to the beginning—but it wasn't a beginner's kind of kiss. Deeper, long, lush kisses followed— lasting for ever. His hands moved, played up her back, and then slipped round her front, his fingers seeking her softness. The ache in her breasts intensified, wanting more.

He spoke her desire aloud. 'I want to touch you. How do I get this off?' He tugged at the material.

'It's complicated. I…'

His groan sounded half smothered. 'Later, we'll get rid of it later.'

Regret whistled through her. There would be no later. But the thought was wiped from her mind as his hands encircled her braless breasts, and his mouth found her nipple with killer precision.

Raw need ricocheted through her. She felt the pull in every limb. Her brain forcing her entire body to attend to the sensation in her nipples. Never had she felt so desired. Never had her breasts received such attention. Such deliberate and devastating touches. Lovers were usually distracted by then—by the scar. Tonight, despite the thin, slippery fabric covering her, she could feel his desire, the wet heat of his mouth as he caressed her with a physical want she knew would wane if he ever saw her in entirety.

She rocked her pelvis against him—an unconscious desire to soothe the ache that had sprung there. Then she realised her body, her very sex, was demanding the same kind of attention her breasts were receiving. The essence of her wanted his fingers, his lips, his tongue to delve and devour the way they were her rounded flesh.

She wanted everything he had. All of his body. All of his strength.

The scent of the room, the sound of her, the softness of her skin and the heady darkness all combined to give Rhys the feeling he'd left this earth and entered some sort of heaven.

He ran his hands over her breasts and back, partly wanting to pull her into him, partly wanting her on a pedestal so he could worship each delicious bit of her.

He was spinning so far out of control. He needed to step back. Regroup a little. Hell, he couldn't even remember if he had a condom in his wallet. Did he have one? Think, brain. *Think.* But she was kissing him again and rational thought was becoming impossible. In this darkness, the cool room wasn't that cool at all. Her long hair tickled his skin and he found himself weaving his hands into it again and again. Running fingers through its silky softness as she kissed his chest, her hands firmly smoothing down his abs. And suddenly he could see it—there was nothing in his mind but the bright, burning gold. Flaxen flames. A gorgeous mess that was so striking and so seductive. He pulled her close for another deep kiss, couldn't keep away any longer, wanting to touch her most intimate space. From the way her hips writhed against his he knew she wasn't about to say no.

He bent his knees so he could place a palm on each leg, halfway up her thighs. He heard her breathing hitch. He kissed her softly, kept close so he could catch every nuance of her reaction as he slowly slid his hands towards home. Her legs were slim but he could feel their supple strength. As he traced up towards where they gently curved together he saw them in his mind's eye—a heaven-sent pillow. After this, when they were in his bed, he would rest his head there and explore the treasure at the top—at length. Right now, his fingers were sending him the images, his ears supplying the audio. Her shallow snatches of air accelerated as he neared his destination. Little gulps turned into little groans and he was seized by the desire to hear her sounds as she came. He'd make sure that happened very, very soon.

He reached the curve of her bottom, the cleft of her sex. And his pleasure in assessing her reaction was totally toppled by the realisation she wasn't wearing any underwear. He had complete access. His mind blanked. But his body knew what to do—make use of it. He traced through her wet warmth, and the scent of her secret space slipped out, filling him, tempting him. He had to taste her. He had to take her. He'd plunge deep into this woman, no matter what.

He was so busy concentrating, so busy deciding, he didn't really register she'd been fiddling at his waist, not until he felt his belt pulled away. How she got his zip down he didn't know but it was blessed relief as his erection sprang free from the denim prison.

With surprising strength she placed one hand on the back of his head, pulling him into a kiss while the other grasped his straining penis. Her hand was warm and firm and she was stroking him and he choked a growl into her mouth. He needed to pull back for a moment or it would be all over in a few more seconds.

And then she jumped. Literally jumped into his arms. Instantly, instinctively, he moved, righting his balance, spreading his legs wide so he could bear both his weight and hers. He had no choice but to have his hands under her bottom, supporting her as she wrapped around him.

God, it felt good. He felt her wetness right on him. Agonisingly close. Then she shifted. He heard the little noise—a cross between a sigh and a cry—as she wriggled and slid onto him. Right down, naturally adjusting her angle so she took him in to the hilt. Her legs locked around him.

Oh, yes!

Sudden. Shocking. And so incredibly satisfying he almost came right away.

Not yet! Not yet! Not yet!

Sucking in air, he fought it. Holding back with an effort sure to shave a few years off his life. His heart thundered. She was so hot, so wet and so wanting. But he couldn't think about it, couldn't indulge immediately. His breath calmed as control returned to him—although he knew it wouldn't be for long.

'You OK?'

Hell, he'd wanted to ensure she was really ready for him, had half planned not to do this until they were in a bed rather than some tiny cupboard at the back of a bar.

But there was no way he could stop now and here she was the one asking if he was coping all right.

'Too fast?'

'A little.' Answering honestly, he pushed out some air. 'But I've got you now.'

He sure did. Hot and sweet. He kissed every inch of her he could reach, squeezed her sweet rounded bottom as he supported her. He wanted this to go a little slower but she was riding him, pressing him home to victory in a way he couldn't resist for much longer. He groaned. Reminded himself this was just the appetiser. The prelude to a fantastic evening ahead where they would lie and roll in a bed over and over, again and again. A room where he would rip the clothing from her if he had to so he could see her as well as feel her, hear her without the backdrop of noise from an overcrowded bar in full party mode. And with that thought relieving him he gave in to the desire to simply take what she was offering. To plunge in deeper and harder and hold her so he could claim her with all his strength.

Her legs curled tighter around him, vice-like she gripped him. Her whimpers of delight turned into cries of celebration as her tension snapped. He felt the waves washing over her, radiating out to him, threatening to swamp him.

And incredibly he didn't explode. Instead he found himself in a new phase, even more intense, where he had even more energy, strength to keep holding her, supporting her while she contracted around him again and again. He pushed inside, further and further, the heated silk of her body absorbing him, the strokes of pleasure almost sending him out of his mind.

More, more, more!

She was coiling tighter again, uttering soft, broken murmurs that sounded like screams to him, they pierced him so intensely. He wanted them louder, wanted her harder.

He growled as he adjusted his stance, tightening his fingers on her, no longer able to keep from bruising, just needing with a kind of possessive and primal instinct that was as foreign to him as it was raw.

He switched his hold, freeing one hand so he could grasp her by her hair, pulling her mouth to his, taking it in a kiss that was hard and hungry and utterly unrestrained.

She gave as good as she got. Her tongue came out—eagerly searching, tasting deep into him, and as he released her from the kiss she came after him, her tongue seeking his lips, tracing their curve and then nipping at them. Her fingers curled into his hair, tugging, holding him so he couldn't escape the heat of her kiss. She took all his breath and demanded more. She was devouring him—raw, relentlessly seeking and giving pure physical pleasure.

And he could fight it no longer. Gave her what she sought. A male body, aroused beyond control, possessively thrusting, pulsating with pleasure, pouring in everything he had until he was utterly, utterly spent.

The bright, burning gold light exploded in his head.

And then there was blackness.

Her weight was no longer his sweet burden. Her legs were gone from his waist. His hands hung, unusually useless, as he tried and failed to get his body working again. He whistled air into his burning lungs—rough and ragged.

He felt her fingers on his neck as she pulled his head down to hers. He felt her warm breath in his ear. He heard the jerky whisper.

'Thank you.'

Before he could reply, she'd slid back the bolt and opened the door, escaping into the passage between bar and restaurant and pulling it shut again quickly behind her.

Rhys blinked. Colour spots floated in front of him, caused by the split second of harsh light. Plunged into blackness again, he reached forward. Palms hit wood.

Hell. She was gone.

He braced his hands on the door, light-headed from the expenditure of energy and sheer disbelief over the intensity of the moment he'd just experienced. Blood rushed all over. To his body, not his brain. That he couldn't seem to work. He couldn't seem to move at all. Stunned. Sapped of all strength.

Then he felt the sweat running off his brow. Felt the way his shirt was sticking to his back. Felt the burn in his thighs and arms, his muscles now seizing from the effort of taking her weight, taking her completely for he didn't know how long.

He pressed the light on his watch. Hell. They'd been in here over an hour. Had she turned him into some tantric sexpert? Rhys was no stranger to a sustained sex session, but he'd never managed quite such a marathon before. And the thing was it wasn't enough. He wanted more. Incredibly he wanted more this minute. He straightened. His body recharged in only those few milliseconds and filled with the need to seek and conquer. Again. Now.

He found the light switch, fastened his jeans, and stuffed a couple of shirt buttons through holes. He gave a quick glance round the cold store—amazingly not a thing appeared out of place. In the small square foot of space in the centre of the room the earth had shifted, reality had receded, and yet not one grain of rice had hit the floor. For a second he frowned—had he just imagined that whole thing? Maybe the hospital had been right and he really, really needed this holiday. Was his brain reduced to feeding him the ultimate fantasy? Losing it, definitely losing it.

Then he caught sight of the slip of black. He bent and retrieved it. A faint, tantalising scent whispered to him. It registered and hit hard in the groin. Her panties. She must have slid them off right at the start. He smiled at their size—a scrap of lace and nothing. He paused, thinking the encounter through. She'd known exactly what she wanted from the start. His smile faded, frown returned. What had gone on tonight? Had she had a hidden agenda? But she'd seemed so genuine. She'd seemed as blown away as he had. Doubt rushed in with anger hot on its heels as an evil thought occurred to him. Maybe she did know who he was. Maybe she'd known his identity exactly and targeted him. And he'd been the fool. Had he just fallen prey to the biggest honey trap ever? And was a million-dollar baby her prize? The Mandy mess would be nothing compared to that.

His blood pumped faster. He knew nothing about her. And he'd just had unprotected sex with her. Stupid. Reckless. Risky. Rhys didn't do risk. He always ensured he retained control of a situation—never allowing circumstance to change so vulnerability could be possible. Vulnerability led to disaster. That he did know.

But he hadn't been in control of that situation—she had. She'd sprung on him, surprised him and—got what she wanted? For once he'd just let go, gone with something that had felt so incredibly good he hadn't had the strength to fight it. Been tempted by the whole holiday idea, the fun of forgetting who he was for a while. Was he now going to pay the price?

Seriously angry with himself, he yanked his belt. Angry with Tim for bringing him to this hellish haven for traveller types. Hell, he couldn't even blame booze for that moment of madness. It had been all-consuming lust. He'd been unable to think beyond having her, hearing her, being in her.

Again. He still wanted it.

Jaw clamped, he stuffed the delicate garment into his jeans pocket. He'd better find her damn fast. And find out exactly what kind of game she was playing. He burst out of the pantry—ignored the startled yelp of the bartender who, with unfortunate timing, happened to be walking past the door.

Rhys strode into the bar. Only a few seconds had passed but that could be her make-or-break advantage. And she had wanted to escape. But the bar was thick and crowded. Thankful for his superior height, he soon spotted the divine stretch of skin that was her back as she slowly threaded her way through. She was almost at the door. He barrelled through the masses, uncaring of knocking someone, hearing the glass fall. He muttered an unintelligible apology that wouldn't have been heard anyway, given he was already three paces past. His eyes were glued to the prize. But then she was out the door. Left. She turned left.

He reached the exit and whipped his head to spot her. There. Several yards along. Even from the distance he could see she was struggling. Her hand rose to her head, fingers knotted in her hair to hold it back from her face. She seemed oblivious to the storm that threw wind and rain at her.

Humidity's hold had been shattered, but until now Rhys hadn't noticed either. The sound of thunder had been disguised, not by the beat of the band, but by the cacophony of their sighs and whispers in the cold store. Her song still rang in his ears, driving him to follow her. Fast. The large drops of rain pelting him were a relief, cooling his lust and anger-heated body.

Something stopped him from calling out to her. He wanted to see where she was going first. Hoped like hell she wasn't about to disappear into a taxi—he could see the lights of one at the stand not too far ahead. Only the one vehicle. Damn.

But instead she turned, stepping through the brightly lit doorway. He read the sign in a second. A hostel. Backpacker paradise. So maybe one part of her story checked out. On the surface at least she was on holiday.

He entered in time to see her ankles disappearing up the stairs. He went to follow but the guy on Reception nobbled him.

'Can I help you?'

'The woman who just went past here. Slim, strawberry-blonde.'

The doorman blinked lazily.

'She's staying here?' Rhys rapped out the question.

'I can't give out information about our customers.'

'So she is staying?'

The bland expression remained.

'More than one night?'

No answer again, but there was a suspicion of a wink.

Rhys savoured the slight satisfaction but it wasn't enough. He'd get all the answers, thank you very much. Utter irritation, unquenchable desire, undeniable need to know forced his actions. 'Got any vacancies?'

'Dormitory or own room?'

He thought for a moment—wicked intent winning over cold curiosity. 'Got any doubles?'

The door guy grinned. 'Sure.' He pulled a form and started filling it in. 'I need name and details, how many nights you want and I need ID—passport or driver's licence.'

Damn. He didn't want to reveal who he was. 'Can't I just pay up front? Cash?'

'We still need ID.'

Rhys deliberated for a nanosecond. Privacy was precious— but the guy on the desk was an American. He'd have no idea who he was. He'd be in the clear. Just one night—so he could find her over breakfast and ask what the hell was going on. So he handed over his driving licence. Filled in the forms. Got the key.

He finally got to go up the stairs she'd ascended ahead of him. He unlocked his room. He even had his own mini-bathroom. Not bad for a cheap-as-they-come hostel. Although he was paying the 'premium' rate for his own room and *en suite*. He wondered where she was right now. Under this roof—but in a room full of bunks or on her own? Was she thinking of him?

Hell—was she with someone else?

He rejected that idea immediately. There had been hesita-tion—he was sure he'd seen that in the blue sea of her eyes. She had said she didn't usually…

What? Go for millionaire heirs? It wouldn't be the first time some stunner had used him to bag herself a fortune. Different style from Mandy, same result. Money. Only this would be even more damaging. He'd be left with a permanent reminder of his folly—no child deserved to be brought into being purely to serve as a bargaining chip, a commodity. He had to find her and fix this.

He swore. How had he managed to lose control so entirely? Irritated, he stood for as long as he could under piping hot water. Sluicing the sweat from his body, he also rinsed his shirt while he was at it, hanging it up where it would dry quick-time. The storm had abated, the temperature would only rise again.

He thought about her parting words. *Thank you.* Simple. Strangely heartfelt. He hardened his own heart. He was not going to be suckered by a burning blonde. Just because she had a nice hint of vulnerability in her eyes that threatened to soften even his roughened-up skin.

But in the steam of the room, memories of their dark encounter flew at him, tormenting him. He turned the tap to cold, glanced at his watch and groaned. It was going to be a long few hours. But no way was she getting away with whatever the hell she had planned.

Although what he was going to do about it, he had no idea.

CHAPTER FOUR

SIENNA sat on the sand and watched the sun rise. The dawn of a new day, and a different Sienna. She chuckled at her dramatic moment. But she felt changed. And she would always thank him for it. She'd escaped the dorm as early as she could, not wanting any kind of post-mortem with Julia and Brooke. Last night was not for analysing. She'd feigned sleep when they'd stumbled back in at stupid o'clock. Really she'd lain awake almost all the remainder of the night.

She stretched out on the sand, rotating her ankles in circles. Half tempted to ease the slight stiffness with some exercises, but mostly tempted not to. Deciding to keep the gentle aches as a reminder of the most physical and intense experience of her life. Her body still felt warm and pliant from the contact with his. Still felt wet and wanting.

She'd never had a one-night stand before and she refused to regret it. She only regretted that it couldn't be more. She grabbed her day pack. Sipped from her water bottle and pulled out her new journal. She never went anywhere without it. She'd kept one for years—had volumes locked away in a suitcase in the attic of her mother's house. It wasn't so much a 'today I did x, y and z' kind of diary, but a personal place to explore her dreams and fears. For years it had been largely fears. She'd recognised early on that she couldn't talk to her mother, brother or even her best friend about those fears because doing so upset them. They worried about her enough. So she developed the skill to listen to others, talk but keep her own anxieties to herself.

Writing was her way of making sense of what was happening in her life. But despite the weightiness of past events, for the first time she felt unable to pen a word, let alone a sentence. She stared unseeing across the sea, flashes of the previous night filling her mind. Impossible. She could never capture that beauty in words. Unable to record what had happened, let alone how she felt about it.

She looked back down to her book, with a thinly protected heart read over the list of her life's must-dos. The list she always wrote at the start of each year in the front of the new journal. Always hoping to cross at least one or two off in the course of the year. As the years had progressed the list had grown longer not shorter, more fanciful, humorous, outrageous.

But she'd done it. Number One could be crossed off. The one that had made her simultaneously blush and giggle as she'd written it. A joke. A fantasy. And it had been more fantastic than she'd ever imagined. Hell, she'd never imagined it could actually be a reality. Despondent, she recapped her pen. To record it would diminish it and it had been so profound, so perfect. She stared again at the water, watching the sun sparkle on the rippling waves. She wished she weren't such a girl over this. Wished the niggle of guilt would leave her.

She had no idea how long she'd been sitting there, but she wasn't alone any more. There were people arriving with sunscreen and shades. She should get up and get some breakfast. Face the world again. But she didn't move—couldn't be bothered and she sure wasn't hungry.

She played with the sand, drawing up a handful and letting it run through her fingers. She'd feel better soon. She had so much to look forward to—this was merely a wait in the wings before her adventure. But she wished for more of last night's adventure—more of him. She felt bad for not explaining things to him. He'd been wonderful and she'd just disappeared. It wasn't her usual style. None of it had been her usual style—and that had been the whole point. To have been able to have it like that she'd had to leave.

She'd struggled to find her way out of the bar at first. Disoriented. Dazed. The crowd had seemed crazy. She'd forgotten other people existed. She'd felt so cocooned in that darkness. She hadn't wanted to go. Her body had ached to lie with his, to sleep curled beside his. It had hated the fact she was walking away. It had not been what was meant to happen. They had been supposed to rest. And then do it all again.

She shook off the sand, picked up the pen again, pulling the cap off and replacing it, over and over.

'Did you sleep well?'

She jerked her head up, dropping the pen and her jaw as she looked at the tall person towering over her.

Oh, God, it was him.

'What—you didn't expect to see me again?'

She snapped her journal shut, and her mouth. Stuffed the fabric-covered, hardbound book into the bottom of her bag. Bought some more time by hunting for the lid of the pen, but it was lost for ever in the sand. Hot blood burned in her cheeks. 'Um. I…um…'

'I didn't sleep too well, actually, thanks for asking.'

She cleared her throat, but still couldn't get words to come out.

'You see, I met this girl—'

'Rhys,' she croaked.

'Oh. You remember my name.'

'Of course I remember your name!'

He squatted down beside her. And she saw into his face properly. Got a shock. He was looking ferocious. Angry as hell.

She got in quickly then, words flying. 'Look, I'm really sorry about last night.'

'I'm not. Yet. I hope I'm not going to be.'

Confusion deepened the burn in her face.

His eyes, mainly slate, captured hers. 'Like, in nine months time going to be sorry. The mother of all honey traps, was it?'

'What?' Her clammy hands covered her inferno-like flush. She grasped his implication. Nine months? As in B-A-B-Y? He thought she used him to get pregnant? As if.

'Contraception is covered, trust me.' She choked the words out. Marriage and children might be on most people's list of life ambitions but they'd never be on hers. She didn't want any child of hers living the kind of cloistered life she'd suffered and she didn't want to commit to someone only to have to leave them too soon—as her father had left her mother.

The hardness in his eyes didn't soften a jot. 'It's a dangerous game you play.'

'I don't. I…I really don't do that,' she stammered. Annoyed with her mortification. Annoyed that she felt the desperate need to defend herself against his thoughts. It shouldn't matter. But it did. He'd been amazing. And she'd just snuck off. She wanted to slink away now. But couldn't. He thought she was some hideous tramp?

'I meant it when I said I didn't usually…' She faltered under his implacability, finally looking away. 'I'm so embarrassed. I got carried away. It was the tequila slammers.'

'You only had one.'

'I had more before you arrived.'

'Rubbish. I was watching you from the moment you walked in.'

She swallowed. Nerves stretching taut—how could she possibly explain this to him?

'You spend all your holidays having one-nighters with people you hardly know?' He laughed. It sounded dangerously like a snarl. 'It wasn't even one whole night, just a turgid hour. A quick lay and you're off. Did you find someone else for the rest of the night?'

'No!' Anger settled in her. She would not have him demean their experience. OK, so she hadn't been particularly thoughtful, but there was no need for things to turn nasty. 'No. That's sleazy. What we did was not sleazy.'

'What was it, then?'

'A beautiful memory.'

He paused at that. When he spoke again it was softer. 'Past tense?'

She looked back to the sea, not wanting to see him and suffer the bitter temptation of something she couldn't ever have again. 'Past.'

There was a long silence. She hoped he'd take the hint and leave. Her heart was fraying round the edges. Was this why so many women regretted one-night stands? There really was no such thing as 'just walk away'. Things always got complicated.

She wasn't naïve enough to think you could fall in love with someone after a one-night stand. But she certainly cared about what he thought. Too much. It was only because he'd done something for her that no one else ever had been able to. The stars had been aligned, maybe there had been a full moon—some sort of mysterious magic? Anyhow, it was a one-off—those circumstances couldn't be repeated.

He didn't leave, rather he sat on the sand, stretched his legs out alongside hers.

He still had the same shirt on but it was looking rumpled. His tanned arms were tense. More stubbly shadow darkened his jaw. The cold light of day—and he was even more gorgeous. Wilder looking than last night, but that, she suspected, was because he was feeling a little wild. With her.

Fair enough.

She felt compelled to talk honestly. 'I didn't expect to see you again.'

He lay back, resting on his elbow, the length of his beautiful body shown off. Hers went all soft inside and she overcompensated—tensing on the outer.

'You just ran into the night like Cinderella, only you didn't leave me a glass slipper, you left me these.'

Mortified, she watched as he pulled her panties out of his pocket. A scrap of lace and elastic. Looking a lot like something a streetwalker would wear.

It was an effort to speak—a squeak, really. 'Can I have them back?'

'No.' A half-smile quirked the corners of his mouth up. 'I don't think you can. Because, unlike you, for me that hour wasn't anywhere near enough.'

'I'm sorry?'

'Last night was an appetiser. My appetite is well and truly whetted. I want you in a bed, my bed, with all the hours of darkness ahead of us.'

Colour flooded her. Top to toe. She knew it did. She could hear blood beating in her ears, feel it in her cheeks, the palms of her hands. Even her ankles were blushing—her knees. Actually blushing. And it wasn't just embarrassment.

It was the most words he'd strung together in the short time she'd known him and she wished he hadn't because his voice was rich and deep and she couldn't help but listen—and be seduced. And she couldn't help but look at his mouth as it moved and really those lips alone were seductive enough.

As for what he'd actually said…

The blush deepened. But she didn't have a chance in succeeding a second time. She'd have to get naked—and that she didn't want to do. She'd never forgotten the look on Neil's face. The way he'd recoiled. *Everything* would change.

'One night. What do you say? Finish off what we started.'

She melted more into the sand.

'It was only the beginning, you know.'

If she had any kind of backbone she'd stand and walk away. But her bones weren't there any more, there was just mush. Wanting, so badly, what she couldn't have.

He sat up. 'Tell you what, I think we've done this all round the wrong way—topsy-turvy. Back to front. Did the sex before the date. Let's do the date now.'

'I'm sorry?'

'I'm serious. Dinner, a drink, some conversation. I think you owe me that at least.'

It was so tempting. And she did owe him. Could she even manage telling him the truth? No. She didn't want to, didn't want to see desire fade. She wanted to maintain the memory. Maybe, if she was careful, she could add to it just a teeny bit.

Rhys watched the conflict cross her face. She wanted to, but didn't want to. Sitting there blushing like a schoolgirl. Apparently mortified over her wildness the previous night. Not her usual behaviour—that was for sure. You couldn't fake a bodily reaction like that blush. Just as you couldn't fake the fire between them.

He felt happier than the moment he learned he'd come first in his final med exams. Initial instinct had been right. It wasn't a ruse. She had no idea who he was. She wasn't out for a million-dollar baby. He believed her about the contraception. She'd wanted him. Still wanted him. So why the up-and-vanish act? He knew he shouldn't be pursuing this. He was running a risk—the longer it went on, the more likely he was to be caught out. But as he sat near to her now, his body made up his mind for him, shoving the prickling doubt away with ease. He wanted to know her. Last night humour had sparkled in her eyes. She'd watched her friends flirt with the band with an unholy twinkle. He wanted in on her joke. And, OK, he'd lain awake the entire night harder than titanium, lusting after her again. He'd have her again right now if he could. But he was happy to do the conventional courting thing if that was how she wanted it this time. Given her all-over colour, he figured she wasn't lying when she said she didn't usually have one-night stands. So why had she? She'd been so bold. A contrary woman who had secrets. There were definitely secrets in those eyes. Rhys had secrets of his own and he was used to holding them close. But he wasn't used to others holding theirs back from him.

He inched closer, her nearness not enough. He badly wanted to feel her hair with his fingers again—glorious colour, divine length. From the way her pulse was beating, she was not immune to his proximity. He shifted again so their legs almost brushed. He had her attention. Awareness arced between them. Why did she want to run from it? 'You know, when I get close to you, you breathe a little faster.'

She nodded. 'Fear.'

'Maybe, but I don't think that's entirely true. What are you afraid of? You were fearless last night. Utterly fearless.'

She looked up at him. 'I won't say it was a mistake. But it was something that can't ever be repeated.'

His blood ran cold. 'You have a boyfriend?' He looked at her hand. 'A husband?' A ridiculous knot of jealousy pulled tight in his belly.

'No!' She flashed a hurt look at him. 'What kind of woman do you think I am?'

He relaxed, amused by her fire. 'Well, I'm not really sure. That's why I want to spend some time with you. So I can find out.'

'I'm surprised you want to spend another minute with me, you're so keen to think all these horrible things—first I'm out for a baby, then I'm cheating…'

'OK.' He held up a hand and grinned. 'Believe me, I want to spend more time with you.' She didn't soften. He needed to change tack. He ruefully rubbed his hands over his face as he tried to think of a way to break through. 'Look, let's just start over. Completely fresh. Forget all this even happened.'

'Forget *all*?'

'Let's temporarily forget last night, and totally forget the last five minutes.'

He finally got a glimmer of a smile. He leant a little closer. 'I've just sat next to you—wanting to borrow some sunscreen.'

'Sunscreen? Oh, come on, surely you can do better than that.'

He laughed. 'OK, but it's early morning and I had a sleepless night—' he gave her a meaningful look '—and it will do.' He continued with his latest façade, getting the feel for it. 'So it's sunscreen. You're a nice person, you smile, say sure, and pass me the bottle.'

'You didn't want me to rub it in for you?'

He blinked. *Hell, yes, rub right where I'm aching.* 'Let's not get ahead of ourselves again, OK?'

'Too fast?'

'A little.'

Her gurgle of laughter hit him in the solar plexus.

'Anyway, we get to chatting. We swap names. I'm Rhys and you're…'

'Sienna.'

'We chat idly. I tell you I'm here on holiday and isn't the weather fantastic? You smile, nod, agree.' He paused, looked at her expectantly.

She laughed. 'OK. Yes, it is.'

'Finally I get around to it. I ask. Have dinner with me.'

She went back to serious.

'We're two people on holiday. Why not join forces and see some sights together? Do a little dinner. Maybe we could hit a club afterwards?' He caught her eye. She was blushing again and quickly looked away. Damn, he should've put the damper on the gas jet.

But then she spoke. 'What about lunch?'

Lunch. She was playing safe. Tortoise speed rather than hare. He figured he should be glad it wasn't 'maybe a coffee'. Right now he was happy she was still in the game. Besides, a long leisurely lunch could lead to a long lazy afternoon— or not so lazy. A chilled bottle of sauvignon blanc and seafood perhaps? They could go to…

He halted. No. He was supposed to be as much of a tourist on holiday as she was, foreign to this town. They'd have to go to a place foreign to him. Actually he'd prefer they didn't go to a restaurant at all. He wanted to keep out of the spotlight, to stay in this small stretch of beach. An idea bubbled. He answered. 'Lunch would be fantastic.'

She smiled warily. 'OK.'

It was his turn to look wary. 'So it's a date? You're not going to disappear?'

'No.' She seemed both decisive and apologetic. 'I'll be there.'

'The foyer of the hostel over the road? Midday? You're sure?'

Her smile peeked out again. 'As sure as you are.'

He couldn't hold back any longer. Reaching out, he took her hand. The fire flashed. He looked at where his skin touched hers. Looked back to her face and saw it in her serious expression. No exaggeration. The current rippled from her through every inch of his body. 'Good.'

He got away then. Needing some space to think, to plan, to perfect his new persona. He approached Reception quickly. Happy no one else was around. It was the same guy, looking ragged around the edges. He got a smile this time.

'Maitland, wanting to check out?'

'Call me Rhys. Don't you ever stop working this desk?'

He shrugged. 'I need the money.'

'I need a few more nights.'

'Sure. How many?' He tapped at the computer with a cunning smile. 'Find what you were after?'

Rhys gave him a narrow-eyed glance. 'Maybe.'

He walked out of the hostel again, straight to the taxi rank—soon in the back of a car and heading to his apartment. He pushed away the guilt with determination. Rhys Maitland didn't want to be Rhys Maitland for a couple of days. He wanted to be free and on holiday and able to do whatever— just Rhys. Maitland, Monroe, Smith—what was in a name? Justifying it because he couldn't not. He'd gone a step too far to backtrack now and he wanted to be with Sienna more than he wanted to risk being honest with her.

He stuffed a few casual clothes into a small carryall, paused when his mobile beeped. He checked it. A text from Tim.

'Where the hell r u?'

Rhys laughed. He'd forgotten about Tim and the others. He'd just gone after Sienna without thought of anything or anyone else. He was supposed to have helped pack the band's gear away. He was supposed to be at some barbecue Tim was organising for the new crop of interns this afternoon.

But now he had other plans. Better plans. He was having time out. He pushed at the buttons with his thumb.

'On holiday.' He sent the message, waited for the confirmation it had gone. And then, with a broad smile, he hit one last button—*'Off'*.

CHAPTER FIVE

TROUSERS were the only option. Together with the obligatory high-necked, long-sleeved top. Hell, Sienna was going to swelter. But she was going to be steaming up anyway—just from being within three feet of Mr Sex God. She took off the note wedged into the straps of her pack. Scanned it.

'We have lots of questions. We want answers. Later!'

She grinned and grimaced at the same time, then started the rummage through for some suitably unsexy outfit for her 'date'. She should have said no. She should have been rude. She should have let him think what he liked.

Impossible.

Mouth like that, eyes like those. She didn't want them frowning at her and looking icy. So she'd go. Have lunch. Do as Rhys suggested and play the game in reverse. But there'd be no re-match, pre-match or after-match frills. No resumption of body contact. But maybe she could give him the kiss goodbye she'd forgotten last night.

She pulled out her quick-dry, billion-pocketed, zip-off-leg, multi-climate, all-terrain, all-purpose pants and stared at them.

Never in a million years. Even if contact was off the menu she wasn't going looking like such a frump. They'd be great for trekking at altitude. But for a lunch in a hip Sydney café in the middle of summer? Whether accompanied by off-limits sex god or not, it was definitely a no to the trousers. Had to be a skirt. She'd go denim. It was slightly longer than the quick-dry equivalent of the combat travel pants, and no way could she wear the number from last night. Then it was just a matter of selecting which high-neck slim tee she'd team it with.

She tried to blow away the helium floating her hopes. But every breath in had them rising higher. So stupid. This was the finale—the bitter-sweet end to a fantasy come true. She sat on the bunk bed and stared into nothing.

Just go and enjoy the first half of the date that you missed out on last night. Let him see you're not some scary serial slapper or some desperate-to-get-pregnant wench. Then walk away.

Who was she kidding? It wasn't about what he thought. It was about what she wanted—more time in his company. And it wasn't just that he oozed a raw sexuality that had her hot in the ping of a bra strap. She didn't just want him, she wanted to get to know him. There was more going on in those greeny-grey eyes that she wanted to explore.

Exactly midday she left the room and went downstairs, met his gaze across the foyer. He was over by the reception desk watching as she descended the last few steps. He made her feel as if she were supermodel beautiful, as if the eyes of the world were on her—watching, wanting. No one had ever looked that way at her before. Everyone had always *known*. For once she was centre-stage, not in the wings—actively involved rather than in the audience.

She walked up to him as with deliberation he looked her up and down and back up again. Ordinarily his mouth held sensual promise; right now, the smile stretching it was utterly carnal. She had no idea if anyone else was around, all she could see was him, all she could sense was the force of his presence, his breadth, the awareness crackling so near the surface. He looked up the length of her legs once more and the desire in his eyes had her wobbling. Deep inside her body was soft and hot and aching with emptiness. But the pounding of her heart reminded her. That look in his eyes would be snuffed out the instant he saw her scar. He might lie, as Neil had, and say it made no difference. But it would make every difference—he wouldn't treat her as real any more. She broke the eye contact, looked down to the ground, registered the big red chilly bin beside him.

He finally tore his eyes from her legs and nudged the bin with his foot. 'Tell me you like seafood.'

'I like seafood.'

'Really?'

She nodded.

'Good. Should have asked earlier.'

'We're having a picnic?'

'That OK? I thought it was such a great day…' He trailed off, attention back on her legs.

She clamped her upper thighs together, halting the warm urge to swing them open, and managed a cool friendly smile. 'That's great.'

She took the blanket that rested on top of the container. Hugged it in a protective hold. He took the chilly. They crossed the road and wandered down to the beach. Hunted out a nice spot to park their burdens and themselves.

She was glad of the crowds. Glad of the broadness of the daylight—because she seriously needed to get a grip. When he was with her she had the crazy feeling that anything was possible. And it wasn't. He didn't know about her. And when he did, everything would change. Better for him never to know so she didn't have to witness that change. Better to end it before it began. He'd been right—this was just the beginning, but of a fantasy. She would have to finish it so she could treasure it for ever—before it turned into a nightmare.

He set up the umbrella that had been strapped to the side of the chilly.

'You've gone to a lot of trouble in a short time.'

He grinned. 'Not at all. The umbrella is from the hostel. I bought the chilly bin from the store down the road and the food is from a great seafood market I found. They packed everything.'

She spread the blanket for them to sit. She was glad she'd gone with the skirt option. Even though the umbrella shaded them, the temperature was still hitting hot—her internal heat going way higher.

'Drink?' He'd unscrewed the lid off a bottle of sauvignon blanc, deftly holding two glasses in one hand while pouring the wine into them.

She glanced at him, catching his eyes for the first time since leaving the hostel, read the challenge.

'Thank you.'

Her fingers touched his as he gave her the glass. With more luck than skill, she managed not to drop it. All that raced through her head was the memory of those fingers brushing across her back.

Sensible speech was impossible. So she asked a few meaningless, ice-breaker questions. Barely heard his meaningless, ice-breaker answers. Relief came as he unwrapped the food—a fabulous platter of deep-sea delicacies. He piled a few chunks of French bread on a plate, added a swipe of butter to each.

Cool, tasty, satisfying. The succulent seafood slipped down her throat—mussels, prawns, shredded lobster. He handed her an oyster, artfully sitting in its half shell. He winked.

A spurt of mirth bubbled in her. 'Are you trying to feed me aphrodisiacs?'

He laughed aloud. 'I'm doing everything in my power to seduce you.'

He'd already done that. And she'd succumb again this minute if there were any way to maintain the level of excitement and enjoyment evident in his eyes. He was out for a little holiday fun—that was obvious. And if only she was truly able to escape her history, she'd do the same.

They ate, talked a little more, looked a lot more—he was so handsome, she couldn't help but stare, until she could no longer take the need slicing through her. She concentrated instead on the beach volleyball game a few yards away, amazed the women actually managed to stay decent in the teensy, eensy, weensy minuscule strips of Lycra that they passed off as their bikinis. They must use tape. Had to.

He was watching her, amusement apparent. 'You want to play?'

'Oh, no.'

'No?'

'I'm not good with ball games.' Never played. Never allowed. Always on the sidelines while her overprotective mother and brother told her she couldn't and shouldn't. Consequently she was hopeless and not about to show him and a beach full of others how bad she was at catching a ball.

His amusement had increased—he wasn't in on her teen angst.

'Really?' His mind seemed to have gone in another direction entirely. 'You know, if you want, I can give you some help with that.'

She looked at him.

His grin was wicked. 'Ball skills.'

She cleared her throat, narrowed her eyes at him but ducked the challenge. 'I didn't do team sports as a kid.'

'No?' He let it slide. 'What did you do?'

'I was in the orchestra—percussion.'

'You were the girl clanging the cymbal, huh?'

She giggled. 'Yeah, waiting the entire length of the piece for my one moment of glory.'

Much like now. And the satisfaction couldn't be repeated.

'So no team sports. Were you a runner or something? Track and field?'

She laughed aloud. Her mirth rather more than the question merited.

'I'm guessing no, then. But you're fit. You're very fit.'

She nodded. She liked feeling strong. She'd taken years to get strong. 'Yoga.'

'Really?'

'Yeah. And Pilates, Thai Chi. All sorts, really. Anything good for strength and flexibility.'

'Flexibility?' He drew in an audible breath. 'Interesting.'

She paused, aware of the extra charge in the already electric air. He was looking at her legs again. She could almost see into his mind. See the mental movie he was playing there.

The atmosphere was so humid and heavy not even a scimitar sword would slice it. Breathing utterly impossible. With great deliberation, and sheer force of will, she turned and stared at the volleyball players some more.

This had been a terrible idea. How had she thought she could seriously sit and lunch with the sexiest guy ever to walk the earth and rein in temptation? Especially when he was making it more than clear that he wanted to tempt.

But he started chatting again. Asking idle questions that had her answering, soft laughter ensuing, relaxing. God, she needed to find a reason not to like him. And fast. But he was making it impossible with his warm eyes, attentive, listening close. Quite some time passed before she realised she wasn't getting to know anything much about him—other than that he looked fantastic in long shorts. He was all questions, all ears, not offering up a lot of himself in return. Usually she was the listener, the one steering the conversation with questions and open-ended comments. She liked it, liked learning about other people, what made them tick, what made them the way they were. She decided to ask a few questions of her own.

'What are you doing on holiday here?'

He shrugged. 'I needed a complete change.'

'Catching up with old friends?'

He looked confused for a moment. 'Oh, Tim. Yeah. A mate from school.'

The book titled Rhys was closed again. Still not much info to process. She looked at him, trying to read more from his expression. But, although friendly, he was guarded. There were secrets in there. Well, OK, she had a few too, but this was simply the conclusion to a wonderful night—she wasn't asking for his deepest thoughts or fears. Couldn't he be a little more forthcoming?

And then he smiled. She couldn't help but notice his mouth again. He had such an advantage. That smile, those lips. The green in his eyes sharpened. She ran a light hand over her forehead, tried to remember what she'd been going to ask him.

He leant towards her. 'Feeling the heat?'

Just a tad.

'Want to go for a swim?'

Yeah, right. Splashing with him in the waves? Visions of them lying in the surf at the shore, limbs entwined like in some old Hollywood movie, rolled in her head. But there was a huge crowd at the beach now. And sand itched. And she'd have to reveal the very thing she wanted to conceal.

'I don't have my swimsuit on.'

'Damn, I was hoping to get you in your bikini.'

Definitely not going there. 'I don't wear a bikini. Don't want to get too much sun.'

He looked at her tanned legs, brows slightly raised.

Doh. She blandly stared him out.

Finally he shrugged. 'Well, as it can't be a swim, I'm going to go get us an ice cream.'

He rose, long limbs lazily moving with innate grace. She watched him walk towards the vendor over on the footpath, then lay back on the blanket, absurdly at ease in spite of the insane awareness. She enjoyed the faint scent of him left in the air, glanced down at the dent in the sand where his legs had rested. The warmth of the sun, the satisfaction from that delicious lunch, had a soporific effect. The sleeplessness of the night before had its after-effect now. Drowsy, she closed her eyes. Relaxed. She thought of him, of what could have been if things were different. Dreamed dangerously pleasant dreams.

'Hey, sleepy.'

He'd returned. She smiled. Kept her eyes closed. Wanting to extend the fantasy for a few more moments. She heard the scrunch of sand as he sat. She felt something cold touch her mouth. She licked her lips, tasted the creamy ice.

'Nice?' His voice sounded very near, very low, very husky.

'Yes.' Her tongue traversed her lower lip again.

'More?' Even lower, even huskier.

'Yes.'

His warm finger daubed cold ice on her mouth.

He muttered. 'You mind sharing?'

She didn't get the chance to reply. Only to sigh faintly as his tongue flicked the sweetness from her. She sent her tongue out to meet his. She couldn't resist his kiss. Just a little more of a man who wanted her in a way she'd never been wanted before. His fingers went to her jaw, turning her face towards his. She opened her mouth. Let him in. Their tongues met and mated and a tempting touch became total turn-on. Deep, hungry kisses that felt divine and promised even greater pleasure could come. She didn't want him ever to stop kissing her, didn't want to stop kissing him. The sensual caresses drove everything from her mind. Only this, only him. She lifted her hand, combing fingers into his hair, holding him so she could kiss him back as fiercely as he was kissing her.

Her curves melted into his hard planes, her body instinctively recognising his muscles. The way they felt around her, their strength at holding her. Making her his prisoner and his keeper. His hot body lay close; he threw his knee across hers. Teasingly heavy. She wanted the rest of his weight over her. She couldn't prevent the parting of her legs, couldn't stop the arch of her pelvis towards him. She moaned into his mouth.

She wanted. Wanted, wanted, wanted…

His hand came to rest on her lower belly, pressing on her, the weight a tiny taste of the delight of having his whole body over hers. His fingers spread on the flat of her stomach. Smoothing upwards. Skin on…*skin.*

She pulled back sharply. Flashed open her eyes. Stared up at him in horror as she saw him looking down the length of her body. No, no and no again.

She wrenched out of his hold, sitting up and scooting away. His surprise was total.

'Sienna?'

'I'm sorry. I can't. I'm really sorry.' Her heart thudded. Her eyes threatened to spill tears of apology and frustration. 'I really am sorry.'

Rhys watched her run across the sand and swore sharply enough for the family group several feet away to turn around and frown at him. He felt a vague flush, slid back under the shade of the umbrella and strove for control. Anger, frustration and plain shock hit him. She'd done it again. Run out on him. Hell, was she some kind of warped tease?

Instinct told him no. She'd felt genuine desire, genuine regret. Well, damn if she didn't owe him an explanation—again. He packed away the remnants of the picnic with precise movements, then headed for the hostel.

He walked straight into the dorm room he now knew to be hers. There seemed to be a mass of women hanging there. They turned and stared at him as if he were an invading Martian. But Rhys was well used to walking into a room full of women—at the nurses' stations, or the new interns. Addressing a bunch of women who were sending a variety of looks from under their lashes wasn't something that intimidated or really even interested him. What interested him was that one woman.

'Is Sienna here?' He addressed them collectively.

'Sure is.' He recognised the speaker as one of the friends at the bar the night before.

It was like the parting of the Red Sea. He looked where they separated and to where she sat on a bottom bunk, quiet and red-faced. Her annoyance and embarrassment were obvious and, yes, her upset. What was she afraid of? Surely not him?

She stood. 'Rhys, you can't come in here.'

'Bet you want to, though, don't you?' The South African again. Caustic delivery.

Rhys ignored the stifled giggles. Time to turn on the charm. He was a Maitland—had the genes, the upbringing. He might loathe it but public speaking was a skill he could call on.

'I'm sorry to butt in on you ladies, but I need to explain something to my friend here.' He didn't take his eyes off Sienna, but sensed the slight hostility in the room. It was as clear to them as it was to him that she was feeling edgy and that he was the cause. He needed to claim back some points— penitent man would be a good start. 'You see—' he gave a small shrug '—I owe her an apology.' He didn't know what for yet but they didn't need to know that.

All seven heads swivelled to Sienna. He felt the atmosphere soften.

'You want to say sorry?'

'Yeah. I'd say it all right now but I need some time with her to explain things properly. Alone.'

He swallowed his smile at her obvious discomfort. Her big blues were fixed on him and the incredulity warring with anger was unbelievably amusing.

'This is way better than any movie.' A different South African this time, she got a low murmur of agreement.

Sienna's cheeks were redder than a fire engine. 'Stop it, Rhys.' She addressed the girls. 'It's me who owes the apology. Again.' Contrite eyes pleaded with him and the rest of the room. Hmm. She was good. A little honesty mixed in with a sidestep.

She turned back to him. 'I'm sorry, Rhys.'

He heard the finality she was striving for and tensed. He wasn't about to let her go. 'Let's get coffee and talk.'

'I can't now. I've promised to go to an art gallery with Brooke this afternoon.'

He was not letting her slip away a third time—he'd have his answers. 'That's OK. You can make it up to me later.' He studied the now silent audience. They could be more of a help to him than her if he played it right. 'Don't you think she should?' He cast a soulful gaze around; it wasn't much of a stretch to play the part of crushed suitor—not hard at all given he actually felt it.

'Oh, yeah, Sienna. You must.'

He had them now, eating out of his palm.

'Give the guy a break.'

'She'll see you later at that bar.' Caustic South African again. More on his side than he'd realised. 'We'll make sure she's there. Six p.m. Have her drink waiting.'

'Yes, ma'am.'

He didn't stick around to let Sienna try to argue, but her eyes flashed her thoughts in the final moment he met them. Anxiety, anger, reluctance—and, at the bottom of it all, desire.

CHAPTER SIX

SIENNA didn't go to the gallery. She went shopping. She was pathetic. But she wanted him again so badly and she wanted it to be as good as the night before. So she was on a mission for a new top—anything that might work. She stopped at the make-up counter. Stage make-up could create a fabulous scar—couldn't it hide one too? She tried on a variety of in-season style tops. There was none with a polo neck. Everything was summery—low-cut and revealing. Exactly what she didn't want.

In despair she went to the lingerie section of the department store. New frillies were supposed to help with confidence, weren't they?

'How was the gallery?' Rhys was waiting. Clad in jeans and a different shirt. Cool beer in a glass, half empty already. Steely eyes lanced her with questions that she knew he wouldn't hold back on. That she knew she was going to have to answer. Honestly.

'I didn't go. Went shopping instead.'

'Buy anything interesting?'

'No.' A new bra. She was wearing it now. Figured if she was going to go down she might as well do it in a hot outfit.

And her sensible travel numbers didn't have the requisite lace ratio. This one did. She could feel her budded nipples pressing against the slightly scratchy stitching even now.

'Sienna—'

She didn't want to be here. Didn't want the pretence. Didn't want the girls from the hostel, whom she hardly knew, watching and wondering. This was going to end in tears—for her anyway. She might as well just get it over with right now.

She grabbed him by the hand. 'Let's get out of here.'

He let her lead, walking beside her but in the direction of her choice. She marched down the street not having a clue where she was headed. Just wanting away from eyes and those memories only recently made but that were going to be the best of a lifetime. Right now she was going to ruin them.

The contact of his hand around hers meant her blood was travelling at high speed to every outlying inch. Making her feel more aware of her body, making her feel more alive than she ever had. It didn't frighten her. It seduced her. Frustration and want and bitterness forced her. She wanted him enough to risk it.

She went into the alleyway a shop down from the hostel. Ducked into a doorway partly along. Turned to face him. He was right behind her.

'Sienna?'

She shut him up with her mouth, passionately pressing against him. His arms clamped around her. He pivoted to lean against the door, taking her weight with him. Hot, intense, searing kisses—as if the moment on the beach had never been interrupted, only intensified. Burning, aching, she swept her hands across his shoulders, rotated against him, driving her hips against his. Wanting to reconnect, taking his mouth with a depth of passion she relished and wanted to relive again and again.

He jerked his head back. 'What the *hell* is going on, Sienna?'

She pulled him back to her. Not wanting to think. Not wanting to admit to anything just yet. Wanting to drown her doubts for moments longer in his kiss.

'You want this?' He groaned against her. 'You want me? Say it.'

'Yes.' She clawed him closer. 'I want you.'

His fingers pulled in her hair, holding her still so he could plunder, pressing a hard kiss that left her in no doubt of the frustration he'd been feeling all afternoon. A kiss that left her utterly without breath.

The lack of oxygen, the fever, sent her crazy. She reached for him. Reckless. If she'd been able to get away with it once, couldn't she do it again? If she could somehow keep his hands occupied—like the way she had last night, forcing him to take her weight, to take her. God, she wanted that again. His strength. His glorious width. Frantic, furious and fast. She fought with his belt. Once more. Just once.

He pulled back sharply, grabbing her hands, stopping them with his. 'No.'

She looked up at him in surprise. Stepped back when she saw the anger in his eyes.

He shook his head at her. 'Too fast.' A savage whisper.

She tried to get her hands back but he tightened his grip. 'If we're going to do this, we're going to do this properly.' He eyeballed her, stepping closer. 'My room or yours?'

She looked away. Damn. Honestly she wanted nothing more than to lie in a comfortable bed and be able to explore him freely and at leisure, but it wouldn't be the same. He'd be like Neil—freeze, then run a mile. Or he'd treat her like some fragile piece of glass and she hated being wrapped in cotton wool.

He stepped even closer, so his body pressed against hers. His erection teased her. His question terrified her. 'Why won't you let me see you naked?'

She tried to pull away but he moved closer still—pushing her back against the wall, keeping hold of her hands, his body leaning into hers.

Her breathing shallowed—half from fear, half from desire.

'You're willing to let me kiss you. You're willing to let me *inside* you. But you won't take your clothes off.'

'Rhys…' Amazed at his acuteness, she pleaded with him not to go there despite knowing it had been inevitable—from the moment he'd strode onto the sand beside her this morning. She'd been kidding herself to think she could get away with not telling him. But it was exactly what she didn't want to have happened. Exactly why she'd run into the night after their encounter.

'Why?'

She stared into his searching eyes, at his sensual mouth now pulled into a hard line. She reached up on tiptoe, pressed her hand to his lips. Finally felt them soften and part. He kissed the tip of her fingers—his mouth moving slowly, warm and teasing.

Desire raged through her veins, coupled with painful anger over what was to come. But she knew no matter what happened, no matter how things would change, she couldn't walk away from him a third time. She was as human as the next person and the temptation was too strong. She had to run the risk so she could have the chance of feeling his erotic intensity again.

She pulled her hand away. He straightened, watching her, waiting for her answer.

She stared at his shirt buttons. 'I have a scar.'

There was a bit of a silence.

'So do I.'

She jerked her head up.

He looked down at her. Mouth twitching. 'You show me yours, I'll show you mine.'

She stared back at him and watched his humorous touch fade. His brows lifted. 'Big scar?'

'Pretty big.' Actually it wasn't. More like hairline, it was what it represented that was huge.

'It can't be as big as mine.' He firmed his grip on her.

He still wasn't getting it. Unable to handle it any more, she grabbed the neckline of her tee in a tight fist. Pulled it down so it exposed the vee of skin all the way from her neck down to the dainty bow decorating the point where the cups of her bra met in the middle. The scar ran from the base of her throat. A straight line right down the centre of her body. Defining her.

She saw the shock register in his face. And recognition. And then she saw it. The look she'd known was unavoidable. Fear. He hid it quickly. Shutting down. Closing off. But it had been there. She tensed.

He said nothing. Just stood frozen. Staring at her chest. His mouth opened a fraction and the buttons on his shirt jumped about as she heard the sharp intake of breath.

Anger and pride held her head high. Her chin lifted higher—underlining the challenge he'd already failed. As she'd predicted, as she'd known, the flame of desire was snuffed out in a flash.

She pushed him back against the wall. Met no resistance, almost as if he'd stepped back at the moment she pushed. She ran, feet light in her sandals. She didn't look back. She didn't need to. He didn't come after her. Didn't call out. Didn't seem to stir even.

She dragged in deep breaths, pushing the sobs back deep into her chest. *Forget it, forget it, forget it.*

She scurried past Curtis on Reception, raced into the telly room, knowing at this time on a Saturday night it was bound to be empty, everyone would be out partying. She chose a big chair on the far side of the room, curled into it like a cat, hiding from the world. She reached into her small day pack and pulled out her journal.

The list of wannabe life achievements she'd scrawled on page one stared at her, making a fool of her. She told herself it didn't matter. Tried not to let it ruin everything. Failed. With anger and misery she relived past revelations.

Neil had been like that. Backed off the instant he'd seen it. Eventually he'd returned. But he'd been hesitant, treating her gingerly. Then he'd made it worse. He'd told the world. She'd only just escaped her hometown and the notoriety of being the 'heart-girl'. Wanting to start over with anonymity. Be normal, like anyone else at university. She'd thought she could trust Neil to see past it. He didn't. And her secret had become common knowledge—the looks, unwanted, undeserved pity sent her way again. And rather than understanding more, Neil had understood less. Become more protective, more and more stifling until he was as bad as her mother and brother combined.

She wanted freedom. She wanted to be the same as anyone else—and to be treated like that. Part of the reason she was going overseas was to start over—again. She read over the list again. Then, for the first time in all her years of keeping a journal, she ripped a page right out.

Rhys rested back on the warm bricks as a range of emotions rushed through him. Shock, anger and desire but mostly disappointment. In himself—what had happened to his renowned beside manner? His unflappable charm? So much for an uncomplicated summer fling. He'd known what he was looking at. For a second after the shock he'd even admired the skill of the surgeon who'd done it. As neat a job as you could get. Then the ramifications set in. You got that kind of scar from a major operation. Open-heart surgery. The thought of her lying on an operating table had made him recoil. Not someone as young and full of vitality as her.

Stupid, when every day at the hospital he was confronted with mortality—he knew full well it could hit anyone any time. He knew that from his own brush with it as a kid. With Theo.

He hadn't been joking about having a scar of his own. It was a mess, but it had left an even bigger mess on the inside. While Sienna's heart might have been operated on, his was the scarred one—one that had never fully healed. He tried so hard to make it right. And failed every time. Roughly healed, puckered tissue formed a protective barrier and he didn't want anyone to penetrate it. He wasn't going to be vulnerable. He'd never reveal the depth of that pain—to anyone. Nor did he want to set himself up for more of that kind of hurt.

He headed back to the hostel. Maybe he should just check out. She'd be feeling pretty mad with him and he was mad with her for not giving him a chance. For springing it on him and then skipping out.

But the more he thought of her, the greater his need to see her again grew. As the shock faded, he felt the resurgence of desire. If anything he wanted her more. He wanted to kiss away the pain he'd seen in her eyes. He wanted them heavy with passion and the glow of life. He refused to analyse why. Just pegged it on desire. Tim had told him to lighten up, to take a break. He rationalised, remembered she was only in town for a few days. This could still be a holiday fling. They weren't talking for ever and babies. Being with her once more couldn't do him any more damage—or her. Maybe they could both forget about their scars for a while.

Curtis was in his regular position behind the reception desk.

'Did they concrete you in place here?' Rhys muttered.

Curtis looked up from the old gossip mag in front of him, his eyes narrowing when he saw it was Rhys. 'She's in the TV room. Looks like you're in trouble.'

Rhys acknowledged the truth with a grunt and went in search of her. He looked into the room, saw her in the far corner, her fine-boned figure folded into the armchair. Her head jerked up as he approached and he saw her stuff a piece of paper into her book, snap it shut and then jam the whole thing into her bag.

'You running out on me is a really bad habit.'

'Be honest, this time you were happy to be run out on.'

'No, I wasn't, and I really don't want you to run out on me again.'

She stared up at him, the blue in her eyes shadowed with the purple of pain. Looking all the more intense in the unnatural pallor of her face.

He boxed on. 'I never did get to show you my scar. You walked away before I had the chance.'

'You froze over. Colder than, than…'

'I was unprepared.'

'It's good that way. Then I get an honest reaction.'

'It's not fair to set someone up. What was I supposed to do? Of course I was going to be shocked. How could I have predicted that? Anyway, it looks to me like some kind of life-saving scar.'

She looked away from him then, seeming to focus on a speck of dust hanging in mid-air.

'Did it work?'

'Clearly.'

He hid his smile at her caustic tone. 'Come on.' He tugged on her hand, hauling her out of the chair. 'I've got something to show you.'

'Rhys, I really don't want—'

'Come with me.' He spoke quickly and then gave a cheeky grin as he realised the *double entendre* of his words.

She looked less bruised, more baleful.

'Please.' He kept hold of her hand and led her up the stairs, away from Curtis' grin and to the privacy of his own room.

'You know, yours isn't really much of a scar. Mine is much bigger.'

She blinked. He'd taken her aback. He undid his jeans and pushed them down so he could step out of them. He hadn't bothered with boxers so his erection thrust up. He suppressed his satisfaction as he saw her eyes widen at the sight of him. Her deadened look disappeared. Her cheeks flushed. Yes, he still wanted her. Now she knew it.

He twisted his leg to show her the place on the outside of his thigh where the glass had gone deep. The scar was old and jagged but still angry-looking.

She was totally diverted. Frowning at it. 'That's not a life-saving scar.'

'No.' It had been a life-taking scar. A constant reminder to him of that day of youthful folly and painful helplessness. The kind of day he'd determined never to experience again. The mistakes he'd never repeat, the inability to do a damn thing…

'I don't really want to talk about it either.' He pulled back his leg. 'So, I win on the scar stakes.' He shut out the memories, shut away the emotion. No room for that kind of emotion here. Only fun—a fling with the sexiest woman he'd ever seen.

They'd just forget their wounds for a few moments. He reached out to her, touching his fingers to the back of her hand, sliding up her arm, stepping closer. But she held back, stiff, head away, not melting into his embrace. He thought he knew why. So they weren't going to be able to forget the scars just yet—at least not hers. He kissed the corner of her mouth. Spoke right into her ear.

'Sienna, for the record. You are not ugly. Your scar is not ugly.'

'I don't think I'm ugly.' She pulled back and he saw vehemence in her eyes. 'That's not what worries me. It's more that people take one look and start acting like I'm going to collapse in a corner any moment. When I wear a low-cut top, I see their curiosity. People look at me, then quickly look away thinking either I'm a circus exhibit or I'm on borrowed time.'

'And are you?'

'Well, I might be able to do the splits but it's going to take me years to learn to juggle.'

'You can do the splits?'

The big blues glinted back at him. 'Three ways.'

'OK, you can prove that to me later, but for now you're saying you're not a circus exhibit and you're not going to collapse in the corner in the next five minutes?'

'You got it.'

He waited, knowing there was more. Despite the gentle humour she wasn't ready yet and he wanted to hear all she had to say.

She stumbled her way through it. 'Last night…last night was amazing.'

'Yes.' He agreed quietly—major understatement.

'You didn't know.'

He thought for a second, trying to figure where she was going—she thought it was amazing only because he didn't know? 'You think it's going to change now I do?'

The flush in her cheeks deepened but she looked him square in the eye—he found himself understanding the expression 'true blue' precisely, such was the painful honesty reflected there. 'I just want to fully enjoy everything like normal people do,' she mumbled.

He started to see even clearer. 'You don't want any soft treatment because of your history.'

She nodded.

'You want to be just like anybody else.'

She nodded again.

He chuckled. 'I'm sorry, honey, but there is no way on this earth you'll ever be just like anybody else.' He finished his thought before her mad look got madder. 'You're special.' Very special and his body was harder than it had ever been. He asked, 'Do you want to be pushed to extremes, Sienna?'

She stared. 'What sort of extremes?' She sucked in a breath as if she were tasting fresh mountain air for the first time. 'Like last night sort of extreme?'

It was his turn to nod—slowly. 'Yeah.' He slid his hands to her hips, wanting to keep her near him. 'Shall we find out exactly how much pleasure your body is capable of?'

The shiver shook her from head to foot. Huge blue pools stared up at him, mirroring her thoughts—incredulity at what he'd said, excitement, temptation.

He couldn't quite believe he'd said it himself, but now he had, he knew it was exactly what she needed. And what he needed—the most wonderful challenge. The opportunity to forget himself, his life, and just bury deep into her, make her forget the trauma her body had been through, show her how much fun she could have.

He saw the moment she was sold—the flash in her eyes, the parting of her mouth.

'OK.'

He hugged her, holding her close to the beat in his own chest, savouring the satisfaction in knowing she wouldn't be running out on him again, that he'd have all the time he needed to quench this lust. Thank God they were finally in agreement.

No one had ever stared at her before with such a look of want. Did he really not mind it? Did he even notice it? Did he not wonder?

'Is it OK if I touch it?'

So he definitely saw it. He ran his finger down the white line that bisected her from base of her throat to diaphragm. Then he looked to the side. He grinned. 'Is it OK if I touch these?' He cupped her breasts; his thumbs stroked her nipples through her bra. 'Very pretty. Pretty flowers, but what's underneath is even prettier.' He pulled the lace down so her nipples played peek-a-boo over the top. Bent and pressed kisses along the rising slope of one, stopped just shy of her nipple—it was so hard it hurt. He slid his hands around her back, loosened the catch and let the straps fall from her shoulders.

'Extreme…' he muttered. 'Let's see if we can do extreme.'

She held her breath, refusing to let her body sway towards his, one last doubt needing to be dealt with. 'I don't frighten you?'

He laughed. 'A slim little thing like you?'

'No.' She jabbed a finger at her chest. 'This doesn't frighten you?'

'Honestly?' He stared straight into her eyes. 'No.' He

grazed the back of his knuckles against her nipples. 'I'll tell you what frightens me. The thought of not having you for one whole night where I can lie with you and we can go at it like rabbits.'

She giggled, spontaneous effervescence bursting through her solemnity. 'How do rabbits do it?'

'I don't know but they do it lots. Let's just go with the lots for now, OK?'

'OK.'

He pulled his tee shirt over his head. Then he returned to her breasts, finally fitting that heaven-sent mouth around her pointed tip and letting his tongue rough over it.

She marvelled at the feel of his hands on her body, the way he was struggling with his passion. He really wasn't fazed by her scar at all—his desire not lessened by any degree. If anything he was even more aroused than the night before. She figured that was because, in one way, he didn't care. He just wanted her. Wasn't worried for her. Because there was nothing invested here—they weren't talking futures or relationships or anything remotely serious. Hell, they weren't even talking tomorrow. They were talking sex—good, hard sex, right now.

That was OK. In fact, she reasoned in the last seconds she could still think, that was perfect—they were living life right in this moment. Exactly how she'd decided she had to live. No guarantees, just go with the now.

He undid the button on her skirt and tugged at it, his fingers catching her panties underneath as well. Slowly, he slid his hands down, kneeling before her as he pulled both skirt and underwear off.

'You have the most magnificent legs I have ever seen.'

She looked down. Six foot three of strongly muscled, extremely naked man was at her feet and gazing at her with unconcealed lust—despite her scar. She was as naked as he. The answering desire inspired in her meant she could hardly stand. She reached a shaking hand out to his shoulder, needing the support.

He stood, scooped her up. 'Do you have any idea the thoughts I've had these last twenty-four hours?'

She let her head fall back on his chest, willingly doing the featherweight female act. 'Do I want to?'

'Sure you do. But—' he grinned as he spread her on the bed to his satisfaction '—I'm not going to tell you, I'm just going to do it.'

He started with a kiss that tasted of his smile and his promise of maximum pleasure. She kissed him back, hungry to take the satisfaction she knew he'd give. His determination, his intention, was unmistakable and she was breathless with just the thought of it, let alone the accomplishment.

He left her lips, left her gasping, while he kissed her cheeks, her jaw, down her neck—kissing all over her shoulders and chest until her entire torso had been touched by his beautiful mouth. His hands worked in accompaniment— trailing fire, teasing, tending to the parts of her that his mouth wasn't fixed to. Meantime she tried to take in air.

He slid down the bed, between legs she'd happily parted. He placed one knee over his shoulder, so he could kiss along the inside of her leg. 'That OK for you?'

Nothing beat the sensation of his stubble gently rasping against her inner thighs. 'Uh-huh.'

He lifted her other leg over his other shoulder so his head was cradled between her thighs. She was hot and wet and he hadn't even touched her yet—not there. She could hardly wait. She raised her hips, wanting to rock them, wanting him to rub and rotate and reach right into her.

His lips curved and her desire to have them press against her became paramount. 'Rhys.'

He bent his head and she stopped breathing altogether. When she started again, it was even faster and shallower. Her entire body beat to the pulse of his movements, to the rhythm of the blood in her veins. She'd never lain like this. Never wanted anything or anyone the way she wanted him doing this, like this.

His fingers stroked, his mouth teased. And all the while she got hotter and wetter and way more vocal about what she wanted—for once in her life she had someone listening, who was willing to take her where she wanted to go at the speed she wanted to go at. She was on the journey and he was the chauffeur. She called out, encouraging him, so close.

He raised his head. 'Need to slow down a second, honey.'

Why?

His half-smile at her expression inflamed her. When he gave her the reason he nearly sent her over the edge. 'I want you really ready.'

She was ready alright. She was beyond ready.

Suddenly he rose, kneeling, hands on her calves. As if she were a doll, he scissored her legs, pushing one right above her head. He looked intrigued. 'You weren't kidding about the splits.'

She grinned and shook her head. Pliant, she stretched for him. He wound her other leg around his waist. The position had her so exposed. His hand hardened round her ankle, the look on his face intensified as he gazed down the length of her leg with wicked intent. Aroused beyond bearing, she could hardly stand the wait.

He arched over, bringing his hips into line with hers. 'This is going to be as deep as it can get. That OK?'

Of course it was OK. She was just damn glad she'd done all that yoga and had no problems with flexibility. 'Yeah.'

He edged in a fraction and then, with his other hand pressing on the mattress beside her hip, penning her in place, he caught her eye and thrust fiercely.

She cried out. Deep wasn't the word.

His eyes narrowed; she could see the tension in his jaw. 'OK?'

She nodded. More than OK. More than anything she'd ever known. Her body half lifted off the bed with him as he tilted back, pausing before pushing in again.

She couldn't hold back the whimper—of delight and of desire. This was incredible.

'You want physical, Sienna?' He gulped in air. 'I can do physical.'

She picked up what he'd left unsaid. 'Just physical?'

He puffed out. 'Yeah.'

Fine. At least he was honest. Besides, she'd be gone in a week, and she was living *right now.* 'So do it.'

He didn't need telling again. Slowly, but with the impact of a ten-tonne truck, he surged into her, grinding deep before pulling back inch by devastating inch.

She'd never been so totally possessed. She couldn't move, couldn't even embrace him back, instead she reached her arms up above her head and took hold of the railing of the headboard—trying to keep as in control as him but with every deep, powerful thrust he took a little more from her.

'You like it?'

'Yes.'

'Want more?'

'Yes.'

'Harder?'

'Yes.'

And from then she couldn't speak, could only moan and not even do that consciously. All she could see was him. All she could feel was him—he was touching her innermost core, and it was so sensitive, so exquisite, she honestly thought she couldn't cope. The heat in her body was so intense she shied from it, shook her head, wanting it to stop, never wanting it to stop.

He spoke. Growled at her as he slowly pulled out. 'Give me that fearless response I had last night. You don't want fear from me—well, I don't want fear from you either.'

He pushed harder on her leg, parting her further so she was so open, so that each time his body slammed forward as much of him entered her as was physically possible—and then some. His pace increased and her consciousness receded. His pelvic bone rubbed against hers—tormenting her, bringing her closer and closer to an oblivion she couldn't contend with.

She held tighter to the rail. She couldn't take it, couldn't…

'More?' His hand gripped, his muscles bunched, his expression showed his thin grip on his self-command.

She couldn't resist. Gave in to the overwhelming instinct to surrender. 'Yes. Oh…'

He pounded. She lost it. Closed her eyes against him, screwed them tight in the agony of ecstasy, her scream sounding around the room.

His body locked rigid as he uttered one word before giving in to the tension, the demand to drive deep and hard that one last time and pour his all into her.

'Perfect.'

CHAPTER SEVEN

'WE NEED to rest a while.' Rhys reached down to the side of the bed, brought back up a bottle of water and held it for Sienna to sip before drinking deep himself. He caught her eye and winked. 'Not bad.'

She lay, gasping for air, wondering if she'd ever catch her breath again. Knowing that when she did, she was asking him to do that again. And again. Blood pounded through her body, singing through her veins. She'd never felt so alive.

'Tell me about it now.'

'The scar?'

He nodded.

Why hold back? He hadn't been lying when he'd said she didn't scare him. He'd just taken her apart and put her back together and shown her she worked just fine. She could tell him it all, knowing he wasn't going to treat her any different— he'd proved that magnificently. 'I was born with a heart condition. My valves didn't work properly and eventually I had to have a couple replaced.'

'Valves?'

She nodded.

He nodded with her. 'How did they find out about it?'

'My dad died from a heart condition when I was little. He

was young—it was really hard on my mum. She got worried that my brother and I might have inherited a weak heart. So she got us checked out and they found it.' She grimaced. 'Then it was all on.'

'What was on?'

She understood the way her mother had reacted, why she'd gone so over the top—she'd never got over her husband's death. She didn't want to lose another of her loved ones. Seeing her pain had made Sienna's decisions for her own future—she couldn't control how Jake and her mother felt, but she could stop how other people felt about her. She refused to burden anyone else with that kind of worry, that heartache. And she refused to let anyone else try to restrict her life the way they had hers—even with the best of intentions. Her relationship with Neil had cemented that decision. It had proved she couldn't have it all. So no long-term relationships, no marriage. Certainly no kids. She didn't want them to inherit this crummy heart. It was the price she'd pay to have the freedom to do as she wanted.

'Mum was terrified she'd lose me. She had a terrible time losing Dad. I know she didn't mean to but her fear made my life a nightmare. So did Jake—my brother. I understand it, I do. But they were so restrictive, totally overprotective. And everyone knew about it. It defined me. Seems like that was who I was, that was all I was. The girl with the dodgy ticker.'

She pulled the sheet up, covering her cooling body. 'I was at the doctor's my whole life. Second opinions, check-ups— any hint of something as little as a cold and I was packed off to the damn doctor—again and again and again. Sidelined from all the fun things.' She paused to draw breath so she could speak with greater force. 'I hated it. Hated them. Constant prodding. Constant questions. Telling you what you can and can't do—all the time. Not that Mum listened too close anyway—she only heard the can't not the can.'

She got a grip on her emotion, tried to look to the future. 'I've had the operation now. I've got my degree. I'm well and strong and I want to move on.'

She still disliked doctors. Knew it was ridiculous when they'd effectively saved her life. But she'd been coddled for so long, eventually the rebellious teen moment had hit and they'd been a good target—better than hurting her family for simply loving her. But her brother and mother still hadn't seemed to have adjusted to her new status, even though the operation was a few years ago now. Same with everyone else she knew. Which was why she'd decided to move away and to keep moving.

'And boyfriends?'

She tightened the sheet about her. 'Not so good.'

'What happened?'

'I don't like everyone knowing.'

'And he told people.'

She nodded. 'And he was overprotective. *Really* overprotective.' Her sigh came from deep within. 'People change when they find out. I don't want this to be all that I am. Yes, it's part of me. But it's not all of me. I have more to offer than that. It's better if people don't know.'

'So what, you're going to stay covered up for ever?'

'Maybe.' She smiled. 'I'm going to start somewhere new again.'

'What if you fall in love and want to settle down?'

Settling down wasn't an option for her. Her own family had been to hell and back for her. She wasn't doing that to anyone else and she wasn't giving up her newly grasped freedom. She shrugged the question off. 'That's not on the horizon. I just want to live life now.'

'How do your family feel about your trip?' Unerringly he zeroed in on her weak spot—he seemed to have a real knack for that. She felt the blush. They didn't know the half of it. Thought she was in Australia for over a month and then heading straight to the UK. She hadn't told them about her detour on the way. Not wanting to worry them unnecessarily. She wasn't taking outrageous risks. She'd present it to them afterwards as a *fait accompli*—when her confidence was stronger. 'They're OK with it.'

Despicable. That was him. He should tell her. The truth. Now. But telling her would make her mad with him and he got the vibe she'd be less than impressed with his MD qualifications. Kind of ironic, seeing most women liked the idea of being with a doctor. Given they were usually rich and all. But Rhys was beyond rich too. And he liked the fact she didn't know either of those things about him. He liked the fact that she simply shared the raw physical attraction. It was basic. Why should they have to go any deeper than that? But already they were going deeper. Her words had an effect on him. 'Yes, it's part of me. But it's not all of me.' They had more in common than he was willing to admit. They'd both experienced trauma, defining them. She was determined to overcome hers. He could never leave his behind. Could never forget. Except when he was in her arms he felt better. Recharged. Couldn't he have that for just a little longer?

Rhys hadn't had such a selfish urge in a really, really long time. But, he reasoned, she need never know. They'd have this fantastic holiday fling together. Have a great time. He'd help her learn how wonderfully well her body worked. How desirable she was. Then she'd go and he'd head back to work refreshed and satisfied. Her company was invigorating. He hadn't had this much fun in what felt like for ever. He'd come back to life.

'Tell me about yours.'

He wondered what she meant for a moment. Then saw what she was looking at. His thigh. His scar. Memories flew at him. He wasn't ever rid of them for long. He never talked about it. Never would, with anyone.

'Skateboard accident.'

He heard it all. The squeal of the wheels as the brakes were slammed on—too late. The crunch of bone on concrete, the spattering sound of blood, the pulse weakening, the look in Theo's eyes as the life had literally bled out of him—the silent plea that Rhys had been unable to answer. If only he'd listened ten seconds before. If only he'd stopped when his kid cousin had asked. If only he hadn't been so hell-bent on being the fastest, the best…

He stopped the replay with the strength of mind that had got him through years of study, years of guilt.

He did not discuss the scar. Not with anyone.

He realised he'd been silent a while. She was watching him, watching whatever he'd let slip across his face. She looked serious and he knew she'd seen more than he'd intended. He flashed her a smile—charm mode. But the questions didn't leave her eyes. Her serious look intensified. Not buying it.

He needed a better method of distraction—for both her and him. He moved quickly, picked her up and carried her to the bathroom—the weight of her transforming the moment of angst to a moment of masculine pleasure. They just managed to fit in the shower.

She giggled at the ridiculously small cubicle. 'Practising for the Mile High Club, are we?'

'I think that'd be a piece of cake after this.' He hoisted

her up against the wall. 'I like carrying you. Makes me feel all he-man.'

'And I'm the little woman? That is not a PC thing to say.'

He shrugged. 'What are you going to do? Sue me?' He scooped her higher so her breasts were almost at mouth height. 'Besides,' he added with unashamed arrogance, 'you like it.'

He kissed her body, let her slide down the wall so he could kiss her mouth. The pathetic trickle of water from the shower head was barely enough to wet her majestic hair. Man, he wished they were in his apartment. His bathroom was built for more than one occupant and had fantastic water pressure. He'd take the hose and spray the water all over her lithe limbs and then follow it with his hands and mouth. His appetite for her was huge and hardly filled.

She seemed to share the hunger for him. She swept her hands over his chest, traversing the indentations and ridges of muscle and bone.

'What do you do to keep fit?'

'Sail.'

On the few days he had away from work he'd spend hours on the water, in the water. Finding freedom with wind and sun and silence.

'You get muscles like these from sailing?' She started exploring them with her mouth as well as her fingers.

'It's not all just sitting around holding the tiller eating crab cakes.'

She mumbled as she kissed down his sternum. 'I've never been sailing.'

'We should go some time.' They should do everything.

'Would you take me below deck?'

She was heading south now and he could hardly answer.

'I'd take you above…below…in the cupboard where I keep the sails. You'd look sexy on my spinnaker.'

'Where do you sail?'

'On the…' *harbour.* He jerked out of the daze of desire. He wasn't supposed to live in Sydney. What had he said— had he said? He'd thought Melbourne. Hell, he couldn't think at all when she did that. She didn't seem to have noticed his lack of answer. She was trailing her hands down his belly, watching as his body responded. Her eyes glazed, the flame in her face growing. He could think of nothing but her. 'What do you want?'

She didn't reply with words. Instead she made like him and let her actions speak—touching him with the hunger he had for her. She raised her head from where it had been deliciously close to where he really wanted her. 'Are you sore at all? From last night?'

Actually, yeah, his legs had been feeling it a bit today.

'Maybe you should lie down, let me do the work this time.'

He lost all ability to think, couldn't come up with a thing to say. She could be the boss. Fine. 'Uh, OK.'

They abandoned the shower, didn't bother with towels, just landed back on the bed in a hot, damp tangle. Her smile was so full of eager anticipation he had to close his eyes against the power of it. He lay on the bed and she knelt above him. Slowly roving over him from top to toe with her hands, her trailing hair, her hot mouth. Her roughened hands killing him with their firm grip and determined action. Exactly where he'd wanted her. Keeping control was such an effort—one certain to slice even more years off his life.

She guided him home. He gasped as she rode him hard. 'We're supposed to be pushing you, not me.'

She laughed, shook her head at him as she kept it crazy,

fast, slow, faster again, keeping him on the edge until the heat was intolerable and his breath came harsh.

Sienna propped up her head by placing four of the thin pillows in the one pile, looked down her body to where he lay sprawled halfway down the bed. He'd spread her legs around him. Was seemingly having a wonderful time focusing on one at a time and exploring it—running smooth fingers down her thigh, twirling round her knee and back up again, fingers playing on her occasional freckles. She was almost reluctant to break into his enjoyment, but she couldn't resist talking to him, wanting to get to know him better. Wanting to break through his quiet charming façade and beyond into the vast reservoir that she sensed was there. There was a lot more going on with Rhys Monroe than he let show.

'You have such smooth hands. No calluses from hammering?'

He looked up, confusion flashing in his face.

She held up her hands to him. 'Look, hardly sexy, is it?' The calluses from hours and hours keeping the beat, from holding the drumsticks. Yet his palms were soft and smooth, surprising given he must spend hours and hours holding hammers and tools.

Dark shadows lurked in his eyes before the green light chased them away again. 'Actually, your hands are very sexy. You have a hold that is unique.'

'A hold?'

'Good friction.' He grinned wickedly.

'You like them?' She looked at the raised welts of toughened skin in amazement.

'There's nothing about your body I don't like.'

'How come you don't have workman's hands?' He didn't.

He had the fine hands of a pianist. Long-fingered, smooth-skinned, neatly manicured.

He shrugged. 'I spend more time working inside than out these days.'

She was about to ask more but he diverted her, leaning over to follow the path of his deftly moving fingers with his mouth. She couldn't concentrate on finding out about him, only what he was doing.

But he was learning about her—body and mind. His fingers probed while he posed questions. 'How come you ended up playing the drums?'

She leaned back on the pile of pillows, luxuriating in the wantonness of her position. Loving looking down and seeing his head nestled between her thighs. Delighting in the freedom to lie back and let him taste her as if she were the most delicious thing. 'I wanted to do something. I wasn't allowed to play sports. And I didn't have the puff for a wind instrument. I thought piano and strings were dull. I wanted to make the biggest, baddest noise I could.'

'Prove you were there, huh?'

She lifted her head to look at his expression. His astuteness was acute—and fascinating to her. He understood her so quickly and she had no hesitation in opening up further to him. Yes, she'd wanted to declare her existence to the world. Not wanting to have a mouse-like existence on the edge of life, hardly daring to move for fear her heart wouldn't cope with action. She'd wanted to claim her place, make enough noise to let others, and herself, know she was *there*. 'I like loud.'

'Do you, now?' His fingers climbed higher and his chuckle warmed her skin. 'I think I knew that.'

She giggled. He wiggled closer. Nuzzling the very top of her thigh.

'So why the holiday in Australia?'

'I wanted a week to relax before starting the big bit of my trip. Sydney has shopping, sun, surf…so long as I don't see any of your spiders and snakes I'm a happy tourist.'

He laughed. 'They don't tend to show themselves in the city much. You're in the clear, I think.'

'Maybe from the snakes but not the spiders. And they're all poisonous, aren't they? I'm terrified every time I shower one will scuttle out of the drain.'

He nipped her tender skin, then licked it, soothing and seducing. 'Tell you what, I'll shower with you the rest of your holiday and scare them away.'

She grinned. 'OK.'

'And what's the big bit of your trip?'

She lay back, enjoying the delightfully slow way he was toying with her—the thin thread of desire being pulled ever tighter. 'Checking a few things off my list.'

'List?'

'Yeah, things I want to achieve before I die.'

His head jerked up. 'I thought you weren't about to die.'

'Well, hopefully not.' She gave him a reassuring grin. 'But it's time to take control of my life and do the things I've always thought I'd never be able to do.'

He looked at her for a long moment. 'Like what?'

'Silly things.' She felt her cheeks heat. She wasn't going to tell him he'd just helped her achieve something she'd never imagined would really be possible. 'I don't mean climb Everest or be the first person on Mars or win a Nobel Prize. I mean, play in a fountain on a sunny day type of things. Eat too many hotdogs at the fair.'

'That's not that silly.' He kept his eyes trained on her, his hands gently stroking up and down her inner thighs. 'You're not planning on doing dangerous things, are you? Like swimming with sharks, or walking on burning embers—in search of some extreme adrenalin rush? Prove your existence that way?'

'Hell, no.' She shuddered. 'It's not about risk. It's about knowing I'm alive and loving it, that I'm not taking life for granted. I want to live here and now, make the most of every moment.'

There was a long silence. She peeked down at him. Serious and contemplative, he seemed miles away. He looked up and saw her watching him. 'Are you ready to make the most of this moment?' His hands slid back to the top of her thighs. Heat flooded her—ridiculous that she should feel any embarrassment now they'd been in this bed for so many hours, being as intimate as it was possible for two people to physically be. But this intimacy wasn't just physical. She was talking with a freedom she hadn't had before. He didn't judge, he simply listened and all the while made her feel sexier than hell. Killer combo. She'd never seen lust so raw like this. Never imagined a guy could even look this way—let alone at her. Never realised how intoxicating it was when she felt it in return—threefold.

Unable to stop, she tilted her hips up to him, silently issuing the invitation—access all areas.

She sprawled back on the flat mattress, having swept away all the pillows in her fight for release, a film of sweat on her brow. But he wasn't done. His gentle exploration, of both her body and life, began again.

'You have a job?'

'Not now. I worked all sorts to save for this trip—in bars, temping, gigs, session recordings.' She'd worked hard—not wanting to use her brother's money although he'd offered time and time again. She wanted to be free of his concern, his well-intentioned control. She wanted to do it all by herself. And while she had good grades and talent, right now she was factoring in the 'me-time'.

'You don't want to be a full-time musician?'

'Music is great but the lifestyle isn't.' And she wanted something more—to make a difference somewhere, somehow. Now she had a life she wanted to achieve something with it.

'Why not teach?'

She frowned.

He laughed. 'Come on, short work days, all those holidays…'

She threw him a sceptical look. 'Which shows how much you know about teaching.' It was a great profession but she'd have to do more study. She couldn't afford that time-wise or dollar-wise at present. Top of her agenda was travelling to the places she'd dreamed of for too long, then she'd work in the UK and decide. Ideally she'd like to work in a voluntary sector—helping out in areas where little help was usually available or affordable. But she still had to eat.

'So what are you going to do?'

Something important. Something useful. Something fulfilling. 'I don't know yet. Does it matter?'

'Yes—to you. That's what you're looking for, isn't it? A way to make your mark? Something positive.'

Too astute by half.

'You'd make a good teacher,' he persisted. 'Teachers are really important.'

'I know.' She sighed. 'You sound like my brother—actually he's a builder, or was. Now he's into commercial property development.'

'Great.'

A bland response if ever there was one. But Sienna wanted

to hone in on some commonality—wanting something to link them besides the physical ache for each other. And he was so damn reticent when it came to talking about himself. 'You do residential property? People's houses?'

'Uh? Yeah.' He looked away from her, down her legs again. 'Tell me more about this list of yours. Is multiple orgasms on it?'

Rhys was still deep inside her, the overwhelming sensations still reverberating in his brain and body when she spoke.

'What about you? You have some things you want to do before you die?'

'I guess.' He could die now a happy man. No. Correction. He needed to experience her softness again. It registered that he wasn't going to be happy again until he'd had more of her. A lot more.

She'd said she wanted to live life in the moment—to make the most of it. He realised that he felt more alive when he was with her like this than he had done in years. She was more addictive than the most dangerous narcotic. The way she felt, the way she smelt, the sounds she made, the touch she gave. All combined to hit him with a natural high that he wanted again and again.

But it was just sex. He hadn't focused like this in a while, that was all. Hadn't lain in bed all night and half the day with a woman and done everything and anything on a whim.

But it wasn't quite just sex. She was interesting. He was interested in learning more about her—and not just her body. She had a refreshing outlook, a different drive from other people he knew. She wanted to make the most of every moment. He wanted a piece of her attitude for himself. 'I think we should trade.'

'Hmm?' She was drowsy, looking dazed and sleepy.

'Something I want to do. Something you want to do.' Hell, she wanted to frolic in a fountain. As if that'd be hard. But he could give her some challenges. He could set up some things she'd never forget. It seemed important she never forget because he had the discomforting feeling he'd never forget her. Never forget the moment he'd first laid eyes on her. Certainly never forget the moment his lips first got to touch hers. 'Deal?'

The blue in her eyes deepened. 'What kind of things?'

He shrugged. 'All kinds of things. Like on your list. Let's cross a few off this week.'

'You want to trade items on our life to-do lists?'

He was intrigued to see colour flood into her cheeks. 'Exactly.' He raised a brow at her blush. 'What do you say?'

'Oka-a-ay. But I'm a tad nervous about what might be on your list.'

He laughed. 'Nothing illegal, honey.'

CHAPTER EIGHT

SIENNA woke early and found her body ached all over—serious workout stiffness. Rhys hadn't been kidding when he'd suggested testing how much she was capable of. He'd pushed her to the edge and beyond.

A huge chunk of her loved the hedonism of it—her body revelling in the physical release. But inescapable thoughts niggled at her. There was a part of her searching for more. Wanting more from him.

A couple of times in the night he'd turned to her, saying nothing but taking her again with an almost desperate desire. As if he was seeking something from her, but she didn't know what it was. She wished he'd open up. She was used to listening to people, getting their stories out, but he was that guarded, didn't offer up a thing—not verbally. His actions told her. He drove inside her as if the physical satisfaction she gave pacified some other, deeper demon inside him.

She rolled over and watched him sleeping. His expression was relaxed, dark lashes curved on his cheek, his mouth soft and sensuous in repose. She was sure he had needs, certain he had hurts, but she couldn't figure them out—couldn't figure him out. She didn't know if she was going to have time to. But she was damn well going to try.

He opened his eyes, looked about with a fidgety air that signalled he wasn't quite a natural hedonist either. 'We need to get out of this room.' He threw back the sheet and slid from the bed. 'Come on, we'll come back and shower. Right now I've got something you've got to do at least once in life.'

She pulled on her skirt, then hunted for her tee—a crumpled mess half under the bed. With a grin Rhys handed her one of his shirts. The relaxed intimacy of his action made her gooey inside. She didn't bother with a bra, just slipped a couple of buttons through. Suddenly not concerned about covering the scar. It was early, there'd be no one about and Rhys had seen it all. The loose cotton was cool and wearing his clothing made her feel sexy. His sparkling expression hinted he liked it too.

'Let's go before I get a better idea.' He laughed and she felt freedom—to explore everything with him.

Barefoot, he led the way down the stairs. She watched, amused at his vitality and good humour. He grabbed a bag from the back of the reception counter—the light was on but for once it seemed Curtis wasn't home. They snuck out across the quiet street and onto the beach.

She followed him across the sand. 'What?'

'Beach volleyball.'

'Oh, no.'

'The tiny bikini is not mandatory.' He winked. 'Well, it would be if this was our own private beach—actually then we'd be having a naturist tournament. Sadly, it's not, and as you are is just fine.'

'Rhys, I really suck with balls.'

He froze. Shot her a look. Started to laugh.

Fire-engine-red, she laughed too.

'I have a feeling you'll do just fine. Anyway, it's early, no one's around to watch.'

Yeah, just you. It was all right for him. She watched the way he bent and pulled a ball from the bag. He had effortless grace, natural style.

He tossed the ball from one hand to the other, obviously amused by her reluctance. 'I thought you wanted to live now?'

She lunged for the ball as he threw it. 'You were one of those guys who could do any sport, weren't you? Rugby in the winter…'

'Cricket in the summer.' He laughed. 'Basketball, swimming, sailing.'

'And you were good all round.' She retrieved the ball from where it had rolled along the sand, lobbed it back.

'Excellent all round.'

She raised her brow.

He threw it back and spread his hands in mock humility. 'Well, that is the family motto.'

'You have a family motto?'

His humour dimmed and his grin became barely there. 'Do the best, be the best—excellence all round.'

'Wow.'

'We have a duty to perform.'

'A duty?'

'Sure. A responsibility.'

She dropped the ball. Again. It took less than three minutes for him to realise she hadn't been kidding about her lack of skill. Laughing, he resorted to even simpler passes. 'A little practice, you'll go far.'

He chuckled at her 'yeah right' expression and abandoned the game completely. He toyed with the ball as they walked along the edge of the water. She gazed across the blue to the high-rise buildings. Loving the vibrancy of the city. Bright-eyed, she turned back to him. 'I've thought of something for the list.'

'Yeah?'

'I want to walk over the Harbour Bridge. You done that?'

'Hundreds of times. And I've driven over it thousands.' Sydney Harbour Bridge—the world-famous landmark and fairly key to being able to move around the city.

She giggled. 'I mean climb it. You know, they put you in harnesses and you climb up the arches.'

Rhys stared back at her, his good mood sinking. Of all the places in the whole city, she wanted to go there? Too high profile. They took endless photos on that thing. Rightly so, it was a great experience, but he wasn't going to be caught in the company of a woman—especially one as beautiful as Sienna— and have the snaps sold. This was his holiday, his escape, his moment of fantasy out of his real life and he wanted to protect it. He wanted to have time with her—just her and him and no interference. No prying eyes. 'I have a better plan for today.'

'What's better than the view from up there? It's not too hot, it's not windy.'

'Yeah, but I have something that can only be done today. Right now, in fact. Let's go!'

She was giving him a funny look but he didn't care. Right now he was too busy thinking over what he was going to come up with list-wise that could be done without attracting too much attention. And the guilt was eating him up. But he'd spent most of his adult life swallowing back guilt—why was he gagging now? He was in serious trouble. The only way he could assuage it was to do the things to her that had her shaking in his arms, shaking in joy. If he kept her in a state of bliss, he'd be absolved.

'Come on.' He pulled her to him, planted a kiss. Got way-laid as usual—he couldn't ever have just one kiss from her. He pushed at the shirt she wore, running his fingers along her delicate bones, wanting to take it off completely. His desire for her was in no way diminishing. He finally pulled back, stared into her flushed face. 'We need to get moving.'

Back in the hostel they darted past Reception, nodding at Curtis who was looking strangely edgy. For a fleeting moment Rhys felt sorry the guy had to work so many hours. Sienna tripped into the little bathroom. He let her monopolise the shower for a few minutes while he scratched round for an action plan. Hell, he must be able to think of something. Then the sound of the water spraying clued him in. Waterfall. Fountain. There must be one somewhere in the city.

Sienna followed a pace behind Rhys as he headed to the train platform. He'd hustled her out of the bathroom and got them back out the door. Curtis on Reception had said hi as they passed again. She'd seen the speculation in his eye. The overly keen interest as he watched them depart. What did he care? Surely they weren't the first hostel inmates he'd seen get it together.

They got on a train, mixing in with a few commuters, shared a secret smile as they sat close on the seat. Enjoying the rocking motion. Sienna secretly enjoying a fantasy of being alone in the carriage with him, late at night, with no threat of other passengers arriving and—

'Ever had sex on a train?'

Apparently they were wired into the same fantasy. She shook her head and grinned at him, admitting with her eyes she'd been dreaming about that exact scenario.

He bent his head and kissed her. 'We'll add it to the list.'

The park was beautiful—surprisingly green. It smelt fresh but the humidity was on the rise again. They walked through, around one corner into an isolated spot—trees and bushes forming a natural canopy. Then she heard it, the gentle trickle of water. Behind a small railing was the most pathetic fountain she'd ever seen.

'We came to see this?'

His grin was slightly shamefaced. 'You're in Sydney at the height of summer. You can't go expecting amazing waterfalls and fountains. We have water restrictions.'

She leant at the railing, struck dumb by the idea that he thought this was better than climbing up the Sydney Harbour Bridge. 'A kid couldn't splash in that, let alone two full-grown adults.'

He stared at it. 'No.'

'And though the morning's warm already it's not quite hot enough.'

'No.' He turned her in his arms to face him. Kissed her gently.

She pulled back to look at him in reproach. 'You think a few kisses are going to turn this into the experience of a lifetime?'

He didn't appear remotely abashed, green twinkling in his eyes.

'You must rate yourself pretty high.'

'I'm sorry, Sienna.' He sighed then, and it was a sigh of genuine regret. 'I'm not myself around you.'

He pulled away, picked up her bag from where it sat beside them, neatly clipped it onto his own. She grinned as he did so, not really minding at all. Just liking spending time with him, getting to know him, feeling more relaxed and content than she ever had. It was nice walking with nothing on her shoulders, feeling the warmth of the breeze through her tee shirt. It used to annoy her no end when her brother insisted on carrying her bag or heavy things. But Rhys taking the burden didn't bother her at all. He wasn't doing it because he was worried for her. He was just being nice. Really he'd been nothing but nice to her from the moment they'd met. He offered nothing more. Expected nothing more. He'd been honest from the beginning. He wanted her. And when she was gone, it was done. She was the one who'd have to get over it. And as the moments passed there was even more of an 'it' to get over.

On impulse she turned to him. 'Thank you, Rhys.'

'What for?'

'Everything.' She smiled. He was so straight up. 'I can really trust you.'

His face hardened. The green sparkle faded behind the slate. 'Sienna.'

Her smile faltered. She was used to him closing over when she attempted to inquire into his life, but just then she hadn't asked anything and right now he had the most remote expression she'd ever seen on him. 'What is it?'

'There's something I have to tell you.'

For a second all her vital organs stopped. Something was wrong. 'Don't tell me you have a girlfriend.'

'No, I don't have a girlfriend.' He flashed a tight smile. 'Want to offer yourself for the part?'

'OK. But I'm only in town for another few days. And so are you.' *Don't start messing with the arrangement, Rhys.* Not when she was only just keeping it real for herself. His deathly serious look panicked her. She couldn't cope with serious. She had to get on.

'That's just it. I'm uh…'

'You're not married.' Sure she was right on that one. He wasn't able to open up even a little way, he'd never open up to marriage.

'No.'

'OK, so you're not married and you don't already have a girlfriend. Are you in trouble with the law?'

'No. I…' He sighed. 'Sienna, please, let me finish.'

She should. Hell, what was she doing? Here he was finally trying to say something important and she was stalling him. Because, she realised, she didn't want to hear it. Didn't want this illusion shattered. And he was about to smash it—she could see it in his eyes.

He opened his mouth, drew in a deep breath.

And then they heard it. The ear-piercing scream. Startled, they stared into each other's eyes as if questioning whether the other had heard it. And then sound came again—shouts and cries. They both turned and ran. Around the hedge encircling the fountain, through the trees.

They came upon masses of people. A pile of them bunched near one of the swing sets. Wisps of conversation came to them—disjointed commands filtering through the crowd. 'She's bleeding…she could be concussed…someone phone an ambulance.'

'Excuse me. Make way, please. I'm a doctor.'

Sienna stopped. The crowd parted. Rhys walked through.

The next few seconds were like a series of still shots in her mind. All she heard was his voice—'I'm a doctor'—over and over. She pulled herself together, walked closer as the crowd dispersed, parents relieved to be able to deal with their own upset kids now there was someone taking charge.

She looked about twelve, had blood spilling from a gash on her head. Was flat on her back. One of her legs was bent at a hideous angle below her shin. Sienna shut her eyes a moment, knowing that she'd just caught a glimpse of snapped bone. She opened them again, focused on him.

Rhys was on his knees next to her, talking softly. 'What's your name, sweetie?'

She looked stricken. He pushed back her hair with the lightest brush of his fingers, compassion clear in his expression, gentle warmth in his smile.

'Katie.'

'Katie.' The child and the white-faced woman on the other side of her, presumably her mother, spoke simultaneously. Sienna understood. When he looked at anyone that way they'd talk. They'd trust—just as she had.

'Hi, Katie. My name is Dr Rhys Maitland, but you can call me Rhys, OK?' He was feeling over her body with deft hands. Sienna saw the way he was concentrating on other things while he chatted to her, saw the keen look in his eye. She recognised that look. Assessing. Evaluating. Deciding on his approach. When he got within range of her leg the child cried.

'OK, sugar. We're going to get you all fixed up, OK?'

He kept talking to her low and quiet. The low, quiet tones he'd used with her, but they were still audible across the grounds.

'My friends are going to come and pick us up in the ambulance. Have you ever been in an ambulance before?'

One of the remaining bystanders next to Sienna turned to her. 'He's a doctor?'

'Apparently so.' Sienna looked back at Rhys. His experience and skill were obvious to everyone.

'Is he good?'

'Rhys is good at everything he does.' Especially lying.

It couldn't have been much more than five minutes till the ambulance arrived, by which time Rhys clearly had everything under control. He even had the mother smiling, and the girl—weakly through her tears. Sienna clenched her teeth, holding back the grimace. The crew leapt out, bags in hand. One had a toy koala that she gave to the girl to cuddle. The kid buried her face in the soft fur.

The other officer grinned at Rhys. 'Hey, hero. Can't keep away from it, can you? Not even on your holidays.'

Aside from a slight wry twist to his lips you wouldn't have thought Rhys had heard the comment. Instead he focused on introducing them to Katie, then talking through her condition.

Sienna watched as he rapped out information. Cool, calm, still polite but so in control. The ambulance officers quickly getting onto it.

Dr Rhys. Spouting medical jargon and utterly at home in a scene of chaos and carnage.

Clinical.

She'd known he'd held something back from her, but this brought home just how little she knew of him. Had anything in the last few days been real?

Yes. Her stupid heart cried bitterly. Those moments in his arms had been the most real thing she'd ever experienced.

But she pushed it away—sex. That was all it had been. Some stupid game. For whatever reason—and what the hell reason it could have been was utterly beyond her—he'd fabricated his entire life. And the thing was he'd done that right from the very beginning.

Why hadn't he told her? He'd lied. And at no point had he withdrawn from that lie. The only thing that appeared to be true was that he was on holiday—but from his job in *this* city, as a damn doctor. Tears of shock and hurt, wounded pride and wounded heart sprang in her eyes. He must have thought she was such a fool. Why, why, why? When she'd been so honest with him?

Rhys worked alongside Melissa and Simon to make Katie comfortable. Grateful it was a team from his own hospital. He'd figured it would be. They were in his catchment area.

Hadn't allowed himself to even think of Sienna until now—needing to focus entirely on stabilising the situation. Needing to keep control of his own careering emotions. He always struggled when it was a younger patient. He always saw Theo's eyes—the unmistakable plea for help, the light fading. This time he could help. This time it would be OK. But his heart still thundered and he kept the sweats at bay with a level of self-command that had taken some years to perfect.

He knew his control would be even more precarious if he stopped to think about what Sienna was making of it all. He'd been about to make a clean breast of it. Unable to hold back from her, wanting her to know the truth because he couldn't stand it any more, he had needed to fix it. It had been such a stupid idea in the first place—making up a new name, a different job—and yet, he couldn't wholly regret it.

But, damn, she'd just found out only half the truth in the most unfortunate way. He finally braved a glance her way. Saw her white face. Saw the furious hurt in her eyes.

He looked away again super quick. He wasn't free from his duty yet and until he was he couldn't work on Sienna.

He heard Melissa talking to the mother.

'Don't worry. She's in great hands.'

Rhys flashed a silencing look but Melissa was in full reassurance mode, taking the woman's arm and leading her to the open doors of the ambulance, her high tones carrying halfway across the park. 'Your daughter was lucky to have the city's best ER doctor on a walk in the park today. Dr Rhys is brilliant. She's going to be just fine.'

'OK, Melissa.' *Shut up.* 'Load up, we need to get to the hospital.'

'We can handle it from here if you want, Rhys. You don't need to come with us.'

'Of course I do. I need to clean up and do the paperwork anyway.'

He'd never leave a patient. He looked around again before stepping into the back of the ambulance. Wanting to at least offer a smile, call that he'd see her back at the hostel. Knowing it wasn't enough, but better than nothing. He scanned the crowd.

She was already gone.

CHAPTER NINE

Rhys' hands itched. He hadn't got back to the hostel for hours—waylaid by people at the hospital who had seemed to think he'd fallen off the face of the earth because he hadn't been at work 24/7 as usual. Regardless that he was supposed to be having a holiday. They had seemed stunned that he actually had. Teased that he still couldn't keep away—not even a full week. If they'd only stopped talking to him he'd have been out of there a lot sooner. For once he hadn't wanted to be there a second longer than necessary.

There'd been no sign of Sienna when he'd got back to his room. Her stuff had vanished. She hadn't appeared the rest of the afternoon or evening. He'd patrolled the place, but hadn't dared enter the dorm room in the middle of the night—imagining all too well the scandalous headlines that might cause. So now, the next day, he was in for the sit and wait. He could hardly raise a polite response to Curtis' idle chat. But no way was he leaving Reception until he'd seen her. Desperate to explain. Determined to get her over that anger. Disproportionately upset that she was mad at him.

He sighed in frustration. Why should it matter? She was his holiday fling. She'd be out of here in just a few days. But

it mattered an awful lot. How the hell could he make it right?
He'd been such a fool. He glanced at her day pack parked next
to him on the sofa.

Anxiety ate at him. Where the hell was she? He didn't
know if she was on meds. After an op like that a patient was
usually on drugs long-term. Had she missed them? He unzipped the bag, needing to check.

A fabric-covered book was at the top. He knew what it was.
He concentrated fiercely on his integrity. He'd been enough
of a jerk. Not going to be tempted. Not going to pry into her
personal thoughts. Much as part of him would love to. Purely
to understand.

But as he lifted the journal to look underneath for any
medicine packets, a piece of paper fluttered from it to the floor
and as he picked it up his eyes automatically scanned it.
Computed it. Sealed it in his brain. And acidic disappointment
flooded his entire body.

It wasn't until after two p.m. that she appeared. Flanked
by the inevitable army of girls from the hostel. She saw him
as soon as she walked into Reception. Her eyes flashed and
her cheeks flushed redder than they already were. She
looked hot and bothered. Well, she wasn't nearly as bothered as him.

'Had a good day?' He managed to grate the words out,
leaping to his feet and intercepting her.

'I don't think I'm talking to you. In fact, I don't think I even
know your name—do I?'

'Rhys. My name is Rhys.'

'Rhys Monroe?'

'No.'

'And are you a builder, Rhys?'

'No.'

'Naughty, naughty Rhys,' Mistress South Africa said.

He ignored her. Held up the day pack in front of Sienna. 'Want this back?'

Her eyes flashed fire. 'Yes.'

'Then come with me now and I'll give it to you.'

'You can give it to me here.'

'No. I'll give it to you once we've sat down and talked about this like adults.'

'I really don't see that we have that much to say. You lied. End of story.'

He studied her. Wanting to throw his own accusations but conscious of the greedy interest of the others, conscious of how tired she looked. She seemed to have got thinner overnight. 'I'm walking out of here right now. If you want this back, you're coming with me.'

He wanted away from all the observers. He wanted just him and her again. He knew she'd come. Hell, if nothing else, he had her medication—and her passport.

She said nothing. Just turned and marched ahead of him. Waited on the footpath outside for him to point out the direction. Despite his own fury he couldn't stop the grudging smile inside. What would she do if he told her how beautiful she looked when she was mad?

Sienna sizzled all the way along the street. Fuming. She'd had an awful night's sleep, and an even more miserable day trying to take in some exciting tourist stuff, but all her mind would let her see was the sight of Rhys in full doctor mode. She replayed the moment of realisation over and over as she searched for reasons—consistently failing to figure answers.

That was why she was walking with him. She wanted

answers and that was all she was after. She didn't want anything more from him now—right? Certainly not any more of his hot body.

Except that was all she could think about right this very second. How different he seemed. As gorgeous as the day before but now even more energy bounced off him. He exuded an aura of barely leashed passion. It had her on edge. It had her excited. In turn, that made her even madder.

He stopped a few yards along from the hostel.

'What's this?'

'My car.'

She stared at the shiny black convertible. 'Car? You brought your car on holiday with you? All the way from… where was it you said you were from again?' She raised her brows at him—attempting a look of cool inquisition but any *faux* haughtiness evaporated at his angry expression. How dared he look so cross when he was the one who'd fibbed his way through the last four days?

'We're not here to discuss my car, Sienna. Get in.'

Her mouth dropped. 'Ever heard of the word please?'

'Get in. Now.'

If he didn't have her most precious things in his hand, she'd walk away this instant. If he didn't have a hold on something even more precious of hers she'd be running like an Olympian. Then again, given he actually had all this precious stuff of hers, she should be flying.

Instead, she got in the passenger seat and slammed the door behind her.

He started the engine and drove. She had no idea where. But after half an hour of simmering silence he pulled into a park and got out of the car.

He walked ahead of her, brandishing her bag. She marched

after him. Quite happy by now to give him one hell of a piece of her mind because he was really, really, asking for it.

He turned into a doorway. She blinked as she stepped out of the dazzling sunlight and into a gloomy interior. They were in a small bar. Guitar music played softly. Spanish. He led her to a table at the front, with booth seats ninety degrees to the window. He didn't sit, just gestured for her to and then, not bothering to wait for the waitress, went straight to the bar and ordered.

Sienna sat, studiously stared out the window, pretended she wasn't remotely interested in what he was doing.

Two cool beers in long glasses were plonked onto the table. He slid into the bench seat across from hers.

Much as she wanted to she couldn't refuse the drink—parched. She picked it up and drank deeply. He did the same. Half-empty glasses returned to the table with equally violent bangs.

'You lied to me.'

He sat back, seeming to relax a little. 'Yes.'

'You made up a name. You made up a whole story about yourself.'

'Yes.'

'And you think that's OK?'

'Of course not. But what about you? What about your *list?*' Scathing to say the least.

She sat up. 'What about it?'

'What about number *one* on your list?'

Blood pounded through every vein. 'You read my journal?' She watched, immobile and enraged, as with calm movements he unzipped her bag. 'Hand that over this instant. That is not your property. You have no right to read that.'

'I didn't. This page fell out when I opened your pack.'

'Why were you going through my pack?'

'I was worried. I wanted to see if you had any medication you'd missed.'

She stopped, jaw dropping; the world she saw was suddenly stained red. *Dr Rhys*. Interfering already.

'Anyway, so what if I read it? You wrote it to be read. That's why people write things down—so they get read.'

'Rubbish,' she snapped. 'Writing goals down helps make them real. Helps you realise them.'

'And that's what this was? Some *goal?*' He picked up the page and read in cutting tones. '"*1. To have wild, abandoned sex with someone who doesn't know about my heart condition.*"'

'And?' With superwoman strength she hid the cringe. OK, it sounded trashy read aloud, but so what? What business was it of his? It was a fantasy, for heaven's sake. One she'd never imagined would ever actually happen.

'So *anyone* would have done? You just wanted the experience of being with someone who didn't know about you. Well, lucky me. Right place, right time. Good thing I got to the table when I did or would you have gone for Tim, or Gaz or some other sucker on the dance floor? Anyone so long as it was dark and he could satisfy you?'

Incensed, she threw it back on him. 'Well, as I remember it you weren't exactly complaining. Don't make out like I've used you any more than you've used me.' She choked the words out. 'Don't you dare come across all holier than thou. It's not like you were out looking for a serious relationship either. Were you? You can't even tell me your real name. For days you've been lying to me. I was up front a hell of a lot sooner than you.' And, no, of course she wouldn't have gone for Tim or Gaz or anyone else in the whole entire world. Because she'd never felt that instant, unstoppable attraction to another before. Not that she was about to tell him that. How dared he judge her? 'It was a one-night stand. That was all either of us intended.'

'How do you know?'

Astounded, she stared. 'How can you say that? We'd known each other thirty seconds before we had sex. Conversed on nothings for a minute max. Relationships don't start that way, Rhys. And we're certainly missing out on the fundamentals of any kind of relationship—like honesty, like trust.' Utterly defensive, she stormed at him. Of course it had meant more and secretly hadn't she dreamed? Stupidly. But now she was out to salvage what little pride she had left. She'd downplay it—how it had felt and what it had meant—because he hadn't even been honest with her about his name.

Besides, she needed to protect herself. Serious relationships weren't for her, remember? She couldn't offer happy ever after to anyone. She might not have the ever and after.

He jerked, sitting bolt upright, glaring at her, looking as if he was about to launch a blistering attack. His eyes glowed green but his jaw clamped. For a long moment he sat rigid. Finally, vehemently, he threw her words back at her. 'What we did wasn't sleazy.'

She met his gaze then, held it for a moment, and then they both looked to the glasses on the table.

'OK.' He spoke more softly. 'So neither of us has been entirely honest.'

She looked back at him, anger refuelled. 'I might have had secrets but I have been honest. You're the one who hasn't. Why lie? What have you got to hide?' She gave a mocking laugh. 'Do tell me, who are you really, Rhys?'

'Here are your tapas, Rhys.' The waitress stood with a tray covered in tiny dishes, her glance flicking between the two of them—her attempt to maintain a bland expression a complete failure.

Sienna turned to the woman. 'What's his surname?'

'I'm sorry?'

'His surname. What is it?'

'Sienna.'

'Maitland,' the waitress replied just as Rhys interjected.

Sienna sat back in the seat and stared at him through narrowed eyes.

'Thanks, Tracey, that's fine.' Rhys smiled at the waitress, who was looking at Sienna as if she were some crazy lady. She'd set the dishes across the table and given them a plate each and after Rhys' words she turned and practically ran to the bar where the other waitress was lounging, watching.

Rhys stared back at Sienna. Eyes hard, the glow gone. 'Eat. You need it.'

She needed answers more. 'Who are you and why did you lie to me?'

'Stuff some chorizo into your mouth and I'll answer. Maybe then I'll have a chance of finishing before you interrupt me.'

Mutinously she picked up the fork and stabbed the sausage several times. His lips twitched.

He picked up an olive and, ignoring his own etiquette advice, put it in his mouth and talked at the same time. 'My name is Rhys Maitland and I'm a doctor. I work in the ER department of the hospital down the road and I've lived in Sydney all my life.'

She swallowed. 'Why didn't you tell me that at the start?'

Rhys thought about his response. No matter how he framed this he was going to come across as a jerk. Then again, that might be an improvement on her current perception of him. 'I just wanted to escape.'

'What on earth have you got to escape from?'

He decided to give her the easy answer—the only answer he'd be able to tell anyone. 'I'm the heir of a multi-million sportswear empire.'

'What?'

'I'm worth millions. I have a trust fund I inherited from my grandfather and I'll inherit most of the company shares from my father. My family is…well-known in Sydney. We're in the society pages, my cousin's wedding was in the weekly women's magazines, that sort of thing.'

She looked blank. 'Are you telling me you're some sort of celebrity, Rhys?'

'Not by choice. No, not really.' He sighed. 'A little. I try to avoid that rubbish. But sometimes, there are events I have to go to, and the press are there and because of the money, the name, they write about it.' Like the eligible bachelors spread some rag had done a couple of months ago that had made life a living hell at the hospital for some time.

'So you have all this money but you work as a doctor.'

He nodded, could see the thought processes. The next question was obvious.

'Why?'

'Why what?' He stalled. He knew where she was going and he didn't want to answer. Some things you could never escape from.

'Why medicine? Why not the family business?'

'I wanted to do something useful.' Instantly he saw more questions leap in her mind but he headed her off. 'Anyway, back to why I lied. I get sick of people only being interested in me because of my bank balance. I wanted to be away from me, from the preconceived ideas people have. I think that's something you can understand, isn't it?' He looked at her pointedly.

He'd got away all right. He'd been acting in a manner totally unlike himself—acting crazy. It wasn't just about her not knowing who he was; it was about him being free to do whatever he fancied. And he fancied her. He continued the confession. 'I am on holiday this week. Tim works at the hospital with me and is in his band for fun. I went along to help with the gear for the gig. Met you. Knew you weren't from town—' He broke off. Realising he was heading into mud the way he was telling it.

'So *I* was the lucky one,' she carried on for him softly. 'Right place, right time. Right tourist.'

Not true. He'd never behaved like that in his life. Never wanted someone the way he'd wanted her—in the very instant he saw her. It was as if she'd switched the on button to his main power source. Until now he'd been functioning at fifty per cent. But he wasn't about to tell her that. Not when she was wearing a frown that would rival Attila the Hun's. Not when he was still irrationally angry with her. It bothered him beyond belief. The idea that she'd just wanted to have sex with someone—anyone—who was ignorant of her history, was utterly galling. He wanted to be more than that. This *mattered,* and he wanted it to matter to her too. He couldn't hold back the bitterness in his tone. 'I guess we're even.'

Her hand wobbled out to her glass. Despite the food she looked pale, unhappy and beautiful. His anger evaporated in the warmth of concern and the heat of desire. He wanted to get out of here, wanted to take her to his apartment so they could lie down—rest and relax. He wanted his holiday to come home. Wanted to see her there. Definitely wanted her in the bathroom.

But the strain in her eyes slowed his libido down. She'd argue it till she was blue in the face but the fact was she was vulnerable. She did have to take extra care. There were higher risks for her—a trip to the dentist could cause her problems.

Rhys shifted on his seat. He didn't have room in his heart for her kind of vulnerable. He couldn't afford to get too involved. He had to protect his bruised heart as much as she literally had to protect hers.

'Have something more to eat.' He took her wrist in his hand as he spoke. Surreptitiously keen to read her pulse, but initially thrown by the erratic beat of his own heart, he held on that little too long.

'Why are you holding my wrist like this?' She stared at his fingers. 'Are you taking my pulse? You jerk. How dare you?'

He felt the beat quicken even before her words were all out her mouth. 'You look like hell.'

'Any wonder? And you've been doing the overprotective bit this whole time, haven't you?'

'What? Don't you accuse me of mollycoddling you or treating you any different from how I'd treat anyone.'

'That's just the point though, isn't it, Rhys? You're a doctor. You *treat* people.'

He lowered his voice. 'You know exactly how far I've pushed you—the extremes I've pushed you to.' And himself. If he was honest, he was going beyond his comfort zone even now. But he couldn't seem to stop. He wanted to make things right with her.

But she was off on a bender. 'This is why you stopped me from doing the bridge walk. You've been protecting me?'

'No.'

Sienna laughed harshly. 'You really are incredible, you know that, Rhys? You thought I couldn't do it, didn't you? That I couldn't even manage some stairs?'

'That is not why I didn't want to do the bridge walk,

Sienna.' He breathed out heavily. Damn the woman and her incessant interrogation. He wanted to be honest but still felt the usual constraint about telling her anything. The last thing he wanted to do was relive the Mandy experience. And he didn't want to put ideas into her head—about selling her story. But at the same time he wanted to straighten this mess out. Reluctance swamped him but the need to resolve things with her won over his reservations about inviting her into his world. 'It's complicated.'

'Is everything complicated with you?'

'No more than it is with you.'

'I'm not that complicated, Rhys.'

'That's not true, Sienna. There are depths in you. Areas you don't let anyone into.'

Sienna looked across the table at him. She might have a few dark corners, but his no-go areas were vast fields. 'That's true of anyone.' She picked up an olive. 'Anything you told me in the last few days—the sailing, the family motto. Was any of it true?'

'Every word.'

She paused, the olive halfway to her mouth. She really wanted not to believe him. But the intensity in his answer was compelling. She could feel him willing her to see him as genuine.

'Can't we just forget about all this rubbish? You know me, Sienna. I know you. I want to keep challenging you.'

She sat back. He was all challenge. He was the challenge of her life. And she couldn't walk away. 'I don't think I know you at all, Rhys.'

'Look. Come back to my apartment with me now. Let me show you.'

She shifted on the seat. Not sure what he meant by 'show'—not sure how she felt about letting him in again that way.

He read her mind. 'I'll run you back to the hostel any time you want—you just say the word.'

CHAPTER TEN

IT WAS a two-minute walk to his apartment. They swept past the security guard who managed to keep his curiosity marginally better hidden than the waitress had. They got in the lift. Rhys pressed several buttons on the keypad and then the lift ascended.

There was another keypad outside his apartment door. Another series of buttons were punched. He looked up and caught Sienna's look of surprise. 'I value my privacy.'

'I could never remember a code that long.'

Once inside she looked around his apartment. He hadn't been kidding about the money thing. Her brother was rich, but this was on a whole other level. The fittings, the furniture, the air, the art—it all screamed extreme amounts of money mixed with good taste.

He watched as she took it all in. 'Does it make a difference?'

'Not to me,' she answered, irritated that he'd think it would. 'Why? You think I'm going to ask you to pay me?'

'No!' he snapped.

His flare irritated her more. 'Then don't insult me. The only person this makes a difference to is you.'

'You're probably right.' A hint of apology crossed his expression as he stood in the centre of the room. 'So this is me.' He gestured wide, a little self-consciously.

She looked at him, rather than his home. She knew some things now, more made sense. But she also knew he had stuff still buried deep that he chose to ignore. It was in his eyes, the mirror reflecting his reticence. His dislike of the media and attention might answer some of it, but there was more to it and she, like the proverbial cat, was curious. That, together with concern, motivated her decision to be here.

Now that he'd invited her here he seemed a little at a loss to know what to do with her. She helped him out. 'You going to make me a coffee?'

He moved then, reminded of his host duties. 'You don't want wine?'

She shook her head. The beer she'd had at the bar had been enough. She needed to keep her wits about her and her will firm. Already she was in danger of forgiving all and letting him get away with anything. There was something so irresistible about his strength and silence and in the occasional vulnerability she saw in his full, sensual mouth. Part of her was so tempted to make a move—this was merely a holiday fling, after all. But she was deluding herself and she knew it. So instead she'd give them a moment for closure and then go back to the hostel. If she stayed around him she'd slip further under his spell and that would be stupid. Falling in love wasn't an option—marriage, kids and a white picket fence were off the list. For the well-being of everyone.

Aside from the art and the opulence there was little to distinguish his apartment from any other bachelor pad. Overflowing bookcases, a state-of-the-art entertainment system that included games console, stereo, masses of CDs and DVDs.

She followed him into the kitchen area and as she turned to admire the gleaming espresso machine she saw what hung on the dividing wall.

It was covered with black and white photos printed on canvas blocks. Varying sizes. Varying groupings. Formal portraits, family snaps. All had been digitally enhanced, then printed onto the canvas. Occasional stripes of colour had been painted on, or tiny details filled in. Some photos were left plain, others had been added to. The effect as a whole was striking—a dramatically different sort of 'rogues' gallery'.

Sienna stared and stared. Finally asked, 'Family?'

He nodded. Eventually gave some more detail. 'My sister did it for me. She's a photographic artist. She does some interesting stuff.'

'This is really cool.' She walked closer, wanting to see if she could guess. She pointed to one shot of a young couple in older style wedding clothes. 'Your parents?'

He nodded, slowly coming to stand beside her.

She pointed to a roly-poly baby. 'You?'

Again a jerky affirmative.

There was a shot to the side of two wide-smiling boys aged maybe eight and ten, the elder one clearly Rhys. 'Your brother?'

He walked, angled away from her, arms folded across the front of his body. She could see his hands were curled into fists. 'Cousin.'

She stared at him. His 'conversation closed' body language couldn't be any louder. She glanced again at the picture then moved on. 'Which is your sister?'

He came back. Obviously reluctant. Pointed, but immediately pulled his head back so his arms became bars across his chest.

'She's younger?'

He nodded.

She smiled. 'Are you a bossy, overprotective older brother?'

'She'd probably say so. I'd say I'm the responsible one.'

'Responsible.' Not the first time that had come up. She

turned to him. 'It's a balance, isn't it? Yes, you have to be responsible but you also have to *live*. And let others live their lives too.'

'Yes, but you also have to recognise you have responsibilities to others—especially those you care about and who care about you.'

Sienna knew that. It was precisely why she didn't want someone getting too close. She didn't want to be stifled. And, ultimately, she didn't want to let them down.

Rhys stared back at the wall. 'You also have a duty to help where you can. A duty not to hurt, not to let people down.' As his last words echoed her thoughts, his gaze landed on the picture of him with his cousin.

Sienna was hit by a horrible thought. 'Is that why you came after me? After I showed you my scar—you felt a duty?'

'Not a duty. No.'

'No? You didn't feel bound not to leave me feeling bad?'

'No.' He turned away from the pictures and faced her. 'I came after you because I couldn't not.'

'So it was a duty.'

His gaze locked with hers. 'It was desire. It's still desire.' He stepped closer, his reserve breaking. 'I like how I feel when I'm around you.' He put his hands on her shoulders, his fingers firm. 'I like how I feel when I touch you.' He drew closer still, speaking quietly yet every word rang loud. 'I can't help but want to touch you.'

He kissed her then, a soft brush that had her parting and wanting. So much for closure.

He looked down at her, his lips a fraction from hers, his eyes burning bright. 'You have no idea how much I want to make love to you.'

Her gasp was soft and in that very instant his mouth was

back on hers, preventing her response, stopping her from voicing her doubt. Sending that doubt packing.

They kissed and kissed and kissed again. A couple of times he pulled away from her lips, kissing down her throat but as quickly he was back to her mouth as if unable to keep away, as if needing to taste the sweet intimacy.

Her resistance melted in the onslaught. As his hands framed her face, cradling her as he kissed her so tenderly, a wave of emotion rose in her and was more than enough to drown her hesitation and hurt. She closed her eyes and absorbed the care he was taking. She was too overwhelmed by sensation to realise he'd been slowly walking them somewhere. Not once breaking the kiss, not giving her the chance to take breath and reclaim sanity, he guided her to his room. With desire-drugged eyes she took in vague details. Just a glimpse of the bed had her knees pathetically weakening.

'I'm sorry I lied.' And she knew that he was. And she wanted to forgive him. She did. But he was still holding a part of himself back, and she knew it and she couldn't quite say it didn't matter.

'Rhys…' She should go back to the hostel. She shouldn't let this become anything more. But the change was already happening; she could feel it swirling around her.

'Let me show you.' He made it so utterly impossible to say no.

He gently set about removing her clothes. She raised her arms so he could slide the tee shirt off her, stepped out of the skirt as it puddled around her feet. Naked for him again, baring everything. Could he do the same for her?

Her senses flared as he stripped. The way he touched her, the way he looked at her, she almost couldn't bear it. His tenderness was so intense she felt more bowled over than if he'd bodily picked her up and taken her barbarian-style on the bed. Instead he moved with deliberate leisure over the length of her body, proving a level of passion that she could scarcely believe. She'd been treated gingerly before. This was different. This was genuine—it felt like love.

She tasted his groan as he slowly pushed into her. She twisted her fingers in the hair at the back of his head, letting her other hand slide down the strong muscles of his back as gently, so gently, he moved against her. The press of his pelvis, the lock of his lips on hers, so they were joined and it was so deep, so complete. With arms wound tight about each other, nothing could come between them.

The simplest intimacy. So sublime.

Her head was spinning and the tears started falling before she was even aware of them until finally she had to break the kiss, arching her neck so she could gulp in one last breath before her body shuddered and her mind shattered.

'That's my girl.' His smile was tender and tight.

She stared up at him as she rode to the end of the crest, just as he hit his. Unwavering, fearless, their concentration sealed on each other as their bodies were.

Then there was silence. Stillness. She reminded herself to breathe. She'd just seen into his soul. And knew he'd seen hers.

Fear struck almost immediately. Rhys had good armour in place. Could she really believe in what she thought had been evident in his eyes? Some time soon she needed him to talk. She needed words as well as actions.

Right now she just needed to recover.

He lifted up from her, wiped away the tears on her cheek with the pad of his thumb. 'You OK?'

She nodded. Not wanting to risk a squeaky sob of a reply.

He lay on his side, pulled her hips so she too turned onto

her side, her back to him. He snuggled close behind her, his arm heavy across her waist, his hand pressing against her chest. Relief flooded her—so glad she couldn't see him because she needed the respite. She felt raw and vulnerable, shaking with emotion so exquisite it almost hurt. This had been completely different from the wild abandonment that first night—the moment she'd thought could never be surpassed. She'd been wrong. Nothing could compare to what had just passed between them. And it frightened her more than anything had ever frightened her in her life. It wasn't supposed to have happened like this. Everything had changed.

He could feel her trembling still. He wondered if she could feel the tremors racking him too. He masked it by smoothing his hand down her back, wanting to soothe her. He regulated his breathing in time to the sweep of his hand.

He'd never felt like this. Never felt anything like that. What they had just shared was beyond comprehension. He hadn't been able to think of a single pyrotechnic thing, no technique, no position that would make all the fireworks in China explode in the one hit. He'd just wanted to worship her. To show her how sorry he was. How much he liked her. To treat her as she should be treated—precious, cherished, loved. And so he had. With gentle hands, soft touches, starting at the bottom, slowly he'd savoured his way up the length of her, sliding his hands up her slender calves and to the rest of her beauty. But it was when he'd finally drawn over her and slowly pushed deep inside her that he'd felt it. The world had stood still. And, for one moment, had been perfect.

How was it that this kept on getting better? That first time, in the cold store of the bar, had been crazy—wild and crazy and he'd never thought he'd feel such intensity again. But he had—time and time again with her. Fast, slow, risky or relaxed, it didn't matter, it just got better and better. A woman he barely knew. A woman he didn't know if he could trust. A woman who was vulnerable and whose vulnerability threatened him in his weakest spot. He couldn't be falling for her. Cardio thoracic surgeon he wasn't, but he knew enough. The likelihood of her needing more treatment in the future was pretty high, and he couldn't, wouldn't sit there and do nothing. Only able to watch while someone he loved…

Oh, God, he was in trouble.

Sienna knew it was the middle of the night but she couldn't sleep any more. Her brain had clicked on and was whirring at triple overtime rate. She listened to his regular breathing. She needed some space. Carefully she slid out from under his arm, slipped into the shirt on the floor and padded barefoot out to the lounge. She flipped the switch and quickly dimmed the light. Her bag was at the end of the sofa. She curled into the chair and opened the book. How to make sense of this? The blank page mocked her swirling, chaotic thoughts and emotions. Fear held the words back. Maybe she shouldn't overanalyse. Maybe she shouldn't even try to make sense of what was happening, of the secret desires rising in her. All the things she couldn't, shouldn't have.

Frustrated, she looked about the room. *Write anything to break through it. Describe the damn curtains.* And so she did. Putting order into her mind by describing the room she sat in. Ignoring the important things—like whose room it was and what she was doing in it wrapped in one of his shirts and nothing else. Trying to block out the melancholy that came when bliss was followed by uncertainty.

He'd said he wanted to make love to her, called her his girl.

But these were just words—the soft nothings of pillow talk. This was the man who still couldn't seem to talk. Who was still so reticent and guarded—despite having invited her into his personal domain. Why didn't he trust her? What had happened that made him stay so locked up? She longed to break through to him. She knew she shouldn't, she was getting too involved, but how she wanted to. You always wanted what you couldn't have.

In his dream her belly was gently rounded. She put a hand to it, her secret smile teasing him. Then her belly was swollen tight and she sat naked, her breasts full, nipples darkening with maternal maturity. His body tensed with longing. His child. His family. Indescribable satisfaction surged through him.

But in that flash the picture fled. Suddenly it was images of the hospital speeding through his brain—medications and operations and tubes and beeps. And then it wasn't Sienna on the table, but a kid.

He snapped back. *No. No. No!* The sound of his own voice jerked Rhys awake. He took a couple of deep breaths. Pressed his hands to his eyes, keeping them closed. Not real. The sweat rapidly cooled, leaving him chilled. He tried to rationalise.

Rhys the clinician knew if ever she was pregnant it could be managed. Yes, there were higher risks, but nothing that medication and good care couldn't handle. And, yes, there was the chance that a heart condition might be passed on to her child. The chance was small but it was there.

Rhys the man couldn't handle even the smallest risk. Rhys didn't want to sit uselessly and suffer while his loved ones suffered.

Suddenly his arms ached with emptiness. He reached out to touch her, sat up sharply as his hand encountered the cold, empty sheet. The loss stabbed. How could he give to her if one day he woke to find her gone?

His heart thumped a wild tattoo. Then he saw the faint light coming through the hall. He slipped from the bed and pulled on boxers. Quietly he moved, unable to stop suspicion rising. She was huddled in his favourite chair, her head bent, scribbling in her journal. What details was she recording?

He stood in the shadow. Uncomfortable—with what had happened, with the crazy way his mind was messing with him, with what she was doing. How little he knew of her. Was she another Mandy? Was she transcribing their every word so she could sell it on? Rhys needed privacy. He needed to keep those deepest and darkest desires and secrets well hidden so he could keep their impact under control. But he'd just slipped up. He'd wanted to make up for his lie, but he'd given far more of himself than he'd intended. She'd slipped under his barriers. Had she known? He needed to back-pedal. Needed to get this back to the casual fling it had started as.

'What are you writing?'

She looked up and guilt flashed all over her face. 'Nothing.'

He hesitated. He could hardly demand to read it. He had to go on trust. He wasn't so good with that. 'You should be in bed.'

Get her back in bed, where he could keep an eye on her. She'd admitted she hadn't intended anything serious from this affair. He needed to think the same. Put it in the physical box and keep it there. No more questions, no more depth. No thoughts to a future that could leave him wide open to a level of pain he knew he couldn't handle.

She should be in bed? What was his angle—because he wanted her or because he was concerned for her? The last thing Sienna needed was another doctor. Scenes from the tapas bar tumbled back—the way he'd wanted her to eat, the way he'd tried to take her pulse, the fact he'd gone through her bag to find her medication. He couldn't help himself. Being a doctor was as much a part of him as his legs were. If this continued into a relationship he'd be mollycoddling her as badly as Neil had. She should walk. Go back to the hostel. Stop before the disappointment hit—inevitable as it was.

But his attraction was irresistible. He had such strength. She wanted to borrow some. And she also wanted to break through it, to whatever it was he was so fiercely protecting. She only had another couple of days in Sydney anyway. Live *now*.

But as he flopped back onto the bed and pulled her onto him, she wished for the carefree romp they'd enjoyed at the hostel. This was getting heavy, he was starting to matter too much and he was so far wrong for her. But while the joy he brought was so unimaginable, so indescribable, she just couldn't say no.

They spent most of the next morning lazing, testing each other's general knowledge by reading the questions from a trivia board game. Not bothering with the actual rules. Conversation stayed safe and simple. They shared favourite movies, favourite songs, most embarrassing moments. He joked, teased and laughed. She joked, teased and laughed. And all the while she knew she was finally getting the truth from him, but still not getting to the heart of him. The scar was key. She saw the way he sometimes rubbed at it. The way he avoided any mention of it.

She thought of her airport trek tomorrow. Hell, her backpack was still at the hostel, padlocked shut but still vulnerable under her bunk in the dorm room. While Rhys was in the bedroom she found the phone and called Curtis on Reception. Got him to put it in the secure room for her.

Fobbed off his attempt at chit-chat and enquiries as to what she was up to.

'Who were you talking to?'

She spun, surprised at the accusatory tone in Rhys' voice.

'The hostel. I just got Curtis to lock my pack away for me.'

'Oh.' He walked across the room, tightened the blinds, keeping them wide enough for light to come in but for the world outside to be blurry.

Sienna couldn't stand it any more. Skirting around issues wasn't something she was good at. She was good at getting people to talk, and she wasn't going to have Rhys, someone who actually mattered, be her only failure.

She even had a plan. His bathroom was magnificent and already they'd spent quite some time investigating how much hot water was in the cylinder—lazing for hours under the shower. So in the late afternoon she suggested they return there. This time when she went in she eyed the double basins and twin towel racks with mock disfavour. 'You entertain here often?'

'No.' He grinned. 'I told you I like my privacy. I don't tend to have people over much.'

'I'm honoured.'

He laughed. 'You are not.'

'No, I am, Rhys. You letting me in here.' She shot him a not-so-innocent look from under her lashes. 'You must trust me.'

His smile remained on his mouth but his eyes went wary. 'Maybe a little.'

'How much?' She walked towards him. 'How much do you trust me?'

The wary look spread. He knew she wasn't joking around. 'Why, what do you want to do?'

'Not me, Rhys. You.'

'What do you want me to do?'

It was so easy, yet he seemed to find it so hard. 'Talk.'

He looked nonplussed. 'What about?'

'How you're feeling.'

'Oh, my God.' He looked at her as if she'd grown two heads.

She laughed. 'It's not that bad. How about this? I touch you, and you tell me how it feels.'

'Touch?' His brows were up, she could tell he could cope with the touch bit. But he didn't know where she planned to lay her hands yet. 'OK.'

'Great. Let's start simple.' She cocked her head on the side and studied him. 'Where to begin... How about if I touch you here? How does that feel?' She ran her fingertips along the breadth of his shoulders.

'Not bad.'

'What about here?' She slid them down to his nipples, circled around them.

'Getting better.'

She went a little lower, crossing abs that went taut at her touch.

'Mmm hmm.'

'Words, Rhys, use your words.'

He grunted. 'You've got to be kidding me.'

She felt a touch of guilty amusement at his expression— half of him wanting her, half of him wanting her to shut up. She paused the downward trajectory of her fingertips and looked up to him, waiting.

The wanting half of him won. 'Isn't it obvious?'

She stayed silent.

He sighed. 'Would it make this simpler if I told you that anywhere you touch me feels good?'

'Well, now, that was a sweet thing to say.'

She squeezed some shower gel onto her hands, rubbed them together in circles to lather it up into a silky, bubbly mass. She skipped over the middle of him entirely. Dropped to her knees. She heard him suck in a quick breath.

She smiled up at him as she knelt before him.

'OK, I'm quite liking this.' He looked back down at her, cheeky grin on the full lips.

Yes, but he didn't know what she had planned. She spread her soapy hands and placed them on the front of his thighs, ran them down over his knees. Switched both hands to one leg and wrapped around his calf, sliding down with sensual slowness and back up.

He'd gone quiet again. She'd known he would. She gave the other leg the same treatment, loving the spray of the water from the multiple shower jets warming her. This was way better than standing in some freezing fountain.

With nervous fingers she went back up his thigh with both hands. Slipped to the side and gently touched his scar. With light fingers she went back over it.

She sensed the change instantly. His tension was palpable, his body rigid. Silence. Even his breathing held in check. She brushed her lips against the puckered skin. Swept across it with a soft, open mouth.

He jerked away. 'Don't, Sienna.'

She ran soothing hands down his legs. 'Does it hurt?'

'No.' Brief.

She touched the scar again. His fists curled at his sides.

She knew he wanted her. But she sensed his anger as well. As sure as steam rose, it was rising, nearing the surface. He had such a seemingly impregnable veneer—quietly charming. But he used it to keep everyone at bay, granting no opening to his true emotion. She wanted to shatter it. Pierce through the layer to the passion and pain she knew simmered deep, deep below. So she traced over the scarred skin once more, first with a quick finger, then with lips, then with the tip of her tongue.

She heard him suck in a breath, struggle to rein in his temper.

'Sienna—'

She couldn't ignore the warning. She stood, laid a tender palm on his chest. Felt the strong, regular beat of his heart beneath. 'Does it hurt here, Rhys?'

Tension hung in the room. His face was like a mask. She let her fingers brush the scar again.

He jerked. 'Back off.'

She stepped after him. 'No.'

His arms crossed his chest. He took another step away. She walked forward another pace, and another half. Until his back was against the bathroom wall.

'Tell me.'

He stared down, eyes heavy-lidded. Almost shut. 'There's nothing to tell.'

She put her hands on his chest. 'Talk to me. Your challenge this time, Rhys. Talk to me.'

'Damn it, don't you know when to leave it alone?'

He moved fast. Spinning around, spinning her around so it was her turn to be pinned against the wall. His body slammed up hard against hers. The tiles were cold on her back. His thighs were hot between her own.

'I don't. Want. To talk.'

'Fine!' she yelled. Right in his face. 'Don't. Don't say a damn thing. Keep your secrets. Don't let anyone in. Don't let anyone get anywhere near you!'

'Near me? How near me do you want to get?' His hands went to her hips, pulling her hard against his. 'This near?' He jerked her closer so his erection dug hard against her lower belly. 'This?'

She rose on tiptoe, wrapped one leg around his waist so he couldn't step away. 'Closer.'

He kissed her then, hard and angry. She was angry too but it was whisked away when she sensed the hurt he was trying to hide. So she opened for him, and he took. Boy, did he take. The ferocity of his passion literally made her weak. It was as if the stronger he was, the softer she became. Her legs were no longer able to support her—gut instinct demanded she lie down and welcome. They slid to the floor, swiftly he moved, entering with a hard thrust and a harsh growl. Any pretence at foreplay was forgotten. She pulled him even closer. Pushed him further.

The water sprayed down on them and as she gazed up at him it was like being under that fountain of her dreams. He could make her feel so wonderful, could make her feel as if she wanted to share everything with him. Most of all she wanted him to share with her. But this was only his body. She understood what he was seeking. The relief, the release, the joy that would obliterate the angst—momentarily. He wanted this to make him feel better. Why couldn't he understand that he'd feel so much more if he opened up completely?

He shuddered, rigid, his groan wrenched out from deep within. She wrapped her arms and legs tight around him. Kissed the side of his face over and over. He'd buried it deep into her neck. She turned into him, wanting to kiss his beautiful mouth. But he kept it locked in the ridge above her collarbone. So she kissed the skin she did have access to—his neck, his jaw, his cheek. She paused—sure she'd tasted salt. Sweat or tears? Maybe both.

'Rhys?'

Silence. For long moments she felt his heart thunder

against hers, felt his ragged breathing. Finally he pulled out, pushed away. Stood. Said nothing. Took a towel and left.

She lay where she was, on the floor, the streaming water keeping her warm, washing away the taste of her own tears.

CHAPTER ELEVEN

BY THE time Sienna braved the bedroom Rhys had already finished there. She pulled on some clothes, feeling colder than she had the entire time in Sydney. Summoning courage, she walked into the living area. He was standing by the window, looking out through the thin lines of the blinds. He must have heard her because he turned immediately.

'I was thinking Thai for dinner. What do you say?'

She stared at him. The smile was there, there was even a slight twinkle in his eye. But his heart was missing.

Her own heart sank. Useless. She'd tried and failed. He'd never let her beyond the barriers and into the reserves he held so deep. She shook her head a little. Such a shame. He was a man who could offer so much—to someone. If only he'd stop for a second and let that someone in. But it wasn't going to be her. And, she acknowledged sadly, nor should it be. She was going beyond her own boundaries as it was. Why blur his as well?

'Tell me about your trip.'

So she was going to be doing the talking—again. And she did. Talked to him about the plans for South America, her desire to see the ancient Inca settlement. Then she was due to fly to London. Hopefully get some work there. Maybe travel about a bit. Ireland? The Continent? She really didn't know but she kept up the chatter. Not wanting the situation to descend into awkward silence. A couple of times he looked about to say something. Then stopped. She looked away, tried to ignore her own hurt. He wouldn't talk to her. He wouldn't trust her. He couldn't love her. The sense of futility grew. There was no point any more. And she shouldn't hang around to go from bruised to broken.

Rhys found the curry utterly tasteless. Might as well be chewing cardboard. This slop was from his favourite Thai restaurant? Maybe he was coming down with something and his taste buds were the first to be infected. He watched Sienna spoon more sauce onto her rice. She was talking, as much as usual, but with restraint. Being careful not to cross any lines. He knew she was holding back over what had happened in the bathroom. In her particularly unique way she'd asked him about the scar, invited him to confess to her. And the thing was he'd been tempted, so tempted. Still was. But it wasn't possible. That was what had made him so angry.

He knew he hadn't hurt her in a physical sense. The way her hips had risen to meet his, matching his energy, his rhythm. The way her hands had pressed him closer, the way she had cried his name as sensation had overruled everything. Despite his anger, his lack of finesse, she had still taken him, enveloping him in her softness, wanting him no matter what. It made him think that maybe, even if she knew it all, she'd still embrace him. That thought was so heady, so intoxicating, he could hardly reason. He wanted it—to confide in her, to take her comfort. And he was beginning to think he wanted it long-term.

But it couldn't happen. He drank deeply from his glass of

water. Trying to cool down, calm down. It ripped him apart that the one person to whom he longed to give everything was so vulnerable. And her vulnerability would make him vulnerable. And that he couldn't allow.

So he couldn't talk about it. He tried to switch back to usual mode—of trying to forget it at all times. Some things ran too deep ever to be touched, not by her. Yet somehow she'd got so close. He'd had to push back—barely hiding the hurt. He just wanted to feel better. Wanted to find that physical relief.

But it was only temporary. And now he felt worse.

He pushed his plate away, overcome by a sense of foreboding. Something really, really bad was going to happen if she went on that trip. He knew it in his bones. 'Are you sure you should do it?'

'Do what?'

He'd interrupted her mid-flow and was ashamed to admit he hadn't caught up with her last sentence. He was still struggling with the whole concept. 'Your trip. South America.'

'I'm sorry?'

'Are you sure it's wise? I mean, maybe you're not up to it yet.'

'Not up to it? What do you mean not up to it?'

He'd got her back up just like that. He wasn't getting this out right. 'I—'

'Are you saying you don't think I can do it?'

'No, but—'

'Don't you dare lecture me on what I can and can't do.'

The snap came quicker and sharper than he'd anticipated. 'Peru isn't the easiest of destinations. The ruins will be wonderful but it's a hard trek—the path to the top outlook is steep and narrow.'

'So?'

'You have a heart condition, Sienna. You have to be careful when travelling at altitude. You're not trekking all the way up there, are you?' His mind sped into medic mode. 'What about antibiotics? Have you got some with you? You're at greater risk of—'

'I'm well aware of what I'm at risk of. I don't need you to tell me.' She put her fork down. 'You might be a doctor, Rhys, but you're not my doctor.'

'I'm not lecturing you in my professional capacity. I'm talking common sense.' He glared at her. 'You're a woman travelling alone. What if you got in trouble?'

'Oh, please, we're living in the twenty-first century. Women travel alone everywhere all the time.'

'That doesn't make it sensible. I'd be saying the same thing if you were going Outback or to Asia or…anywhere.' He clamped his jaw shut and glared some more. Anger continued to rise. What the hell was she doing on this trip anyway? What about her friends, her family, her life? 'Even your mates at the hostel travel with someone. Why aren't you doing this with a friend?'

'That's the whole point, Rhys. I want to do this on my own.' Hurt glistened in her eyes and he knew it wasn't just from this line of conversation. 'I don't need anyone, Rhys.'

'But you might. What if you have an accident? What if you get in trouble?'

'I'm not going to get in trouble. I am not weak, Rhys. I can do anything.'

'Fine! Smash your head against that wall. Go on. Do it. Just to prove you can.' He pointed to the wall dividing the kitchen from the living room. 'No? Not going to? Because it's a dumb thing to do. And so is jetting off to who knows where all by yourself. A dumb thing to do.'

'It is not. This is what I want.' Her eyes were bright. 'I want this. I'm leaving. I'm living my life. *Mine.* I'm not sharing it. And I will not be told what I can and can't do by you or anyone else. OK?'

'Well, I…' *don't want you to* '…think it's stupid,' he said lamely.

'Well, we're just going to have to agree to disagree.' She pushed her plate away, food half eaten. 'Maybe I should go back to the hostel.'

'No!' He felt like banging her head on the wall for her. 'No.' He repeated it, less loud but just as vehement. He thought of another point. 'There are snakes there, you know. Lots and lots of snakes. And spiders. Big ones.'

'Why are you doing this?' She positively smoked at him. 'We have a few hours left, Rhys. Can't we just enjoy it? Forget about my trip. Why do you want to ruin this last day?'

Good question. Why did he? Because it was all wrong. Everything felt wrong all of the time. Except when he was deep inside her. Then it was all very, very right. But that couldn't be right. She was not the one to want more from. He was filled with the desperate need to be with her and the stark knowledge that it couldn't be for any more than this one last night. No way could it be more. He could not take the risk.

He stood up from the table so fast he knocked over his chair. 'Forget it. Forget everything. Let's not waste another minute.'

But the hesitation in her face was unmistakable now. That first night, it had been the merest flicker, gone again under the weight of desire. Now, he saw, the desire had been stamped out by the burden of insecurity. He didn't blame her but still he tried. He speared her gaze with his as he stepped forward, wanting the physical attraction to overrule their heads and hearts. He wanted to hold her close, kiss her, make the doubts disappear in the heat of the moment. Just once more.

Her gaze slid away, avoiding him. He'd held back and now she was shutting him out. He understood but he hated it. He wanted to restore her openness, her wide-eyed honesty. But to do that, he'd have to be the honest, open one.

Could he give just a little of what she was asking? Could he talk to her? She seemed to offer so much if he did.

He ran his fingers through her hair. Wanting to imprint the feel of her, the scent of her, the very essence of her, in his mind and body.

He was so close to caving in, so close to confessing. So torn. Wanting to trust her. Knowing he shouldn't. What had she said? Relationships didn't start this way. Could there be the level of trust he needed? Could he commit to someone who might not be around for as long as he needed?

He pushed away the thoughts, concentrated on actions, on sensations. He traced the line of her jaw with his finger. Nudged her chin so she faced him again, but her lashes brushed her cheek and she wouldn't lift them.

Sienna. His blue-eyed Siren. Even now, in silence, she called to him. Tempting him to surrender that which he had locked away for so long—his secrets, his heart. He inched nearer. If he kissed her the passion would override the promise of the tranquillity that might come if he talked with her. But, much as he wanted to taste her, a piece would still be missing and finally the need to fix things was stronger. He wanted to explain, just a little—wanted to right the wrong inside. Wanted her to understand why this could only be physical, and only for now.

Still she wouldn't meet his gaze. It made him feel worse than anything. He didn't want her to step away. Didn't want her to go back to the hostel. He needed to buy some time. They needed respite from this all-consuming intensity.

He twirled her hair some more. Became aware of the way

she was standing so still before him. Almost as if she was holding her breath.

'Why don't we go see a movie?' he muttered. 'We could go for coffee after and…' Silence fell again. He lightly stroked across her high cheekbones, the silky soft skin so smooth under his fingertips.

'And what?' Her prompt was quiet. Her expression still hidden.

'Talk.' He wanted to. God, the longing. Her lashes swooped up. Her eyes were like deep pools and he wanted to bathe in their healing beauty. Still the fear held him back— the pain of loss and the desperate need to avoid more of that kind of pain. The pressure in his chest was immense. Everything was bubbling so close to the surface, closer than it had ever been. And he wanted to be free of it. But his burden was heavy and she was so slight and he couldn't quite be sure. Not yet.

She was silent a long time.

'Please. Just something light. I know a great café for after. The music's not too loud and it has comfy sofas you can curl up in.' If she curled at one end he could sit beside her. Maybe he could touch her hand, or toy with her hair, and maybe, just maybe, he could talk to her about what had happened on the day that everything had changed.

Don't walk out on me just yet.

What he had to say might hurt her, but if he didn't try he'd probably hurt her even more. And even though this had to come to an end, he didn't want to upset her more than he had to.

'OK.' She put a hand to her chaotic hair. 'Let me go and freshen up.'

He felt a spurt of relief, an easing in the ribcage, sent her a small smile. 'I'll find out what's on.'

She left the room and after a deep breath he went to the kitchen counter where he'd chucked the mail that had been delivered with lunch. He pushed around the stack of letters and the advertising circulars and found the day's paper in the pile. Unfolded it and started leafing through the pages to find the entertainment section. He got to the social pages. Stopped. Stared at his own face in full colour. They were on the beach and he was looking at her and his feelings were there for the world to read. On the other side of the headline was another picture of Sienna alone—smiling straight at the camera.

Maitland's Mystery Match

Single women of Sydney sigh with despair over this. It seems the city's hottest bachelor has been snagged at last. Rhys Maitland, heir to the Maitland millions, was snapped in his favourite haunt with a strawberry-blonde who, as the pictures show, had him spellbound. What began as an ill-concealed argument became a tentative reconciliation with the blonde giving him a hard time. They finally left the tapas bar and walked to Rhys' nearby luxury apartment—where the Maitland magic must have worked as the blinds have yet to be opened!

Our source tells us Rhys checked into the hostel she was staying at, determined to catch up with the beauty. And as our pictures show, he certainly did that…

Rhys stopped reading, stared sightlessly across the kitchen as it sank in. Source. Sienna. The drivel was merely an add-on to the steamy photo of them kissing on the beach the morning they'd failed to play volleyball. He'd been taken for a ride. Once was unfortunate. Twice was sheer stupidity.

The fear that had been raging within rose and transformed into a fury that was blinding. With excessive force he scrunched the paper in his hands.

Sienna ran the brush through her hair and tried not to let the feeling of elation grow beyond all proportion. Take it easy. Keep it slow.

Something had changed. Her lover, with the world's most impenetrable security system around his heart, might just be about to unlock a gate—a cat-flap, perhaps. A tiny opening into the vast reservoir on the other side. He was so very strong but just then he'd softened—a slight touch. There was hope. She couldn't help but hope. All too easily she flicked her own doubts out of her mind. Focusing on him, she could forget about her own rules.

She jumped out of her skin when she heard him shout her name.

He appeared in the doorway. 'You're just like all the rest, aren't you?'

'Rhys?' Shocked, she watched as he strode towards her, his hands shaking. He shoved the newspaper in her face. She grasped it but couldn't read—too thrown by his expression, the menace with which he towered over her.

'Is that what you were writing earlier? More details you can sell for part two of your exposé?'

'Rhys, what are you talking about?' Frantic, she glanced down over the headline, saw the picture of herself looking so cheekily at whomever it was taking the photo. Oh, no. 'Rhys, this wasn't me.'

'Yeah, right. When did you tip them off? You've known all along, haven't you?' He swore. 'God, how guilty I felt. I really thought I'd hurt you. And you've been laughing at me this whole time.' He stepped back, strode around the room. 'You've played me for such a fool. What is it you're really after—fifteen minutes of fame? Money?'

'Rhys, look at me.' He couldn't think this had been her. He just couldn't.

'Look at you? Like I am there—*in love?*' Bitterly scornful, he stopped pacing, gestured to the paper. 'Never.' He spun away, swore some more—ferociously.

She shrank from the vehemence in his voice and the frown on his face. Violently hurt by his words and how quick he was to believe so badly of her. For a second their gazes met—steel lancing tremulous blue.

'No, don't give me that look. Your eyes tell lies.' He turned away from her again, fingers curling back into fists. 'How could I have been so stupid?'

'Rhys—' Panicked that he wouldn't stop and think.

'Take the rubbish you helped them write and go.'

'Rhys!' She had to talk to him. Had to get her head round what the hell had happened, but he was wild and wasn't going to listen and wasn't giving her a second.

'I can't believe I was such an idiot. And to think I wanted to tell you…to think I was going to—' He turned sharply and headed to the door.

'What, Rhys?' she cried after him. Her voice breaking as she tried to make him stop, make him hear her. 'Whatever it is you can tell me!'

'I can't!' He whirled to face her. Stepped towards her with such barely held fury she instinctively moved back. He shouted. Every word wounded. 'I can't trust you!'

She stared into his face. Cringing at the blazing anger, the hate she saw there. Crushing hurt swamped her. Her heart ached so hard she thought it would burst. She couldn't take any more. She wanted to give to him. Wanted him to lean on her the way she had him.

She wanted to love him.

And he thought she'd betrayed him?

They could offer billions and she'd never let him down. But she could say nothing. Do nothing. Could only try to escape the absolute agony she felt at his words. She wanted to hide from the bitter way he looked at her. Wanted to hide from the fact he'd never care for her the way she did for him. Oh, how that hurt.

She tried to bite back the sobs, but they burst out anyway. Deep, racking gulps that stole her fight and her energy. Hardly able to see, she grabbed at her bag, crushing the pages of the paper against her. Scalding tears spilled. Blindly she ran.

CHAPTER TWELVE

THE emergency department was overflowing as always. Rhys had rung in. Not wanting a minute more of his wretched holiday, so out of sorts and unhappy that he'd be best off working crazy hours and having something—anything—to occupy his brain and fill in the void where his heart should be. He needed a sense of purpose—saving a few lives ought to be enough. Wasn't that the whole reason he went into medicine? To make amends?

Despite the fact he was busy he still felt hollow—lonely in the crowded corridors. He dealt with crises and walked through the waiting areas. Used to recognition in the eyes of passers-by, he was able to let the obvious speculation slide over him. He kept up his reserved but amiable demeanour. Hid behind the 'Doctor' title. He watched the patients, the worried faces of family and lovers, witnessed the reunions, the fears, the loss, the relief, the recovery.

Usually he drew satisfaction from the effort of his work. Even if he failed to help someone, he knew he had tried. And it tired him enough to keep the demons at bay. But now it wasn't working. Instead the emptiness inside was growing.

He was haunted.

In every patient he saw the hurt in her eyes. The plea to

stop, the shock, the truth. And with every passing moment the certainty grew that he'd been so wrong. So completely wrong he didn't know how he was going to make it right.

He ignored the sidelong grins and glances of his colleagues. They were his friends. He knew he had their respect. But he also knew their curiosity would get the better of them. It was Tim—inevitably—who broached the topic as they walked through the ward. 'So you really hit it off with the drummer girl.'

Rhys gave a noncommittal grunt and hoped it was enough to signal 'end of conversation'.

'What was the surgery?'

Rhys frowned. 'Surgery?'

'You know, the pictures in the paper.'

Pictures. He hadn't got much past the opening paragraph. Hadn't seen beyond the teasing grin she'd given the camera. There'd been other pictures?

Tim drummed his fingers on his chest. 'I'm thinking heart?'

'Valve replacement,' Rhys answered shortly. 'I have to go check something.'

He strode to the staff room, rifled through the stack of papers and magazines on the table. *Please, please, please.* And there it was. Folded open, well read by the look of it. Gritting his teeth, he skimmed over the first few lines, going straight to the later paragraphs.

No stranger to tragedy, has Rhys set himself up for more heartache by falling for one of his patients?

He froze, icy fingers slipping across his skin. He looked for the first time at the photos along the bottom of the page. They'd snapped her in his shirt when they were on the beach in the pale light of dawn. It was only buttoned at the waist—she looked hot and there was no hiding her fresh-from-bed hair. And there was no hiding her scar in the open vee of his shirt either. To make it worse they'd blown up the part of her chest and added it as a pop-up pic, circling the mark of the long incision.

The scar suggests the mystery beauty has had major surgery.

Hot guilt mixed with the icy dread. The words confirmed what he already knew. What had kept him tossing and turning at night. Sienna would never have sold him out.

His knuckles clenched, the skin turning white as he read on. Media intrusion was something he was used to. He disliked it and worked hard to avoid it, but it came with his name. She had no experience, had no defences built for this kind of invasion. They had no right to destroy her privacy. She would hate to have her scar revealed to the world.

He had been such an idiot. She must surely hate him. She should have been angry, should have yelled, should have put him in his place good and proper. But she'd been hurt—too hurt. And he'd been a fool to throw away someone who could care like that.

He should have been helping her—consoling her over having her life ripped open for the entertainment of the masses. Instead he'd accused her of orchestrating the whole thing.

And why? He'd been like a trapped tiger searching out something to attack. It gave him a way of shoving her back. Because he'd been on the verge of letting her right inside and it terrified him.

He raked fingers through his hair as frustration and futility ravaged his heart. Sienna hadn't deserved that, just as she didn't deserve this. She'd be mortified by these pictures. He looked closely at the head and shoulders shot of her at the top of the page—the one where she smiled so freely. He could make out part of the sign on the wall behind her. Recognised it hung in Reception at the hostel. Of course, it was obvious now. Curtis—who had to work all those hours because he 'needed the money'. He'd known all along who Rhys was. The creep. With sadness Rhys read on. Not only had they debated on her history, they'd printed the details of his accident with Theo. And then they'd reprinted some of Mandy's more painful comments. He blanched as he skimmed over them. So inevitable. So predictable. So true?

Sienna read the article again and again and again. She had no chance of sleeping on the plane. Couldn't concentrate on any in-flight entertainment. The cabin steward was wonderfully kind and provided an entire box of tissues and a cool pack for her eyes.

Rhys, fourteen at the time, and his twelve-year-old cousin Theo were skateboarding down the street. A car, speeding out of its driveway, collided with both boys. Rhys was tossed to the side while Theo was crushed, dying at the scene...

She stared at the photos, not of herself, but of Rhys, of the way he was smiling at her—in love? So the gushing journalist said. But she knew otherwise. He'd *told* her otherwise. He'd never opened up. She'd asked. He'd refused. Not trusting in himself, in her, or in the bond she'd thought they had. All the while she'd been so open, he'd kept part of himself locked away. But what else could she expect when they'd started so casually? She couldn't demand anything more serious from him just because she then wanted it.

She wished it had stayed purely physical—that searing attraction. It had been a wild coming together that had blown her mind. In the hostel they'd channelled the energy, deliberately fuelling it, pushing it. Since the first time in his apartment, she'd been unable to control anything, not least the entirety of her response.

For it was no longer just physical. Her mind was involved. And so was her heart. And all she could hear right now was her head telling her how bad her heart was feeling.

His ex-girlfriend Mandy says he's emotionally crippled, claiming the city's wealthiest bachelor will never wed as he's already married to his job...

Deep anger gripped her as she read the comments. No wonder he was so untrusting, when his ex could so blithely say such cutting things. He wasn't crippled, he was warm and caring and funny and *hurt*.

Now she knew his history she saw it had been for the best. They could never have had a relationship beyond a brief affair. She couldn't give him what he needed—serenity, security, stability. There were things on her list that she'd never written down. Rules she had to live by—no marriage, no kids. She couldn't promise her life to anyone, not when she wasn't sure she had the power to see it through. But she needed to be a little better at observing those rules. Instinctively she'd known long-term wasn't for her, thinking it was because she didn't want anyone else to worry over her the way her mother and brother did. But now she knew the real reason was because she couldn't cope with the heartache herself. She just wasn't strong enough. And she couldn't bear to see Rhys hurt more than he already was. He needed someone whole and well and who would be reliable. She couldn't guarantee that. She didn't know what her future held.

Their parting was definitely for the best.

That didn't stop the tears rolling.

Taking several deep breaths, Rhys ducked into the supply cupboard for some space, raised shaking fingers to his face and massaged his forehead. *Sienna, Sienna, Sienna.*

He could no longer keep the lid on his emotions. For the first time his personal life was affecting his ability to work. He'd almost choked up over that patient. Had seen the startled look the nurse had given him. He couldn't go on like this. Every second it got worse, not better.

He closed his eyes and caught the memory of when he'd first seen her.

The blood had pumped in his veins. His senses had gone supersonic. Everything was brighter when she was around. Hell, he was pathetic. He'd made up the whole Monroe thing to escape himself more than anything. It wasn't about her. It had been about him. And it had backfired completely.

His world was all about life and death. He witnessed both—every day, every night. But that was just it, he was witnessing. Facilitating. Fighting for others. But not actually doing it himself. He'd been driven to make a difference—to give, to help. But he was so busy trying to save, he no longer lived his own life. He stood on the sidelines, spectating. Bound by fear. Afraid of losing. But he'd already lost.

Sienna had been forced to spectate for most of her life. He had chosen to. Now she was fighting to live it—reaching out and taking it on with both hands. Rhys couldn't, he felt duty-bound not to waste the life he'd been given. Not when he'd been instrumental in Theo losing his. He'd work and help and never be useless again.

But didn't he have a duty to Sienna as well? At the very least, she deserved an explanation and an apology. He couldn't leave it unfinished. He owed her answers. He owed her honesty.

He banged his creased forehead with his knuckles. She didn't want duty from him. She'd said he had a responsibility to live his own life. What about his life's to-do list? He'd never even thought about it seriously. He'd never been to Peru either. Why shouldn't he go too? Wasn't it as much a waste of a life to focus so completely on only one aspect—in his case, work? Shouldn't he be embracing all avenues of his life? How she tempted him. Made him long for everything.

In the gloom of the supply room it dawned on him that he'd used her—wanting the moments of bliss to break up the lifetime of guilt. And hadn't she used him too? To have those moments of freedom? Be treated normally? But then she'd wanted more—she'd wanted him to open up to her. Why? If it was just a fling, an affair—an extended one-night stand…

Because it wasn't just a fling. Because she cared.

And he'd hurt her. And in hurting her, he'd hurt himself more. The least he could do was apologise. See her, explain it all the best he could. He'd never been able to apologise to Theo. He should take the opportunity to apologise to her while he had it. He had to take a leaf out of her book and seize the day. Make the most of every moment, and leave no room for regret. He locked his knuckles together. Right now he re-gretted everything he hadn't done.

He didn't know what the future held. No one did. All he knew was that he couldn't go on in the present as it was. He couldn't hide any more. It was too late. She was already there, lodged deep in his heart, and he had to fight to stop his heart from breaking.

A nurse came into the cupboard. Stopped as she saw Rhys leaning against the cabinet. Glanced round to see if there was anyone else in the tiny room. 'Sorry, I—'

'It's OK. I was just leaving.'

CHAPTER THIRTEEN

SOMEHOW it was so typical that after five days of fairly tiring travel, a lifetime of dreaming and a huge chunk of her life savings spent, the ruins of Machu Picchu would be shrouded in mist the one day Sienna had to visit them. She'd known it would be a possibility, it wasn't the optimum time to travel there weather-wise, but she'd wanted to go so much and hadn't wanted to wait any longer. She'd wanted it to be the first major step on her big adventure. New year, new life. But she'd stepped into her adventure with far more of a jump than she'd planned.

And there would be no view for her. Not today. She wouldn't be climbing the steep track. The one that Rhys had become so 'lecturing doctor' over. She hadn't wanted to anyway, she'd just wanted to walk in the ancient ruins and marvel. And she hadn't trekked all the way. She'd taken the train, taken her time, got used to the thinner air, ensured she rested as well as she could. Despite what he thought, she knew her own limitations. And it was enough to be here. Wasn't it?

But the void couldn't be filled—no view to fill it, no one to share it, no one to laugh about it. She was mad with him for ruining what should have been one of her life's most marvellous moments. Mad with herself for letting him.

She sat in the damp air and wallowed. She was pathetic. Other tourists walked on by. She hadn't banded together with any of them. Just wanted her own company—as she'd told Rhys. But she'd lied. She'd wanted his.

Finally she stood, deciding to go down to the village below where she was staying. Maybe she could add another day there, hope for better weather tomorrow. She could laze in the thermal pools this afternoon and try to jolly herself out of it.

As she went she saw someone walking up the other way.

He was staring straight at her. Not smiling. Not frowning. Just looking kind of frozen. Oh, man, she was hallucinating. Thought it was him. Wishful thinking. She blinked a few times. Maybe she had some weird form of altitude sickness?

'Sienna.' Not a question, but a call—a command for attention.

'Rhys?' For the first time in years she nearly fainted. She consciously tensed every muscle in her body, refusing to let the light recede. 'What are you doing here?'

He didn't reply until he was right in front of her. He really was there. Wearing khaki trousers, a long-sleeved tee and at least three days' stubble. 'There was something I wanted to tell you.'

She waited—for once in her life struck dumb.

As Rhys drew in his breath, all the sentences he'd mentally rehearsed in the aeroplane disappeared into the mist. 'I, uh, didn't want you to go.' With relief he saw the colour flood back into her cheeks.

'Pardon?' She stood, feet planted firmly on the ground, in front of him.

The words forced their way out from deep inside. 'I didn't want you to leave. I wanted you to stay.' He puffed the air out. There. He'd done it. He'd said it.

She whirled on him. 'That's it? That's all you have to say?'

She unzipped the pocket to the side of her thigh, pulled out the wrinkled pages from the paper.

'I'm sorry I thought…I'm sorry I couldn't…I'm sorry.' He wanted to talk but the words weren't coming. The blockage in his chest had risen to his throat and it hurt. He just wanted to reach out and pull her home to his embrace. If he could hold her tight to him, maybe he could whisper it all in her ear. God, how he needed her comfort and how he longed to comfort her. She was close enough to touch but she was looking mad and now words were flying from her.

'You know, you're the one who needs the surgery. You're the one whose heart needs cutting open—to free the blockages. Let the blood flow. Let the love flow.' Tears spilled down her face; the pages rustled in her shaking hands. 'I opened up to you—really opened up. And you held back from me the whole time.' She sniffed, scrubbed a tear away with a fist. 'Even when you told me who you were, you still held back.'

Defensive anger rose. 'No, I didn't. Not in bed. I gave you everything there and you know it.' He'd shown her, again and again.

'So what about sex, Rhys? There was more to us than sex. Don't you get it? It would never have been that fantastic if there wasn't more.'

He stopped. Of course there was more than sex—that was just one tangible facet of a deeply profound bond. They connected on many levels, not just the physical. He ran his hands through his hair. This wasn't going anything like he'd imagined. He was supposed to have apologised to her and then it would all have been OK. He'd tried to prepare. Knew he'd have to talk. But now it had come to the moment, he still didn't know how to say it, didn't know where to start.

'I just wanted to forget it all.' He ached to enfold her in his arms, needing to feel her length against his. To be certain they weren't ever separating again.

'Trying to forget doesn't work—*does it?*' She stared at him sadly.

He looked away from the accusation in her gaze, the astuteness, the question she'd asked before and would ask again. She'd pierced through. He could feel his tension building, demanding to be let out at last. He'd come so far for her. He was already committed. And if he didn't talk now, he'd lose her.

'Actually I have a photographic memory.' A slight lift of his shoulders as he started. 'And like an elephant, I can't forget.'

After a stretch she spoke again, softer this time. 'What can't you forget?'

He looked up the path to where she stood square on, facing him. Slim but so strong. Stronger than he'd ever imagined. Those brilliant blue eyes of hers stared intensely, seeing right through him, willing him to share his burden. The ultimatum—giving him no choice.

And finally he did it. Told her. The one thing he'd never told anyone—the awful truth. 'It was my fault.'

'What?'

He glanced at the paper in her hand. 'My cousin. Theo.'

'How?'

He looked down at the ground, not wanting to see her frown. 'We were skateboarding. I was in front. We were racing. A car came out the driveway.'

He'd got such a fright from the noise he'd come off his own board, landed roughly on the edge of the footpath, right on pieces of broken bottle. He'd skidded, the bits of glass embedded deep in his thigh, ribboning the skin and muscle, marking him for life.

'I don't see how it was your fault, Rhys. That car came flying out of the driveway—straight across the footpath. The driver was the person who was going too fast, who should have stopped to check. You were just playing in your neighbourhood like all kids do.'

'But if I hadn't challenged Theo to a race. If I hadn't been showing off and going so fast, calling out to him to hurry. We didn't hear the car. He was asking me to wait up and I didn't—'

He broke off suddenly. Head bowed, he tried to fix his blurry vision by focusing on one tuft of grass poking through the muddied track. Cold sweat slid over him. And as he talked he didn't know if she could hear him any more. All he felt was the agony. The fear. 'I couldn't do anything. I couldn't help him. I just sat there and held his hand and watched while he slipped away. He looked at me and then he just—'

They'd tried to tell him Theo wouldn't have known anything. But Rhys knew better. He'd seen it in his eyes, seen the plea for help.

He hated going over this. Hated the memories. Wanted to keep it all buried deep where he could try to forget about it. Even though he failed day in, day out. But trying to forget was better than grinding through this rotting mess that tasted foul as he spoke of it. *If only, if only, if only.* Thousands of times he'd replayed it. Thousands of hours feeling horror and dread and guilt.

'And now you're a doctor.'

She understood already but still he voiced it, realising now how much he *wanted* to tell her, hoping comfort would come with confessing everything. 'I was so useless. He was dying and I couldn't do anything. I won't be in that position again. At least now I can try to help. Not do *nothing.*'

* * *

Sienna longed to touch him, wanted to wrap her arms around him, but he stood so defensively. Not looking at her, fists clenched, sweat shining on his forehead. She saw how hard this was for him. How deep the feelings were buried. While she didn't want to stop the flow, she couldn't let him go on blaming himself. She stepped a little closer.

'You didn't do nothing, Rhys. You held him. You were there for him. You were with him. He wasn't alone.' That, she knew, was huge.

It was Rhys who had been alone. A scared child, burdened with a guilt no one would have expected him to carry. Not many people could handle holding someone who lay dying— not in circumstances like that, not without help. She understood his mission now, the need that drove him to work in the field he did, with the dedication he had. So busy fighting he'd forgotten how to have fun.

Her heart ached—for him, and for her. He'd paid a price high enough—he didn't need to be with someone who might only cost him more. She breathed little, quick breaths, trying to be strong. Maybe they could talk. It might help. But after that she knew she had to walk away.

She definitely didn't want a heart that worked properly if it was going to hurt this bad.

'How many?' She focused on him.

'How many what?'

'How many do you have to save before you feel better about Theo? You can't bring him back.'

'I know that.'

'It wasn't your fault. You were a kid—you weren't responsible for him. The person responsible was the person behind the wheel of the car.'

He stood like a statue and she had no idea whether she was getting through to him.

'You can't go beating yourself up over this the rest of your life. I'm sure he'd hate that.'

He flinched. She couldn't tell what he was thinking. The silence grew and this time she waited.

'I just wanted to help him.' The words came out low and so full of need she could hear the bleed in his heart and the tears in his soul.

Very gently she replied, 'You did.'

'How was the view from the top?'

Change of topic. That was as much as she was going to get. He was so on edge she didn't know whether to push much more. He stood rigid as he battled to keep everything in.

'I didn't go up.' She gestured at the mist. 'Didn't seem much point with the weather like this.'

'Will you try tomorrow?'

'I'm supposed to be leaving. But I was thinking I might go up in the helicopter in the morning, if it's a clear day.'

He swore sharply, long and loud. 'You can't do this.'

Stunned, she stared. 'Do what?'

'Mess me around. You know, you say you're going to go off and do this, that and the other and people who care about you worry the whole time and then you don't do it anyway so they didn't have to worry after all and then you turn around and say maybe you'll do something even more stupid and then they have to worry all over again.'

She frowned, flummoxed by the verbal onslaught she'd never have expected from him. People who cared about her? Her family didn't even know she was here. The only person who knew she was here was—

'Who cares about me, Rhys? Why are you so worried about my heart?'

'It's not your heart I'm worried about!' he roared. 'It's mine!' His tension snapped. Anger, frustration and uncontrollable emotion poured out of him as he stood in the path and yelled. 'I worry about you. I want to take care of you. That's what people who love each other do. It's not because I think you're sick. It's because I love you!'

He stopped. The sound of his passion reverberated around them.

How could it be that those three little words could have one half of her soaring higher than the sky-touching peaks around them and the other half of her sinking fast into despair and remorse? Raw honesty shone in his face. He was utterly exposed, had opened up completely, for her—inviting her into a place she had no right to be.

What had she done?

'You can't expect me to just sit back and agree to whatever stupid scheme you've come up with,' he growled, muscles bunching. 'You can't do this emotional blackmail thing—accusing me of mollycoddling when I'm just pointing out common sense.'

Her silly bruised and battered heart beat stronger than it ever had. But her brain screamed—she was wicked to have let this happen. She wished she'd known about his past sooner. She'd have stayed away then, steered well clear so she wouldn't hurt him.

'Sienna, I am *sick* of this talking.' He strode towards her, words abandoned as his body went into action.

'Rhys.' She stumbled and he swiftly pulled her into his arms.

His grip hurt and he lifted her clear off her feet. His mouth pressed hard on hers. And it was so wonderful it blocked the fears scurrying in her head. For a spell it was simply bliss. She reached up with both hands, threading them through his thick hair, and strained to give as well as to take. He raked in her body, pressing her close with a hug that was so tight she struggled to suck air into her squeezed lungs. She couldn't tell who was shaking more. He was muttering, the words muffled as he kissed her face. It took several moments, many kisses, to decipher what it was he was saying again and again.

'Don't.'

'Don't what?'

'Don't go without me.'

'Rhys.' She pushed with all her might, pulling her head away and raising tortured eyes to him. 'I can't promise you that.'

CHAPTER FOURTEEN

'LET'S go.' She pulled away from Rhys, starting to head down the track.

He looked stunned. 'Sienna—'

'That site guard has been looking at us like we're loco and about to leap onto the ruins and do something sacrilegious.'

'If kissing you is sacrilegious, then I intend to be the biggest sinner there is.' His mouth moved into a sort of smile but his eyes showed his seriousness—and uncertainty. 'OK, now we have to talk about this. You have to talk.'

'I know and I will. Let's just do it somewhere private, OK?' She didn't want to stand in the middle of a major tourist attraction, pour her heart out to the love of her life, and then walk away from him. She needed privacy. So did he.

She walked briskly to the entrance to the ruins and got straight on the waiting bus. It wasn't a long trip down to the town below the ruins, but today it would take for ever.

'Sienna.'

She didn't want to look at him, didn't want to be tempted. She had to be strong—it was for his own good, damn it. But she hated herself. He'd just told her he loved her and here she was running again, leaving him hanging. She blinked, wanting rid of the sting in her eyes. She spoke quickly, not wanting stilted silence. He didn't deserve that. 'How did you get here?'

'Helicopter.'

'*Helicopter?*' Amazed, she spun to look at him then. 'Why?'

'I needed to get here quickly.'

'You haven't had time to acclimatise. You might get altitude sickness.'

'It's not the altitude that's making me feel...' His voice trailed away.

Hurriedly she turned back and looked out the window, her cheeks flaming. Her innards had gone mushy and she fought to maintain her resolve. Only then did she realise how hard he was going to make this.

As the bus moved she chanced another look at him. Less stunned. A lot determined. She had a fight on her hands, but for his sake she'd better win it. She couldn't bear to hurt him more than he already had been. Guilt ripped through her. She had forced him to open up. She loved him for it. But wasn't being with her going to hurt him beyond repair?

'I'm sorry they showed your scar.' He nodded at the pages still in her hand.

She shrugged. 'It's OK. I guess I'm never going to escape it.'

'No, but you'll learn to live with it. It's only a small part of who you are, Sienna.'

She looked at him keenly. 'Ditto.'

She led him to her hotel, straight in and up the stairs to her room.

He looked about, took in the double bed. 'No dorm room this time?'

'I needed some space.'

She recognised the glint in his eye and moved back into the other half of the room. She needed space from *him* now.

If he came any nearer she'd melt into his arms. Not allowed. She had to think of him rather than herself. She picked up her journal, waved it at him like a sword. 'New year, new journal, new me.' She laughed—bitter and brittle. 'I wrote my list, as you know. But there were some things I didn't write down. The really important things.' She took a deep breath. 'I can't be with someone for ever, Rhys. I can't ever have kids or a family or anything like that. I decided I was going to live life *now*. I can't make promises for the future—not to anyone.'

'Why not?'

'Because there might not be a future.'

His colour drained. 'What are you saying?'

She sighed. 'I remember when Dad died. Mum was devastated. It nearly killed her too. She was great with us kids but her heart went into the grave with him. You can still see it in her eyes.' She looked to him, pleading for him to understand. 'You've already been through enough, Rhys. You don't need to hook up with someone who might not be around for you. I don't want you to go through that. I don't want to leave a husband without a wife, children without a mother.'

'Who says you will? Who says you won't live to be a hundred? Hell, bits of your heart are practically bionic. They keep coming up with better treatments all the time. Why do you have dibs on dying first? I could get hit by a bus tomorrow.' His colour had returned, and he flashed his easy smile.

'Don't, Rhys.' He wasn't taking this seriously. And she meant it, she really meant it.

He sobered. 'Sienna, a few days ago I might have agreed with you. But now I know I have to be with you for however long fate decides it is we have together. I thought I couldn't bear a future with you in it. Because of the possibility I might lose you. But the fact is, I can't bear a present without you. I'm alive now. I want to live now.'

He pointed to her chest. 'I know the risks. You know the risks. They're there but they're not that big. And we're at risk of a million other things we don't even know about. We have to live life, Sienna, for as long as we have it. We have to create life—lives even.' His smile was soft. 'And we have to let them take their courses. No more sidelines.'

He stepped nearer, spoke up some more. 'It isn't your job to protect me. You can't—not like this.' He took the journal from her hand, tossed it onto the floor where it landed with a thud. 'You once told me that people write things down to help make them real. But you didn't write this down. Why?'

She stared. 'Because it was...so fundamental.'

'No.' He shook his head. Took another step nearer, his voice another notch louder. 'It's not. This isn't some goal, Sienna. It isn't meant to happen and you know that.'

The thing she wanted most was the thing she didn't want the most. Torn and trapped by her conflicting emotions and by his relentless advance across the room, she stood immobile and mute.

'No one truly wants a lonely life. Not many people choose to reject the possibility, the hope of love. You say you want to live every moment to the full and yet you won't let someone share it with you? I never thought you of all people would be so defeatist!' With each word his volume increased. They'd be hearing him up at the ruins. Sienna could hardly bear to hear him at all.

'People like me didn't spend years studying, years working to fix you, for you to then chicken out. You are whole, Sienna. And you have to let yourself live a whole life.' He stopped right in front of her, breathing hard, eyes glued to hers.

She was afraid to move. 'I'm broken, Rhys.'

'No, you're not.' He gave a half-smile and a half-shrug. 'No more than me. No more than most other people.'

'You'd always want to take care of me.'

'Of course I would. I love you. And I expect you to take care of me too. But I've never stifled you, Sienna, and I never will. When you're booking your flight in the helicopter, make sure my seat's right next to yours.'

'You want to go with me?'

'Everywhere.'

Her eyes watered. Could she really have it all? For so long she'd thought not and this was too much. She pressed her palms together, tried to take some deeper breaths. She couldn't seem to think any more. She felt frozen on the edge of a precipice and she didn't know if she was going to be able to take the leap.

'You know what I think?'

She looked at him, unable to voice the question.

'I think you're scared. Scared to really let yourself fall.'

Of course she was scared. Terrified. Petrified. Far more fear in her here than any stupid snake or spider could arouse.

'I'm scared too—the whole thing is crazy. We've known each other what—a week? But this is right, you know it is. Let's live *now*, Sienna. Jump with me.'

He wasn't going to let it go. Wasn't going to let her go. She tried to speak. Twisted her lips even. But failed to produce sound.

He stepped nearer. Spoke softly this time. 'It's too late, you know, we're already in free fall.'

At last, squeaky and raw, her voice worked again. 'Do you think either of us remembered a parachute?'

He took her hands in his, held them firm, and smiled. 'Honey, you are my parachute, and I'm yours. So long as we hold onto each other, we'll be fine. I've never been more certain of anything. You've turned me on—and I don't just mean *that*.' He grinned. 'You *make* the trees sing, the air sweet. You make my life. Hell, I don't know how to say it.'

'You're doing OK so far.' The tears overflowed, two fat trails tripping down her cheeks, followed rapidly by twin rivers.

'No fear, remember?'

She returned the grip of his hands, needing to be honest about what frightened her most. 'One day the mechanical bit in this heart might need replacing. I might have to be opened up again.'

'Maybe. And if that happens I'll be holding your hand when you go under.'

Her eyes snapped to his. Intently she focused on him. 'Holding someone's hand can be the best thing you can do for them. The only thing you can do.' She squeezed his tightly, whispered, 'So they're not alone.'

The shadow darkened his eyes and she knew he thought of Theo. 'Yeah.' She knew he understood. The hint of green appeared again as he looked at her. 'Well, I'll be holding your hand when you wake up too.'

She smiled, a little wan, but right back at him. 'Apparently I can get a little stroppy when I wake up.'

He released her, lifting his fingers to frame her face. 'It'll be a good challenge.'

One of her hands crept up and held his to her cheek, the other curled against her chest. 'Then, for as long as it's beating, this heart is staying right beside you.'

The kiss was the sweetest she'd ever experienced. He held her face to his and as their lips joined it was as if their very souls had opened up and embraced. Warm relief mingled with hot desire. Her knowledge that this being together was the beginning of for ever brought an enduring, unlimited joy. She reached for him, caressed him with both gentleness and strength, wanting to express the depth of her feelings.

Inevitably, the sweetness was overtaken by sensual, strident need. But there was a tacit understanding to keep the brakes on for once. They undressed—item by item, as if unveiling everything to each other for the very first time. The love and wonder in his eyes as magnetic as the raw lust that also registered there. When they lay naked on the bed there was nothing but deep kisses for a long, long time. Murmurs of love and mutters of laughter followed. Then no more talking, just action.

His arms, his body, imprisoned hers, but his love didn't bind her. He didn't suffocate her with concern but rather gave her freedom. When she was with him she had the courage to attempt things she'd never before contemplated. While she knew she was whole, having him beside her gave her the push to prove it. Life would never be the same again. Life would never be boring.

'You know, I had some thoughts about what you could do for a job.'

She managed to open an eye and look half enquiring.

'If you were serious about doing something positive, I mean.'

'Yes?' Both eyes opened and she lifted her head a millimetre off the pillow.

'Don't say no straight away. Hear me out.' He sat up on one elbow, enthusiasm seeming to send energy back to his body. 'You know how bored kids in hospital get. How scared?'

'Yes.'

'And you know how much fun it is to make a big, big noise?'

'Yes?'

'Music therapy. I can't believe you haven't thought of it yourself.'

She stared at him blankly. Then her mind worked through

the suggestion. 'You mean I go into the hospital and get the kids to bang some drums?'

He beamed. 'Yeah!'

'I can't believe you think I'd want to work in a hospital!'

'Not just any hospital. My hospital. I'll be there.'

'And that makes all the difference?'

'We can have lunch together.'

'As if you take lunch breaks.'

'We can snatch a few moments in the supply room.' He laughed. 'Think about it. You know I'm right.' He stroked her arm. 'You'd be making a difference.'

Her heart flooded and so did her eyes. Again. Actually the idea wasn't bad. She quite liked the possibility of having a van full of xylophones and swanni kazoos and drums and tambourines and noise, noise, noise. She buried her face in his chest, listened to the solid, rhythmic thud of his heart. He was so strong. His drive as a doctor wouldn't be changing. He needed to do it, and he'd sensed that she sought something as challenging and as rewarding for herself. That she wanted to put back in to others' lives as well as her own—just as he did. And he'd worked out a way they could do it together—he wanted her in his world and him in hers, wholly.

He breathed deeply, fingers teasing through her hair. 'Love at first sight. Never thought it happened. Never thought it would happen to me.'

'Tell me about it.' She sighed, contentment cloaking her. 'I walked into that bar and there you were looking ferocious and I blinked and my heart was no longer mine. Just like that.' She nuzzled his neck. 'I love you, Rhys.'

He clamped her to him, arms like a vice, as he spoke low and rough in her ear. 'Marry me, marry me, marry me.'

They lay bonded for a long moment, listening to their

quickened breathing, their galloping hearts. She whispered, hardly loud enough for him to hear, hardly able to believe she could feel this happy. 'OK.'

His arms tightened even more. 'No getting out of it now. We'll do it as soon as it can be arranged. The family will want big and pomp and the damn media will want photos.'

She lifted her head to look at him, humour sending a smile to her face. 'That's the real reason you want to marry me, isn't it? So you can bow out of the hellish glare of life as Rhys Maitland, bachelor heir.'

'Darling, you know me so well.'

She rolled her eyes, rolled her hand down his chest, and knew the bliss of limitless love.

The sky was clear and cloudless. One opportunity. Holding her hand tightly, he looked at her and felt an overwhelming sense of togetherness. He hadn't realised just how alone and isolated he'd become. He had a wide circle of friends, an endless supply of dates—had he wanted them—respect and authority at work. He was invited to every party, never stuck for something to do. But, hell, he'd been lonely. There was only one body his arms wanted to encircle. Only one person he wanted to have alongside him.

'We have to draw up a new list.' He saw the question in her eyes and explained. 'We never did get very far on yours. We could check them off—keep up the zest for life.' He grinned. 'I never want to take it for granted. Never want to take us for granted.'

'OK.' She thought for a moment. 'I want to do life-drawing classes. You can be my model.'

'OK.' He'd always be happy to get naked for her. 'I want to make love on a train.'

'Swim with dolphins.'

'Make love on a plane.'

'Be an extra in a movie.'

'Make love on a boat.'

'See the pyramids.'

'Make love on a bus.'

'Go to Rio for the Carnival.'

'Make love on a motorcycle.'

She rolled her eyes. 'Shave my head.'

'Make love in a car.'

'Swim with sharks.'

'Make love in a gondola.'

'Walk on burning embers!'

Undeterred he winked and checked off his fingers. 'Make love in a horse-drawn carriage, a hovercraft, a helicopter.'

'I'm sensing a theme here, Mr One-Track Mind. Haven't you run out of transport options yet?'

'No. Make love in a blimp.'

Giggles erupted from her. 'Gee, that sounds so romantic.'

He turned to her, leaned his face so close their noses brushed. 'Making love with you is *always* the experience of a lifetime.'

Her eyes shone bright. He wanted to tell her again how he loved her, but nothing was needed. She understood. Besides, you couldn't hear a thing above the noise of the rotor blades starting up. The helicopter rose high into the sky. She sat by the window and he was in the middle, nicely anchored with his arms tight around her. They circled around the ruins. Her profile was in the foreground, wisps of her hair fluttered across the blurry backdrop.

The view was incredible.

NOT-SO-PERFECT
PRINCESS

MELISSA MCCLONE

For Tom

Special thanks to:
Elizabeth Boyle, Terri Reed,
Schmidt Chiropractic Center
and the Romance team for
letting me tell Julianna's tale!

Melissa McClone has published over thirty novels. She has also been nominated for Romance Writers of America's RITA® award. She lives in the Pacific Northwest with her husband, three school-aged children, two spoiled Norwegian Elkhounds and cats who think they rule the house. They do! Visit her at www.melissamcclone.com.

CHAPTER ONE

"THREE ARRANGED marriages and not one has made it to the altar. That is unacceptable!" King Alaric of Aliestle's voice thundered through the throne room like a lion's roar. Even the castle's tapestry-covered stone walls appeared to tremble. "If men think something is wrong with you, no amount of dowry will convince one to marry you."

Princess Julianna Louise Marie Von Schneckle didn't allow her father's harsh words to affect her posture. She stood erect with her shoulders back and her chin up, maximizing her five-foot-eight-inch-stature. The way she'd been taught to do by a bevy of governesses and nannies. Her stepmother didn't take a personal interest in her, but was diligent in ensuring she'd received the necessary training to be a perfect princess and queen.

"Father," Jules said evenly, not about to display an ounce of emotion. Tears and histrionics would play into her country's outdated gender stereotypes. They also wouldn't sway her father. "I was willing to marry Prince Niko, but he discovered Princess Isabel was alive and legally his wife. He had no choice but to end our arrangement."

Her father's nostrils flared. "The reason your match ended doesn't matter."

Jules understood why he was upset. He wanted to marry her off to a crown prince in order to put one of his grandchildren on a throne outside of Aliestle. He was willing to pay a king's ransom to make that happen. She'd become the wealthiest royal broodmare around. Unfortunately.

He glared down his patrician nose at her. "The result is the same. Three times now—"

"If I may, Father." Indignation made Jules speak up. She rarely interrupted her father. Okay, never. She was a dutiful daughter, but she wasn't going to take the blame for this. "You may have forgotten with all the other important matters on your mind, but you canceled my first match with Prince Christian. And Prince Richard was in love with an American when I arrived on San Montico."

"These failed engagements are still an embarrassment." Her father's frown deepened the lines on his face. The wrinkles reminded Jules of the valley crags in the Alps surrounding their small country. "A stain on our family name and Aliestle."

A lump of guilt lodged in her throat. Jules had been relieved when she found out Niko wouldn't be able to annul his first marriage and marry her. From the start, she'd hoped he would fall in love with his long-lost wife so Jules wouldn't have to get married.

Oh, she'd liked Vernonia with its loyal people and lovely lakes for sailing. The handsome crown prince wanted to modernize his country, not be held back by antiquated customs. She would have had more freedom than she'd ever imagined as his wife and future queen. But she didn't love Niko.

Silly, given her country's tradition of arranged marriages. The realist in her knew the odds of marrying for love were slim to none, but the dream wouldn't die. It grew stronger with the end of each arranged match.

Too bad dreams didn't matter in Aliestle. Only duty.

Alaric shook his head. "If your mother were alive…"

Mother. Not stepmother.

Jules felt a pang in her heart. "If my mother were alive, I hope she would understand I tried my best."

She didn't remember her mother, Queen Brigitta, who had brought progressive, almost shocking, ideas to Aliestle when she married King Alaric. Though the match had been arranged, he fell so deeply in love with his young wife that he'd listened to her differing views on gender equality and proposed new laws at her urging, including higher education opportunities for women. He even took trips with her so she could indulge her passion for sailing despite vocal disapproval from the Council of Elders.

But after Brigitta died competing in a sailing race in the South Pacific when Jules was two, a heartbroken Alaric vowed never to go against convention again. He didn't rescind the legislation regarding education opportunities for women, but he placed limitations on the jobs females could hold and did nothing to improve their career prospects. He also remarried, taking as his wife and queen a proper Aliestlian noblewoman, one who knew her role and place in society.

"I'd hope my mother would see I've spent my life doing what was expected of me out of respect and love for you, my family and our country," Jules added.

But she knew a lifetime of pleasing others and doing good works didn't matter. Not in this patriarchal society where daughters, whether royal or commoner, were bartered like chattel. If Jules didn't marry and put at least one of her children on a throne somewhere, she would be considered a total failure. The obligation and pressure dragged Jules down like a steel anchor.

Her father narrowed his eyes. "I concede you're not to blame for the three matches ending. You've always been a good girl and obeyed my orders."

His words made her sound like a favored pet, not the beloved daughter he and her mother had spent ten years trying to conceive. Jules wasn't surprised. Women were treated no differently than lapdogs in Aliestle.

Of course, she'd done nothing to dispel the image. She was as guilty as her father and the Council of Elders for allowing the stereotyping and treatment of women to continue. As a child, she'd learned Aliestle didn't want her to be as independent and outspoken as her mother had been. They wanted Jules to be exactly what she was—a dutiful princess who didn't rock the boat. But she hoped to change that once she married and lived outside of Aliestle. She would then be free to help her brother Brandt, the crown prince, so he could modernize their country and improve women's rights when he became king.

Her father eyed her speculatively. "I suppose it would be premature to marry you off to the heir of an Elder."

A protest formed in the back of her throat, but Jules pressed her lips together to keep from speaking out. She'd said more than she intended. She had to maintain a cool and calm image even if her insides trembled.

Marrying a royal from Aliestle would keep her stuck in this repressive country forever. Her children, most especially daughters, would face the same obstacles she faced now.

Jules fought a rising panic. "Please, Father, give me another chance. The next match will be successful. I'll do whatever it takes to marry."

He raised a brow. "Such enthusiasm."

More like desperation. She forced the corners of her mouth into a practiced smile. "Well, I'm twenty-eight, father. My biological clock is ticking."

"Ah, grandchildren." He beamed, as if another rare natural resource had been discovered in the mountains of Aliestle. "They are the only thing missing in my life. I shall secure you a fourth match right away. Given your track record, I had a backup candidate in mind when you left for Vernonia."

A backup? His lack of confidence stabbed at her heart.

"All I need to do is negotiate the marriage contract," he continued.

That would take about five minutes given her dowry.

"Who am I to marry, Father?" Jules asked, as if she wanted to know the person joining them for dinner, not the man she would spend the rest of her life with in a loveless marriage negotiated for the benefit of two countries. But anyone would be better than marrying an Aliestlian.

"Crown Prince Enrique of La Isla de la Aurora."

"The Island of the Dawn," she translated.

"It's a small island in the Mediterranean off the coast of Spain ruled by King Dario."

Memories of San Montico, another island in the Mediterranean where Crown Prince Richard de Thierry ruled, surfaced. All citizens had equal rights. Arranged marriages were rare though the country had a few old-fashioned customs. She hadn't been allowed to sail there, but the water and wind had been perfect.

Longing stirred deep inside Jules.

Sailing was her inheritance from her mother and the one place she felt connected to the woman she didn't remember. It was the only thing Jules did for herself. No matter what life handed out, no matter what tradition she was forced to abide by, she could escape her fate for a few hours when she was on the water.

But only on lakes and rivers.

After Jules learned to sail on the Black Sea while visiting her maternal grandparents, her father had forbidden her to sail on the ocean out of fear she would suffer the same fate as her mother. Two decades later, he still treated Jules like a little girl. Perhaps now he would finally see her as an adult, even though she was female, and change his mind about the restrictions.

"Am I allowed to sail when I'm on the island?" she asked.

"Sailing on the sea is forbidden during your engagement."

Hope blossomed at his words. He'd never left her an opening before. "After I'm married…?"

"Your husband can decide the fate of your…hobby."

Not hobby. Passion.

When she was on a boat, only the moment mattered. The wind against her face. The salt in the air. The tiller or a sheet in her hand. She could forget she was Her Royal Highness Princess Julianna and be Jules. Nothing but sailing had ever made her feel so…free.

If La Isla de la Aurora were a progressive island like San Montico, she would have freedom, choice and be allowed to sail on the ocean. Her heart swelled with anticipation. That would be enough to make up for not marrying for love.

"Understand, Julianna, this is your final match outside of Aliestle," he said firmly. "If Prince Enrique decides he doesn't want to marry you, you'll marry one of the Elder's heirs upon your return home."

A shiver shot down her spine. "I understand, Father."

"You may want to push for a short engagement," he added.

A very short one.

Jules couldn't afford to have Prince Enrique change his mind about marrying her. She had to convince him she was the only woman for him. The perfect princess for him. And maybe she would find the love she dreamed about on the island. Her parents had fallen in love through an arranged marriage. It could happen to her, too.

She'd avoided thinking about tomorrow. Now she looked forward to the future. "When do I leave for the island, sir?"

"If I complete negotiations with King Dario and Prince Enrique tonight, you may leave tomorrow." Alaric said. "Your brother Brandt, a maid and a bodyguard will accompany you."

This was Jules's last chance for a life of freedom. Not only for herself, but her children and her country. She couldn't make any mistakes. "I'll be ready to depart in the morning, Father."

Lying in bed, Alejandro Cierzo de Amanecer heard a noise outside his room at the beachfront villa. The stray kitten he'd found at the boatyard must want something. He opened his eyes to see sunlight streaming in through the brand-new floor-to-ceiling windows. Most likely breakfast.

The bedroom door burst wide-open. Heavy boots sounded against the recently replaced terra-cotta tile floor.

Not again.

Alejandro grimaced, but didn't move. He knew the routine.

A squad of royal guards dressed in blue and gold uniforms surrounded his bed. At least they hadn't drawn their weapons this time. Not that he would call another intrusion progress.

"What does *he* want now?" Alejandro asked.

The captain of the guard, Sergio Mendoza, looked as stoic as ever, but older with gray hair at his temples. "King Dario requests your presence at the palace, Your Highness."

Alejandro raked his hand through his hair in frustration. "My father never requests anything."

Sergio's facial expression didn't change. He'd only shown emotion once, when Alejandro had been late bringing Sergio's youngest daughter home from a date when they were teenagers.

In spite of the security detail accompanying them, Alejandro had feared for his life due to the anger in the captain's eyes.

"The king orders you to come with us now, sir," Sergio said.

Alejandro didn't understand why his father wanted to see him. No one at the palace listened to what Alejandro said. He might not want to be part of the monarchy, but he wasn't about to abandon his country. He'd founded his business here and suggested economic innovations, including developing their tourist trade. But his ideas clashed with those of his father and brother who were more old-fashioned and traditional in their thinking.

A high-pitched squeak sounded. The scraggly black kitten with four white paws clawed his way up the sheet onto the bed. The thing had been a nuisance these past two weeks with the work at the boatyard and renovations here at the villa.

"I need to get dressed before I go anywhere," Alejandro said.

"We'll wait while you dress, sir." Sergio's words did nothing to loosen Alejandro's tense shoulder muscles. "The king wants no delay in your arrival."

Alejandro clenched his teeth. He wanted to tell the loyal captain to leave, but the guards would use force to get him to do what they wanted. He was tired of fighting that battle. "I need privacy."

Sergio ordered the soldiers out of the room, but he remained standing by the bed. "I'll wait on the other side of the door, sir. Guards are stationed beneath each window."

Alejandro rolled his eyes. His father still saw him as a rebellious teenager. "I'm thirty years old, not seventeen."

Sergio didn't say anything. No doubt the captain remembered some of Alejandro's earlier…escapades.

"Tell me where you think I would run to, Captain?" Alejandro lay in bed covered with a sheet. "My business is here. I own properties. My father's lackeys follow me wherever I go."

"They are your security detail, sir," Sergio said. "You must be protected. You're the second in line for the throne."

"Don't remind me," Alejandro muttered.

"Many would give everything to be in your position."

Not if they knew what being the "spare" entailed. No one cared what he thought. Even when he tried to help the island, no one supported him. He'd had to do everything on his own.

Alejandro hated being a prince. He'd been educated in the United States. He didn't want to participate in an outdated form of government where too much power rested with one individual. But he wanted to see his country prosper.

"Guard the door if you must." Alejandro gave the kitten a pat. "I won't make your job any more difficult for you than it is."

As soon as Sergio left, Alejandro slid out of bed and showered. His father hadn't requested formal dress so khaki shorts, a navy T-shirt and a pair of boat shoes would do.

Twenty minutes later, Alejandro entered the palace's reception room. His older brother rose from the damask-covered settee. Enrique looked like a younger version of their father with his short hairstyle, tailored designer suit, starched dress shirt, silk tie and polished leather shoes. It was too bad his brother acted like their father, also.

"This had better be important, Enrique," Alejandro said.

"It is." His brother's lips curved into a smug smile. "I'm getting married."

About time. Enrique's wedding would be the first step toward Alejandro's freedom from the monarchy. The birth of a nephew or niece to take his place as second in line for the throne would be the next big step. "Congratulations, bro. I hope it's a short engagement. Don't waste any time getting your bride pregnant."

Enrique smirked. "That's the plan."

"Why wait until the wedding? Start now."

He laughed. "King Alaric would demand my head if I did that. He's old-fashioned about certain things. Especially his daughter's virginity."

"Alaric." Alejandro had heard the name. It took a second to realize where. "You're marrying a princess from Aliestle?"

"Not a princess. *The* princess." Enrique sounded excited. No wonder. Aliestle was a small kingdom in the Alps. With an abundance of natural resources, the country's treasury was vast, a hundred times that of La Isla de la Aurora. "King Alaric has four sons and one daughter."

"Father must be pleased."

"He's giddy over the amount of Julianna's dowry and the economic advantages aligning with Aliestle will bring us. Fortunately for me, the princess is as beautiful as she is rich. A bit of an ice princess from what I hear, but I'll warm her up."

"If you need lessons—"

"I may not have your reputation with the ladies, but I shall manage fine on my own."

"I hope the two of you are happy together." Alejandro meant the words. A happy union would mean more heirs. The further Alejandro dropped in the line of succession, the better. He couldn't wait to be able to focus his attention on building his business and attracting more investors to turn the island's sluggish economy around.

"You are to be the best man."

A statement of fact or a request? "Mingling with aristocracy is hazardous to my health."

"You will move home until the wedding."

A demand. Anger flared. "Enrique—"

"The royal family will show a united front during the engagement period. Your days will be free unless official events are scheduled. You'll be expected to attend all dinners and evening functions. You must also be present when the princess and her party arrive today."

Alejandro cursed. "You sound exactly like him."

"They are Father's words, not mine." Rare compassion filled Enrique's eyes. "But I would like you to be my best man. You're my favorite brother."

"I'm your only brother."

Enrique laughed. "All the more reason for you to stand at my side. Father will compensate you for any inconvenience."

Alejandro's entire life was a damn inconvenience. Besides, he would never be able to get the one thing he wanted from his father. "I don't want *his* money."

"You never have, but when Father offers you payment, take it.

You can put the money into your boats, buy another villa, donate it to charity or give it away on the streets," Enrique advised. "You've earned this, Alejandro. Don't let pride get in the way again."

He wasn't about to go there. "All I want is to be left alone."

"As soon as Julianna and I have children, you will no longer be needed around here. If you do your part to ensure the wedding occurs, Father has promised to let you live your own life."

Finally. "Did you ask for this or did Father offer?"

"It was a combination, but be assured of Father keeping his word."

"When am I to move back?"

"After lunch."

Alejandro cursed again. He had a boatyard to run, investment properties to oversee and the Med Cup to prepare for. Not to mention the kitten who expected to be fed. "I have a life. Responsibilities."

"You have responsibilities here. Ones you ignore while you play with your boats," Enrique chided.

Seething, Alejandro tried to keep his tone even. "I'm not playing. I'm working. If you'd see the upcoming Med Cup race as an opportunity to promote—"

"If you want to build the island's reputation, then support this royal wedding. It'll do much more for the economy than your expensive ideas to improve the island's nightlife, build flashy resorts and attract the sailing crowd with a little regatta."

"The Med Cup is a big deal. It'll—"

"Whatever." Enrique brushed Alejandro aside as if he were a bothersome gnat. Like father, like son. "Do what you must to be here after lunch or Father will send you away on a diplomatic mission."

The words were like a punch to Alejandro's solar plexus. Not unexpected given the way his father and brother operated sometimes. The threat would be carried out, too. That meant Alejandro had to do as told to secure his future. His freedom.

"I'll be back before your princess arrives."

But he would be doing a few things his way.

Once the black sheep, always the black sheep.

And let's face it, Alejandro didn't mind the title at all.

A helicopter whisked Jules over the clear, blue Mediterranean Sea. The luxurious cabin with large, leather seats comfortably fit the four of them: her, Brandt, Yvette her maid and Klaus their bodyguard. But even with soundproofing, each wore headsets to communicate and protect their ears from the noise of the rotors.

Almost there.

A combination of excitement and nerves made Jules want to tap her toes and twist the ends of her hair with her finger. She kept her hands clasped on her lap instead. She wanted to make her family and country proud. Her mother, God rest her soul, too. Presenting the image of a princess completely in control was important, even if doing so wasn't always easy.

She glanced out the window. Below, on the water, a Sun Fast 3200 with a colorful spinnaker caught her eye. She pressed her forehead against the window to get a better look at the sailboat.

Gorgeous.

The crew sat on the rail, their legs dangling over the side. The hull planed across the waves.

Longing made it difficult to breath.

What she wouldn't give to be on that boat sailing away from the island instead of flying toward the stranger who would be her husband and the father of her children… But she shouldn't wish that. Jules had a responsibility, a duty, the same that had been thrust upon her mother so many years ago. Marrying Prince Enrique had to be better than being stuck in patriarchal Aliestle for the rest of her life. At least, she hoped so. If not…

Jules grimaced.

"You okay?" Brandt's voice asked through her headset.

She shrugged. "I think I'm cursed. When my godparents offered gifts at my christening, one of them must have cursed me to a life of duty with no reward. A loveless arranged marriage."

And an unfulfilled yearning for adventure and freedom.

"Look out the window," Brandt said. "You're not cursed, Jules. You're going to be living on a vacation paradise."

Crescents of postcard-worthy white sand beaches came into view. Palm trees seemed to stand at attention, except for the few arching toward the ground. The beach gave way to a town. Pastel-colored, tiled roofed buildings and narrow streets dotted the hillsides above the village center.

She glimpsed rows of sailboats moored at a marina. The masts, tall and shiny, rocked starboard and port like metronomes. Her mouth went dry.

Perhaps cursed was the wrong word. All these sailboats had to be a good sign, right? "Maybe life will be different here."

"It will." Brandt smiled, the same charming smile she'd seen on a cover of a tabloid at the airport in Spain. "Your fiancé will be unable to resist your beauty and intelligence. He'll fall head over heels in love with you and allow you to do whatever you wish. Including sailing on the ocean."

She wiggled her toes in anticipation. "I hope that's true."

"Believe," he encouraged. "That's what you always tell me."

Yes, she did. But this situation was different. Jules knew nothing about Prince Enrique. She'd been so busy preparing for her departure she hadn't had time to look him up on the internet. Not that she had a choice in marrying him even if he turned out to be an ogre.

For all she knew he was old with one foot in the grave. Okay, now she was overreacting. Her father had always matched her with younger men because he wanted grandchildren. This match shouldn't be any different.

Jules hoped Enrique was charming, handsome and would sweep her off her feet. She wanted to find him attractive and be able to love him. She also wanted his heart to be free and open to loving her in return.

Her concern ratcheted. Prince Richard and Prince Niko had been in love with other women. If Enrique's affections were attached to a girlfriend or mistress that wouldn't bode well for their match reaching the altar or, if it did, love developing between them.

Jules shifted in her seat. "I do hope this island has up-to-date ideas about women."

"It has to be more contemporary. Aliestle has been asleep since the Middle Ages." Brandt cupped one side of his headset with his hand. "Listen, I hear Father snoring now. The tyrant could wake the dead."

A smile tugged at the corners of Jules's mouth. "Too bad we can't wake him."

"Along with the entire Council of Elders."

Nodding, she stared at her brother who was more known as a playboy crown prince than a burgeoning politician and ruler. "When you're king, you'll change the way things are done."

Brandt shrugged. "Being king will be too much work."

"You'll rise to the occasion," she encouraged.

He gave her a look. "You really think so?"

"Yes." Her gaze locked with his, willing him to remember their previous discussions and their plan. Okay, her plan. "You will bring our country into the twenty-first century. If not for our younger brothers and subjects, then for your children and theirs. Especially the daughters."

"I don't know."

"Yes, you do. And I'll help." The bane of his existence was being crown prince. Brandt wanted all the perks that went with being royalty without any of the responsibility. One of these days he was going to have to grow up. "Once I marry someone outside of Aliestle, Father's reign over me ends. I'll be able to represent our country to the world and gain support to help you enact reforms when you are king, even if the Council of Elders is against them. We must change Aliestle for the better, Brandt."

He didn't say anything. She didn't expect him to.

"We are approaching the palace," the pilot announced over the headsets.

Goose bumps prickled Jules's skin.

Full of curiosity at her new home, she peered out the window. A huge white stucco and orange-tile roofed palace perched above the sea. The multistoried building had numerous balconies and windows.

But no tower. Another good sign?

A paved road and narrower walking paths wove their way through a landscape of palm trees, flowering bushes and manicured greenery. Water shot at least twenty-five feet into the air from an ornately decorated fountain.

The Mediterranean island and palace were a world away from Aliestle and the stone castle fortress nestled high in the Alps. Living somewhere lighter and brighter would be a welcome change from the Grimm-like fairy-tale setting she called home.

"Father may have finally gotten this right," Brandt said.

Jules nodded. "It's pretty."

"At least on the outside."

She sighed. "Don't forget, dear brother, you're here for moral support."

"And to make sure the honeymoon doesn't start early," Brandt joked.

As if she'd ever had that opportunity present itself. She glared at him. "Be quiet."

"Sore spot, huh?"

He had no idea. Engaged three times, and she'd never come close to anything other than kisses. Besides making out with Christian while a teenager, she'd been kissed once as an adult. Prince Niko's kiss while sailing had been pleasant enough, but nothing like the passion she'd overheard other women discussing. Perhaps with Prince Enrique…

The helicopter landed on a helipad. The engine stopped. The rotor's rotation slowed. Her hand trembled, making her work harder to unbuckle her harness. Finally she undid the latch. As they exited, a uniformed staff member placed their luggage onto a wheeled cart.

"Welcome to La Isla de la Aurora, Your Royal Highness Crown Prince Brandt and Your Royal Highness Princess Julianna." An older man in a gray suit bowed. "I am Ortiz. Prince Enrique sends his regrets for not meeting you himself, but he is attending to important state business at the moment."

"We understand." Brandt smiled. He might not be the typical statesman, but no one could fault his friendliness. "State business comes first."

Jules looked around at the potted plants and flowering vines. A floral scent lingered in the air. Paradise? Perhaps.

"Thank you, sir." Ortiz sounded grateful. "I am in charge of the palace and at your service. Whatever you need, I'll see that you have it."

Jules glanced at Brandt, whose grin resembled the Cheshire cat's. She would have to make sure he didn't take advantage of the generous offer of hospitality.

"The palace grounds are lovely, Ortiz," she said. "Very inviting with so many colorful flowers and plants."

"I am happy you like it, ma'am." His smile took years off his tanned, lined face. "Please allow me to show you and your party inside."

Klaus nodded. Her bodyguard, in his fifties with a crew cut and a gun hidden under his tailored suit jacket, had protected her for as long as she could remember.

"Lead the way, Ortiz," she said.

As they walked from the helipad to the front door, Ortiz gave her a brief history lesson about the palace. She had no idea the royal family had ruled the island for so long. No doubt the continuous line of succession had impressed her father who would want to ensure a long reign for his grandchildren and the heirs that followed.

"Prince Enrique has done so much for the island," Ortiz said. "A finer successor to King Dario cannot be found, ma'am."

If only Jules knew whether the compliments were truthful or propaganda. She knew little about her future husband besides his name. "I'm looking forward to meeting Prince Enrique."

Ortiz beamed. "He said the same thing about you at lunchtime, ma'am."

A third good sign? Jules hoped so.

When they reached the palace entry, two arched wooden doors

parted as if by magic. Once the heavy doors were fully open, she saw two uniformed attendants standing behind and holding them.

Jules stared at the entrance with a mix of anticipation and apprehension. If all went well—and she hoped it did—this palace would be her new home. She would live with her husband and raise her children here. She fought the urge to cross her fingers.

With a deep breath, she stepped inside. The others followed.

A thirty-foot ceiling gave the large marble tiled foyer an open and airy feel. Stunning paintings, a mix of modern and classical works, hung on the walls. A marble statue of a woman sitting in the middle captured Jules's attention. "What an amazing sculpture."

"That is Eos, one of the Greek's second generation Titan gods," Ortiz explained. "We are more partial to the Latin name, Aurora. Whichever name you prefer, she'll always be the Goddess of the Dawn."

"Beautiful," Brandt agreed. "Eos had a strong desire for handsome young men. If she looked anything like this statue, I'm sure she had no trouble finding willing lovers."

"Close the front doors," a male voice shouted. "Now."

The attendants pushed the heavy doors. Grunts sounded. Muscles strained.

"Hurry," the voice urged.

The people behind Jules rushed farther into the foyer so the doors could be shut. The momentum pushed her forward.

A shirtless man wearing shorts ran toward the doors. Something black darted across the floor.

Yvette screamed. "A rat, Your Highnesses."

"There are no rats in the palace," Ortiz shouted.

The ball of black fur darted between Jules's legs. Startled, she stumbled face-first.

"Catch her," Klaus yelled.

Too late. The marble floor seemed to rise up to meet Jules though she was the one falling.

She stopped abruptly. Not against the floor.

Strong arms embraced Jules. Her face pressed against a hard, bare chest. Her cheek rested against warm skin. Dark hair tickled her nose. The sound of a heartbeat filled her ears. He smelled so good. No fancy colognes. Only soap and water and salty ocean air.

She wanted another sniff.

Ortiz shrieked. "Your Highnesses. Are either of you hurt?"

Highnesses? The man must be a prince. Her father had only spoken of the crown prince. No other brothers had been mentioned. Oh, if this were Enrique...

CHAPTER TWO

"JULES?" BRANDT sounded concerned.

"I'm fine," Jules said quickly, more interested in the man—the prince—who saved her from hitting her face on the floor and still held her with his strong arms. Such wide shoulders, too.

Awareness seeped through her.

"My apologies." His deep, rich voice and Spanish accent sent her racing pulse into a mad sprint. "The kitten darted out of the room before I could grab him."

Ortiz raised his chin. "As I said, there are no rats in the palace, Princess."

The prince inhaled sharply. She found herself being set upon her feet. But he kept hold of her, even after she was standing.

"Stable?" he asked.

She nodded, forcing herself not to stare at his muscular chest and ripped abs.

He let go of her.

A chill shivered through Jules. She wasn't used to being in such close contact with anyone, but she missed having his nicely muscled arms around her.

She studied him, eager for a better look.

Over six feet tall with an athletic build, he looked more pirate than prince with shoulder-length dark brown hair, an earring in his left ear, khaki shorts and bare feet.

His strong jawline, high cheekbones and straight nose looked almost chiseled and made her think of the Eos sculpture. But his full lips and thick eyelashes softened the harsher features.

The result—a gorgeous face she would be happy to stare at for hours. Days. Years.

Jules's heart thudded. "Thank you."

Warm brown eyes met hers. Gold specks flickered like flames around his irises. "You're welcome."

Everyone else faded into the background. Time seemed to stop. Something unfamiliar unfurled deep inside her.

He swooped up a black ball of fur with one hand. The look of tenderness in his dark eyes as he checked the kitten melted her heart. She would love for a man—this man—to look at her that way.

The kitten meowed. As he rubbed it, he returned his attention to her. "You're Princess Julianna from Aliestle."

It wasn't a question.

"Yes." Jules had never believed in love at first sight until now. She hoped their children looked exactly like him. A smile spread across her lips and reached all the way to her heart. Her father *had* gotten this right. She would realize her dream of marrying for love. A warm glow flowed through her. "You must be Enrique."

"No." His jaw thrust forward. "I am Alejandro."

Alejandro held on to the kitten as confusion clouded Juliana's pretty face. He was a little confused by his own reaction to this so-called ice princess. She had practically melted against him, and he'd yet to cool down from the contact. The woman was gorgeous, with a killer body underneath her coral-colored suit, long blond hair and big blue eyes a man could drown in.

She smelled sweet, like a bouquet of wildflowers. He wondered if her glossed lips tasted…

Not sweet.

He forced his gaze off her mouth. Julianna's marriage to Enrique and the children she conceived would remove Alejandro from the line of succession. She was his ticket out of his obligation to the monarchy. He couldn't think of her as anything other than his future sister-in-law.

That shouldn't be difficult since she wasn't his type.

Beautiful, yes, if you liked the kind of woman who knew how to apply makeup perfectly and could give any supermodel a run for her money. But he wanted a woman who didn't care about the trappings of wealth and royalty. A woman who was down-to-earth and didn't mind the spray of salt water in her face.

"Alejandro," Julianna repeated as if he didn't know his own name.

He couldn't remember the last time anyone had mistaken him for Enrique. Polar opposites didn't begin to describe their differences. But the fact Julianna didn't know what her future husband looked like surprised Alejandro more. Arranged marriages were still a part of royal life in some countries, but agreeing to marry someone without seeing their photograph struck him as odd. "Yes."

She stiffened. The warmth in her eyes disappeared. The expression on her face turned downright chilly.

Ice princess?

He saw now why she'd been called that. The change in her demeanor startled him, but he shouldn't have been surprised. Alejandro had dated enough spoiled and pampered royals and wealthy girls to last a lifetime. This one, with a rich-as-Midas father, would most likely rank up there with the worst. He almost pitied Enrique. Emphasis on almost.

She drew her finely arched brows together, looking haughty not curious. "That makes you...?"

The kitten chirped, sounding more bird than cat. Alejandro used his thumb to rub under the cat's chin.

Impatience flashed in Julianna's eyes.

He took his time answering. "Enrique's younger brother."

Alejandro waited for her look of disdain. No one cared about the second in line for the throne, especially a woman meant to be queen.

"Oh." Her face remained expressionless. But royals were trained to turn off emotion with the flick of a switch and not display their true feelings. "I didn't realize Enrique had a younger brother."

That Alejandro believed. "My family prefers not to talk about me."

Ortiz cleared his throat.

"The princess will be family soon enough, Ortiz." Alejandro would be counting the days as soon as the official wedding date was set. He couldn't wait to live his own life without interference from his family. Of course, an heir or two would need to be born until he would be totally free. He shifted his gaze to the princess. "She'll hear the stories. Whispers over tea. Innuendos over cocktails. Nudges during dessert. No sense hiding the truth."

Tilting her chin, she gave him a cool look. "What truth might that be?"

"I'm the black sheep of the family."

Julianna pursed her lips. "A black cat for the black sheep."

"Not by choice," he admitted. "The cat chose me."

She stared at the kitten, but didn't pet him. Definitely ice running through her veins. "Such a lucky kitty to be able to choose for itself."

"It's too bad royalty doesn't get the same choices," Alejandro said.

He waited for her to reply. She didn't.

"Eat, sleep, play." A man in his early twenties with dark, curly brown hair stepped forward. He had rugged features, but his refined demeanor matched his designer suit and Italian leather shoes. "The life of a cat seems perfect to me. Much better than that of a prince."

"Well, the kitten is a stray," Alejandro said. "Caviar isn't part of his diet."

The man grinned. "It's only part of mine on occasion."

Julianna sighed. "Prince Alejandro, this is—"

"Alejandro," he corrected. "I don't use my title."

"Wish I could get away with that," the other man said. "Though the title does come in handy when it comes to women."

"That is the one benefit I have found," Alejandro agreed.

Julianna rolled her eyes. "The two of you can compare dating notes later. Now it's time for a formal introduction."

The princess's words told Alejandro she was cut from the same cloth as Enrique. Both seemed to hold an appreciation for royal protocol and etiquette. Something Alejandro saw as a complete waste of time. The two stuffy royals might live happily ever after.

"Alejandro," she continued. "This is His Royal Highness Crown Prince Brandt. One of my four younger brothers."

Brother? Alejandro studied the two. He couldn't believe they were so closely related. Brandt was as dark as his sister was fair.

"Half brother," Julianna clarified, as if reading Alejandro's thoughts.

That explained it. But nothing explained why his gaze drifted to the curve of her hips. A nice body would never make up for an unpleasant personality that was the female version of his older brother. Maybe he'd been spending too much time working at the boatyard and not enough time out partying with the ladies. Perhaps later…

Right now he wanted to return to his room. Being surrounded by royalty was suffocating.

"It's been nice meeting you." His obligation to be here when the princess arrived had been met. He cradled the now napping kitten in the crook of his arm. "I'll see…"

Julianna stroked the kitten. The move took him by surprise. The soft smile on her face reached all the way to her eyes and made him do a double-take. His pulse rate shot up a few notches.

He'd always been a sucker for a pair of big baby blues. "Would you like to hold him?"

She drew back her hand. Her French manicured nails had no cracks or chips. "No, thank you."

Alejandro didn't know whether to be intrigued or annoyed by the princess. Before he could decide which, a cloud of strong aftershave hit him. He recognized the toxic scent, otherwise known as the expensive designer brand of cologne his brother wore.

Enrique turned the corner. He strode across the floor with quick steps and his head held high. Whereas Brandt looked regal, Enrique came across as pompous.

He stared at Julianna as if she were a red diamond, a rare gem meant only for him. Dollar signs shone in his eyes. Enrique's priority had always been La Isla de la Aurora. Women were secondary, which was why an arranged marriage had been necessary.

After an uncomfortable moment of silence, Enrique glared at Ortiz, who introduced everyone with lofty titles and more middle names than Alejandro could count.

Enrique struck a ridiculous pose, as if he were at a photo shoot not standing in the foyer. "I hope you had a pleasant journey from Aliestle."

"Thank you. I did." Julianna's polite smile gave nothing away as to her first impression of her groom. "The palace is lovely."

Leave it to Enrique to turn meeting his future wife into such a formal event. Alejandro couldn't believe his brother. Didn't he remember their charm lessons with Mrs. Delgado? If Enrique had a clue about women, about Julianna, he would kiss her hand and compliment her on her shoes. He would make her feel as if she'd arrived home, not treat her like a temporary houseguest. But Enrique only did what he wanted, no matter how that affected anyone else.

"Alejandro." Irritation filled Enrique's eyes. "What are you doing with that animal?"

"He's a kitten. And I'm only following your instructions, brother," Alejandro explained. "I'm here, as requested, to meet your lovely bride."

Enrique's face reddened. "You could at least have taken the time to dress."

"He escaped while I was changing." Alejandro petted the sleeping cat. "I assumed Father wouldn't want a kitten tearing through the palace unattended."

Enrique started to speak then stopped himself. Their guests

must be keeping his temper in check. At least the princess and her entourage were good for something around here.

"I'll take him to my room," Alejandro added. "See you at dinner."

"Formal attire," Enrique reminded, his voice tight. "In case you've forgotten, that includes shirt and shoes."

Alejandro rocked back on his heels. "I know how to dress for dinner, bro, but thanks for the reminder."

The air crackled with tension.

Twenty years ago, they would have been fighting while Ortiz called for the palace guards to separate them. Ten years ago, the same thing might have happened. But Enrique would never lower himself, or his station, to that level now. Even if his hard gaze told Alejandro he wanted to fight.

"At least your younger brother knows how to dress, Enrique. Not all of mine do." Julianna sounded empathetic. "I don't know about you, but sometimes it's hard being the oldest."

Her words may have been calculated, but they did the trick. Enrique's jaw relaxed. He focused his attention on Julianna.

Alejandro was impressed. Diffusing the situation so deftly took skill. And practice.

"It can be difficult." The corners of Enrique's mouth lifted into a half smile. "Younger siblings don't take things as seriously or have the same sense of duty."

Idiot. Alejandro wondered if his brother realized he was also slamming Brandt, another crown prince, with his words.

"Some don't," Julianna agreed. "But others just need to understand their responsibilities a little better. Isn't that right, dear brother?"

Brandt nodded, looking more amused than offended. Alejandro liked the guy already.

Enrique's mouth twisted, as if he finally understood how his words could be construed. "I was talking about Alejandro."

Julianna smiled at Enrique. "Of course, you were."

The woman was smooth. Alejandro had no idea if her skills came from dealing with her brothers or boyfriends, but he'd never seen anyone handle Enrique so well. Not even their mother who had separated from their father years ago. Maybe Julianna could rein in the future ruler's ego and temper. If she had a brain in that pretty head of hers, as she seemed to, she could stop him from making bad decisions, like focusing on projects that aggrandized himself, but did nothing to help the island.

The ice princess might be exactly what Enrique needed.

Alejandro would have to make sure his brother didn't blow this engagement.

For both their sakes. And the island's.

"Thank you for escorting me to my room." Standing with Enrique, Jules glanced around. The pastel pink and yellow decor was bright and cheery. Maybe some of it would rub off on her because right now she was feeling a little...down. She forced a smile anyway. Replacing Enrique's aftershave and teaching him a few manners wouldn't be difficult. It could be much worse. "The suite is lovely."

"I asked Ortiz to put you in this room." Enrique pulled back a curtain. "I thought you might like the view."

She stared out the window at rows of colorful flowers below. A burst of hot pink. A swatch of bright yellow. A patch of purple.

Another wave of disappointment washed over her. The same way it had when she'd discovered her hottie rescuer wasn't going to be her husband, but her brother-in-law.

Don't think about that. About him. Otherwise she might find herself back in Aliestle.

"A garden." She hoped she sounded more enthusiastic than she felt. A bush of red roses captured her attention until she noticed the large thorns on the thick stems. Ouch, that would hurt. "How nice."

"The garden is the closest thing I have to a hobby now. A majority of the flowers are in bloom," Enrique explained. "When you open the window, the breeze will carry a light floral scent into your room."

"Picking out this room for me is so thoughtful of you." Even if she would have preferred the smell of salt water, a view of the sea, Alejandro.

No, that wasn't fair.

Enrique was handsome. He looked more like a fashion model from Milan than a crown prince in his designer suit, starched shirt, silk tie and leather shoes. If he'd been shirtless and she found herself pressed against his hard chest…

She tried to imagine it. Tried and failed.

He wasn't Alejandro, who had appeared in the foyer like the Roman god Mars come to life and looking for a fight. Well, until he held the kitten in his hand, and then he'd looked…perfect.

Not perfect. No one was perfect.

But the two brothers were tall, dark and handsome. They shared the same brown eyes, but the similarities ended there. One was sexy and dangerous, the black sheep. The other was formal and Old World, the future king.

Jules might be inexperienced when it came to men, but she wasn't stupid. Even if thinking about Alejandro made her pulse quicken, Enrique would make the better husband and father. He was the logical choice, the smart choice.

The only choice.

She was here to be Enrique's bride and his alone. She would be his wife and one day a queen. Whatever she may have felt in Alejandro's arms didn't matter. No one could ever know she found him attractive. As for her fiancé…

So what if he had similar mannerisms and speech as her father? Perhaps Enrique's formality stemmed from nervousness. Crown princes were human, even if few would admit it.

He had selected this room for her. Granted, the view wasn't the one she would have preferred, but he'd had his reasons for choosing it. And he was still better than marrying anyone from Aliestle. Jules smiled genuinely at him. "Thank you for welcoming us into your home."

"It'll be your home soon enough."

She nodded, trying to muster a few ounces of happy feelings and peppiness. She hoped they would come.

"I look forward to seeing you at dinner," he said.

"As do I."

He took her hand and raised it to his mouth. He brushed his lips over her skin.

Jules wanted to feel the same passion and heat she'd felt in Alejandro's arms. She would settle for a spark, tingles, warmth at the point of contact, even a small shiver. But she felt…nothing.

Enrique released her hand. "Until later, my princess."

Later. The word resonated with her.

As he left and closed the door behind him, she remembered what she'd told Izzy, Princess Isabel of Vernonia.

Remember, just because you don't love someone at the beginning doesn't mean you won't love them in the end. Love can grow over time.

Jules needed to listen to her own advice.

My princess. She would be Enrique's princess. She needed to act like it, too.

Just because she didn't feel anything with him now, didn't mean she wouldn't ever. Physical attraction and chemistry weren't the same as love. Passion could be fleeting, but love remained. Prevailed. This first meeting was only the beginning.

Love could grow between her and Enrique.

She had to give the relationship time, keep an open heart and remember how love had blossomed with her parents.

But to be on the safe side until love bloomed with Enrique, Jules realized with an odd pang, keeping her distance from Alejandro would probably be a good idea.

Dinner was exactly what Alejandro thought it would be—a total drag. Each course of the gourmet meal took forever. He enjoyed good food, but by the time the meal finished, he'd be falling out of his chair sound asleep. The conversation about international trade agreements would make a rabbit in heat want to nap.

Across the table, Julianna sat next to her brother, Brandt. She looked stunning in a blue evening gown that matched the color of her eyes. The dress didn't show a lot of skin, but the flowing fabric gave enough of a hint of what was underneath to make a man want to see more.

He tried not to look at her.

Enrique was doing enough staring for both of them.

But Alejandro heard her voice drone on. She tried to sound interested in what others were saying, but her tone lacked warmth. Yes, she was going to be an excellent match for his superficial brother.

Five formally dressed staff members set plates of pan-seared sea scallops in front of each of them at the exact same time. Two wine stewards circled the table filling wineglasses from bottles of Pinot Gris.

What Alejandro wouldn't give for plates of tapas and a pitcher of sangria right now.

Enrique laughed at something Julianna said. So did his father.

"Who knew your bride would be an expert in trade?" Dario said.

"Thank you, sir." Julianna's smile didn't reach her eyes the way it had when she'd petted the kitten. "But trade is a hobby."

A hobby? Maybe a geek lived inside the beauty's body. Or maybe she was trying to impress her future father-in-law. Either way, Alejandro wanted nothing to do with her.

"Now that is a worthy hobby." Enrique pinned Alejandro with a contemptible look. "Unlike *some* of the hobbies others of us have."

He stared over the rim of his wineglass. "Care to wager how my hobby turns out during the Med Cup, bro?"

Julianna's fork clattered against her plate and bounced off the table. Her cheeks turned a bright shade of pink. "Excuse me."

Alejandro studied her. Strange. The stumble in the foyer aside, Julianna didn't seem like a klutzy princess. It was unusual for someone as elegant as her to drop her fork in the middle of dinner and make a spectacle of herself.

Two servants rushed to her side. One picked up the fork from the ground. The other placed a new fork on the table.

"Thank you." She raised her half-filled water glass. "So you sail, Alejandro?"

"I sail. I also build boats. Racing sailboats." He noticed the glance exchanged between Julianna and Brandt. "Do either of you sail?"

She looked again at her brother.

"We sail," Brandt answered. "On local lakes and rivers. For pleasure. Unlike many of our royal compatriots who enjoy the competitive side of the sport."

Alejandro couldn't understand why Julianna needed her brother to answer such a simple question. She'd had no problem talking about trade.

Enrique swirled the wine in his glass. "Some royals take sailing too seriously. I enjoyed the few regattas I competed in, but I no longer have time to sail with so many other obligations."

"Horse racing may be the sport of kings," Brandt said. "But many royals have sailed for their countries in the Summer Games. I'm sure more would have liked to."

Dario nodded. "I've always preferred the water to horses."

"As have I," Enrique added hastily.

Julianna leaned forward. The neckline of her gown gaped, giving Alejandro a glimpse of ivory skin and round breasts. He forced his attention onto the sea scallops instead.

"Will one of your boats be entered in the Med Cup?" she asked, as if trying to draw him into conversation.

He appreciated her taking an interest. "My newest design."

"A bit risky, don't you think?" Enrique asked.

Alejandro shrugged. "You never know until you try."

A smug smile curved Enrique's lips. "I may take you up on that wager."

"My sons take the opposite sides on everything," King Dario explained. "And if they can figure a way to bet on the outcome…"

"They sound like my brothers, sir." Julianna's smile lit up her face. The result took Alejandro's breath away. She looked more like the woman he'd held in his arms, not the cool, proper princess. "Brandt isn't as bad as the younger three. At least not any longer."

Brandt raised his glass to her. "Thanks, sis."

"So will you be sailing in the race, Alejandro?" She sounded not only interested but also curious.

"Possibly." The change in her intrigued him. "I'm trying to find the right mix of crew. But the boat can be sailed single-handedly, too."

"Doesn't sound like much of a racing boat," Enrique said.

"The best boats can perform with varying numbers of crew." Her eyes became more animated as she spoke. "I'm sure it'll be an exciting race."

Alejandro thought he heard a note of wistfulness in her voice. "Racing is always exciting. I'd be happy to take all of you out sailing. You could see the boat for yourself."

Julianna straightened.

Brandt smiled. "Thanks, that sounds like fun."

"Yes, but a sail isn't possible right now." As Enrique spoke, Julianna leaned back in her chair with a thoughtful expression on her face. "I don't need to sail on your boat to know what the outcome of the race will be."

Alejandro didn't know why he tried.

"Enough sailing." Dario gave a dismissive wave of his hand. "We have more important things to discuss, like wedding plans. King Alaric says there is no need for a lengthy engagement."

"Our father is satisfied with the marriage contract," Brandt said. "Whatever wedding date you decide upon is fine with him."

"Outstanding. A short engagement, it'll be." Dario beamed. "How quickly do you two want to get married?"

Enrique and Julianna smiled at each other, but neither said a word.

"If I might make a suggestion, Father," Alejandro offered.

"Go on."

"Set the wedding date a week after the Med Cup, sir."

"That would be a short engagement. Why then?" Dario asked.

"Because two people have never seemed more perfect for each other." Oddly, the words felt like sandpaper against Alejandro's tongue. But the sooner the two were married, the sooner he would be free. "Having the wedding after the Med Cup will allow me to focus all my attention on my responsibilities as best man."

"Excellent suggestion," his father said. "Enrique, Julianna. Do you agree?"

"I do." Enrique stared at Julianna. "I can't wait to marry."

"Neither can I." Julianna sounded like she meant it.

Dario clapped his hands together. The sound echoed through the large dining room. "I'll call King Alaric in the morning."

"I'll start planning our honeymoon," Enrique said.

The thought of Julianna in his brother's bed left a bad taste in Alejandro's mouth. But heirs were necessary if he wanted to be left alone by his father.

Julianna didn't seem to mind. A charming blush crept up her long, graceful neck.

He remembered what Enrique had said about King Alaric's daughter being a virgin. That didn't seem possible unless he had used his wealth to protect her virtue. But was the seemingly in-control princess ready for some passion?

Alejandro couldn't forget the way she'd pressed into him and how her heart pounded against his chest when he'd held her in his arms or the excited tone of her voice and the gleam in her eyes when she talked about sailing. Only a talented actress could feign that kind of interest.

Maybe there was more to her than Alejandro realized.

Not that it mattered. He picked up his wineglass and sipped. Not much anyway.

CHAPTER THREE

AFTER DINNER, Jules stood out on the terrace alone. Cicadas chirped. A breeze rustled through the palm fronds. The temperature had cooled, but no jacket was required.

She glanced inside through the open terrace doors to see Brandt having a brandy with King Dario. Enrique must still be on his telephone call with the ambassador to the United States.

Jules enjoyed the moment of solitude, a break from the endless conversation at the dinner table. At least the topic had finally turned to something interesting.

With her hands on the railing, Jules gazed up at the night sky. The stars surrounding the almost full moon winked at her. A smile graced her lips.

Perhaps she wasn't cursed.

Enrique hadn't said yes to the sailing invitation, but his words "right now" filled Julianna with hope. He'd raced sailboats. Alejandro built racing sailboats. Her wedding date was a couple of weeks away.

What were the odds of so many things working out so well? Not only was she marrying into a family of sailors, she would soon be Enrique's wife. She could say goodbye to being submissive for the rest of her life.

On La Isla de la Aurora, she would be able to do what she wanted. Personal freedom, yes, but she could also help Brandt to show the world Aliestle was more than an eccentric, backward country. Maybe by doing that, Jules would be able to live up to the spirit of her mother.

Laughter bubbled up inside her.

Oh, she'd visit her homeland, but she would no longer be expected to live by all the restrictive laws and traditions.

The only thing missing was falling in love, but given how well everything else was turning out she believed it would happen. She would fall in love with Enrique and he with her. The same way her parents had fallen in love after their arranged marriage.

It was all going to work out. "I know it will."

"Know what will?" a male voice asked from the shadows.

Jules jumped. "Who's there?"

"I didn't mean to startle you."

She squinted. She couldn't see anyone, but recognized the voice. "Alejandro."

He ascended the staircase leading to the terrace where she stood. "Good evening, Julianna."

Her heart lurched. She fought against the burst of attraction making her mouth go dry. It wasn't easy.

The stubble on his face made him look so much like a sexy pirate. She could easily imagine him standing behind the wheel of a sailing ship trying to capture a vessel full of gold or pretty wenches.

He'd removed his jacket, tie and cummerbund. The neck of his dress shirt was unbuttoned, the tails hung out of the trousers and his sleeves were rolled up. The high rollers decked out in the finest menswear on the Côte d'Azur had nothing on Alejandro. Even with his bare feet.

"How long have you been lurking in the shadows?" she asked.

He moved gracefully like a dancer or a world-class athlete. "Long enough to hear you laughing."

Heat enflamed her cheeks. "If I'd known you were there…"

Alejandro crossed the terrace to stand next to her. "No need to apologize for being happy."

Maybe not for him. But happy wasn't an emotion Jules was used to experiencing let alone expressing. Sharing that moment embarrassed her. Still she owed him for what he'd said at dinner about sailing and the wedding. But one was more important than the other. "Thank you for suggesting a short engagement."

"Afraid you'll change your mind?" he asked.

"Worried Enrique will."

"Not going to happen."

Jules wished she shared Alejandro's confidence. "I've heard that before."

"He'd be a fool, a complete idiot, if he didn't marry you."

His compliment made her feel warm all over. His opinion shouldn't matter, but for some reason it did. "Well, intelligence has never been a requirement to be a crown prince."

The deep, rich sound of his laughter seeped into her and raised her temperature ten degrees. "You're a contradiction, Julianna."

"How so?"

"Your dress and demeanor present the image of a proper, dutiful princess, who dots her I's and crosses her T's. Yet you show glimpses…"

No one had ever looked beneath the surface or beyond the label of dutiful princess. She wouldn't have expected Alejandro to, either. Full of curiosity, she leaned toward him. "Of what?"

"Of being a not-so-perfect princess."

It was her turn to laugh. That wasn't who she was. Oh, well… Perhaps Enrique would recognize the real her. "You're reading too much into my words and deeds. Women are second-class citizens in Aliestle. We must obey the men in our lives or deal with the consequences. Duty becomes our way of life. But that doesn't mean we don't have the same hopes and dreams, the same sense of humor, as women in more contemporary lands such as this island."

"As I said, a contradiction."

She eyed him warily. "Thank you, I think."

"It's a compliment." He glanced back toward the sitting room. "Your groom has returned."

Jules looked behind her to see Enrique holding a brandy and talking with the others.

"I should leave you." Alejandro took a step toward the

staircase. "I don't want my brother to think I'm trying to steal his princess bride."

Would Alejandro do that? Her pulse skittered thinking he might.

Stop. Now. She couldn't allow herself to be carried away with girlish fantasies. She raised her chin. "Enrique wouldn't think—"

"Yes, he would."

"Have you stolen his girlfriends in the past?"

His eyes raked over her. "No, we have different taste in women."

Alejandro's stark appraisal should have made her feel uncomfortable, but he also made her feel sexy, a way she'd never felt before. She wet her lips. "Would your being the black sheep and all the gossip have something to do with Enrique feeling this way?"

Alejandro grinned wryly. "Possibly."

"So the rumors and stories are true."

"Some are," he admitted. "Others are exaggerations."

He was a gorgeous prince. That often led people to act out of…"I'm sure a few tales are due to jealousy."

He eyed her curiously. "Has this happened to you?"

"Oh, no. I'm about as proper a princess as you'll find."

"Proper with obvious skills of manipulation."

"Proper with practiced social skills and manners that help others get along."

"Yet you downplay your intelligence by saying your knowledge about international trade is nothing but a hobby."

His perceptiveness made her feel like a mouse caught in a trap. He might be a black sheep and prefer to go barefoot, but he was sharp. She'd have to watch herself. "Education opportunities for females in my country exist, but are limited. Women are allowed to hold only certain jobs. We must work within the system. I've been more fortunate than others and able to use my time traveling abroad to…expand my knowledge base. But the last thing my country wants is their princess spouting off how smart she thinks she is."

Laughter lit Alejandro's eyes and made her temperature rise ten degrees. "You'll be good for Enrique. Keep him on his toes. But he won't mind."

"I hope not. What about you?" Jules liked the easy banter between them. Earlier when she'd arrived, she thought Alejandro didn't like her. "Will you mind not being second in line for the throne after Enrique and I have children?"

He glanced inside once again. "I can honestly say the more children you and my brother are blessed with, the happier I'll be. I've been hoping to be made an uncle for years."

His words sounded genuine. She ignored her disappointment that he wouldn't want her himself. That was stupid. Her father would never approve of a man like Alejandro, and she needed to be a queen to best help Brandt and Aliestle. "That's sweet of you."

"The kitten is sweet. I'm not." He took two steps down the stairs. "Enrique's on his way out here. That's my cue to fade back into the shadows."

Alejandro's cryptic words intrigued her. "Do you usually hang out in the shadows?"

"Yes, I do."

She watched him disappear into the night.

Behind her, footsteps sounded against the terrace's tile floor. A familiar scent of aftershave enveloped her. She didn't like the fragrance. Still better than the alternative, she reminded herself.

Jules leaned forward over the railing, but couldn't see Alejandro. "I hope your call went well.

"It did." Enrique stood next to her. "But you needn't worry about state business. The wedding should be your focus."

"I've been thinking about our wedding." She wondered if Alejandro was listening from below. Not that she minded if he eavesdropped. A part of her wished he was here with her instead of his brother. "And children, too."

"We are of like minds." Enrique placed his hand over hers. His skin was warm and soft. His nails neatly trimmed. Not the hands of a sailor or gardener. "Heirs would please my father."

"Mine, too." Her duty was to extend the bloodline. But Jules also wanted babies of her own. She remembered helping the nurses with each of her brothers. She wanted to be more involved with raising her children than her stepmother.

Enrique's eyes darkened. "Once we are married we shouldn't waste any time starting a family."

His suggestive tone made her shiver. Not a surprising reaction given she'd never discussed sex with any of her matches before. Offspring had always been assumed. "I would like a big family. At least four children."

He tucked her hair behind her ears. "I hope they all look like you."

His compliment was nice, but the words didn't make her feel warm and fuzzy the way Alejandro's had. "Thank you."

"My brother will be pleased to know you want so many children," Enrique said. "He can't wait to fall lower in the line of succession. I believe if he could give away or relinquish his title he would without a second thought."

"I can't imagine anyone wanting to do that," she admitted. "But Alejandro does have his boats."

She envied his ability to follow his dreams.

"Nothing matters but those damn boats. Sailing has consumed him. He works as a manual laborer, a commoner, refusing to take advantage of the free publicity being a royal engaged in business always brings."

Enrique's critical tone didn't surprise Jules. The two brothers seemed to always be going at each other. But sometimes that might keep them from seeing a situation more clearly. "If Alejandro wins the Med Cup, he'll earn respect. New customers."

"He won't win with a new design," Enrique said. "Competition is fierce. The best crews are going to be on well-known, tested designs. Too bad my brother is too stubborn to use the same boat as last year. But he always wants something newer, better. That's one reason I doubt he'll ever marry. He upgrades the women in his life like they were cars."

The picture Enrique painted of his younger brother was not flattering. Jules wondered if this was one of the stories Alejandro had mentioned. The two brothers needed to get along better. That gave her an idea.

"Sail his other boat for him," she said. "The one he sailed last year."

"I haven't raced since my duties became expanded. State business takes up the majority of my time."

His curt tone rebuked her. "It was only a suggestion."

"Racing in open water isn't without risks."

"I've never sailed in the ocean." Just dreamed about it.

"Your father told me he's forbidden you to sail on the sea. That's why I didn't accept Alejandro's invitation to go sailing."

"You and Brandt can go."

"Not without you," Enrique said, and she appreciated his courtesy. "Your father mentioned your mother's accident. So tragic."

Jules knew information would be exchanged during the marriage negotiations, but she'd never been privy to it. "My mother's death was an accident, a freak occurrence."

"No matter the circumstances." Enrique's voice softened. "Your father said he was deeply affected by the loss."

"I've been told he changed after she died. He loved my mother very much."

"He loves you, too."

Hearing the words from someone outside her family made Jules feel as if all the sacrifices she'd made to live up to the expectations of her father, family and country had been worth it. Her tongue felt thick, heavy, so she nodded.

"A lesser man might not have recovered from such a tragedy," Enrique continued.

She appreciated the admiration in his words. "My father is a king. He is a strong man. He mourned my mother's death, but he remarried less than a year later. He needed a male heir. I was a young child who needed a mother."

"Understandable."

Jules wondered if that meant Enrique would do the same should she die. Probably. "La Isla de la Aurora seems more progressive than Aliestle."

"It is, though we are a little old-fashioned about a few things," Enrique said. "Do not worry. I intend to make sure you like it here, Julianna.

His words fed her growing hopes. She gathered her courage. "My father said you would decide whether I could sail on the ocean after we are married. You told Alejandro we couldn't sail right now. Does that mean you've given some thought to my sailing after our wedding?"

"Your father also discussed this with me. I've already made my decision."

Her heart raced. She held her breath.

Please, oh, please. Say yes.

Enrique squeezed her hand again. "Sailing on the sea is too dangerous."

Jules felt as if someone had wrapped a line around her heart and pulled hard. She had to make him understand, to see how important this was to her. "I am a careful sailor. I would never take undue risks."

"You are on the ocean. Weather can change. No one, not even the best sailors in the world, can remove all the risk."

She understood that. She wasn't a complete idiot.

Desperate to make this work she sought another test. "Sailing is a pleasurable leisure activity. Something we could do together in our free time."

"I don't have a lot of free time."

"It wouldn't have to be that often. Only once in a while."

"We may have just met, but I must admit I understand your father's concerns." Enrique spoke to her as if she were a child. "You are to be the mother of my children, my wife, my queen. I wouldn't want anything to happen to you as it did your mother."

Disappointment settled in the center of Jules's chest, but she didn't allow her shoulders to slump. Being here was still better than Aliestle. "So I'm only allowed to sail on lakes and rivers?"

"I've seen what sailing has done to my brother. The sport

killed your mother. Once we are married, I do not want you to sail again."

The air rushed from Jules lungs. Tears stung her eyes. She clutched the railing. "But I've always been able to sail. Just not on the ocean."

"That was your father's decision. This is mine."

No! Her chest tightened. This was so much worse than she imagined. It wasn't only the sailing. The tone of Enrique's voice told her she would be exchanging her controlling father for a controlling husband. Her freedom would be curtailed here, too.

"Don't look so disappointed," Enrique chided. "This isn't personal. I'm not trying to be cruel."

"What are you trying to do then?"

"Be honest and help you," he said. "It's time for you to grow up and put childish things aside, Julianna. You may believe sailing is good for you, but it's been brought to my attention that sailing brings out a wilder side in you."

She drew back. "What have I done?"

"Kissed Prince Niko."

"One kiss. We were engaged at the time."

"There have been other reports," Enrique said calmly, as if they were discussing business and not her life. "Such a pursuit is inappropriate for a future queen. You must embrace the bigger duty you'll now have."

Jules forced herself to breathe. Carving a new life for herself and helping Aliestle would be an uphill battle. She would be constrained here on the island, too. "What is to be my role here? My bigger duty?"

"You are to be my wife. You will provide me with heirs."

Both of those things she'd known about. Accepted. But she doubted that was all Enrique would want from her. "And?"

"You will be a conventional princess and queen the people can respect. It's in your best interest to do what I say and not bring any embarrassment to our name."

Her best interest? What about their best interest? Enrique seemed to want to tell her what to do, not have a real relationship with her. How could love grow out of that?

Emotion clogged her throat.

What was she going to do?

Returning to Aliestle in disgrace and marrying a nobleman would be the worst choice for her, Brandt, her country and her future children. Doing something more drastic didn't appeal to her, either.

Other women might run away. But if she turned her back on her responsibilities she would be exiled. Her father would keep her brothers from seeing her. Not only that, her father would also denounce her. Conditions would worsen for the women in her country. She couldn't give up on everything she'd sacrificed her whole life for and her family.

That left one choice—going through with the wedding. Her stomach churned.

Think of the bigger picture, the future, others.

Jules would be able to help Brandt and Aliestle. Her children would have a better life and more choices on the island. Those things would make up for everything she was giving up. In time, Jules would see she made the right decision.

But right now, it still…hurt.

In an apartment on the ground floor, Alejandro tried to relax. But being back at the palace made him antsy. So did something else. Someone else…

Julianna.

Maybe she wasn't as bad as he originally thought. She seemed different tonight, warmer and more genuine. But if that were the case, he couldn't understand her icy facade earlier.

Not that he should be thinking about his brother's fiancée at all.

Alejandro sat on the floor and used a laser pointer to play with the kitten. This was the same room he'd had as a teenager, though the furniture had been replaced, the floors refinished and the walls painted. The decor wasn't the only change. Back when he'd been a teenager, a guard had always been stationed outside the back door that led to the beach path to keep him from running away. Not that a guard had been able to stop him. At least his father hadn't posted anyone there tonight.

The kitten sprinted across the hardwood floor after the red dot, pawing and pouncing until he plopped onto a hand-woven rug and purred. His eyes closed.

As Alejandro moved from the floor to a chair, a flash of blue passed outside the window. The same blue as Julianna's gown.

He stood to get a better look.

Silky fabric and blond hair billowed behind her as she hurried down the path leading to the beach, making her look almost ethereal with the starry night sky as her backdrop.

Not his type, Alejandro reminded himself.

He glanced at the clock. Eleven o'clock. A little late to go beachcombing. Not that what she did was any of his business.

But no one seemed to be with her. Not Enrique. Not her bodyguard.

That didn't sit well with Alejandro.

She shouldn't be alone. It was dark. She could lose her way.

On a lighted path, an inner voice mocked.

Something could happen to her. Alejandro ignored the fact that he could find his brother and send him after Julianna.

Alejandro stepped outside onto the patio. The tile was hard beneath his bare feet. Planters full of fragrant flowers lined the edge. Lanterns hung from tall wrought-iron poles.

Maybe Julianna wanted a closer look at the water, or to dance on the beach under the moonlight...or skinny-dip.

As his blood surged at the thought, he quickened his pace. Now that he would like to see. Ice princess or not.

The lighted path stopped at the beach. Alejandro's bare feet sunk into the fine sand. Thanks to the moonlight, he saw Julianna standing at the water's edge holding her high heels in one hand. The hem of her gown dragged on the sand. Wind ruffled her hair and the fabric of her dress. Waves crashed against the shore, the water drawing closer to her. She didn't move.

Mesmerized by the sea or thinking? About him?

He scoffed at the stupid thought. She would be thinking about Enrique. Her fiancé. Alejandro should leave her alone.

Yet he remained rooted in place, content to watch her.

Being here had nothing to do with the way her dress clung to her curves or the slit that provided him with a glimpse of her long, smooth legs. He was here for her protection. Even though this strip of white sand was private, reachable only from the palace or by water. He didn't see any boats offshore, only silver moonlight reflecting off the crescents of waves.

Still he stood captivated by the woman in front of him. The individual, not incarnations of women she would become. Future sister-in-law, mother of his nieces and nephews, queen.

He longed to go to her, pull her into an embrace, taste her sweet lips and feel her lush curves pressed against him.

What the hell was he thinking?

Disgusted with the fantasy playing in his mind, Alejandro turned to leave. Julianna moved in his peripheral vision. He looked back. She sat on the sand, resting her head in her hands. Her shoulders shook as if she were crying.

A sob smacked into him. His gut clenched.

The instinct to bolt was strong. Tears made him uncomfortable. He'd been in enough short-term relationships to know crying women were to be avoided at all costs. He never knew what to say and feared making a situation worse.

Yet he walked toward her anyway as if pulled by an invisible line. Compelled by something he couldn't explain. "Julianna."

She didn't look up. "Go away, please."

Her voice sounded raw, yet she was polite, always the proper princess. He saw her behavior wasn't an act like his brother's. His respect inched up for her. "I'm not going away."

"I'll pretend you aren't here then."

"It won't be the first time that's happened." He plopped onto the sand next to her. "I've been becalmed many times. Having the boat bob like a cork while waiting for wind to return used to drive me crazy, but I've learned to enjoy the downtime."

She remained silent.

As waves broke against the shore, Alejandro studied the stars in the sky. He drew pictures in the sand. A boat. A crab. A heart. He wiped them away with the side of his hand.

Julianna raised her head. "You're still here."

"Yes." Tears streaked her cheeks. The sadness in her swollen eyes reignited his desire to take her in his arms and kiss her until she smiled. "I may have some of the same stubborn streak shared by other members of my family."

She sniffled.

He wished he had a tissue for her. One of those handkerchiefs his brother and father carried in their pockets would come in handy. "When you're ready to talk…"

A new round of tears streamed down her face. She looked devastated, as if someone she loved had died.

Her vulnerability clawed at his heart, made him feel useless, worthless. He couldn't sit here and do nothing.

Alejandro turned toward Julianna and lifted her onto his lap.

She gasped. Stiffened.

A mistake, probably, but he'd deal with that later. He needed to help Julianna.

The moment he wrapped his arms around her something seemed to release inside her. She sagged against him, rested her head on his shoulder and cried. He rubbed her back with his hand, the same way his mother used to do whenever he'd been hurt by something Enrique did or his father had said.

Julianna's tears didn't stop, but that didn't bother Alejandro. She felt so perfect nestled against him. Her sweet scent enveloped him. He would have preferred to be in this position under different circumstances, but he knew that wasn't possible. She had a fiancé—what she needed tonight was a friend.

He could be a friend. That was all he could ever be to her.

Her tears slowed. Her breathing became less ragged.

"Thank you," Julianna muttered. "I'm sorry for inconveniencing you. This is so unlike me."

Alejandro brushed the strands of hair sticking to her tearstained cheeks. "You're in my arms and on my lap. Formalities and apologies aren't necessary."

She stared up at him. Even with puffy, red eyes she was still beautiful.

But she was almost family. She would be his sister-in-law.

Julianna scooted off his lap. "I'm better now."

He missed the warmth of her body, the feel of her curves against him. "Tell me what's wrong."

She looked at the water. "It's nothing."

"Let me be the judge of that."

A beat passed. And another. "Did you hang around after Enrique joined me on the terrace?"

"No." Maybe Alejandro should have.

She took a slow breath. "I thought coming here and marrying Enrique would be so much better than staying in Aliestle. I believed things would be…different."

"I don't understand."

"It's difficult to explain. Do you recall at dinner when you asked if we sailed, and Brandt answered?"

Alejandro nodded. He'd thought that odd.

"Brandt spoke because he knows how much sailing means to me, and I would've gotten carried away. I love it. I'd rather sail than do anything. Being on a boat is the only time I can be myself. Not a proper princess or a dutiful daughter and sister." She gazed at the water. "It's heaven on earth for me."

The passion in her words heated the blood in his veins. The longing for independence, for a freedom from all the expectations of being a royal matched the desire in his heart. This perfect princess was as much a black sheep as him. She just kept the true color of her wool hidden. "I know exactly how you feel."

She studied him. "I thought you might. My father has never allowed me to sail on the ocean due to my mother dying during a race. That's why Enrique turned down your invitation to go sailing. My father said once I married, Enrique could decide whether I could sail or not."

"You'll be living on an island," Alejandro said. "Why wouldn't you sail?"

"That's what I thought. After you left the terrace, I asked Enrique about being able to sail." Her lower lip quivered. "He has forbidden me to sail. Not only on the ocean, but ever again. He says sailing brings out a wildness in me that's not appropriate for a future queen. I'm to be a conventional wife and princess."

Tears gleamed in her eyes.

Damn Enrique. His brother was a complete moron. A total ass. As usual. "He has spoken without thinking."

"He was quite serious about his expectations of me."

"My brother might be a cad, but he isn't a monster. He'll come around."

Tears slipped from the corners of her eyes. "I don't think he will."

Alejandro's chest tightened. "I'll talk to Enrique. Make him see how much sailing means to you."

"No," she said. "He might change his mind about marrying me."

Not likely given her dowry. But Julianna was so much more than the money she brought to the marriage. She might act like a cold, dutiful princess, but underneath the perfect facade was a passionate woman looking to break free of the obligations that came with her tiara and scepter. La Isla de la Aurora deserved a queen like Julianna. Too bad Enrique didn't deserve a woman like her.

"Ask to be released from the marriage contract." Alejandro couldn't believe those words had come from his lips.

"I can't."

"You won't."

"If I don't marry Enrique, I'll be sent home to marry one of the sons of our Council of Elders." The way her voice cracked hurt Alejandro's heart. "In Aliestle, it's against the law to disobey your husband. I'd rather raise my children in a country that is more progressive. At least in principle. This is my fate. I must learn to accept it."

Alejandro hated seeing her so distressed. She deserved to be happy, to have the freedom to do what she wanted to do.

"Not so fast," he said. "In spite of a few traditional mindsets here, La Isla de la Aurora is a progressive country. That includes our laws. Enrique can't throw you in prison or lock you away in a tower if you disobey him and go sailing."

"This isn't only about my sailing."

"I'm not only talking about sailing. My mother left the island fifteen years ago." Alejandro had learned an important lesson the day his mother left. Never rely on anyone but yourself. "Separation is an option here, even for royals."

"That's very modern compared to where I come from." She wiped her eyes. "You see, I'd hoped to use my position as future queen to effect change back home without embarrassing my country and family."

Alejandro remembered what she'd told him. "Working within the system."

She nodded. "Royals can't be selfish and ignore the people who look up to them."

"That's noble of you," Alejandro said. Too bad most royals didn't feel that way. "But you shouldn't be too upset. My brother's pulling one of his power plays with you. He's done it to me many times and will change his mind. Your life will be better here than in Aliestle. You'll have royal obligations, but you'll also be able to do what you want to do, including help your country and sail."

Her shoulders remained slumped. "Enrique could annul the marriage if I defy him. I'd have to return to Aliestle."

"I don't see a ring on your finger."

"Not yet anyway." She glanced at her left hand. Straightened. "No ring."

"What?" Alejandro asked.

Her gaze met his. "Maybe Enrique will change his mind about things or maybe he won't. I can't change anything that will happen once I marry. But if I go sailing now, I wouldn't be disobeying my husband since Enrique is only my fiancé."

Her tone sounded different. Not as distraught. "You lost me."

Julianna's gaze met Alejandro's with an unspoken plea.

Understanding dawned. He leaned away from her. "No. No way. I can't get involved in this."

"You're already involved." She scooted closer. "All I need is a boat for one sail."

The flowery scent of her shampoo filled his nostrils and made him waver. He leaned backed to put some distance between them. "If you're caught disobeying your father…"

"I'll make sure I'm not," she said. "You believe Enrique will change his mind, but you didn't see the look in his eyes. It's worth the risk for one last hurrah before I get married."

"Maybe to you, but not to me." Alejandro would be in deep trouble. That had never bothered him in the past. But the stakes were higher this time.

"What do you have to lose?" she asked.

His chance at freedom. He hated the way Enrique was treating Julianna, but Alejandro didn't want to cause an even bigger problem between the couple. He needed the two to marry and have children.

A deep shame rose up inside him. He was thinking of himself while Julianna was trying to do her duty even if it made her unhappy.

"I'm sorry," he said. "But I won't be the reason you get in trouble."

Disappointment shone in her lovely eyes.

"Fine." She flipped her hair behind her shoulder with a sexy move. "I'll find a boat myself."

She would, too. He pictured her heading to the marina and going out with anyone who'd take her. That could end in disaster. If he helped her…

Alejandro couldn't believe he was contemplating taking her out, but he didn't want to think only of himself. "Sailing is that important to you?"

"Yes."

The hope and anticipation in the one word made it difficult for him to breath.

"Please, Alejandro." Julianna stared up at him with her wide, blue eyes. "Will you please help me?"

A long list of reasons why he shouldn't scrolled through his mind. But logic didn't seem to apply in this situation. Or with Julianna.

He thought about it a minute. Taking her sailing wasn't that big a deal. "I suppose it would be against my character and ruin my bad reputation if I turned down an opportunity to do something Enrique was against."

She leaned toward him giving him another whiff of her enticing scent. "So is that a yes?"

CHAPTER FOUR

YES. I'll take you sailing tomorrow night.

Jules fell asleep thinking about Alejandro's words. She woke up with them on her mind, too.

Sunlight streamed through the windows. Particles in the air gave the rays definition, as if a fairy had waved her magic wand to make the sunshine touchable. She reached out, but felt only air.

With a laugh, she rolled over in the queen-size bed eager to start her day. She couldn't wait to go sailing tonight. Of course if she was discovered…

Don't think about that.

She needed to do this. Everything else in her life, from her education to her marriage, had been determined for her. Not out of love, but because of what tradition dictated and what others believed to be best for Aliestle.

Going sailing tonight was the one decision she could make for herself. She was desperate enough for this one act of disobedience. A secretive rebellion of sorts, the kind she never did as a teenager.

Jules tossed back the luxurious Egyptian cotton sheet and climbed out of bed. Her bare feet sunk into a hand-woven Persian rug. Only the finest furnishings for the grand palace.

She entered the large bathroom. Yvette had set out her toiletries on the marble countertop. The gold plated fixtures reminded Jules of every other castle she'd stayed in. Gold might be considered opulent, but didn't any of the royal interior designers want to be creative and try a different finish? Then again, royalty could never be too creative or different. The status quo was completely acceptable.

Jules stared at her refection in the mirror. Today she would maintain that status quo. People would look at her and see a dutiful princess. Even if she would be counting down the hours until her first and last taste of…

Freedom.

Her chest tightened. She had no idea what true freedom would feel like.

So far, Jules's choices in life had been relegated to what she wanted to eat, if it wasn't a state dinner, what books she wanted to read, if she'd completed all her assigned readings, and what she purchased while shopping. Perhaps that was why she'd become a consummate shopper.

Choosing what she wanted to do without having to consider the expectations of an overprotective father and a conservative country would have to feel pretty good. She couldn't wait to experience it tonight.

Jules had thought about what Alejandro said about the island not being Aliestle, about the legal rights she would have here and about his mother leaving his father. Those things had led her to devise a new plan.

She would sail tonight, then return to being a dutiful princess in the morning and marry Enrique after the Med Cup. Once they had children, she would work to improve her position, get Enrique to be more cooperative and try to change things.

Thirty minutes later, Yvette clasped a diamond and pearl necklace around Jules's neck. "Excellent choice, Yvette. You have quite an eye when it comes to accessories."

"Thank you, ma'am." The young maid stared at their reflection in the mirror. "You look like a modern day Princess Grace."

Jules felt a little like Princess Grace, who had been forced to stop acting because someone said the people of Monaco wouldn't be happy if she returned to making movies. Life for many royals didn't always have a happy ending.

"Thank you, Yvette." The retro-style pink-and-white suit had been purchased on a recent trip to Paris. Jules tucked a strand of hair into her French roll. "I'm sure the hairstyle helps."

"Prince Enrique will be impressed."

"Let's hope so." Jules tried to sound cheerful, but her words felt flat. She doubted Enrique would be impressed by anything she did. He was nothing like…Alejandro.

She couldn't imagine Enrique cradling her in his arms and offering sympathy while she cried. He would have cursed her tears, not wiped them away as Alejandro had.

A black sheep? Perhaps, but he was taking her sailing. She guessed he was more of a good guy than he claimed to be.

She smiled. "Perhaps I'll make an impression on the entire royal family."

"Not Prince Alejandro." Yvette sounded aghast. "I've been told to stay away from him."

The words offended Jules. She would rather spend time with Alejandro than Enrique. "Who said that?"

"One of the housekeepers. She's young. Pretty," Yvette explained. "She said Prince Alejandro has a horrible reputation. Worse, his taste in women is far from discriminating. Royalty, commoner, palace staff, it doesn't matter."

Alejandro had warned her about the gossip. But the words stung for some reason. "That could be a rumor. The press loves to write about royalty whether it's true or not. People will believe almost anything once it's in print or on the Internet."

"The housekeeper sounded sincere, ma'am," Yvette said. "She's especially concerned about you."

"About me?" Jules remembered the warmth of Alejandro's body and the sense of belonging she'd felt in his arms. He could have taken advantage of the situation and her emotional state last night, but he hadn't. He'd acted like a friend, not a man who wanted some action. She'd actually been a tad bit disappointed he hadn't found her desirable.

Silly. Pathetic, really. She straightened. "I appreciate the warning, but I'm going to be Alejandro's sister-in-law. He doesn't see me in the same way as he sees other woman."

Doubt filled Yvette's eyes. "I hope you're correct, ma'am."

Jules didn't. She wouldn't mind being wrong about this. Alejandro was…attractive, but the way he'd made her feel on the beach—understood, accepted, safe, ways she'd never felt before—intrigued her the most. After tonight, following the housekeeper's advice and staying away from him would be the best course of action. No matter how much a tiny part of Jules wished he were the one she was marrying.

Better squelch that thought. Alejandro was going to be her brother-in-law. Nothing else.

"Don't worry." She raised her chin. "I'm not about to risk my match with Enrique for a fling with a self-avowed black sheep."

Even one who was gorgeous and sailed and sent tingles shooting through her. More reasons to keep her distance.

After tonight.

Tonight would be her first chance to experience freedom. The initial step in figuring out how to be an influential princess and her own person.

"That is smart." The tight lines around Yvette's mouth relaxed a little. "Being matched to a man outside Aliestle would be a dream come true for most of our countrywomen, ma'am."

Be careful what you wish, or in this case, ask for.

Jules recognized the maid's wistful tone. She'd sounded the same way on more than one occasion. The weight on her shoulders felt heavier. She wanted life to be different for her countrywomen. "Has a match been secured for you?"

"Yes, ma'am. A very good match." Yvette gave a half smile. "One that will be advantageous to my family."

"That's excellent."

"Yes, ma'am. We marry in two years, after I complete my obligations on the palace staff." The look in Yvette's eyes didn't seem to agree with her words. "I am…most fortunate."

Most likely as fortunate as Jules. Her heart ached. She wanted men to treat the women of Aliestle with respect, consideration and love. Not like commodities.

When Brandt became king…

Yvette adjusted her starched, white apron. "I transferred the contents of your handbag into the purse, ma'am."

"Thank you, I'll…"

A high-pitched noise sounded outside the bedroom door. Not quite a squeal, but not a squeak, either.

Yvette's forehead creased. "It sounds like a baby, ma'am."

Jules hurried to the door and opened it. The noise sounded again. She glanced around the empty hallway. A black ball of fur scratched at the door across the hall.

"You're correct, Yvette. It is a baby. A baby cat." Jules picked up the kitten who pawed at her. A long, white hair above his right eye bounced like an antenna in the wind. "I can't imagine someone let you out into this big hallway on purpose. Did you escape again?"

The kitten stared up at her with clear, green eyes.

Her heart bumped. She'd always wanted a pet. This one was adorable.

"I can see where he belongs, ma'am," Yvette offered.

"I'll return him." The kitten wiggled in Jules's hands. She cuddled him closer in hopes of settling him down. He rested his head against her arm and purred. "I know where he belongs."

With Alejandro.

Anticipation spurted through her. She wanted to see him. Because of the sailing, she rationalized. That was the only reason. Anything else would be too…dangerous.

"Cat?" Alejandro checked the closet, the bathroom, under the bed and beneath the other furniture. No sight of the furball anywhere.

The kitten didn't come running as he usually did.

Maybe he was locked in the bathroom? Alejandro checked. No kitty.

The last time he'd seen the kitten was before his shower. He glanced around the apartment again. A vase with colorful fresh-cut flowers caught his eye. Those were new.

Only Ortiz knew about the kitten. If whoever delivered the

flowers had left the door to the apartment open, the kitten could have gotten out.

Alejandro ran to the door and jerked it open.

Julianna stood in the doorway.

He froze, stunned to see her.

A smile graced her glossed lips. Clear, bright eyes stared back at him. Her pastel-pink suit made her look like the definition of the word princess in the dictionary.

She was the image of everything he didn't like in a woman—royal, wealthy, concerned with appearances. He shouldn't feel any attraction toward Julianna whatsoever. But he couldn't stop staring at her beautiful face.

Awareness buzzed through him. Strange. Alejandro didn't usually go for the prim and proper type. But this wasn't the time to examine his attraction to her. He needed to find a kitten. "I—"

"I was about to knock," she said at the same time. "Look who I found."

Alejandro followed her line of sight. The kitten was sound asleep in her arms.

Relief washed over him. "I was on my way out to look for him. Where did you find him?"

"In the hallway trying to squeeze under the door across from mine. A futile effort given his size, but he made a valiant attempt." She smiled at the kitten. "I figured he must have escaped and you'd want him back."

"Yes." Alejandro tried focusing on the cat, but his gaze kept returning to her. He wanted to chalk his reaction to her up to gratitude but knew better. "Thanks."

"You're welcome."

Alejandro waited for Julianna to hand over the cat. She didn't. He needed to go to the boatyard, but he wasn't in that much of a hurry. He motioned into the apartment. "Please come in."

Julianna looked to her left and then to the right. "Thanks, but I'd better not."

He gave her a puzzled look. "You have plans."

"No," she admitted. "I don't want to upset Enrique."

Alejandro ignored the twinge of disappointment. He understood her concern. "You're right. We don't want to add fuel to the fire."

"Especially with tonight," she whispered. Excitement danced in her eyes.

He was looking forward to the sail. He wanted Julianna to like it here. For his sake as much as hers. She'd realize she wouldn't be a prisoner on the island. Enrique didn't know how to treat women properly; a combination of selfishness and lack of experience. His brother would settle down eventually.

"Rest up today or you'll be exhausted," Alejandro said.

"Like the kitten. He fell asleep on the walk over here. He must have tired himself out during his adventure."

Alejandro wouldn't mind tiring himself out with Julianna. He imagined her beautiful long hair loose and spread across his pillow, her silky skin against his, the taste of those lips…

His blood heated and roared through his veins.

He pushed the fantasy out of his mind. Thinking of Julianna in a sexual way was wrong and dangerous. They both had too much to lose.

"I've been wondering what the kitten's name is," she said.

Good, he could think about something other than her in his bed. "Cat."

"Cat is the kitten's name?"

"Yes."

Julianna drew her delicately arched eyebrows together. Her pretty pink mouth opened then closed, as if she thought better of what she wanted to say.

"What?" he asked.

"It's nothing."

Alejandro recognized the look in her eyes. "Tell me."

Julianna hesitated. "You're doing me a favor taking me sailing. I shouldn't criticize."

He'd been criticized his entire life by his father and by his brother. He never could live up to what the people wanted him to be, either. The bane of being the spare. Nothing he did was ever good enough. Alejandro had grown immune to the put-downs. "I want to know."

"You might get mad."

He didn't want her to be afraid of him. "Enrique might get a little heated at times. You don't have to worry about that with me."

She squared her shoulders, as if preparing for battle. A one-hundred-eighty-degree difference from her sobbing on the beach last night. "Cat isn't a proper name for a pet."

That was what this was all about. Alejandro almost laughed. He thought it was something serious. "Cat doesn't seem to mind the name."

"That's because he loves you."

The warmth in her voice wrapped around Alejandro like a soft, fluffy towel. He couldn't remember the last time anyone had made him feel so good. But he knew better. The feeling was as fleeting as the love she spoke about. "Love has nothing to do with it. He's a cat. He comes because he's hungry."

"He'd come no matter what you call him," she continued.

"Cat isn't a child."

"No, he's your pet."

Children and a family weren't something he'd considered before. Saying he had a pet was pushing the level of commitment he was comfortable with. Love and commitment didn't last so why bother? His mother had claimed to love him. But she'd abandoned him to a father who disapproved of him and a brother who antagonized him. Alejandro rocked back on his heels. "Cat's a stray."

"Living in a palace."

Her voice teased. Okay, she had a point. "If I give the cat a proper name, I'll have to keep him."

She pursed her lips. "Do you plan on releasing him when he gets bigger?"

Alejandro fought the urge to squirm under her scrutiny. He hadn't done anything wrong or irresponsible. At least not yet. "I haven't thought that far ahead. But cats take off when they get tired of you."

She peered around him and motioned to the sock tied in a knot, piece of rope and empty boxes strewn across the floor. "You're going to need to buy a suitcase when he goes so he can take his toys with him."

"I just had that stuff lying around." Alejandro shoved his hands in his pockets. "I'll probably keep him. At the boatyard when he gets older," he clarified.

"Then you might as well come up with a more original name for him."

"He's a cat. The name fits."

"True, but look at his green eyes. His handsome face. The white boots on his paws." She held the kitten up as if he were a rare treasure. "He is so much more than a generic cat."

Alejandro laughed, enchanted by her tenacity. "If you ever get tired of being a princess, you should become a trial lawyer."

She scrunched her nose. "I've never considered such a career, but I would be happy to provide more evidence for changing the kitten's name."

"For someone who wants *me* to take them sailing," he lowered his voice, "you're not very agreeable."

Her eyes widened. Her complexion paled. "Oh, I'm—"

"Kidding." Alejandro didn't think she would take him seriously. But he could make it up to her. He thought about her description of the kitten. One word popped out at him. "Boots."

A line creased above her nose. "Excuse me?"

"Cat's name is now Boots. Satisfied?"

"Very." She smiled, visibly relieved. "Thank you."

Pleasing her felt better than it should. Just trying to make her happy so she'd want to marry Enrique.

Yeah, right. Alejandro leaned against the doorjamb. "It's the least I could do after the way you argued for his rights. Perhaps you should do the same for your own. And your countrywomen."

Her smile disappeared. So did the light from her eyes. He didn't like the change in her.

"I would if I could, but that's not the kind of princess Aliestle or your brother wants." She touched one of the kitten's small paws. Her expression softened. "The least I could do was support a fellow underdog."

"I don't think Boots would like to be associated with anything having to do with a dog."

The corners of her mouth slanted upward. "You're probably right about that."

Alejandro reached out to pet the kitten. His fingers brushed against the bare skin on Julianna's arm. Tingles shot outward from the point of contact. He jerked his hand away.

She didn't seem to notice.

Good. He didn't want her to know she had an effect on him. "You like cats."

"I do, but I've never had one." She rubbed the top of the kitten's head. "My father didn't want any animals in the palace. He claimed they were too dirty and too much trouble."

Alejandro hadn't expected to have anything else in common with her except sailing. "We had a dog growing up, but after she died my father didn't want another one. He said dogs were too much trouble."

Julianna eyed him with curiosity. "Yet you have Boots."

But Alejandro didn't live in the palace. He doubted his family would want Julianna to know he was here for appearance sake and would be departing after the wedding. "Black sheep, remember?"

"I haven't forgotten. I hope your reputation means you're an expert at subterfuge and not getting caught."

He winked. "You're in experienced hands, Princess."

"Excellent." The sparkle returned to her eyes. She glanced behind her as if to make sure they were still alone. "Have all the arrangements been made?"

The princess's hushed voice made it sound as if they were going to undertake an important, secretive mission. Alejandro realized in her mind they were. The least he could do was play along.

"Almost," he whispered back. "Check your closet this afternoon. Everything you need for tonight will be in there."

Her mouth formed a perfect O. "My closet? You're going to go into my room. Isn't that risky?"

"No one will see me."

"You can't be certain. My maid might be—"

"There are secret tunnels and passageways throughout the palace." He didn't want her to worry. "You access them through hidden latches in the closets."

"Oh."

The one word spoke volumes of her doubt.

"Do you trust me?" he asked.

She handed the kitten to him. "I don't have a choice if I want to go sailing."

"No, you don't."

Alejandro felt like a jerk. He was the last person she should be putting her faith in. He had the most to gain by her marrying Enrique. She had the most to lose by saying "I do." Okay, his brother wasn't that bad. But she was still sacrificing for the marriage.

"Not many people would understand how important tonight is to me," she said. "I trust you won't let me down."

He appreciated her earnest expression and words. He was used to those in the palace being unable to see past his rebellions as a teen and his wanting to change the monarchy from the archaic monolith it had become.

But Julianna was far too trusting. She must have lived a sheltered life in Aliestle. Things would be better for her on the island. "You're the perfect fairy-tale princess."

Defiance flashed in her eyes, but disappeared quickly. "A princess, yes. Perfect, not so much. Though I try my best."

"Trying is an admirable trait, but not if it makes you unhappy."

"Doing what is expected of me is all I know."

Julianna was nothing like he imagined she would be. She wasn't jaded in spite of being a royal prisoner her entire life. She was the closest thing to perfection he'd ever met. Alejandro would make sure Enrique treated her fairly. "You do a good job."

She rewarded him with a closemouthed smile. He would have

preferred to see one with her straight, white teeth visible. "I plan to continue to do so."

Except tonight.

Crossing the line had become second nature to him growing up. Alejandro didn't do it as often now. Still he didn't care what anyone thought about him. The lovely princess did care. The way she dressed, spoke and acted made it clear. She might feel the need to rebel in this one-time act of defiance. A brief escape from an impending arranged marriage and a curtailed freedom. But he didn't want Julianna to have any regrets over what they were going to do.

"Are you certain you want to go against your father and sail tonight?" Alejandro whispered.

"Most definitely."

"You may regret—"

"I'll regret not doing so more," she interrupted. "This is the right thing to do. Even if I'm caught."

Julianna was saying the right words. Alejandro hoped she meant them. Because if she got caught, the price she would pay might be higher than either of them imagined.

That evening, the hands on the clock in the dining room moved slower than the Council of Elders. King Dario sat at the head of the table. His two sons sat on his left with Jules and Brandt on the king's right.

She tapped her foot, impatient the meal was taking so long. Servers scurried about with wine bottles and platters. She wanted dinner to end so she could excuse herself and prepare for the sail with Alejandro.

He sat across the table from her. No tuxedo, but a designer suit and dress shirt sans tie. He looked more like a CEO than a boatbuilder. Well, except for his hair. The dark ends brushed his shoulders. She preferred his casual, carefree style to Enrique's short, conservative cut.

She kept hoping Alejandro would say something to turn the dinner conversation away from the upcoming royal wedding and onto something more interesting.

He didn't. He barely spoke or glanced her way.

No doubt trying to keep anyone from guessing about the rendezvous later. Jules suppressed the urge to smile about her impending adventure.

King Dario yawned. "I'm going to skip having a brandy."

Alejandro straightened. "Are you feeling okay, Father?"

The king waved off his son's genuine concern. "I'm fine. Just tired."

"Dealing with the demands of the island takes a lot out of a person." Enrique narrowed his gaze as he spoke to Alejandro. "Something you would know little about, brother."

Jules waited for Alejandro to fire back a smart-assed comment. He took a sip of wine instead. When he finished, he wiped his mouth with a napkin. His dark eyes revealed nothing of his thoughts. "Sleep well, Father."

With that, King Dario departed.

Silence filled the dining room. The servers seemed to have vanished along with the king. Jules counted to one hundred by tens in Japanese. When could she say good-night without drawing suspicions to herself?

"I have work to attend to." Enrique scooted his chair away from the table. "If you do not mind," he said to her as if an afterthought.

Perfect! Her entire body felt as if it were smiling. "I don't mind."

"I was planning to hit the clubs," Brandt said with eager anticipation in his voice.

Yes! She couldn't have arranged this any better if she'd planned it. "Take Klaus with you."

Brandt rolled his eyes.

"Listen to your sister," Alejandro suggested. "You'll be thankful you have a bodyguard should things get out of hand."

"My brother knows the island's club scene intimately." Derision dripped from each of Enrique's word. "He's often at the center of the melees."

Jules didn't like his tone. She often gave her four brothers a hard time and teased them, like any big sister, but she never spoke with such disrespect.

"Please, Brandt," she said. "Father would never forgive me if something happened to you."

"And vice versa." Brandt directed a warm smile full of love her way. "I'll have Klaus accompany me."

Relieved, she smiled at him. "Thank you."

Enrique remained seated in his chair, but he looked ready to bolt out any minute. She wished he'd go.

"What will you do tonight, Julianna?" he asked.

"Oh, I don't know." She forced herself not to look at Alejandro. "Read. Watch TV. I'll find something to do."

She wiggled her toes in anticipation of what she would actually be doing.

Enrique rose from the table. "Then I'll bid you good-night and see you tomorrow."

Jules watched him exit the dining room. The atmosphere seemed less stuffy with Enrique gone. Her uncharitable thought brought a stab of guilt. He was her future husband. She'd best accept him as he was.

Alejandro rose. "I'm going to say good-night, also."

"Will I see you later?" Brandt asked.

"Not tonight," Alejandro said. "I have a prior engagement."

Yes, he did. She bit back a smile. In two hours and twenty-two minutes she would meet him at a private dock. The map, a headlamp and everything else she needed were sitting inside a duffel bag she'd found in her closet this afternoon.

"Blonde or brunette?" Brandt asked.

Alejandro laughed at the innuendo. "I wish I could say differently, but unfortunately it's not that kind of…engagement."

Jules tried to figure out what Alejandro meant. That he wished he were seeing a different woman or he wished he were meeting her under different circumstances? Not that he would or she could. But still…

"You can meet me at a club later," Brandt said.

Alejandro glanced her way. "Maybe I will."

"No." The two men looked at her with surprised expressions.

Jules's heart dropped to her feet. She hadn't meant to say the word out loud. "I mean, do you know how long you'll be, Alejandro? Brandt might not want to stick around one club waiting for you to show up."

Brandt shook his head. "Stop being such a big sister, Jules. He can text me when he arrives."

"Oh, right," she said. "You know how often I go clubbing."

"You've never been to a club," Brandt said.

She'd never been allowed to go. She always wondered if her bodyguards were more concerned protecting her or ensuring she remained a virgin so her father could use that in marriage negotiations. "Exactly."

"Your sister's correct, though," Alejandro said. "I have no idea how long I'll be. I may not make it."

Brandt shrugged. "More lovely ladies for me."

"Save some for us tomorrow night."

Her brother grinned. "You're on."

Jules didn't want to think about tomorrow and the life waiting for her as Enrique's bride and future queen. She wanted tonight to last forever. She wanted it to start now.

She rose from the table. "Good night, gentlemen. I hope you enjoy the rest of your evening."

"I hope you're not too bored here alone," Brandt said.

"Don't worry. I won't be bored at all." Her gaze met Alejandro's for a moment. "Tonight is exactly what I need."

CHAPTER FIVE

TWO HOURS LATER, Jules stood in the walk-in closet in her room. The headlamp she wore illuminated the dark space. She wore sailing clothes two sizes too big, a short, dark wig and a cap. She clutched a map in her left hand. With a steadying breath, she searched for the hidden latch with a trembling right hand.

She'd never disobeyed her father or anyone else for that matter. She'd never come close to doing anything illicit unless you counted eating an entire bag of chocolate in one sitting. But this...

Her heart pounded against her chest.

You're in experienced hands, Princess.

Alejandro's words gave her a needed boost of courage.

Jules's fingers brushed across something. She sucked in a breath. The latch. She pressed the small, narrow lever. Something squealed. She stepped backward. A secret door opened to reveal a staircase.

Her insides quivered with a mix of nerves and excitement and a little fear.

She stood at the threshold and glanced down the pitch-black stairwell. The headlamp illuminated the narrow steps.

Jules ventured forward onto the first step with a slight hesitation. Nerves bubbled in her tummy. She found a latch on the inside of the passageway and closed the secret door.

The steep staircase led to a tunnel that looked as if it had been there for decades, possibly a century or more. She wondered what the tunnel had been used for in the past. Had other princesses used it to escape?

Her feet carried her across a packed dirt floor. Weathered, thick wood beams reinforced the walls and ceiling. The map said the tunnel was two kilometers long. The distance felt longer with the inky shadows stretching out in front of her.

Something gray darted across the floor at the edge of the headlamp beam.

Her breath caught in her throat. She shivered with a sense of foreboding. Nothing like being in an underground tunnel with rodents for companionship.

Not rodents, she corrected. Mice.

"No rats in the palace," she muttered. "No rats in the palace."

With the words as her mantra, Jules continued forward. Adrenaline quickened her pace. More creatures scurried across the floor or ran along the walls. Her nerves increased. She wanted out of here. Now.

She came to a wrought-iron gate secured with a combination lock. She pulled the lock toward her and dialed in the digits written on the map: 132823. The lock clicked open.

The sound of freedom.

Jules opened the gate and stepped through with all the excitement of Christmas morning back when she was a child. She exited the tunnel and found herself in a grotto. No one would ever guess inside one of the rocks was a secret tunnel. She memorized the spot where she'd come out.

Following a paved path, her apprehension rose. She had no idea where she was. Insects chirped and buzzed. But she saw no people, no other lights.

Keep going.

Alejandro had planned the outing so she wouldn't get caught. A good thing, Jules knew. She trusted him for the reason she'd told him. She had no other choice if she wanted to sail. She couldn't have pulled this off on her own in spite of her bravado on the beach last night.

She continued walking, unable to shake her uneasiness at being out here secluded yet exposed. Not that she was about to turn around. This opportunity was too important.

Being out here alone, without servants, bodyguards, chaperones or family, was something she rarely got to do. She might be fighting nerves, but the experience gave her a little thrill.

The canopy and walls of rocks gave way to a large field of grass with gardens on either side. The moonlight eased some of her anxiety.

The path led her up a rise. She heard the sound of waves crashing against the shore. At the top, she stopped, mesmerized by the sight of the sea. The beach had to be below her somewhere, but she focused on the water. Light from the full moon shimmered like silver on the crests of the waves.

Jules's breath caught in her throat.

So beautiful.

As she descended the path toward the water, she noticed a light shining. A lone lamppost stood on a short dock with a sailboat moored at the end.

Her pulse rate quadrupled, as did her excitement. She'd found the place without getting lost or caught.

Jules hurried down the path, eager to hop onboard and set sail.

A figure stood in the cockpit of the boat. A man. Alejandro. Her heart gave a little lurch of pleasure.

He waved.

Jules waved back.

Alejandro reached below deck. The running lights illuminated— red on port, green on starboard and white on the stern.

Exhilaration shimmied through her. She could forget about duty and obligation tonight. She could be herself and sail on the ocean like a bird set free from its cage.

With Alejandro.

He motioned for her to join him in the boat.

Shoulders back. Chin up. Smile.

This time it came naturally. No effort required. Jules turned off her headlamp. She no longer needed the light with the lamppost on the dock.

Tingles filled her stomach. She couldn't imagine sharing tonight with anyone else.

* * *

As Julianna walked along the private dock with a clear spring to her step, the tension in Alejandro's shoulders eased. He'd planned her escape from the palace with the precision of a military operation. His efforts had seemed to work. With one foot in the cockpit and the other on the rail, he waited for her to come to him.

She stopped two feet away from the boat. "Your map was spot-on, Alejandro."

He liked the way his name rolled off her tongue. She might sound like the same elegant princess he'd met yesterday, but she looked nothing like the woman who had stared down her nose at him, cried in his arms on the beach and prompted him to rename his cat. The disguise had completely changed her appearance.

He looked beyond her to the path leading up to the cliff, but only saw a few trees. Anyone who ventured out here on this late night would be trespassing. He'd picked this secluded spot for that reason. "Were you seen?"

"Not that I know of," she said. "Though I doubt anyone would recognize me if they saw me."

A satisfied smile settled on his lips. "You're right about that."

Baggy clothes covered Julianna's feminine curves and round breasts. A short, brown wig and America's Cup baseball cap hid her luxurious blond hair. With all the makeup scrubbed from her face, no one would mistake the fresh-faced kid for fashion icon Princess Julianna of Aliestle.

"You look like a teenager," he added.

"A teenage boy," she clarified. "You picked an excellent disguise for me."

She sounded appreciative, not upset. That surprised him a little. Most women wouldn't want to look like a boy. But then again, she hadn't wanted to get caught. A good disguise had been necessary.

"I had no problems, except Ortiz might want to reconsider his claim about no rats in the palace. I saw mice, and something… larger in the tunnel."

"Ortiz doesn't know about the tunnels. Only the royal family knows of their existence and an architect long dead," Alejandro explained. "The tunnels were built by pirates to hide treasure. When the king had them attached to the palace, a hand-selected crew was used. They were blindfolded and had no idea where they were working."

"How did the royal family find out about the tunnels?"

He grinned. "Supposedly my great-great-great grandfather was a king and pirate."

She laughed. The intoxicating sound floated on the air and made him want to inhale.

"You think that's funny."

"A little," she admitted. "But I'm not surprised you come from a line of pirates."

"Not a line," he clarified. "One pirate."

Amusement gleamed in her eyes. "If you say so."

"I do."

"Aye, aye, Captain," she teased.

It was his turn to laugh. Alejandro liked knowing he wasn't the only black sheep in his illustrious family line. He'd embraced the fact he had a pirate ancestor and thought others might, too. The island could capitalize on the colorful past except his father and brother didn't want the knowledge made public. "Ahoy, matey."

With an eager smile, she inspected *La Rueca* from bow to stern. "Lovely boat."

"I'm pleased with how she turned out." Alejandro touched the deck. He'd put everything he knew about boats and a fair share of money into her design. "Though she is untested in an actual race. The Med Cup will be interesting."

"You don't sound concerned."

"I'm not." If he were, he wouldn't have entered *La Rueca* in the race. "I'm confident she can perform and be competitive with the right wind and crew."

Julianna looked at the boat's name written in script on the stern. *"La Rueca."*

"The Spinning Wheel."

"Interesting name."

He stared at her slightly annoyed. "I already caved on the

kitten. Are you going to challenge me on my boat's name, too?"

"No, but I'm curious if it has a special meaning."

"Most boat names do."

"What's the meaning behind yours?"

Alejandro remembered how persistent she'd been about the kitten's name. He had to tell her something. "*La Rueca* is a reminder that I haven't been spinning my wheels when it comes to boatbuilding."

"Spinning your wheels?" she asked.

Wanting to put an end to this topic of conversation, he lowered his one foot to the floor of the cockpit, reached back and started the outboard motor. He left it running in neutral. "Now is not the time."

"Later?"

"Do you always pester so much?"

"I'm sorry." Julianna raised her voice to talk over the idling motor. "Occupational hazard."

"Of being a princess?"

"Of having four younger brothers who never tell me anything unless I pester and pry. They are the only males, men, I'm allowed to be alone with for any extended period so they get the brunt of my curiosity." She looked around, not meeting his eyes. "Being out here with you like this…"

His annoyance disappeared. He appreciated her honesty. He also acknowledged the risk she was taking.

"It's okay. I'm not used to having a sister around." Though he didn't feel brotherly toward Julianna at all. "This is new for both of us."

She smiled softly. "I hope *La Rueca* turns out to be everything you wish for."

"Thanks. It's looking pretty good." And it was. A new sailboat design, a full moon and a beautiful woman to share a sail with tonight. She was so easy to talk to. He liked how she laughed.

Remember, sister-in-law. Julianna belonged with Enrique, not Alejandro. The realization left him feeling adrift.

Time to set a new course. They'd spent enough time talking.

The longer they were out here, the more likely they were to be caught.

Alejandro extended his arm from the cockpit. "Climb aboard."

Julianna's hand clasped and melded with his. Heat shot up his arm. The reaction startled him, but he didn't let go. Truth was, he liked how her hand fit in his.

Her disguise might fool others, but not him. He knew she wasn't a teenager but a grown woman with lush, feminine curves. He'd held her in his arms and smelled the sweet fragrance of her shampoo. He wouldn't mind doing that again.

She stepped onto the boat and released his hand. As Alejandro flexed his fingers, she inhaled deeply. "I love the salty air."

"Wait until you get a taste of the sea spray."

"I'm looking forward to it." Gratitude shone in her eyes. "Thank you for going to so much trouble. Not many people would do this for a total stranger."

"It's my pleasure." And it was. Julianna looked so young, eager and pretty. Very, very pretty. "Besides you're not a stranger. You'll be family soon. My sister-in-law."

Alejandro said the words more for his benefit than hers. He waited for her to respond, but she didn't.

Julianna stared up at the clear, starry sky. The moonlight made her ivory complexion glow. Enrique didn't seem to understand the lovely princess from Aliestle. She was more than a showpiece, more than her dowry. She was a stunning, intelligent woman... Alejandro wondered why King Alaric had picked Enrique to be her husband. His brother had some admirable qualities, even if they disagreed over how best to help their country. But Julianna could do so much better.

"The weather is cooperating with us tonight." Her voice sounded lower, a little husky...sexy. Desire skimmed across his skin. "Lucky," she added.

Getting lucky tonight would be the perfect end to a midnight sail. Not that she would. Or he...

Yes, he would. The thought brought a lump of guilt to his throat.

"Let's get underway. I'll cast off." He motioned to the wheel. "Are you comfortable steering while we motor away from the dock?"

"Yes." She made her way toward the wheel. He moved out of her path, but her backside brushed him.

Heat burst through Alejandro. What the hell?

He didn't understand why he kept reacting to Julianna. She was his ticket to an independent life. He needed to control himself. A mistake could cost him his freedom from his father and the monarchy.

Some distance from Julianna would be good. Alejandro walked forward to the bow.

Maybe he should hit the clubs later tonight and connect with a pretty young thing. That would be the fastest way to get rid of whatever tension had built up and was stirring inside of him.

He pulled up a bumper, removed the bowline from the cleat and tossed the line onto the dock.

She stared up at the wind indicator. "Won't it look weird to be sailing at this hour?"

"No." He stepped over the lifeline, jumped onto the dock and moved to the aft section of the boat. "I always take out my new boats at night so people can't see the designs."

Julianna touched the wheel. "Sounds like boatbuilding is a competitive field."

"Everyone is looking for an edge." Alejandro pulled up the other bumper and unfastened the line from the boat's stern cleat. The rope fell to the dock. He stepped onto the boat with his left foot, shoved the boat away from the dock and hopped aboard with his right foot. "I'd rather they not steal mine."

"Confident."

"If I wasn't, I would crew on someone else's boat for the Med Cup. A boat that was a top contender."

Julianna reached back, shifted the motor to forward and twisted the throttle. She steered clear of the dock and headed out to open water. "Do you race a lot?"

"Not as much as I would like due to my royal obligations, but I hope that will change in the near future."

And it would. After Julianna married Enrique and they had a baby, Alejandro would have as much time as he wanted for business and sailing.

"Looks like there's a nice easy breeze tonight." She shot him an expectant look. "Ready for the mainsail."

It wasn't a question.

Interesting. She knew what to do without him saying a word. He hadn't expected that from her. Saying you enjoyed sailing while sipping a glass of wine and knowing what to do when you were onboard were two completely different things. Alejandro hadn't known what kind of sailor the princess was. So far, he was impressed by her knowledge. "I'll raise the main."

As he moved forward to the starboard side of the mast, she turned the boat head to wind.

Pointing the bow into the wind wasn't something instinctual. That took experience or good instruction. Whichever the case for Julianna, his respect increased.

"You know what you're doing out here." Alejandro yelled to be heard over the motor. He raised the mainsail with the halyard. "How long have you been sailing?"

"Since I was seven." She tailed the halyard and secured the line at the cleat on the top of the cabin. "My grandparents taught me how to sail on the Black Sea. Best vacation ever. How long have you sailed?"

"As long as I can remember." Alejandro shifted to the port side of the mast to hoist the jib, a triangular sail set forward of the main. He saw no other boats on the water. "Both my parents sail."

Julianna turned the wheel right to ease the bow starboard and trimmed the mainsail so it filled with the wind. The boat steadied and glided forward through the water. "I can't imagine anyone not sailing if they lived here."

The awe in her voice made him smile. "Me, neither."

She throttled down the motor, shifted to neutral and killed it.

The sudden quiet gave way to the sound of the hull cutting

through the water and the breeze against the sails. Better get to it and make the most of the time they had out here.

Her sailing skills impressed him, but he wasn't going to assume what she knew or didn't know. "Ready for the jib."

She held the starboard sheet in her hand. One step ahead of him again. "Ready."

He hoisted the jib while she tailed the jib halyard. She secured the sheet by wrapping the rope around a cleat.

Alejandro moved aft to the cockpit. "Nice work."

With a wide smile, she gripped the wheel. "Thanks."

He gave her a compass heading.

Her eyes widened. "You want me to take the helm?"

She sounded like a teenager who'd been given the keys to a brand-new car. He almost laughed. "You've got the wheel."

"I do, don't I?" Her grin was brighter than the full moon. She repeated the heading and turned toward the dock.

"Want to go back?" he asked.

As she shook her head, the cap didn't budge. "I want to make sure I have my bearings and know what the area looks like for our return."

Smart thinking. "You've sailed at night before."

"A few times, but I'd do the same thing if it were daytime."

His respect for her sailing abilities went up yet another notch. Alejandro trimmed the jib, adjusting the sheet to match her course and ensure the sail filled properly. Julianna adjusted the mainsail to match the heading.

He reached back and raised the motor out of the water. Now they would really move.

La Rueca accelerated through the water. Julianna kept her course, making minor corrections as she headed upwind. She seemed to have a feel for the boat as well as the wind.

"I love it out here." The look of pure joy on Julianna's face took Alejandro's breath away. "This is heaven. And you're an angel for doing this for me."

No angel. Not when he was getting turned on watching her sail. The gleam in her eyes. Her smiling lips. Her flushed cheeks.

He focused on the sails. They had filled perfectly, no trimming necessary.

"We're going to need to tack," she said.

He held onto the jib sheet. "Whenever you're ready."

"Tacking."

Alejandro bent over to avoid the boom as it swung across to the other side. The sails luffed, flapping in the wind. He pulled in the sheet. She trimmed the main.

Julianna sailed at a forty-five-degree angle to the wind.

The boat heeled. She leaned over the side to stare at the bow.

As the boat headed upwind, she tacked back and forth to keep the boat moving. With each direction change, the two of them worked together managing the sails with the sheets. Words weren't necessary. They both knew what to do. Perfectly in sync, like they'd done this a hundred times together. Alejandro continued to be amazed by Julianna's knowledge and skill.

He'd never seen someone with such a natural talent. She handled the boat as if it were an extension of herself. She seemed to know when the wind was going to change, and the perfect course to set to maximize the boat's speed.

With the wind on her face, she stared up at the full moon.

His heart lurched. She was truly stunning.

"This is even better than I imagined." Julianna's gaze met his. "Being out here on the sea like this… It's intoxicating."

He felt the same way being around her. "You steer like you've been sailing on the sea your entire life."

"Thanks," she said. "I love the way your boat responds."

"I love the way the boat responds to you." He wondered how she would respond to him, to his touch, to his kisses.

She eyed him curiously. "I'm sure she responds this way with any helmsman."

"Guess again," he admitted. "You handle *La Rueca* better than anyone else."

"Including you?"

"Yes."

She laughed. As before, the sweet sound carried on the wind.

Alejandro wanted to reach out and capture it, a song to remind him of this perfect sail.

He wished the evening wouldn't have to end. As much as he'd like to keep Julianna out here all night, he couldn't. They'd sailed longer than he intended.

"Come about," he said. "And head downwind."

"Can't we head up a little farther?"

"It's time to go back." The disappointment in her eyes knotted his stomach. "You don't want to sneak into the palace when it's daylight. If your maid finds a blond wig and pillows in your bed…"

"That would be a disaster." Julianna gripped the wheel until her knuckles turned white. "Coming about."

The boat turned around. They sailed with the wind at their backs, running with the wind.

But Julianna no longer smiled. The sparkle disappeared from her eyes. She looked so…resigned.

Alejandro didn't like the change in her. Being out here on the water had set her free. The sailor with him tonight was the real Julianna. He didn't want her to put on a princess mask and have to wear it for the rest of her life. "Perhaps another time we can—"

"There can't be another time." She sounded dejected, sad. "This is my last sail. At least until Enrique changes his mind."

Her words echoed through his brain. He firmly rejected them. "I know it's forbidden and you can't risk being caught, but you're so happy out here."

"It's my fate."

Screw fate. Happiness was important, too.

Her last sail?

Not if Alejandro had any say in the matter.

CHAPTER SIX

WITH THE BOAT secured to the dock, Jules stood in the cockpit. She checked a sheet and wrapped it in a figure-eight pattern around a cleat. No way was the rope coming undone. Too bad her future couldn't be secured as easily.

The sail was over. With a sigh, she glanced at the bow. Soon she would be back in the palace. The thought squeezed her heart.

Below deck, Alejandro rummaged around, looking for a sail bag. Before long it would be time to go.

Emotion welled up inside her. She didn't want to return to reality yet. Nothing awaited her except a life of duty. Okay, she was being a total drama princess, but this once she would allow herself that luxury.

As the breeze picked up, the mast, standing so tall and strong, caught her attention. She closed her eyes and breathed in the salt air. The wind caressed her face. She could almost believe she was...free.

"Found it," Alejandro said from below.

Her eyelids flew open.

He climbed into the cockpit. "I need to organize the equipment."

"I'll do it for you now."

"It's too late."

Maybe for him. "I'll help you stow the sails."

"Good idea." Alejandro stood on the luff side of the mainsail. "We'll get out of here faster with two pairs of hands."

Her shoulders slumped. She should have offered to do the sails on her own. Getting out of here faster was the last thing she wanted.

She took the leech side. Together, they flaked the sail, layering the fabric across the boom. He secured the main with ties.

"What about the jib?" she asked.

He turned off the boat's running lights. "I'll take care of it when I get back."

Back? He was going out after this. To a club? The thought made her spirits sink lower. She should forget about it. Him. But she couldn't. "Where are you going?"

"I'm walking you back to the palace."

His chivalry pleased her, but she'd found her way to the dock on her own. She didn't need to be escorted back. A slow walk through the park on the way to the tunnels would keep her free a little while longer. Jules wanted as much extra time outside the palace as she could get. "I can find my own way."

"I know you can, but I'm going to escort you back."

"Okay." Jules caved like a house of cards. Truth was, she liked being with Alejandro and wanted to spend more time with him. Oh, she'd see him around the palace, at events and during meals. But given his relationship with Enrique, this might be their last chance to be alone.

She felt a pang in her heart.

The moonlight cast shadows on his face. With his strong jaw, nose and high cheekbones, he did look more pirate than prince. Too bad he wouldn't kidnap her, sail away with her on his boat and ravish her…

A smile tugged on the corners of her mouth. She couldn't help herself from daydreaming and fantasizing.

Alejandro was a hottie. He'd come to her rescue more than once. He might consider himself a black sheep, but black knight might be a better term after the sail tonight. He'd gone out of his way for her. Jules would be eternally grateful to him.

If only she could thank him, not with words, but a…kiss. A kiss would make tonight's sail more perfect. She stared at his full, soft-looking lips. A kiss under the full moon.

"Julianna?" Alejandro asked.

Desire flowed through her veins. "Yes?"

"You okay?"

"I'm just thinking." Of kissing him. All she had to do was rise up and touch her lips to his. Tempting, undeniably so. But the rebellious act of sailing was more than enough for the evening, for a lifetime really.

At least her lifetime. Jules took a deep breath.

"About our sail." She touched the boat's wheel, running her fingertips over the smooth edge. "I want to remember everything about tonight."

Everything except Alejandro.

Forget about kissing him. If she was to be Enrique's wife, she needed to bury all memories of Alejandro deep in her heart. Otherwise she would make herself and her marriage miserable, wanting what she couldn't have.

Not that Jules had real feelings for him or vice versa. They'd just met. She was getting carried away after a lovely evening with a fellow sailor. Alejandro hadn't flirted with her. He'd barely noticed her beyond her sailing abilities.

The setting with its full moon, starry sky and ocean breeze was perfect for two people to connect, to kiss. Yet he hadn't gotten caught up in the romantic atmosphere. That was a little... annoying. Maybe he didn't find her attractive.

What was she thinking? She shouldn't want him to hit on her.

"It's too bad we couldn't take pictures," he said.

"Yes." But having a photograph of tonight was too big a risk. If Enrique found it...

Enrique.

Maybe he was the reason Alejandro hadn't made a move on her. He might be the black sheep of the family, but he was an honorable man and not about to kiss his brother's fiancée.

She respected that. Respected him.

If only Enrique was more like his younger brother... Jules swallowed a sigh.

Alejandro double-checked the ties. "Ready to go?"

She took a final glance around. Everything had been stowed or secured, but she was in no hurry to leave.

Waves lapped against the hull. The boat rocked with the incoming tide. The sound and motion comforted her. She ran her hand along the deck, a final farewell to *La Rueca*.

Regret mixed with sadness. "I'm ready."

She exited the boat without taking Alejandro's hand. She didn't need his help. Not anymore.

Touching him again, feeling her small hand clasped with his larger, warm one, would make putting tonight behind her harder. Being with him made her feel so different. She didn't know if that was freedom calling or not. But real life beckoned, or rather would with the sunrise.

Tears stung her eyes. Blinking them away, she headed up the dock. Her nonskid shoes barely made a sound against the wood.

Would the memory of tonight fade into nothingness as she embraced her role as Enrique's fiancée and wife? Jules hoped not.

She glanced up at the sky. A shooting star arced across the darkness.

I wish this didn't have to end.

The thought was instantaneous, and her entire body, from the top of her head to the tips of her toes, felt that way. She kept her gaze focused on the sky. The star and its tail vanished.

What a waste of a wish. Jules should have wished for Enrique to change his mind instead. She blew out a puff of air.

Time to stop pretending. She wasn't living a fairy tale, but it wasn't a Gothic novel, either. She needed to face up to her responsibilities.

Climbing the steep hillside, she ignored the burn in her thighs.

Alejandro caught up without sounding winded or breaking a sweat. He walked alongside her, shortening his stride to match hers. "I hope you enjoyed your sail."

"I did." She forced the words from her tight throat. Making small talk wasn't going to be easy. The walk back made her realize how prisoners at the Tower of London must have felt on their way to the executioner. Though Jules faced a life sentence, not death. A sentence she'd chosen for herself, for the sake of her brother, her children and her country. "Thank you so much for tonight."

"I should be the one thanking you."

Alejandro's easy smile doubled her heart rate. She wanted to scream and cry. If he'd been the firstborn... No, a man like him would never need an arranged marriage to secure a bride. No matter what the amount of that bride's dowry.

"Watching you sail tonight has been a true pleasure, Julianna," he continued. "You're very skilled. Amazingly so."

His words made her stand taller. She needed to focus on the positives, not wallow in what-could-have-beens or what-ifs. "Plying me with compliments, huh?" she quipped.

"I'm telling you the truth."

The sincerity of his words lifted her burdened shoulders and lightened her heavy heart. "That means more to me than you can imagine."

His gaze locked with hers. Seconds turned into a minute. The way he looked into her eyes made her think he was going to kiss her. Jules wanted him to kiss her. Anticipation surged.

She leaned toward him and parted her lips. An invitation and a plea.

"You should be at the helm of *La Rueca* in the Med Cup," he said.

Her breath caught in her throat. "What did you say?"

He repeated the words.

A strong yearning welled up inside of her, a longing that didn't want to be ignored. She started to speak then stopped herself.

What he said was impossible. In fact, he looked as surprised at his words as Jules did. He must have been joking.

She pushed aside her disappointment and laughed. "Oh, yes. That's exactly what I should do. Princess Julianna of Aliestle, helmsman."

Alejandro didn't joke back. His smile disappeared. His eyes darkened.

"You're not laughing," she said.

His jaw thrust forward. "I'm not kidding."

Of course, he was. Jules reached the top of the hill and continued along the paved path through the park. "It's been a lovely evening. Please don't spoil it by teasing me."

"I'm serious." The determined set of his chin made him look formidable. A lot like his father. But she remained unnerved by that. "If *La Rueca* places in the top five, the resulting publicity will boost my boatyard's reputation and raise the island's standing in the eyes of the yachting world. To do that I need you steering the boat."

"Wait." What he said confused her. "You said you were confident in the boat. In your crew."

"That was before I saw you sail. I need you, Julianna."

His words smacked into her like an unwieldy suitcase on wheels a porter couldn't handle and nearly knocked her on her backside. No one had ever needed her before.

"I'm floored. Flabbergasted. Flattered." Jules bit her lip to stop from rambling. She needed to be sensible about this, not emotional. "But we both know I can't race with you. The Med Cup is right before the wedding. Enrique and my father are unlikely to change their minds and allow me to compete, even with you."

"This will be our secret."

Jules considered what he was saying…for a nanosecond. "That's…that's…"

"Doable."

"Insane," she countered. "If I get caught—"

"We'll make sure you aren't."

A mix of conflicting emotion battled inside Jules. Part of her wanted to grab the moment and make the most of the opportunity. But common sense kept her feet planted firmly on the ground, er, path. She forced herself to keep walking toward the grotto.

"We're not talking about a midnight sail with the two of us. I'd have to practice with a crew in daylight. They'd figure out I'm not a boy the first time I said anything." Coming up with a list of reasons this was a bad idea was too easy. "Let's not forget the race officials. A crew roster will be necessary. We can't overlook the media coverage. The press will have a field day if my identity is discovered."

"For someone who's never sailed on the ocean you sure know a lot about what's involved with racing."

"I've raced in lakes, and I've followed various racing circuits for years. I know enough…" Her voice raised an octave. She took a calming breath. It didn't help. "Enough to know that with me at the helm, the odds are you'll lose. I'm not experienced enough."

"Are you trying to convince me?" he asked. "Or yourself."

"You."

"I say you're qualified enough. I want you to be my helmsman."

She felt as if she'd entered a different dimension, an alternative universe. Perhaps this was a dream and La Isla de la Aurora didn't exist. She would wake up in her room at the castle in Aliestle, not engaged. "Consider what you're saying, Alejandro. You're crazy if you want to risk the Med Cup on someone like me."

"Maybe I'm crazy. Certifiably insane. But I know what I saw tonight out on the water. No one else handles *La Rueca* as well as you."

"Have them practice more," she said. "It's late. I must get back to the palace before the sun rises."

She quickened her pace, leaving Alejandro behind. The sooner she reached the grotto, the better. She couldn't listen to him anymore. It hurt too much to think racing on the ocean was even a possibility. That had never crossed her mind given her father's restrictions.

The footsteps behind her drew closer. "Don't run away."

"I'm heading in the wrong direction if I wanted to do that."

"Stop."

Jules did. She owed him that much for tonight's sail.

He placed his hand on her shoulder.

She gasped, not expecting him to touch her.

"Please," he said. "Consider what I'm saying."

Warmth ebbed from the point of contact. She struggled against the urge to lean into him, to soak up his strength and confidence. She wanted to, but couldn't. She shrugged away from his hand and counted to twenty in French. "I've considered it. No."

"Racing will make you happy." He wasn't giving up for some reason. "You love to sail."

"I love to sail, but it isn't my entire life." Jules didn't dare look at Alejandro. She couldn't allow herself to be swayed, even if she was tempted. "I have a duty to my family and country. That is more important than some…hobby."

The word used derisively by her father tasted bitter on her tongue. Sailing was a pastime, but it represented the freedom to live as she wanted and a tangible connection to the mother she didn't remember.

"I can't risk upsetting Enrique." The reality of her situation couldn't be ignored. "If he finds out—"

"Do you really think Enrique's going to send you back to Aliestle and walk away from a hundred-million-dollar dowry because you went sailing?"

Her jaw dropped. So did her heart. *Splat.*

Jules knew her father had set aside a large amount of money for her dowry, but not *that* much. She closed her mouth. She'd always known suitors were after the money, not her. Still the truth stung. "I…can't."

"Yes, you can," he urged. "It'll be worth the risk."

"For you, maybe. Not for me." If Enrique didn't marry her, she'd find herself trapped in a worse marriage, in an old-fashioned country with archaic, suffocating traditions. Her efforts to help Brandt and Aliestle would be futile. Plus, she had her children to consider. "I would love to race. But I can't do all the things I want to do. I must consider the consequences."

"Consider the consequences if you don't race."

The word *no* sat on the tip of Jules's tongue. That word would end further discussion. But her heart wasn't ready to do that yet. She wanted to know what racing might feel like. But reality kept poking at her, reminding her what was at stake. "There are no consequences if I don't race."

Alejandro held her hand. "Your happiness, Julianna."

"I'll find happiness."

"Life on the island will be good for you, but Enrique is self-involved. He'll most likely ignore you."

"Ignoring me will be better than trying to control me," she admitted. "And I'll be happy once I have children. I've always wanted to be a mother. Children will bring me great happiness and joy. I'll devote myself to being the best mother I can be. That will make me very happy."

"Will children be enough?"

They had to be.

"I'm sorry, Alejandro." Julianna pulled her hand out of his. "I must find contentment in the life I'm meant to live. If I believe I can or should have more, that will make the days unbearable."

"You're a wonderful, brave woman."

"If I was brave, I'd say yes even though it would be a really bad idea."

"It could be sheer brilliance."

"Or an utter disaster."

"You want to." Alejandro gazed into her eyes. "I can tell."

Her pulse skittered. She flushed. She did want to. More than anything. "I told you. It doesn't matter what I want. I can't."

"What's really stopping you?"

"Common sense." She raised her hand in the air to accentuate each point. "Duty. Obligation."

"Royal duty doesn't mean making yourself a slave."

"It's not slavery, but a responsibility to build something better."

"I'm trying to build something better here on the island. But you can't pretend to be something you're not," Alejandro said. "However much we love people or have loved them, we still have to be the person we are meant to be. Follow your heart," his voice dipped, low and hypnotic.

Emotion clogged her throat. She'd followed her heart once. Tonight. The thought of doing so again made her mouth water. "I…"

"Say yes," he encouraged. "You won't regret racing."

Oh, she would regret it. Jules had no doubt.

But tonight's glimpse of freedom had spoiled her and made her feel carefree and alive. She wasn't ready for that feeling to end.

"Yes." Her answer went against everything she'd been raised to do or be. She needed to reel herself in and set clear boundaries to temper this recklessness. She remembered her plan from this morning. "I'm saying yes for the same reason I sailed tonight. Once I marry Enrique, things will change. I must honor my husband and my marriage. I will step fully into my role of the crown princess who will one day be queen."

"The people of La Isla de la Aurora have no idea how fortunate they are to have you as their future queen."

"Let's make sure I'm not caught so one day I *can* be their queen."

"That's the number one priority," Alejandro said. "I'll take every precaution to keep your identity a secret. I have as much to lose with this as you do."

His words didn't make any sense. This had nothing to do with him. "What do you mean?"

Alejandro hesitated.

"I want to know what you have to lose," she said.

"My freedom," he admitted. "Once you and Enrique marry and have children, I'll be free from all royal obligations. I can concentrate on business and not have to worry about any more princely duties."

Enrique had said Alejandro didn't want to be royalty anymore. She'd thought Enrique had been exaggerating. Maybe that was what Alejandro had meant about being the person he needed to be. "You really want to turn your back on all your duties?"

"Yes."

She admired his being true to himself while dealing with some of the same burdens she had as a royal, but his wanting to break off completely from his obligations and birthright saddened her. Yet she had to admit, she was a tad envious. Alejandro would sail off into the sunset and do what he wanted, whereas she would carry the weight of two countries' expectations on her shoulders for the rest of her life.

At least she knew he would do everything in his power to keep them from getting caught. "I guess we both have something to lose."

"We're in this together, Julianna."

Yes, they were, but the knowledge left her feeling unsettled. Being out here alone with him did, too. His nearness disturbed her. His lips captured her attention. She still felt an overwhelming urge to kiss him. Even if he was the last man she should kiss.

Keep walking. Julianna saw the grotto up ahead. "We'd better get into the tunnel before someone sees us out here."

"No one will see us." Alejandro spoke with confidence. "I own this place."

"What place?"

He motioned to the land surrounding them. "The dock. The park. Everything you see."

She tried to reconcile this new piece of information with what she knew about him. Enrique had made Alejandro sound as if only sailing mattered to him. "You're a boatbuilder and a real estate investor?"

He nodded. "My goal is to turn the island into a travel hotspot. Most of the tourist traffic goes to other islands along the coast of Spain. La Isla de la Aurora doesn't have enough quality hotels, resorts and marinas to attract the big spenders. My father and brother have a more low-key vision of how to improve the economy. But the Med Cup has helped attract the yachting crowd. Now I have to get the travel industry onboard."

Impressive. And unexpected. He was so much more than she'd originally thought. Not that anything he owned or said or did should matter to her.

But it did. A lot.

She chewed on the inside of her cheek.

"As I mentioned, *La Rueca*'s result in the Med Cup could help that happen sooner," he said. "If we finish well."

We. The realization of what she'd agreed to hit her full force. Pressure to do well. Practice time. Being with Alejandro, a man she was attracted to. One who would be related to her when they finished racing. Oh, what a tangled web she was weaving. No way would she be able to escape unscathed.

"This isn't going to work." Doubts slammed into her like a rogue wave. "Someone at the palace will notice I'm not around if we have to practice a lot."

"Don't worry." He tucked a stray strand of blond hair up into the wig and adjusted the cap on her head. "I'll figure everything out. Trust me."

Jules shivered with desire and apprehension. She would have to trust him in a way she'd never trusted anyone before.

"Do you really think we have a shot at doing well?" she asked.

One side of his mouth tipped up at the corner. "With you at the helm, we have a good shot at not only placing, but winning."

CHAPTER SEVEN

THE SOUND OF voices woke Julianna. Lying in bed, she blinked open her eyes. Morning already. The bright sunlight made her shut her eyes again. But she'd glimpsed enough to know this wasn't her room back in Aliestle. She hadn't been dreaming.

Last night had been real. The sail. Alejandro.

A shiver ran down her spine.

She'd agreed to race, to be on his crew.

Somehow, she would have to be Enrique's conventional princess-fiancée and Alejandro's helmsman. And not let the two roles collide. Her temples throbbed thinking about trying to negotiate between the two different worlds without anyone figuring out what she was doing.

"The princess is sleeping, sir." Yvette's voice became more forceful. "I don't want to wake her unless it's necessary."

"This is important," a male voice Jules recognized as Brandt's said.

She opened her eyes and raised herself up on her elbows.

Yvette wore the traditional castle housekeeper uniform—a black dress with white collar and apron. Her brown hair was braided and rolled into a tight bun. She had the door cracked and held onto it with white knuckles, as if to keep an intruder out. Jules pictured Brandt standing on the other side, trying to sway the young maid with a flirtatious smile.

"I'm awake, Yvette," Jules said. "Send Brandt in."

"The princess is no longer sleeping, sir." Yvette opened the door all the way. "You may come in."

Brandt strode in, looking every inch the crown prince in his navy suit, striped dress shirt and colorful tie. He laughed. "I was out clubbing most of the night yet you're the one in bed. Must have been an exciting night watching TV?"

Jules shrugged. The night had been more exciting than she imagined. She hadn't been able to fall asleep when she'd returned to the palace. Too many thoughts about Alejandro had been running through her brain. Each time she closed her eyes, she'd seen his handsome face, as if the features had been etched in her memory.

She watched her maid head into the bathroom. "What is so important?"

"Prince Enrique wants you downstairs now."

Jules glanced at the clock. A quarter past ten. "Nothing is listed on my schedule."

If so, Yvette would have never allowed her to sleep in. The maid always made sure Jules was ready on time for her scheduled events.

Brandt raised a brow. "It's a surprise."

Her brother sounded amused. That set off warning bells in her head. "Care to enlighten me about this surprise?"

"No."

She tossed one of her pillows at him.

He batted it away. "Hey, don't shoot the messenger. I'm only doing as requested. I assumed you'd rather have me wake you than Enrique."

Alejandro would have been better. Especially if he woke her with long, slow kisses... She pushed the thought away as she fought a blush. Steering the boat was her responsibility, not kissing him. "I'll get dressed."

Brandt held up his hand as if to stop her. "That won't be necessary."

She drew back. "Excuse me?"

Mischief filled his eyes. "Enrique said a robe and slippers are fine."

She made a face. "I don't like the sound of this."

"No worries," Brandt said. "Bring Yvette. She and I will ensure your reputation isn't sullied."

If Jules had been caught last night, her reputation would have been more than sullied. "You've been spending too much time with Father. It's influencing your vocabulary."

"I happen to like sullying young maidens."

She rolled her eyes. "Give me five minutes. I'll meet you in the hallway."

"Don't take any longer," he cautioned. "Enrique said this is important."

Worry shivered down her spine. Had Enrique found out about last night? But if that were the case, why wouldn't he want her to dress before coming downstairs?

Brandt strode out of the room and closed the door behind him.

Jules slid out from under the covers and stood on the rug. Her simple white nightgown looked nothing like what a stylish princess would wear to bed. Her father forbade her to wear any sort of pajamas that were too pretty or feminine because she wasn't married. Forget sexy lingerie. She felt lucky wearing underwire bras decorated with lace. The castle's head housekeeper confiscated purchases she deemed inappropriate by King Alaric's standards.

Yvette returned, holding a lavender-colored, terry-cloth robe and matching slippers. "ma'am."

"I'd rather dress."

"I don't think there is time, ma'am."

Jules heard the sympathy in Yvette's voice. "Do you have any idea what's going on downstairs?"

"No, Ma'am." Yvette helped her into the thick robe. "But people have been arriving at the palace since early this morning. I'm surprised the noise didn't wake you."

Jules had been dead to the world once she'd quieted her thoughts of Alejandro and fallen asleep. She couldn't remember the last time she'd slept so soundly. She didn't remember any of her dreams. A rarity for her. "I didn't hear a thing."

"You must have been tired, ma'am."

She nodded.

Lines creased Yvette's forehead. "Are you feeling well, ma'am? Should I request a doctor be sent to the palace?"

"No worries, Yvette," Jules said. "I'm not sick. Let's go see what Enrique's surprise is all about."

Something good, she hoped. And something that had nothing to do with last night.

Alejandro stared at the attractive, stylish women carrying boxes into the palace's large music room. These weren't members of the normal staff. Not with those long legs and short skirts. His curiosity piqued, he decided to take a closer look and entered the Grand Hall.

Enrique paced with his hands clasped behind his back. Wrinkles creased his forehead. Sweat beaded at his brow. The crown prince looked nothing like the oil paintings of the island's rulers hanging on the walls alongside him.

But Alejandro had seen his brother this way once before, when he prepared for what would turn out to be a disastrous date with a famous movie actress. The spoiled, pampered, egotistical couple had clashed from the moment they said hello. Each expected the other to cater to their whims.

"What are you up to, bro?" Alejandro asked.

"I wondered when the scent of perfume would lead you here." Enrique dabbed his forehead with a linen handkerchief. "Look, but don't touch. The women are being paid handsomely for their services."

Alejandro raised a brow. "I didn't realize you paid for female services."

"Not those kind of services, moron." Enrique sneered. "This is a surprise for Julianna."

"A surprise. Really?"

"Don't sound so shocked." He continued pacing. "She is going to be my wife."

Alejandro wasn't about to forget about that. He'd resisted tasting her lips last night for that very reason. But her agreeing to be his helmsman made up for the lack of kisses.

Asking her to join his crew wasn't his smartest move given consequences involved, but he believed *La Rueca* had a better chance of winning with her behind the wheel. She'd also looked so happy sailing. He wanted to show her how beautiful life could be here. All he had to do was douse his attraction for her, and things would be fine.

"I know." He tried to sound nonchalant, even if he was a little...envious. Enrique hadn't had much luck in the dating department, but he'd hit the jackpot finding a bride. Not that Alejandro was in the market for one himself. "But you've never gone to so much trouble for a woman before."

Any trouble, really. Enrique expected women to fall at his feet. Those with dreams of being a princess and queen would until they tired of his self-centeredness. But Julianna was different...

"The royal wedding will generate a tremendous amount of publicity." He lowered his voice. "Julianna must be dressed appropriately for the ceremony and reception."

Too bad Enrique needed to feed his ego, not please Julianna the way she deserved to be pleased and cherished. Alejandro rolled his eyes in disgust.

"The princess is always at the top of the Best Dressed Lists." He hadn't been able to sleep last night. He'd searched the internet to learn more about Julianna. "She is a fashion icon for women, young and old."

"In everyday clothing, yes," Enrique said. "Being a princess bride is different. I have assembled the top experts here. A dress designer and her team, makeup artists, hairstylists and many others. This is all for her."

Alejandro rolled his eyes. "Don't pretend any of this is for Julianna. It's about how you want her to look when she's with you."

"This is important. The royal wedding will change the island's fortune and future. Everything must go perfectly." Enrique sounded more like a spoiled child than a crown prince. "Today's trial run of our wedding day preparations will work out any kinks and problems. The dress designer will also take care of alterations needed on the wedding gown."

Practical, perhaps, but so not romantic. Julianna was practical. Her words last night about her embracing her marriage told Alejandro that. But the woman who had sailed with stars in her eyes also seemed like the kind who liked the hearts, flowers and violin type of romance. Arranged marriage or not.

"Alterations?" he asked. "I didn't think Julianna had a wedding dress yet."

Enrique smirked. "She has one now."

The look on his brother's face worried Alejandro. "What have you—?"

"Good morning, gentlemen." Julianna walked toward them with Brandt at her side and her maid following.

Julianna looked regal wearing a bathrobe and slippers. Every strand of her hair, worn loose this morning, was perfectly placed. She'd applied makeup, too. Not as much as she usually wore, but enough for him to notice the difference from her clean face last night. No one would guess the perfectly groomed princess had another side, one that had taken her out onto the sea with him until early this morning.

She stopped in front of them. "I was told you wanted to see me, Enrique."

Her formal tone contradicted the casual way she'd spoken on the boat and during the walk back to the palace.

"I do." Enrique beamed. "I have a surprise for you, my lovely bride."

The corners of her mouth tipped up, but her eyes didn't sparkle the way they had last night. Of course, no one would notice that except Alejandro. He found it strange she showed no hint of the woman he'd spent hours sailing with. Her mask was firmly in place, a disguise like the sailing clothes she'd worn.

Julianna rubbed her hands together. Excited or cold, he couldn't tell. "I love surprises," she said.

Alejandro didn't think she would like this one. She wanted freedom, not be told what to wear and how to act on her wedding day. He needed to warn her so she would be prepared. "Why don't you grab Father, Enrique? I'm sure he'll be interested in seeing this."

"Father is attending his weekly breakfast meeting with the head of the Courts. Something you would know if you had a clue about what went on around here." Enrique extended his arm, and Julianna laced her arm around his. "Ready for your surprise?"

She nodded with a hint of anticipation in her eyes.

The woman always hoped for the best. Alejandro respected that about her, but he knew she would only be hurt that much more.

The doors to the music room opened.

Alejandro stared at the floor. He didn't want to see her disappointed.

Julianna gasped.

His gaze jerked up. White satin, tulle and miniature white lights covered the walls of the music room. A thick, white rug lay on the hardwood floor. A white silk curtain separated a third of the room from the rest of it. No expense had been spared in transforming the space into a spa complete with a private beauty salon and a massage table.

Impressive. Enrique had managed to get it right this time. If only his motivation had been for his bride and not himself. Alejandro glanced over at Julianna.

She surveyed the entire room with wide-eyed wonder. "What is all this?"

"Everything you'll need to prepare for our wedding day," Enrique said proudly. "This will be your bride room."

"Oh, Enrique." Her smile widened. "I can't believe you would go to all this trouble."

Don't believe it, Alejandro wanted to shout. This was nothing but smoke and mirrors on the part of his brother. Ambition and pride run amuck à la Lady Macbeth. But Alejandro saw how moved Julianna was. He wanted her to be happy, even if that meant she was happy with his brother. Enrique might get Julianna the princess, but Alejandro took fierce delight in getting Julianna the sailor.

"This is amazing, Enrique," Brandt said. "Thank you so much."

Even Brandt had been fooled.

Enrique kissed the top of Julianna's hand, the gesture as meaningless as the over-the-top display in the music room.

"It was no trouble at all." Enrique's smooth tone made Alejandro want to gag. "Anything for my princess bride."

Julianna's eyes didn't sparkle, but they brightened. She looked relieved, pleased with what she saw in the music room and with her fiancé. "Thank you."

Warmth and appreciation rang out in her voice. Perhaps she would be content, even happy, in this marriage. But Alejandro couldn't shake his misgivings.

Enrique's chest puffed out. "There's more."

Alejandro had to admit he was curious, but in a train-wreck-waiting-to-happen kind of way.

With a grand gesture of his arms, Enrique motioned for the curtain to be opened. Two young women, both dressed in the same hot pink above the knee dresses and black sling-back stilettos, opened the white silk curtains to reveal a wedding gown on a busty mannequin wearing a diamond tiara and a long lace veil.

"Surprise," Enrique shouted with glee.

Julianna gasped again. Not in a good way this time. A look of despair flashed across her face before her features settled into a tight smile.

Alejandro didn't blame her for the reaction.

A cupcake. That was his first impression of the gown. The frilly dress with big puffy sleeves, sparkling crystals and neatly tied bows would look perfect on a Disney princess, but not on Julianna. She would look like a caricature of a princess bride in that dress.

Julianna should wear a more sophisticated, elegant gown with sleek lines to show off her delicious curves. He imagined her walking down the cathedral aisle in such a dress and pictured himself waiting for her...

What the hell?

Alejandro shook the image from his head. He wasn't looking for a girlfriend, let alone a bride. Especially one who was already engaged and held the key to his freedom.

Julianna stared at the spectacle of a dress in front of her. Tears welled in her eyes.

"I told you she would like this." A smug smile settled on Enrique's lips. "She's crying tears of joy."

Alejandro balled his hands. He barely managed to keep his fists at his sides. He wanted to punch his brother in the nose and knock some sense into his inflated, ego-filled head.

The guy had to be a narcissist not to realize Julianna was horrified, not joyful. Either that, or Enrique was that dense about women.

"That is my sister's wedding dress?" Brandt asked with a tone of disbelief.

Enrique nodded, visibly pleased with himself. "I told the designer to create a royal wedding dress fit for a fairy-tale princess bride."

"When?" Julianna muttered. "When did you tell her that?"

"A while ago," Enrique admitted. "When my father decided I should wed."

Julianna pressed her lips together. Alejandro didn't have to be a mind reader to know what she was thinking. Enrique had requested the gown for a generic bride, not with Julianna in mind.

More proof this show today was for Enrique's benefit, no one else's. He knew exactly how *he* wanted things. Who cared about anyone else, including his bride who hadn't even been considered in the dress design?

Alejandro had come up against his brother's ego many times. He'd lost most battles and won a few, but he'd never been so angry with Enrique as he was now.

"Try on the dress," Enrique urged.

Alejandro waited for Julianna to speak up, to say she wanted to pick out her own wedding dress.

She squared her shoulders.

He smiled. This should be good.

"Let's go see how the dress looks on me, Yvette." Julianna set off toward the wedding dress with her maid in tow.

Alejandro stared in disbelief. Julianna had no problem

yesterday speaking up to him, showing sass and spunk when it came to Boots's name and being helmsman. He couldn't understand why she remained silent now.

He glanced at Brandt. Surely the crown prince would stand up for his big sister? But he followed Julianna without saying a word.

What was going on? Alejandro watched from the other side of the music room as they approached the atrocious wedding gown.

"I knew this was a good idea," Enrique said in a low, but singsong manner.

Alejandro gritted this teeth. "A bride should choose her own gown."

"This was part of the wedding negotiations with King Alaric."

"The king approves of Julianna wearing a dress you picked out?" Alejandro asked.

Enrique nodded. "King Alaric paid for all of this, including the wedding gown I commissioned months ago. The old fool is so desperate to have grandchildren he agrees to anything I ask for. He's giving me an extra ten million if I keep Julianna from ever sailing again. Imagine that."

"I can't." Outrage tightened Alejandro's jaw until it ached. For that amount of money, Enrique would never change his mind about Julianna sailing again. "Especially since she seems to enjoy the sport."

"She'll get over it." Enrique's brush-off bothered Alejandro more than usual. "Remember, she has me. That will be enough for her."

His brother's uncaring attitude roused Alejandro's protective instincts. Someone had to take a stand for her. "Julianna might be happier if—"

Enrique cut him off. "Her happiness isn't my priority. I only care about her dowry, ability to produce heirs and obeying my orders."

Alejandro had never seen his brother act so callous. "This is wrong."

"I'm treating her the way she expects to be treated. Women in Aliestle are used to being ordered about. It's all they know."

"Enrique, don't—"

"Enough." Enrique sneered. "If you say a word to Julianna or Brandt about any of this, I'll shut down the Med Cup this year."

"You can't cancel the race."

"I can, and I will."

With the threat hanging in air, he strutted toward the others like a proud peacock.

Alejandro seethed. He needed his brother to marry if he wanted to be released from his princely duties and obligations. But what would the cost of that freedom be?

He stared at Julianna. She touched the skirt of the wedding dress with a hesitant hand. She claimed marrying Enrique was better than returning to Aliestle. Alejandro had his doubts.

The women in pink removed the frothy confection of a wedding gown from the mannequin. Julianna and her maid followed them behind a white, fabric-paneled screen.

Enrique's threat made it impossible for Alejandro to take action. Not that he could stop the royal wedding since Julianna wanted to marry his brother. But Alejandro could do something else.

He could make the Med Cup race memorable for Julianna. He could show her how skilled and talented she was. He could make her see she deserved the best from the crew, the staff and most especially, her husband.

That was the least Alejandro could do for the beautiful princess bride. And he would.

I look like a puff pastry.

Jules stared at her reflection in the three-part mirror with horror. She couldn't believe Enrique wanted her to wear this monstrosity at their wedding. She'd thought for a few short moments he'd wanted to make her happy and gone to all this trouble to make her feel…special. But he hadn't.

Do you really think Enrique's going to send you back to

Aliestle and walk away from a hundred-million-dollar dowry because you went sailing?

Alejandro's words reaffirmed what she knew in her heart and her mind. Enrique only cared about her dowry. He'd made it sound like all this had been for her, but it was really for him. She'd overheard the manicurist talking to the hairstylist about putting together a list of improvements for the crown prince. No one cared about Jules's opinion.

Thank goodness Enrique hadn't stuck around long. Otherwise she might have said something impolite. At least she didn't feel quite so guilty about agreeing to sail in the Med Cup and going behind his back.

One of the women in pink raised the hem of the dress. Tulle scratched Jules leg. "We'll need to add another ruffle."

No. Her stomach churned. Not another ruffle. The dress had too many as it was.

She inhaled to calm herself. The potent mixture of the different perfumes the women wore made her cough. Her eyes watered.

Delia, the dress designer, and her team jotted notes and marked the dress with pins.

Jules tried to ignore them. She needed a distraction. A quick survey of the room yielded nothing. Alejandro must have left before Enrique. She would have to rely on her own imagination.

She imagined being on *La Rueca* and holding the wheel in her hands. The metal felt smooth beneath her palms. The boat heeled and water splashed against her face and wet her clothes. Alejandro manned the jib sheet, his flexed muscles glistening from a combination of sweat and water. He glanced back at her. His handsome face filled with pleasure, his dark eyes gleaming with hunger for her. An answering desire sparked low in her belly as the wind whipped through her hair—

"With the dreamy look in your eyes, you must be picturing your wedding day," a woman's voice broke through Julianna's thoughts.

She turned off the romantic scene playing in her head and brought herself back to the present.

"You look gorgeous, ma'am." Delia motioned to the women in pink. "Let's button up the back to see how the gown fits."

Jules didn't—couldn't—say anything. She'd rather daydream about sailing with Alejandro than think about marrying a man who would have a wedding gown designed for a nameless, faceless bride. A dress more suited for a younger woman who wanted to be a fairy-tale princess, not a woman a couple of years away from turning thirty. The thought of walking down the aisle wearing the dress filled her with dread.

Don't think about that. She imagined herself with the wind on her face, the taste of salt in her mouth and Alejandro next to her.

Someone pulled on the left side of dress. "It's a little tight."

Jules pretended the lifeline tugged against her, keeping her attached to the boat. With iffy weather and big waves, falling overboard could be fatal.

As would be continuing to fantasize about Alejandro.

"It'll fit," another woman said.

The pressure around Jules's midsection increased. She felt as if she were caught in the middle of a tug-of-war game. The air rushed from her lungs, forced out by whatever was being tightened around her.

"Can't breathe," Jules croaked.

"Release the buttons and strings," Delia ordered.

The women did.

"Thank you," Jules said.

"Sorry, Ma'am." Delia's cheeks flushed. "The dress is too large in the bust and too small in the waist. I'll take measurements so I can alter the gown."

Enrique must have given the measurements for his idea of the perfect bride. Jules wasn't surprised he wanted an eighteen-year-old woman with the proportions of a real-life Barbie doll. She remembered the room he'd picked out for her with the garden view to make her happy. One of Enrique's problems was he assumed everyone's tastes were the same as his own or should be.

Using a measuring tape, the designer and her assistants took measurements and scribbled notes.

Jules wanted to laugh at the absurdity of it all, but despair crept along the edges of her mind, threatening to swamp her. The reality of what kind of marriage she would have had become clearer.

Running away, giving up duty and family for happiness, no longer seemed like such a drastic measure. She could shuck the awful dress and flee. No more grinning and bearing it. No more doing what everyone else wanted her to do.

But that behavior wasn't any more her than the wedding gown. Jules wanted a better future for her children and her country. She had a plan. She would have to be content with her sailing rebellion.

"That is all we need, Ma'am," Delia said. "I'll start to work on the alterations right away. I shall also remove some of the bows and layers. Prince Enrique talked about a fairy-tale princess dress. That led me to believe you were younger. My mistake."

"You've worked hard on the dress, Delia. The craftsmanship and quality are outstanding. I know you've delivered the wedding dress Prince Enrique asked for," Jules said. "But I'm twenty-eight. Not eighteen. Anything you can do to make the gown a little more…subdued would be appreciated."

Delia bowed her head. "I understand, ma'am."

The woman's empathetic tone told Jules the designer understood. Was that enough to make up for her having to wear the dress and marry an egotistical crown prince? She exhaled on a sigh.

Enrique was to be her husband. She had to make the best of the situation and the most of the opportunity. Jules straightened. "So where am I to go next?"

"The massage table, ma'am." Yvette read from a sheet of paper. "Then you're to have a pedicure and manicure before seeing the hairstylist and makeup artist."

"I'll be all made up with nowhere to go," she said, trying to sound lighthearted and cheerful.

"You do have someplace to go, ma'am." Yvette waved a piece paper. "I received an updated itinerary for today. You, Prince Brandt and the royal family are attending the ballet tonight."

Jules hoped that included Alejandro. Her heart bumped. The thought of seeing him again—make that racing with him—was the only thing keeping her going right now.

Thank goodness she'd said yes to being his helmsman or she didn't know what she would do. The memory of racing would keep her going until she had children to love.

Maybe she would get pregnant right away.

On her wedding night.

With Enrique.

The thought of being intimate with him seared her heart. Tears stung the corners of her eyes. She looked up at the elaborate crystal chandelier hanging from the ceiling and blinked. Twice.

Jules knew better than to let her emotions show. She'd been trained from a young age to hide her true feelings. She had to be more careful or someone might discover the truth about how she felt.

Shoulders back. Chin up. Smile.

She looked at Yvette. "So, which ballet will I be seeing?"

CHAPTER EIGHT

THE SUN HAD yet to peek over the horizon. As Jules made the early morning trek to Alejandro's boat dock, her headlamp illuminated the way through the darkness. The scent of cut grass hung in the air. The smell was new, different from the night before. Someone must have mowed yesterday. Or maybe she was paying closer attention this time.

Knowing where she was going made the walk easier. But the stillness was a little eerie. Even the insects seemed to have called it a night. If only she had gotten more sleep…

Jules yawned.

The four-hour ballet and the dessert afterward had dragged on into the wee hours of the night. She'd slept for three hours before having to wake and prepare for this practice. She felt half-asleep.

Too bad the Lilac Fairy from the ballet couldn't lead a handsome prince to Jules. A kiss might wake her up, especially if the kiss came from a certain prince.

Alejandro.

Warmth balled in her chest.

He'd been at the ballet for the first act, long enough to slip a note about this morning's practice into Jules's beaded clutch. He'd left the royal family's private box before the start of the first intermission, well before the kissing happened in act two. She'd been sad to see him go. Not for any other reason than she enjoyed his company, she decided.

Jules knew she would never be anything more than Alejandro's sister-in-law. Anything more would be wrong. But she allowed herself the luxury of daydreaming about him until her wedding day. A guilty pleasure, yes. But a necessary one if she wanted to make it through her engagement without losing her mind.

Jules wanted to like her future husband. She wanted to fall in love with him. But he wasn't making it easy. He'd paraded her around like a puppet bride on a string during both intermissions. Enrique didn't want a wife; he wanted a fashion accessory.

She shivered with disgust at the way he'd showed her off and talked about her as if she weren't there. At least he hadn't tried to kiss her good-night.

Forget about it. Him. She needed to focus on sailing.

But Jules couldn't muster the same level of enthusiasm she'd felt venturing out here yesterday. Partly because of what had happened with Enrique, but also because she would be meeting the crew for the first. She wouldn't be Julianna, but J.V., a nineteen-year-old male university student from Germany who knew enough English sailing commands to be an effective helmsman.

Jules wore the same disguise as before, but she didn't know if she could pull off her new identity. The waist of her pants slipped down her hips. She pulled the pants up and rolled the band. Maybe that would make it fit better.

A wave of apprehension swept over her.

Alejandro thought she could do it, but the man exuded confidence. He thought he could do anything. He seemed to believe the same of her, too. Jules wished she was as certain, but all she felt were…misgivings.

At the top of the hill, she stopped.

The sun broke through the horizon casting beautiful golden rays of light through the sky. She inhaled, filling her lungs with the briny air.

Dawn brought a new day, a new beginning. This was hers. She needed to grab it with both hands.

Freedom.

Excitement shot all the way to the tips of her toes.

Alejandro needed her. Well, she needed him and *La Rueca*.

Jules would do whatever she had to do until the Med Cup was over to create memories that would last a lifetime, ones she could share with her children, and she hoped, someday, with her husband.

Not even thinking about Enrique could burst the enthusiasm energizing her now. Jules wiggled her toes inside her boat shoes. She wanted to be down on the dock. She wanted to sail.

Jules removed the headlamp, switched off the power and shoved the device in her windbreaker's pocket. She hurried down the path, eager to climb aboard *La Rueca*.

Men stood on the dock and in the boat. Navy, black, red and white seemed to be the colors of choice for their clothing. Two wore baseball caps. Good, she wanted to fit in.

Still butterflies filled her stomach. She kept descending moving closer to the boat.

A few men glanced her way, gave her the once-over, but not in the way she was used to. That was okay. She didn't want them looking at her too closely.

She studied each and every one of the faces. The crew contained a mix of nationalities and ages. But she didn't see Alejandro with them.

Anxiety rocketed through her.

Where was he? Alejandro hadn't mentioned not being here on his note. She couldn't do this without him. Jules wanted to stop moving, but that would look odd. She didn't want to make the crew suspicious. She forced one foot in front of the other.

Please be here.

A familiar head with dark hair popped up from below deck. Alejandro.

Relief washed over her. She quickened her pace to reach him—the boat—faster.

With the dark stubble on his face, he looked very much like a pirate captain and king. His smile made her breath catch in her throat. "Good morning, J.V."

The rich, deep sound of his voice made her heart turn over.

Jules acknowledged him with a nod. The less she said, the

better. She kept her hands at her sides, too. She didn't want to wave back like a girl, or worse, a princess.

"This is J.V.," Alejandro announced. "The one I told you about. Wait until you see him at the helm. *La Rueca* turns as if she's sailing on rails."

Jules straightened, pleased by his compliment. Living up to his words might be hard. What if she'd gotten lucky the other night with a perfect combination of wind and sea?

The others didn't say anything. They eyed her warily.

Jules wasn't offended. She understood their caution. Alejandro had given her the nod of approval, but she was an unknown quantity. She would have to earn their respect with her sailing. She only hoped she could.

"Hi," Jules said in the deepest voice she could manage.

She shoved her bare hands in her jacket pockets. Shaking hands with anyone would be a bad idea. She'd trimmed her nails and removed the polish, but her hands still looked feminine. Maybe she needed a pair of sailing gloves.

"I'm Phillipe." The bald man with clear, blue eyes spoke with a French accent. She recognized him from races she'd watched on television. "Tactician."

Before she could acknowledge him, Phillipe walked away, unimpressed by her. Uh-oh. This could be interesting since they would have to work closely together.

"I'm Mike. One of the grinders." The burly, brown-haired man, whose job was to crank the winch, sounded like an American. He yawned. "I hope all our practices aren't going to be at the crack of dawn."

Wanting to say as little as possible, Jules glanced at Alejandro.

"J.V. can't miss any of his classes at the university," he answered. "The wind is good in the morning."

"This morning," Mike agreed. "But these early wake-up calls are going to mess with my social life, skipper."

"Chatting on Facebook can wait until after the Med Cup, mate." A bleach blond with a tanned face stepped forward. Friendliness and warmth emanated from his wide smile. "I work the bow. Sam's the name. From New Zealand. Welcome aboard, J.V."

She smiled at him, feeling a little strange that no one could tell she wasn't a boy. Okay, she didn't want to be recognized, but it made her wonder. Were her features that masculine? Was that the reason her father had such a hard time marrying her off?

"Dude, I'm not talking about Facebook," Mike said to Sam. "This girl I met at the club last night is so hot. She's interested, too."

Sam laughed. "In getting away from you."

"Yeah, right. That's why she gave me her number," Mike countered. "I'm texting her as soon as we finish practice. Talk about an amazing rack."

As a red-haired, Irish-sounding guy asked to see the woman's picture, heat rushed to Jules's cheeks. She turned her face away so no one would notice. Her brothers didn't talk like that in front of her. Not even Brandt, who probably considered admiring "racks" a pastime.

"No pics right now, Cody. We'll finish the rest of the introductions later," Alejandro said. "Let's take advantage of the wind and have J.V. show us what he can do."

Jules swallowed around the anchor-size lump lodged in her throat. If she messed up...

No, she shouldn't imagine making any mistakes.

The other crewmembers took their positions.

Alejandro had put his faith in her. She couldn't let him down.

With her insides shaking, Jules boarded *La Rueca*. She removed Brandt's sunglasses from her pocket and put them on. The dark lenses would protect her eyes from the rising sun, but also hide them.

She was a world away from the life she lived, but her training would help her today. A helmsman needed to be cool, calm, calculating. Just like a princess.

Shoulders back. Chin up. Smile.

Jules did all three. As her fingers tightened around the

wheel, she widened her stance. The position felt familiar, comfortable.

"Ready?" Alejandro asked.

She would prove to the crew Alejandro hadn't made a mistake by giving her the helm. "Ready, skipper."

Her smile widened. She sounded like a German. Maybe she could pull this off.

Julianna had done it. Pride filled Alejandro. She'd proved her worth as a helmsman with some world-class sailing.

The three hours on the water went by faster than anyone expected. No one wanted to return to the dock. But Julianna needed to get back to the palace before anyone realized she wasn't asleep in her bed as they thought.

Standing on the dock, Alejandro picked up a line. He glanced at the cockpit where Julianna studied one of Phillipe's charts. With her sunglasses on top of her hat, she looked every bit a teenager. No one suspected differently. Maybe people only saw what they expected to see. The disguise made her appear younger, but nothing could hide her high cheekbones, lush lips or smooth complexion.

Alejandro could watch her all day long and never get bored.

"Skipper," Sam called from the bow. "Toss me the line."

Alejandro did.

"The kid's good." Sam hooked the end around a cleat. "Quiet, but he knows what he's doing. The way he maneuvered around that buoy. Sweet. It's like he's got a sixth sense when it comes to wind shifts."

"Told you."

Sam nodded. "But J.V. seems a bit…soft. We need to take him out. Harden him up. Make him drink until he pukes."

Alejandro's muscles tensed. Having Julianna out here without a bodyguard was bad enough. Granted, he could protect her. No doubt his security detail wasn't far away given his sneaking out of the palace hadn't been necessary this morning. But he wouldn't put her in harm's way, not even for a little hazing by the crew. "J.V. is young. He lives with his overprotective family.

If we have some fun with him like that, he won't be allowed to sail with us."

"Okay, but he's wound pretty tight. Maybe a woman—"

"Leave the kid alone," Alejandro interrupted. "That's an order."

"If you change your mind—"

"The kid's a natural. We need to mentor J.V., not introduce him to a life of debauchery."

"You've never had a problem with debauchery before." Sam grinned knowingly. "Let me guess. The kid has a hot sister."

Julianna was hot. Alejandro smiled.

"You dog." Sam laughed. "I didn't know you liked young pups."

Alejandro didn't. "She's a bit older than J.V., but I'll take what I can get."

That was the case with Julianna until she married. Then he'd be free and she'd be with… He didn't want to think about that.

"Okay. I'll put my plans to corrupt the youngster on hold." Sam winked. "Until you've had your fill of his sister."

A good thing Julianna couldn't hear them. She was huddled with Phillipe going over race strategy in German. No one knew the Frenchman was fluent. Fortunately Julianna was, too. Otherwise her cover would have been blown.

Day one had been a success. Only time would tell what the rest of the days would bring.

But Alejandro was…hopeful.

Jules walked back to the palace through the dark tunnel. The four-footed creatures running alongside her beam of light didn't bother her. Meeting the crew and being accepted by them exhilarated her. The image of Alejandro with his eyes full of pride, a wide smile on his handsome face and the dawning sun gleaming in his hair gave her a boost of energy.

The darkness beyond her headlamp seemed to go on forever, but she didn't care. Jules felt as if she'd already been crowned queen. The only thing she needed was a hot shower. Okay, a nap wouldn't hurt.

She reached the staircase to her closet and climbed the steep, narrow steps to the landing.

Alejandro's plan had worked. Relief flowed through her veins. Sailing on his crew was going to work out fine. She could race and then marry Enrique. No one would know the truth.

Jules pressed on the latch. The secret door opened. She stepped out of the dark passageway and into the closet.

She'd told Yvette not to disturb her this morning and allow her to wake up on her own. But Jules stood at the closet door and listened. No sounds. Yes! Her escape and return had gone off without a hitch.

She closed the secret door.

All she had to do was undress, hide the sailing clothes and—

The closet door opened. Yvette dropped the towel in her hand and gasped.

Stunned, Jules jumped back.

No, no, no, no, no.

Heart pounding, she lurched forward and placed her hand over Yvette's mouth. "Shhhh. Don't scream."

Fear filled Yvette's brown eyes. "Waah wuh wah ma puhsa."

Jules struggled to comprehend the words. She hoped being in the closet would mute their voices. "I'm going to lower my hand. Do not scream. Understand?"

Yvette nodded.

Jules lowered her hand from the maid's mouth. "What did you say?"

"Please don't hurt my princess."

Hurt. Princess. Yvette hadn't recognized her. Jules could still escape.

Her relief lasted no longer than a breath. Escaping into the tunnels wasn't an option. An investigation into the mysterious closet intruder might reveal the tunnels' existence. Worse, she couldn't allow Yvette to be traumatized by this.

Jules's best choice, her only choice, was to come clean and hope for the best. A miracle.

"It's me, Yvette," Jules whispered. "Julianna."

The young woman's brows knotted, but fear remained in her eyes. "Princess Julianna?"

"Yes." Jules pulled off the baseball hat, wig and the nylon cap holding all her hair.

Yvette gasped. "I just saw you asleep in your bed, ma'am."

"You saw pillows and a blond wig," Jules admitted. "Not me."

Yvette stared at her as if she was an extraterrestrial with three eyes, two mouths and purple skin. "What are you doing in your closet dressed like a boy, ma'am?"

The knowledge of the secret tunnels remained safe. For now. "I've been sailing."

Another gasp. "That is forbidden, ma'am."

"Which is the reason for my disguise." Jules needed Yvette to understand what was at stake. "Please, I beg you. Keep my secret in your heart. Never repeat a word of this to anyone."

Especially the tabloids or her father. Fear of discovery made Jules's stomach roll with nausea.

"I don't understand why you would disobey the king, ma'am." The maid sounded dumbfounded. "You've never…"

"I felt as if I had no other choice." In for a penny, in for a pound. Jules needed Yvette's help. That required honesty. Perhaps the truth would bring compassion. "Once I marry Enrique, my life will be the same as it is back home, with similar restrictions. Enrique has forbidden me from sailing again. I know I'm disobeying my father, but I need a taste of freedom. When Alejandro asked me to be on his racing crew—"

"You're sailing with Prince Alejandro?" Yvette's eyes widened, as if scandalized.

Jules nodded.

"But his reputation—"

"May be bad, but I assure you, Prince Alejandro has been a total gentleman."

Unfortunately.

"If King Alaric finds out or Prince Enrique—"

"Neither has to find out. Only Alejandro and you know what I'm doing. The crew thinks I'm a college kid from Germany."

Yvette said nothing. Her eyes looked contemplative. Maybe she was too stunned for words. Or maybe she was totaling how much she could make selling this story to the media.

Jules knew her freedom, at least what little she'd found sailing with Alejandro, would vanish with one wrong word. She took the maid's hands in hers. "I know what I'm asking is wrong, but please don't tell anyone."

The seconds ticked by.

"I'll keep your secret, ma'am," Yvette said. "I pledge my loyalty and promise to help you."

Her words nearly knocked Jules over. "Oh, thank you. I'll find some way to make it up to you. I promise."

"That isn't necessary, ma'am." Compassion shone in Yvette's eyes. "I understand."

"You do?"

"Yes, ma'am. I'd love to escape my job as a palace maid, move to Milan or Paris and work in the fashion industry." Wistfulness echoed in the maid's words.

A kindred spirit. "You have the talent."

"Thank you, ma'am."

"I'm sure we aren't the only ones who wish for something different."

Yvette nodded.

"I can't do much about Paris or Milan, but I can see about getting you a job here on the island."

"Thank you, ma'am, but my family needs me in Aliestle. I don't want to hurt my sisters' marriage prospects."

"I understand, but if you change your mind let me know." Jules had more in common with her maid than she realized. She smiled. "Having your help, Yvette, is going to make sailing in the Med Cup so much easier. Here's what we'll need to do…"

CHAPTER NINE

AS THE DAYS FLEW BY, Jules juggled between playing the role of J.V. and being Princess Julianna. Whenever anyone wanted to see her in the morning, Yvette said the princess was sleeping. No one was the wiser, at the palace or on the crew, in spite of a close call when a strong gust of wind nearly blew her cap and wig off her head.

Jules had found a way to do her duty, as was required by her father and country, and experience freedom, as her heart and soul longed for. But guilt niggled at her.

Being on Alejandro's crew was a crazy, fun adventure, but a temporary one. Her wedding day, however, was right after the Med Cup, yet she'd barely thought about it. Or her groom.

Prince Enrique wasn't the man of her dreams, but he was to be her husband and the father of her children. Their marriage would last for the rest of her life. She couldn't ignore her fiancé, even if he'd been ignoring her.

If love was to blossom, someone had to make the first move. That someone was going to have to be her.

With her resolve in place, Jules walked to Enrique's office. The sound of her heels against the marble floor echoed through the hall.

Enrique's assistant wasn't behind his desk, but the door to the inner office was ajar.

She tapped lightly. "Enrique?"

"Julianna." He rose from a large walnut desk. His gray suit, white dress shirt and red tie were a far cry from Alejandro's casual boating clothes and sexy, carefree style, but Enrique looked regal and handsome. "What brings you here?"

Jules entered the office. "I've hardly seen you this week."

She preferred sailing with Alejandro or her own company to being with Enrique. But she needed to make sure their marriage started out on a solid footing even if he saw her as nothing more than his royal broodmare and arm candy.

"True, but I've been thinking about you." Enrique smiled, but the gesture seemed to be more of an effort to placate her. "You must understand, my princess. There is much work to attend to."

"Yes, you have been busy." She wanted him to show her she hadn't misjudged him. She wanted him to do something to make her want to be with him the way she wanted to be with Alejandro. "Will you be joining us for dinner tonight?"

Enrique hadn't eaten with them the past four nights. Not even her father worked that much, and he was king. Aliestle was a small country, but wealthier and more influential than this island.

"I regret missing dinners." Enrique motioned to the papers on his desk. "But I am working more now so I can take a few days off after the wedding."

I, not we. Disappointment weighed her down. For their marriage to work, she needed Enrique to meet her halfway. "Just a few days for our honeymoon?"

He nodded. "I can't afford to be away any longer."

"I understand." Look at the bright side, Jules thought. They hadn't spent any time alone. Whenever they attended an official event, a security detail and the press accompanied them. And each time they were together, Enrique managed to irritate her more. A short honeymoon might be best. "Duty first."

He sat. "Your sense of duty appeals to me, Julianna."

Her obedience was second only to her dowry.

Stay positive. Enrique might want to lead her around like a champion show dog on a leash, but their daughters could be doctors and lawyers if they were raised on La Isla de la Aurora. Jules forced a smile. "Thank you."

"How is the wedding planning coming along?" he asked.

The question struck her as odd. Enrique made most of the decisions about the royal wedding. Either he was trying to be polite or he thought her that clueless. Neither boded well. But she kept her pride in check. "The wedding coordinators seem to have everything in hand. But I manage to keep myself...occupied."

Her day started at 3:00 a.m. in preparation for the morning sails. Jules returned to the palace for more sleep before heading to town to make appearances and attend functions.

"I love going into the capital," she admitted.

The coastal town looked like something from a postcard with its pastel buildings with tiled roofs, the coffee shops with umbrella covered tables and the open-air markets where people could buy everything from fresh fish to vegetables. Businesses closed in the afternoon for siesta. The relaxed pace reminded her of Alejandro.

Don't think about him now.

"The people are charming," she added.

The citizens of La Isla de la Aurora embraced their Spanish heritage. They spoke English and Spanish with ease often mixing the two languages. Wherever she went, smiles greeted her. The genuine warmth of the people touched her heart. Jules felt accepted here in a way she'd never felt back home. That gave her another reason for wanting this marriage to work. She liked living on the island.

"You've been tired lately," he said with what sounded like a hint of concern. She was surprised he'd noticed.

"A little." Jules made do with what sleep she could squeeze in. "I'm working hard to learn my new role."

Here at the palace and on the boat.

"You're doing well." He sounded pleased. "I saw your picture in the paper this morning. You were at the hospital."

She nodded. "I enjoy visiting the patients, especially the children. There's this little boy. His name is—"

"Stop visiting the hospital until after the wedding," he interrupted. "You could catch a nasty germ there."

"I'm sure you wouldn't want to get sick." The words slipped out.

"That's for certain."

She swallowed a sigh. Once again he was only concerned about himself. "I'm just tired, Enrique. Don't be concerned about catching germs, I'm healthy."

"I know."

Jules drew back. "You do?"

"Our palace doctor spoke with yours."

She didn't know what to say. Had all her fiancés been told about her medical record? Not that she had anything to hide, but still… She hated the lack of privacy. That would never happen to one of her brothers.

Enrique glanced at his computer monitor, distracted by whatever had popped up on his screen. "Is there anything else?"

No, you egotistical tyrant-wannabe, Jules would have said if she had a choice, but she didn't say a word. Like it or not, Enrique was going to be her husband. She couldn't spend the rest of her life fantasizing about his younger brother. She had to make this relationship with Enrique work. Somehow.

"Perhaps we could go out," she suggested. "Just the two of us. On a date," she clarified, so he got the point.

"A date. What a sweet thought. But that's not possible with our upcoming nuptials." He placed his fingers on his keyboard. "Don't fret, my princess. We'll have plenty of time for dates after we're married."

Their first kiss would be at the wedding ceremony. Their first date would be on their honeymoon. The thought of her wedding night made her nauseous.

She straightened. "I'll leave you to your work."

Enrique didn't look up. He didn't mutter a goodbye. The only sound was his fingers tapping on the keyboard.

So much for meeting her halfway. She walked to the doorway.

Time to face facts. If not for the PR opportunity at the

wedding, he'd send a proxy to stand in for him as groom at the ceremony.

Enrique was going to have to have a complete change of heart about her and the marriage for things to work. Even then she wondered if love was possible.

But Jules knew one thing. No longer would she feel any guilt for sailing. She'd tried to make things better, but Enrique had shut her down.

Nothing was going to stop her from having the time of her life with Alejandro and the crew. Nothing at all.

Alejandro couldn't focus. All he wanted to do was look at the picture of Julianna on the cover of this morning's newspaper. He stared at the black and white photograph.

No one would call this vibrant, warm woman an ice princess. The smile on her face reached all the way to her eyes. Those same eyes looked brighter, more alive.

Alejandro wondered if he—make that the sailing—had brought about those changes. Or had it been Enrique?

He hadn't seen the royal couple together in a few days. Enrique had skipped several dinners. Alejandro hadn't minded one bit. He enjoyed spending time and talking with Julianna even with his father and Brandt there. The more Alejandro learned about her, the more he wanted to know. He couldn't wait to see her tonight.

He glanced at the clock. Only two.

The thought of waiting until dinnertime to see Julianna didn't sit well. If he returned to the palace early, he could see if she wanted to spend time with Boots. She enjoyed playing with the kitten.

Alejandro liked playing with her. Or would, if he could…

He'd settle for being alone with her.

She might be on his boat every morning, but so was the rest of the crew. They couldn't talk openly or in a language he was comfortable speaking. She had to play a role, and so did he.

Leaving with her from the dock might raise suspicions, so

she always headed back to the palace alone while he went off to the boatyard.

He looked at the clock again.

Why not take the afternoon off? He rarely did so.

After a quick talk with the boatyard foreman about what needed to be completed today, Alejandro returned to the palace. He found Boots sound asleep in the apartment. The kitten didn't stir when Alejandro picked him up. He went to Julianna's room and knocked on her door.

No answer.

Alejandro knocked again. Nothing.

Damn. He felt becalmed, as if all the wind had left his sails.

"Are you looking for Princess Julianna, sir?"

He turned to face one of the palace housekeepers with a feather duster in her hand. "Yes, Elena, I brought Boots by for a visit."

"Every day the princess tells me how much the kitten is growing." Elena's smile deepened the lines on her face. She'd been working at the palace for as long as he could remember. She used to sneak him food when he'd been grounded for some infraction or other. "The princess is right, sir."

Alejandro hadn't noticed any changes in the kitten. He glanced down. Boots may have gained some weight. But they'd only been living at the palace a little over a week. That didn't seem long enough for the kitten to grow.

Then again Alejandro felt as if he'd known Julianna for years not days. He felt so comfortable around her. "The princess has been sneaking Boots treats. That's probably why."

Elena nodded. "I saw the princess head down to the beach about a half an hour ago."

"Thank you."

Alejandro returned the kitten to the apartment and then headed to the beach.

Clear blue waves rolled to shore. Off in the distance, Julianna sat on the sand. She didn't seem concerned about her white Capri pants getting dirty.

A seabird soared overhead. The white wings contrasted against the blue sky. Another bird swooped and dipped its feet into the water, but the talons came up empty.

Julianna wasn't alone. Her bodyguard, Klaus, stood back. Far enough to give the princess privacy but close enough to react if needed. Alejandro acknowledged Klaus with a nod before approaching Julianna.

As he made his way toward Julianna, the wind caught in her hair. Strands went every which way. She pushed the hair off her face.

He would have liked to do that for her. He remembered how her hair felt, soft as silk, when strands had slipped out of her wig. But with Klaus behind them, Alejandro would have to keep his hands to himself. "Hello, Princess."

Julianna glanced up at him. The combination of the sky and her short-sleeved shirt accentuated the blueness of her eyes. She smiled, looking pleased to see him. "Hi."

"Enjoying the peace and quiet?"

"Yes. I was raised to fear being on my own, but I like it." She raised a handful of sand into the air and let the granules sift from her fingers. A hill of sand formed. "Especially out here by the water."

"I don't want to disturb you."

"You're not." She patted the spot next to her. "Sit."

He did.

Julianna carved into the sand until a rustic castle took shape.

"You need a bucket and a shovel to build a proper castle," he said.

She stuck out her tongue. "Who said anything about this being proper?"

He laughed. "My mistake."

"This castle is different. Special."

Her wistful tone intrigued him. "Tell me about it."

"In this castle, you're allowed to do whatever you choose. The only rule is to follow your heart."

Alejandro shoved his hands into the warm sand to help her dig a moat. "A good rule for any castle, proper or not."

She nodded. "Marriage is encouraged, but only if you've found your one true love."

His hands worked right next to hers. If he moved his left hand, he could touch her. The bodyguard would be none the wiser. Klaus couldn't see past their backs or hear what they were saying. Alejandro inched his hand closer. "Weddings must be rare."

One side of the castle collapsed. She knocked the rest away and started over. "Divorces are rarer."

A little farther... Anticipation built.

Alejandro wanted to touch her, to feel her soft skin against his once more, but doing so would be wrong. He moved his hand away from hers.

"That would be a different kind of castle." While she occupied herself making another mound of sand, Alejandro pulled out his phone, typed in a text message for Ortiz and hit Send. "What about royal duty?"

"Royalty does not exist."

That surprised him. Sailing aside, she seemed so keen on being a perfect princess and having little princes and princesses to keep the royal bloodline going.

"All people are created equal in my castle," she continued. "Whether male or female, wealthy or poor."

"Sounds like a nice place to live."

"It would be nice." Jules stared at the sand. "If I could build it."

The longing in her voice touched his heart. "La Isla de la Aurora isn't perfect, but it's an enjoyable place to live. Though you won't have the kind of freedom here as you'd have in your castle."

She laughed. "It's a fantasy. No place like that exists."

"True." But the freedom he craved did. Her marriage to Enrique would give Alejandro what he wanted. No more pressure or orders to fulfill his royal duties and obligations. Yet was marriage to his brother what Julianna wanted?

"Your castle may be a fantasy, but if that's your dream I don't understand why you want to marry Enrique."

"It's my duty."

"You have a duty to yourself."

She stopped digging in the sand. "I was raised to do whatever is best for Aliestle. I've always known a marriage would be arranged for me. That is the custom. And marrying Enrique is what's best for my family and my country."

She sounded genuine. Patriotic. Alejandro's respect for her grew knowing the sacrifice she was making. "You hold duty in a much higher esteem than I do. You're ready to dive headfirst into an arranged marriage knowing you're sacrificing your dreams. I can't wait to escape the demands of palace life. We are very different."

Her gaze met his. "You want what's best for your country."

"Yes."

"So do I. We're just going about it differently."

Julianna might think so, but he knew better. She was far more worthy than him. "My brother doesn't deserve you."

She shrugged. "He would say I don't deserve him the way I've been sneaking around behind his back."

Alejandro sprung to her defense. "You're helping the island. Once we place—"

"Win."

Her confidence pleased him. "Yes, win, I'll be able to draw more attention to the sailing and tourism here. But my father and brother..."

"They have different ideas."

"They have taken a completely different path," Alejandro said. "Enrique thinks my efforts are too radical. He believes a royal wedding will accomplish the same thing as my plans." Alejandro drew lines in the sand. He wanted to make his own mark somehow. "But I'm not going to let them stop me. I'll turn this economy around and show them."

"I'm certain you will."

He appreciated her confidence. He also liked how her blond hair shone beneath the afternoon sun. So beautiful.

One of the garden staff sprinted across the beach with his arms loaded with colorful buckets, shovels and other sand tools.

He placed them on the sand. "Compliments of Ortiz, Your Highnesses."

Julianna's grin lit up her face. "Please thank him for me."

The young man bowed before walking away.

She shot Alejandro a suspicious glance. "You sent a text to Ortiz asking for all this."

"Sometimes being a prince comes in handy."

The gratitude sparkling in her eyes made it difficult for Alejandro to breathe. "Thank you."

He ignored the quickening of his pulse and handed her one of the shovels. "Let's see if we can build you a castle that will last."

CHAPTER TEN

THAT EVENING, Jules floated down the staircase on her way to dinner. Her sling-back heels felt more like ballet slippers as she descended and the hem of her cocktail dress swooshed above her knees. An afternoon with Alejandro had been exactly what she needed. Building a sand castle had been fun, but being with him had made her heart sing. He'd told her about growing up on the island and listened when she spoke. Something men in Aliestle, including her brothers, rarely did.

Jules wondered if he was in the dining room. Anticipation danced through her. She couldn't talk to him as freely as she had on the beach, but being with him during the meal would be enough.

Realization dawned. She had a huge crush on him.

She giggled like a schoolgirl. That would explain her growing affection toward him. Though crushing on her future brother-in-law probably broke every rule in the princess handbook.

Well, she never claimed to be perfect. Besides, she'd never let the crush go anywhere.

She entered the dining room to find Alejandro and Enrique involved in a heated discussion. As soon as they saw her they stopped talking.

She saw three place settings on the table large enough to seat twenty-four. "Is no one else joining us?"

Enrique kissed the top of her hand. He seemed big on that gesture. But he'd made an effort. She shouldn't complain.

"My father is dining with old friends," he said.

"Brandt is dining with new friends," Alejandro explained. "He took Klaus with him."

No doubt with a push from Alejandro. She would have to thank him later. "Lucky me. I'm a fortunate woman to be dining with two handsome princes."

Enrique stared down his nose at his brother. "Though one of us is handsomer than the other."

Alejandro half-laughed. "In your dreams, bro."

Jules wondered what Enrique would do or say. She hoped nothing.

He ignored his brother and escorted her to the table. That pleased Jules. But his stiff formality overshadowed how suave and debonair he looked tonight in his dark suit. If only he would relax and not always be so...on.

A footman pulled out her chair, and she sat. A server placed a napkin across her lap.

Alejandro took his seat in one easy, fluid motion. He was definitely relaxed. Still he looked stylish in his own right wearing a button-down shirt and black pants. Not too fancy, but not casual. Just...right.

Her admiring gaze met his and lingered. The temperature in the room seemed to increase. Her heart rate kicked up a notch.

His mouth quirked.

Oh, no. He must realize she was staring.

Jules looked away. She took a sip of ice water, but the liquid did nothing to cool her down.

Enrique sat at the head of the table in King Dario's place. The ornate chair befit the king with his confidence and majestic splendor better than his son, who didn't quite emanate the right amount of regality and power. In time that would come, Jules told herself. With more...maturity.

The light from the chandeliers dimmed. Lit candles in foot-tall crystal holders provided a warm glow. Platinum-rimmed china set atop silver chargers stood out on the crisp, white linen tablecloth. A stunning bouquet of roses and lilies in an elaborate silver vase added a light floral fragrance to the air.

A table fit for a future king. And queen, she reminded herself.

"Romantic," Alejandro said.

Very. She forced her gaze off him and onto Enrique. This would be the perfect opportunity for her fiancé to show Jules he was willing to make an effort with their relationship. Oh, she wanted to dine with Alejandro, but if Enrique held out an olive branch, or a red rose in this case, she would gladly accept what he offered.

"You know." Alejandro pushed back from the table. "I'm sure you both would prefer an intimate dinner for two."

He glanced at Jules. She didn't know whether to thank him for the suggestion or not. Her heart debated with her mind over the outcome each wanted. She looked at Enrique, holding her breath while waiting for his answer.

"That's generous of you, but the table is set for three. You're already seated," Enrique said. "Please stay and dine with us. I'd like to finish our discussion."

Relief mingled with disappointment. Jules would get to spend more time with Alejandro, but Enrique should have taken his brother up on his offer. If he'd listened to her in his office, he would have jumped at the opportunity for them to share a romantic dinner alone.

But he hadn't, and he didn't.

Was he that dense or was he trying to make some kind of point? Did he want a chaperone present so rumors couldn't start? No matter what the reason, his decision stung.

She stared into her water glass, not wanting to participate in the brothers' conversation about Alejandro's most recent real estate purchase—a run-down hotel on the opposite side of the island.

The servers brought out the first course. Gazpacho.

Jules waited for Enrique to take the first sip, then did so herself. The cold tomato-based soup was one of her favorites. This version had a little more spices than she was used to, but she liked the tanginess.

Enrique wiped his mouth with a napkin. "I heard the two of you were out on the beach building sand castles today."

Jules stirred uneasily. She didn't want to risk saying too much so took a sip of white wine. The Albarino tasted crisp and fresh, a perfect complement to the acidity in the soup.

"Yes, I bumped into Julianna on the beach," Alejandro said much to her relief. "She was having trouble making a sand castle with her hands so I asked Ortiz to send out some proper tools to use."

"Tools." Enrique snickered. "You mean, toys."

Alejandro didn't look at his brother. He picked up his wineglass and sipped, the same way she had.

Jules recognized the impatience in his eyes. He was trying hard not to say anything. She respected him for not losing his temper. It couldn't be easy letting so much roll off his back. Maybe she could make it a little easier on him this time. He'd come to her assistance by speaking up before, now she could return the favor.

"Having the buckets and tools delivered was a sweet gesture." The afternoon had been a pure delight. The time had flown by with all the talking and laughter. She'd shared her dreams with Alejandro, something she'd never done with anyone else. Not even Brandt.

But Alejandro made her feel safe and, like the people on this island, accepted. He seemed to know her so well—better than her own family. It was easy to open up around him. He'd become a good...friend.

"And much appreciated," she added for Alejandro's benefit. "I would have never been able to build my castle without those items. Especially one that..."

"Lasts." Alejandro raised his glass to her. "Now everyone can live..."

"Happily ever after," she said with a smile.

"You shouldn't have been out there so long." Enrique scowled, seemingly oblivious to how close she'd gotten to his brother. "You're sunburned."

Jules touched her face. "Where?"

He studied her as if she were flawed and should be returned to the store for a refund. "Your nose."

"Fair skin," she said.

"I didn't notice it when you were in my office," Enrique said.

Thank goodness this hadn't been the result of sailing. That would have been a total disaster. "I must not have put on enough sunscreen this afternoon."

"The sun is strong here," Alejandro said. "I should have reminded you."

Enrique nodded, one of the few times she'd seen him agree with his brother. "Makeup will hide the redness. But if you get sunburned any worse, the wedding pictures will be ruined."

Jules knew he expected her to make him look good. She'd have to layer zinc oxide on her nose during the race. Not only would that protect her skin from the sun's harsh rays, but the thick, white lotion would help disguise her face better. "I'll be more careful when we're out tomorrow."

Enrique eyed her suspiciously. "Planning to build more sand castles?"

A lot more careful. She swallowed. Another sunburn would be a dead giveaway she wasn't spending much of the daylight hours asleep in her bed. "No, but I plan to be outside. I was hoping you could join me."

Alejandro nodded his approval.

Enrique didn't notice. "I have meetings."

"You've heard about our afternoon, Enrique," Alejandro said. "Tell us about yours."

"It was more interesting than playing in the sand." Enrique described his day in minute detail.

Jules mouthed the word "thanks." She appreciated Alejandro shifting the focus off her and onto Enrique's favorite subject—himself.

Courses paired with wines to complement the flavors of the dish came and went. Enrique droned on with Alejandro chiming in with comments spoken and muttered under this breath.

The differences between the two brothers became more distinct. Enrique was so focused on himself and his role as crown prince and future king, nothing else mattered. She wasn't sure if he cared who sat at the table with him as long as someone was present to hear him speak.

But Alejandro wasn't perfect, either. His blatant disdain for the responsibilities thrust upon him by his royal birth and his lack of respect for the monarchy made her question his priorities. She wished he wasn't so intent on turning his back on his duty.

Still she enjoyed his company. No one had ever made her feel so…good, capable, alive. Underneath his casual, sailor exterior, Jules saw a man—a prince—who loved his country with his whole heart, the same as her. But he'd been pushed aside due to the birth order and forced to live in Enrique's shadow. And for that, he blamed the monarchy and the rules that accompanied it.

Neither brother was Prince Charming, and that was okay. Such a prince was the thing of legends and fairy tales, like the expectation of her being the perfect princess. Being perfect wasn't possible.

Too bad no one else seemed to realize that.

Jules slumped in her chair, overcome by weariness and emotion. She straightened only to want to relax again. She focused on the food and tried to tune everything else out. It wasn't hard to do.

As soon as the servers cleared the dessert dishes, Jules wiped her mouth and folded her napkin. "Thank you for the pleasant company, gentlemen. I'm going to retire for the evening."

Both men rose as she stood.

"Good night, Julianna," Alejandro said.

"Sleep well," Enrique said. "I want to see my bride's pretty blue eyes sparkling tomorrow."

She moved away from her chair and waited for Enrique to offer to escort her, but his feet remained rooted in place.

Alejandro's gaze met hers in silent understanding. "Sweet dreams."

Jules acknowledged him with a smile. She didn't dare trust her voice. She wanted to have sweet dreams, but she feared the wrong brother would be starring in them. Not only tonight.

But every night for the rest of her life.

* * *

Alejandro's temper flared, but he maintained control.

For Julianna's sake.

She walked out of the dining room with her head high, but the disappointment in her eyes was unmistakable.

Alejandro remained standing until she disappeared from sight. He turned to Enrique. "Why didn't you escort Julianna to her room?"

Enrique had already sat. He motioned to the wine steward to refill his empty glass. "She said she was tired."

Anger burned in Alejandro's throat. "That's why you should have walked with her."

His brother's gaze sharpened. "Why do you care what I do with Julianna?"

Good question. Alejandro sat. He downed what remained in his wineglass. He wanted to say he felt indifferent about her, but he would be lying. He enjoyed being with her whether on the boat or here at the palace. But, rudeness aside, that didn't explain why his brother's treatment of her bothered him so much. "I wouldn't want her to leave the island."

That much was true.

"Never fear, little brother." Enrique snickered. "She can't leave."

"Can't?"

"If Julianna doesn't marry me, she'll be forced to marry a nobleman from Aliestle." His lip curled in disgust. "Any woman with half a brain would want out of that backward country."

Alejandro hated that she had only those two options. She deserved so much more. "Julianna has more than half a brain. She's very intelligent."

"That is why she doesn't mind how I treat her. She knows she must marry me," Enrique explained. "She'll put up with anything I do or say to keep from having to spend the rest of her life stuck in archaic Aliestle where men treat her worse."

Julianna had admitted as much to Alejandro, but that didn't excuse Enrique's behavior. "Her misfortunate situation gives you carte blanche to be ill-mannered and rude to her. How... noble."

Enrique snorted. "This is rich. Relationship advice from the man who goes through women as if they were selections on a menu."

"I may have never been involved in a serious relationship for an extended period of time, but I know women. Better, it seems, than you, bro," Alejandro said. "Julianna isn't an obedient automaton. She has feelings. Dreams. She deserves—"

"She deserves what I see fit to give her."

"Enrique…"

"As long as she obeys and provides me with heirs, be assured she'll have all she needs."

"She needs to be loved and accepted for who she is," Alejandro countered. "If you continue treating her poorly and taking advantage of her situation, you'll alienate her until she can't take it anymore. Is that what you want?"

Enrique leaned back in their father's chair. "You've come up with all this about her after spending an afternoon playing in the sand?"

"You've missed dinners this week," Alejandro replied. "You can learn a lot about a person over seven course meals."

Especially Julianna once she let her guard down and opened up.

"Come on, Alejandro," Enrique cajoled. "You don't care about Julianna. You want to make sure I marry."

"With your marriage comes my freedom from royal obligations."

That was the one thing Alejandro wanted more than anything. Somehow with his growing concerns over Julianna's future he'd lost sight of that. How had that happened?

Letting physical attraction and friendship get in the way of what he wanted made no sense. Julianna was hot, but she was also a princess. She might enjoy sailing, but she would never walk away from her title or her duty. Not for anything in the world. She wanted to help her brother, her country and her future children. The fact that she was willing to marry Enrique after his treatment of her spoke volumes about her priorities and was a not-so-subtle reminder…

As soon as the Med Cup finished and she married, Alejandro

needed to say goodbye. She belonged with his brother, not him.

The truth stung. A sharp pain sliced into his heart. He reached for his wineglass, but it was empty.

"Treat her better." If Enrique did that, he would give Julianna what she wanted—more freedom, a throne and children.

Especially children.

I've always wanted to be a mother. Children will bring me great happiness and joy. I'll devote myself to being the best mother I can be. That will make me very happy.

Julianna's words echoed inside Alejandro's head. He wanted her to be happy. That wasn't like him. He'd never considered a woman's happiness beyond the moment at hand. He hadn't worried about how she felt after. That didn't make him much better than Enrique who wasn't considering Julianna's happiness at all.

The truth hit Alejandro like a sucker punch.

He didn't want to have anything in common with his brother.

"Do it for yourself, but for me and the island, too." And Julianna. "Heirs must be your first priority."

Enrique's forehead creased. "You want out of the line of succession that badly?"

"Yes." Alejandro did. But this wasn't about him anymore. Julianna needed babies to love. He was finally figuring out why this had become important to him.

Maybe if she were happy, he might be happy, too.

Alejandro tossed and turned all night. Images of Julianna flashed in his mind like photographs in a digital picture frame. Her long legs exposed by her short dress. Her playful smile on the beach. Her parted lips as she steered *La Rueca*. Her passion-filled eyes as she looked at him.

The last one was pure fantasy.

With a grimace, Alejandro tried to fall asleep for the fourth time. But he couldn't stop the slide show playing in his brain. He kept thinking about her, about wanting to be with her, about wanting to touch her.

Not only touch her.

Alejandro punched his pillow. Maybe if he was more comfortable...

Nothing helped. The harder he tried not to think about her, the more he did. Some of the thoughts were going to require a cold shower if he wasn't careful.

He didn't want to take that chance. He jumped out of bed, dressed for sailing and headed to the boat.

That would keep him...distracted.

La Rueca bobbed in the water. This past week, he'd gotten used to the activity of the crew preparing for a sail or cleaning up afterward. Today, she looked lonely tied to the dock with her running lights off and no crew around.

Better remedy that. Alejandro hopped aboard. The boat rocked with the incoming tides. The wind increased, jostling the lines that secured the boat to the dock. Metal clanked against metal. The waves picked up momentum, hitting the hull with more force.

He glanced at the horizon. Orange and red fingers of sunlight poked their way into the dark sky.

Red sky at night, sailor's delight. Red sky at morning, sailor's warning.

The nursery rhyme used to predict weather played in his head. A red sky might mean a more challenging sail this morning. That would be a good test for the crew with the race coming up.

Especially Julianna.

He had no doubt she'd rise to the challenge. The more situations she was exposed to, the more experience she could rely upon come race day. He'd have to make sure they came up with a good excuse to explain her absence during the three days of races. Sleeping in late wouldn't cut it.

An image of Julianna's twinkling blue eyes, her smiling mouth and her sunburned nose formed in his mind. At least that picture was more innocent than others he'd imagined.

He laughed.

"Care to let me in on the joke?"

Alejandro's heart lurched. He could recognize Julianna's melodic voice anywhere.

He whipped around to face the dock. The beam of light from her headlamp blinded him. He shielded his eyes. "You're here early."

She removed her headlamp, turned it off and shoved it in her pocket. "Couldn't sleep."

Her, too. Alejandro doubted for the same reasons as him.

Lust probably wasn't in the innocent princess's vocabulary. Not that anyone would mistake Julianna for anything but a too thin, gawky teen in those baggy clothes.

Anyone, except him.

He saw a beautiful woman who was willing to disguise herself to experience a taste of freedom. She'd grabbed the golden ring with both hands and wasn't going to let go until she had to. Julianna was…special. He'd never met a woman like her. If only…

Don't go there. He'd decided what he needed to do once she married. But she was here now.

Alejandro shifted his weight. He needed some distance. "I'm going to get the sails."

He stepped below deck without waiting for her to respond. He didn't want to care what she said.

A musty scent filled his nostrils. He'd always found familiarity in the smell, but he would have rather breathed in Julianna's sweet fragrance. Her usual scent when she wasn't pretending to be a teenage boy.

He shook his head. She'd gotten under his skin. He needed to get her out of there.

Alejandro felt a presence behind him. He didn't need to turn around to know who it was. "Julianna."

"I'll help you."

"Thanks." He faced her. The sails, equipment and slope of the hull didn't leave a lot of room. With her down here, the space felt more cramped. Or maybe he was more aware of her. "But I've got them."

"We'll have things ready for the crew faster with two pairs of hands."

He'd said something similar to her after their first sail together. That seemed like a lifetime ago.

The boat tilted to one side, as if hit by a mischievous wind or a powerful surge.

Julianna widened her stance.

The boat jolted and leaned the opposite way. Jules flew into Alejandro. He caught her, as he had in the foyer that first morning when she'd arrived at the palace.

He stared down at her face. Her body pressed against his. "The princess is in my arms yet again."

She was nothing like the woman he'd held then. Or maybe she'd taken off the mask and allowed her true self to show. Whichever, he didn't want to let her go. His arms tightened around her.

Attraction sizzled. A need burned deep within him. He fought against the ache with every ounce of self-control he had.

The race began tomorrow. The royal wedding would occur next week. She would be out of his life…

The same longing he felt filled Julianna's eyes. Her lips parted.

A sense of urgency drove him. He lowered his mouth to hers, capturing her lips with a kiss.

She gasped, but didn't back away.

His lips ran over hers, tasting and soaking up her sweetness. He knew he was crossing the line.

What he was doing was wrong on so many levels. But he didn't care. Maybe he'd care later, but at this moment the kiss consumed him. She consumed him.

Julianna arched toward him, her breasts pressing against his chest, her arms entwining around his chest. She opened her mouth further, deepening the kiss. Her eagerness thrilled him. Blood roared through his veins. He pulled her closer, until he felt the rapid beat of her heart.

His tongue explored her mouth with abandon, burning with

her sweet heat. Sensation pulsated wildly through him. Passion grew. Self-control slipped.

A soft moan escaped her throat. So sexy.

Alejandro wanted more. He wanted all of her. But he'd take whatever she was willing to give him.

He leaned back against the sail bags, pulling her with him. His hands cupped her round bottom. Fabric bunched. Too much clothing was in the way.

Alejandro slid his hand under her jacket and...

Voices sounded above them.

Julianna jerked away so fast she almost fell on her butt. She regained her balance and touched her hand to her mouth. "I-I'm sorry. I shouldn't have..."

Her red cheeks and ragged breathing made her look so turned-on and sexy, but Alejandro couldn't pretend he didn't hear the regret in her voice. He tried to regain control. Not easy with his body on fire and aching for more kisses. More Julianna.

But she was right. They shouldn't have done this.

"I'm the one who kissed you." He knew better, but when he was around her he couldn't think straight. "I apologize."

She stared down her nose at him. "I kissed you back."

Always the princess even when passion filled her eyes, a flush stained her neck and cheeks and her lips were swollen. Alejandro bit back a smile. She would be upset if he thought this was funny.

"Alejandro?" Phillipe yelled.

"Ju—J.V. is helping me with the sails." Alejandro needed to calm down and cool off. Or they would blow her cover. But he couldn't stop thinking how perfect her lips felt against his. He'd kissed many women, but no kiss had ever felt like this. "Be up in a minute," he added, not wanting anyone to come down here.

"What now?" she asked.

More kisses. That was what he wanted. But Julianna wasn't some woman he'd met at a club or on the beach or at a sailing regatta. She was Enrique's future wife and Alejandro's ticket out of the royal life he abhorred. Even if his brother was out of the picture, she wasn't a fling. He wasn't looking to get serious with anyone.

Alejandro had too much going on with his boat business, properties and plans for the island to get involved in a serious relationship with any woman. Let alone with a princess.

He wanted to be freed from his princely duties, not be caught up trying to live up to her expectations. She would want him to remain a prince. She would challenge him to be more and embrace his birthright. He'd seen her act that way with Brandt. That behavior and pressure didn't appeal to Alejandro in the slightest. He'd spent too much of his life justifying himself and his actions. Continuing on that path would be hell on earth.

Julianna was the last woman Alejandro should want to be with. She was a perfect princess, with a royal heart and soul. Duty and country motivated her. She would use her role on La Isla de la Aurora to make a difference in Aliestle. He would never be able to make a princess like her happy. He wouldn't want to try. Even if he liked kissing her.

And wanted to kiss her again.

So what now?

"We sail," he answered.

CHAPTER ELEVEN

THREE HOURS OF sailing with high winds and waves kept Jules's mind off Alejandro's kisses. Thank goodness she'd needed to focus on steering the boat, or she would have been sighing, staring and swooning.

Pathetic.

But she couldn't help herself. The way Alejandro made her feel overwhelmed Jules. Which was why she'd hurried up the dock back toward safety without a word as soon as the crew was ready to leave.

She may have apologized, but it wasn't because kissing Alejandro had felt wrong. Kissing him had felt oh-so-right. As if that was what she should be doing today, tomorrow and every day for the rest of her life. That was why she'd been sorry. Feeling that way while engaged to Enrique wasn't fair to either man.

She jogged through the park, eager to return to the palace and the sanctuary of her room. The suite provided all she needed—a means to escape and a lovely view from the windows. Enrique had been right about that. The pretty, colorful blossoms soothed her. She could use some soothing now.

Enrique.

She wove her way through the rocks in the grotto, passed through the wrought-iron gate and locked it behind her.

She didn't want to think about her fiancé now.

Not with the effects of Alejandro's kisses lingering.

The tunnel seemed darker and longer, and the smell of moisture and mold more pronounced. Each of her nerve endings seemed heightened in sensitivity. Her lips still tingled. The ache deep inside her that had started the moment his lips captured hers had grown exponentially since then.

Alejandro stirred something inside her. She was torn by her desire of wanting more and her guilt of knowing better.

Was this what passion felt like?

If so, the feeling frightened her even as it thrilled her. Allowing herself to be carried away by the strong current of emotion would be stupid. She had to be rational about this.

He hadn't proclaimed his undying love and affection. He'd simply kissed her until she couldn't think straight. He'd made her feel so special, like the only woman in the world.

Would that be the only time she ever felt like that? Her heart hoped not.

"Julianna."

The sound of Alejandro's voice sent a shiver of pleasure down her spine, but brought a twinge of uncertainty, too. She stopped walking. "I thought you were going to the boatyard."

He caught up to her. The beam from his flashlight pointed at the dirt floor. "I wanted…"

You. She held her breath.

"…to talk with you," he finished.

Disappointment squeezed her heart even though she knew his wanting her was as likely as her living happily ever after.

Alejandro reached forward and tilted her headlamp so the light shone up. "We never got a chance to talk on the boat."

Her uncertainty increased three-fold. "A hard day of sailing. We needed to focus."

"You didn't smile much."

"I had a lot on my mind." Like now. She started walking. "I should get back to the palace."

Being so close to him sent her out-of-whack emotions spiraling into the danger zone. His scent made her want to lean in closer for another sniff. His warmth made her want to seek shelter in his arms. And his lips made her want to forget what her future held.

He fell into step next to her, his flashlight swinging at his side. "Tell me what's on your mind."

"You mean on the boat?"

"And now."

Jules didn't know where to start. She took a deep breath. It didn't help.

"Julianna," he prompted.

"You. You were…are…on my mind." There, she'd said it. Even though she figured Alejandro had guessed as much.

"You've been on my mind, too. We're equal."

Not even close. Jules had never felt this way about any man, not even Christian, whom she believed at the time she loved. Of course, she'd been sixteen then.

Not that she was in love with Alejandro. Except…

She wanted to be with him on the boat, off the boat, all the time. She wanted to sneak out of the palace for good and sail off into the sunset with him. And Boots. They wouldn't have to sail—they could walk, run, drive or fly. She wasn't particular on the mode of transportation as long as they were together. The thought of being without Alejandro…

What was she thinking?

Being with him was impossible. What she felt now was a crush. The new sensations he had awakened with his kiss were causing her to feel this way.

Not…love.

"About this morning below deck," Alejandro said.

"It's okay." Jules didn't dare look at him. No one could ever know how much his kisses had affected her. "Each time I exit this tunnel, I enter a whole new world full of wonderful, but forbidden things. Freedom. Sailing. Kissing."

"You've never—"

"I've been kissed." The surprise in his voice made her cheeks grow hot. Jules was embarrassed enough by letting a crush get so out of control. She wasn't about to tell him she could count on one hand the number of times she'd been kissed. "But I'm not…as experienced as you."

"I couldn't tell."

Well, she *could* tell *he* was an expert kisser. That kind of expertise took…practice.

Alejandro has a horrible reputation. Worse, his taste in women is far from discriminating. Royalty, commoner, palace staff, it doesn't matter.

Yvette's words were the cold dose of reality Jules needed. She was probably one in a long line of women who'd come before. A part of her—okay, her heart—didn't want to believe that, but she'd allowed this to go way further than it should. Romanticizing his kisses made no sense. "Kissing you was a nice addition to my adventure."

"Adventure?"

She nodded. "Escaping the palace, wearing a disguise and sailing on *La Rueca*'s crew. It's all been a grand adventure, a fantasy I've been able to experience for a brief time, but I know it's not…real."

"The sailing has been real. Kissing you was—"

"Not real." If the kisses weren't real, neither were her feelings. "I mean, we kissed. But we were caught up in the moment. Two consenting adults in each other's arms. The opportunity presented itself. A kiss was bound to happen."

"Perhaps we should find out if the kisses are real or not."

Jules's gaze flew up to meet his.

His intense gaze seemed to penetrate all the way to her soul. Her breath caught in her throat. She'd never felt so exposed, so naked before.

A chill rushed through her. Goose bumps prickled her skin. "We…can't."

"Why not?"

Her heart slammed against her chest. Logically she knew what she should say, but those words would contradict what her heart and her lips wanted her to do. "This can't go anywhere."

Alejandro traced her jawline with his fingertip. "I know."

His light-as-a-feather touch tantalized. Teased. Tempted. "I'm marrying Enrique."

"I know that, too." Alejandro's rich voice seeped into her, filling all the empty places with warmth. "The race begins tomorrow. This may be our last opportunity to be alone."

Jules's chest tightened. "This has to be the last time."

He nodded and lowered his hand from her face. "That would be for the best."

At least he agreed. Still, nerves gripped her. "But I…"

Silence hung between them, but instead of pushing them apart Alejandro drew closer. "Your move, Princess."

Her move. Jules had never been in this position before, but she knew what she had to do. She raised her chin and pressed her lips against his. Hard.

A mistake? Probably.

But she wanted—needed—to kiss him one more time. She wanted to remember what his kiss felt like and how he made her feel.

Jules wrapped her arms around him and leaned in close. She tasted a mix of salt and heat. So delicious. She wanted to remember every detail, each texture.

As she deepened the kiss, sparks shot through her.

Okay, this kiss was real. She'd give him that.

The kiss made her quiver with pleasure and burn with desire.

But Jules didn't know if the way she felt was real or not. She didn't care. She just wanted to keep kissing him.

Because once she finished, Jules knew she would never kiss Alejandro again.

Tensions ran high the next morning. The first day of the Med Cup had arrived. Alejandro couldn't believe how calm and cool Julianna was. She impressed the entire crew with her composure. She steered like a pro. The entire team worked together. The sweat and hard work enabled *La Rueca* to win their first race. Alejandro's goal was one step closer.

And so was saying goodbye to Julianna.

He ignored the knot in his gut.

His father excused him from eating dinner at the palace that night. But Alejandro didn't feel like celebrating as he sat at a tapas bar with the crew so he headed back to the palace.

Julianna.

She should have been with the crew tonight. With him.

Alejandro wanted to take her in his arms and kiss her until she begged him to stop or give her more. But he couldn't.

This has to be the last time.

He'd agreed. Logically that made the most sense, but the way he felt about her didn't make sense at all.

The kitten was waiting when Alejandro entered the apartment. "Hey, Boots."

The kitten meowed.

Alejandro got an idea. "Want to go see Julianna?"

Another meow.

That was good enough for him. He swooped up the cat and went to Julianna's room.

In the hallway, Yvette sat on a chair outside the door and read. She lowered her book. "Are you here to see Princess Julianna, sir?"

"Yes." He showed her the kitten. "Boots wants to see her."

As if on cue, the cat meowed.

"I'm sorry, sir. The princess is sleeping."

Alejandro looked around. No one else was in the hallway. He smiled. "Please tell her I'm here."

"I'm sorry, sir," Yvette repeated with a hint of disapproval this time. "Princess Julianna has an upset stomach and asked not to be disturbed until morning. Would you like me to tell her you and Boots paid a visit?"

"No, thanks. I'll see her tomorrow." Disappointment settled over the center of his chest. Alejandro wanted to see her now. "Good night."

He returned to his apartment feeling out of sorts. He played with Boots using the laser pointer, but the kitten had more fun.

The entire time, Alejandro couldn't stop thinking about Julianna. The passion in her eyes when they kissed. The exhilaration on her face during the race.

He had to see her for a minute. Yvette wasn't about to let him pass, but he knew another way.

With a flashlight in hand, Alejandro used the secret door in his apartment to enter the tunnels. He wove his way around until he reached the staircase leading to Julianna's room. Each step brought him closer to her. He stood on the landing and pulled the latch. The secret door opened.

Alejandro had been here before to leave her disguise and other gear she needed. He'd never thought twice about entering her closet.

But this time, he hesitated.

This can't go anywhere.

I know.

I'm marrying Enrique.

I know that, too.

His conversation with Julianna echoed through his head. Yes, he wanted to see her. Hell, he wanted to kiss her.

But Julianna didn't want that.

I'm marrying Enrique.

Alejandro might want to see her, but he couldn't. She was determined to marry his brother. He wasn't going to do something that both he and Julianna might regret. He knew better than that.

Alejandro closed the secret door.

This was for the…best.

The morning of the race, Julianna had instructed Yvette to tell anyone who came to the door she was suffering from a stomach virus. No one, especially Enrique, would want any part of that.

Hours later, she stood with her hands on the wheel, nervous and excited. Adrenaline coursed through her veins.

They were halfway through the course, running ahead of their closest competitor.

The tension and noise level had increased from yesterday's match. The winds and waves had, too. Both had turned stronger over the last twenty-four hours. That made her job harder.

Water splashed into the cockpit. A foul weather suit kept her dry. Each member of the crew had a responsibility and knew what to do. Hers was to steer the boat. She focused her attention on the direction the boat sailed. She couldn't think about anything else.

Or anyone else.

But Jules knew where Alejandro had been since the boat had left the dock. Her gaze was automatically drawn to him at midbow. Water dripped from his hair and his foul weather gear. He looked sexy and in his element. The sheer joy on his face tugged on her heart and her dreams.

One more day of racing. A week until her wedding. And it would be all over.

A sense of loss assailed her. She ignored it. Now wasn't the time.

Each of the crew worked to keep the *La Rueca* sailing as fast as she could with adjustments to the sails. Others sat aft, trying to keep the weight on the stern.

The boat sailed downwind, surfing the waves that got bigger by the minute. The up and down motion of the boat reminded her of a thrilling roller coaster ride. More than once her stomach ended up in her throat, but she didn't mind one bit.

Jules tightened her grip on the wheel. She needed to hold a steady course, but didn't want to plow into a wave and risk the possibility of broaching.

Water hit her face and dripped down her cheeks. She tasted salt on her lips and in her mouth.

This was what she dreamed about. Freedom in its purest form.

She had no regrets. Well, one. Alejandro. But that wasn't as much a regret as a what-might-have-been. Kissing him again had left a wound on her heart. One she hoped would heal in time.

"*Dragon Rider*'s broached," Sam yelled from the midsection of the bow.

Jules could barely hear him, but she'd heard enough. Their competitor had heeled too far to one side and was lying broadside. Her stomach clenched. She hoped the crew were tied in. It would be easy to capsize or break the mast in these waves.

Everyone searched for the boat. The sails and waves got in the way. The mast must be in the water or someone would see it.

"Does it look like they are going to recover?" Alejandro's voice sounded strained.

"I see them," Sam shouted.

"Me, too," Mike yelled. "They are knocked down."

Jules inhaled sharply, but held the course.

"Has the boat righted itself?" Phillipe, who was nearest to her, asked.

"No," Mike said.

The answer sent a chill down Jules's spine.

"Man overboard," a voice called over the radio.

"Trimming up for beam reaching," she said without a moment of hesitation.

Alejandro jumped off the deck and grabbed the radio. "*La Rueca* is responding."

The energy level tripled. A sailor was in the water. A life was at stake. The race no longer mattered. Every able-bodied vessel was required to offer assistance.

He looked at Jules. Confidence and affection shone in his eyes. "You can do this."

She nodded once.

As she turned the boat from the starboard side, the mainsail and jib trimmers went to work. No one wanted to waste any time, but they had to be careful. They didn't want to broach as well.

"Get a fix on the person in the water," she ordered Phillipe. With the race on hold, he needed another job. Jules needed to make sure she didn't run the sailor over.

"I've got the beacon," Alejandro said, moving toward the stern.

She knew he was clipped in, but she bit her lip, worried about his safety out there. And the other boat. They'd been fighting the waves all day. *If he went overboard…*

Don't think. Just steer.

"I see him," Mike yelled.

Jules heard the collective sigh of relief, but the sailor wasn't safe yet.

Alejandro threw the overboard buoy toward the sailor in the water. The buoy was state of the art with a lighted pole, life ring, flotation jacket and location beacon.

"Sailor has the beacon," Phillipe said. "You've sailed past him on the aft side."

"Coming about," she ordered. "Trim up."

Jules gave the second order even though it wasn't necessary. They knew what to do. She sailed over the waves. Tacking back, she guided the boat toward the buoy.

Alejandro stood on the bow, clipped into the jackline. Sam was nearby, too. They looked out at the water. Alejandro was too far away for her to hear him so he directed her with hand signals.

She slowed down, luffing leeward of the sailor in the water. The wind against the loose sails sounded like thunder. The crew shouted. The noise level kept rising. She must be getting closer.

Jules focused, pushing the boat to its limits to reach the sailor as quickly as possible.

A helicopter flew overhead.

Mike used a recovery hook to grab the buoy's line, pulling the buoy and the person toward them. Cody grabbed the buoy pole and dragged it back toward the stern.

"The other boat's righted," he said.

Thank goodness, but she couldn't celebrate yet. She kept the sails luffing so the boat wouldn't drift into the person bobbing in the water. Mike and Phillipe hauled the man onboard. His face was pale, but he looked relieved to be aboard. Water poured from his foul weather gear.

"We've got your sailor," Alejandro radioed. "But due to the weather conditions an exchange isn't possible."

"We're dropping out to recover," the voice replied.

Bummer, Jules thought. But two other boats were still racing. Her questioning gaze sought Alejandro's. He smiled at her, sending her heart into a pirouette.

"We'll keep going," he said over the radio.

"Thanks and good luck," the voice replied. "Tell your newest crew member to enjoy the ride."

"Will do," Alejandro said. "The extra weight will come in handy with these waves."

The guy on the radio laughed.

"Time to finish the race," Alejandro announced to the crew.

Everyone took his position with a cheer.

"We can win this." The confidence in Alejandro's voice kept her focused. "J.V."

"Coming about," she said.

It was as if the rescue had never happened. If not for their extra passenger it might have all been a dream.

But as they sailed toward the finish line, Jules knew it was real. Like Alejandro's kisses.

The bow crossed the finish line.

The crew cheered. Jules laughed.

They'd won.

Won!

La Rueca would be in the finals tomorrow.

Excitement rocketed through her. She stared at Alejandro. A grin lit up his face. So handsome. So dear to her heart.

He gave her a high-five. She would have preferred a hug, but being able to touch him was enough. For now.

"I've never seen anyone sail like you did today," he said. "Awe-inspiring."

"You're the best, J.V.," Sam said.

"Thanks for the ride." The sailor they'd rescued, Robert, shook her hand. "We underestimated you, kid. You're one helluva a helmsman."

Jules smiled, but didn't say anything. Her voice would give her away. She couldn't fake a deep tone now. Not with delighted joy exploding like fireworks in her chest.

The boat docked. People were waiting for them. A medical crew stood in front of the crowd.

"Looks like you'll need a checkup," Alejandro said to their guest.

Robert had changed into spare dry clothes down below. "I'd rather hit the bar and wait for my boat to arrive."

"Maybe there's a pretty doc or nurse to keep you company, mate," Sam said.

"One can hope." Robert saluted Jules and the rest of the crew. "Thanks again. Good race, but watch out for us next year."

Alejandro laughed. "We'll have our eyes open looking back at you the entire way."

Robert grinned wryly. "With this kid driving, you might be."

As he left with the medical crew, people pushed forward.

"Look at all these fans, mates," Sam said. "Smile. The media is here, too."

Jules's heart slammed against her chest. A horrible sense of dread replaced the wonderfulness of the moment. The press took pictures, asked questions, followed up.

So not good.

She ducked her head and pulled her cap lower.

"You may find yourself a pretty girl out of this, J.V.," Sam teased with a slap on Jules's back.

Jules forced a smile. Anything would be better than the truth coming out.

"Don't worry," Alejandro whispered so only she could hear.

She appreciated his words, but she was worried. Terrified. Her future, her country's future and her children's future were all at stake. The press circled like a school of hungry piranhas. She swallowed around the spinnaker-size lump in her throat.

The sea of people standing on the dock grew larger. Some held cameras. A few shouted questions in a variety of languages: Spanish, German, French, Italian and English. She understood most of the questions, but she pretended not to hear them.

Her insides trembled, but she maintained her composure. A teenage boy would relish the attention after winning a race, not run away. Still her feet were itching to take off.

Who was she kidding?

If she could jump into the water and swim away without drawing attention to herself, she would.

"We need to get you out of here," Alejandro whispered.

"I can swim."

"So can the sharks." He tried to lead her away from the mob, but the crowd pushed closer. "It'll be okay."

She clung to his words even though her doubts multiplied by the seconds. Camera flashes blinded her. Reporters shoved microphones and digital recorders in her face. Arms reached for her.

Jules cringed. Bodyguards never let crowds get so close. She wasn't used to being touched like this. Her anxiety level spiraled.

Someone touched her cap.

"Please don't." She held it on her head with both hands. "Alejandro."

He tried to help her. "Leave the kid alone."

Another person grabbed the cap off her head. The wig went with it, leaving her wearing a nylon cap.

People gasped. A horrible silence fell over the crowd.

"It's a girl," a man shouted.

"A woman," another yelled.

"Hey," a woman said. "Isn't that the princess who's going to marry Crown Prince Enrique?"

The air rushed from her lungs. Her worst nightmare was coming true. Everyone would know her true identity now. Including Enrique and her father.

Her heart and her head felt as if they might explode.

Hundreds of people surrounded her, but she'd never felt so alone. And she had only herself to blame.

Life as she knew it was over.

Had it been worth it?

She glanced at Alejandro. He'd removed his sunglasses. The warmth in his eyes drove her goose bumps away.

"Do not worry," he said softly. "I'm here. You won't have to face this alone."

His words gave her the strength she needed. She knew sailing with Alejandro had been worth it. No matter what the consequences.

Shoulders back. Chin up. Smile.

Jules fell back into the training that had been ingrained in her since she was a little girl. She removed the plastic cap hiding her blond hair.

Goodbye J.V., hello Princess Julianna.

She answered the questions being shouted at her. Alejandro stood next to her the entire time. He downplayed the situation by answering questions as well. She appreciated his efforts. The rest of the crew stayed by her, too, though they looked confused. Phillipe's brows furrowed. Mike's mouth gaped. Cody scratched his head. Sam stared at her as if she were a ghost.

But Alejandro's presence gave her strength. Courage.

A good thing, too. When her father and her fiancé discovered what Jules had done, she was going to need all that and more.

CHAPTER TWELVE

BACK AT THE PALACE, Jules couldn't stop shaking. Not even a hot shower helped. She put on a conservative pink dress, befitting a princess and future queen. With trembling hands, she applied makeup and styled her hair in an updo.

What was her father going to say? Do about her disobedience?

Yvette fastened a strand of pearls around Jules's neck. "You look like a proper princess, ma'am."

She hadn't been acting like one. "Thank you."

A knock sounded on her door. Jules's heart pounded in her ears. She wasn't ready.

Yvette answered the door. "It's Prince Brandt, ma'am. He's here to escort you to the sitting room."

As soon as Jules stepped into the hallway, her brother hugged her. "Father requests your presence."

She stepped out of Brandt's embrace. "Yvette said he arrived like a bull from Pamplona. Snorts and all."

"I've never seen him so angry." The concern in Brandt's voice matched her own. "I'm worried what he'll do."

She wanted to ease Brandt's concern even though she was apprehensive, too. "Don't worry. Father will be…fair."

At least she hoped so.

"I screwed up." Brandt hung his head. "Klaus is beside himself for leaving you alone so much."

Jules touched her brother's shoulder. Love for him filled her heart. "Neither of you are to blame for this."

Only her.

She descended the stairs, mindful of each step so she didn't stumble.

"But if I hadn't been partying so much—"

"Please, Brandt." Straightening, Jules composed herself. She couldn't duck for cover now. "Don't get in the middle of this."

It would be bad enough without dragging him or Alejandro into this.

Alejandro.

His name brought a welcome rush of warmth through her cold body. She'd survived the onslaught of questions on the dock with him at her side. If she had the same help tonight...

No, that was too much to ask of him. Her father was too rich, too powerful. He could destroy everything Alejandro worked so hard to build.

The sitting room loomed in front of her like a black hole. She entered with Brandt at her side.

A tense silence filled the air. Alejandro, Enrique, King Dario and her father rose from their seats.

Compassion filled Alejandro's eyes. He'd shaved, removed his earring and pulled his hair away from his face and secured it at his nape. He looked regal and princely in his suit, dress shirt, tie and leather shoes. Respectable. Her heart squeezed tight. She missed the pirate.

Enrique had dressed similarly. The two men had never looked as much like brothers as tonight. Enrique glared at Alejandro with accusation and a frown on his lips.

She hated knowing she would push the two men farther apart.

Concern clouded King Dario's face. He pressed his lips together and clasped his hands behind his back. Sweat beaded on his brow.

Her father's gaze burned with fury. His lips thinned with anger. "How dare you disobey me, Julianna Louise Marie!"

Shoulders back. Chin up.

No way could she smile. Jules looked him in the eyes. She wanted to be strong for Brandt's and Alejandro's sake, as much as her own. "I apologize for my actions, sir. I didn't mean to cause any trouble."

"Trouble?" Alaric's features hardened. "You have brought disrepute onto our family and country. Pictures of you looking windswept and wild, hardly the way a princess should appear in public, are everywhere. Papers, television, the Internet."

Jules felt everyone's eyes on her, especially Alejandro's. She tried not to cower, but she'd never seen her father so full of rage.

Enrique sneered. "You looked like a boy."

"It was a disguise," she explained, cutting him with a quick glance.

"The fact you needed a disguise should have been the first sign this was a mistake." King Dario patted his forehead with his handkerchief. "You're the future queen of La Isla de la Aurora, Julianna. This kind of behavior is unacceptable."

"I'll say." Enrique glowered at her. "Your father and I told you not to sail. You're supposed to be a conservative princess. Not a...wild child."

Her temper rose. "I wasn't—"

"You were." Her father's voice boomed like a thunderstorm in November. "I watched a tape of the race on the flight. You not only disobeyed me but put yourself in danger. You could have been killed sailing the way you did today."

Heat stole into her face. Her breath burned in her throat.

"Jules is fine, Father. She saved a sailor's life," Brandt said bravely. He'd never stood up to their father before and she was proud he'd found the courage to do that. "It's my fault Klaus wasn't with Jules. I partied too much, and he was with me."

Her muscles tensed, nervous what her father would say.

"This has nothing to do with you, Brandt," Alaric replied sharply. "Your sister knew what I expected of her. She must accept the consequences."

Dread shuddered through her. Jules knew what her punishment would be—to spend the rest of her life in Aliestle.

She glanced at Alejandro. Her heart cried. She would never see him again.

"King Alaric." Alejandro stepped forward. "I am Prince Alejandro Cierzo de Amanecer. King Dario's second son."

"You mean, the spare." King Alaric's curt voice lashed out. "You're the idiot who put my daughter's life in danger."

Jules drew in a sharp breath at the insult. She couldn't stand the thought of her father taking out his anger on Alejandro.

"Yes, but Julianna's safety is of the utmost concern to me, Your Majesty." The regal air emanating from him made him seem more like a future king than second in line for the throne. "I take full responsibility for what's happened. Julianna disobeying you was one hundred percent my fault. I took her sailing. I asked her to be part of my crew and race in the Med Cup. I'm the one who should be punished, not her."

Jules stared at Alejandro, full of pride and…love.

I love him.

Love was the only explanation for her feelings, ones that went far deeper than friendship and future familial bonds. She couldn't stop thinking about the way he looked at her, kissed her, stood by her side and wanted to take the blame for all of this.

Alejandro had to have feelings for her. Otherwise why would he be standing up for her now? Her heart wanted her to go to him, but too many things needed to be resolved first.

Jules couldn't allow Alejandro to take the blame. She hadn't been a dutiful princess. She'd disobeyed. She needed to stand up and be accountable for her actions, not let a wonderful, giving man suffer consequences meant for her.

Joy provided strength. Love gave her courage.

Alejandro embraced his role as a prince tonight to protect her. She needed to embrace her role as a black sheep to accept her punishment and protect him.

"Thank you, Alejandro." An unfamiliar sense of peace rested in her heart. "But I can't allow you take the blame for my actions."

His eyes implored her. "It's my blame to take."

Her heart melted. She allowed her gaze to linger, longer than what was considered proper. She loved the gold flecks and the concern she saw in his brown eyes. "No."

"Yes," Enrique countered. "All this is Alejandro's fault, King Alaric."

"It's not. I knew what I was getting myself into, Father." Jules stared up at her father, who towered over her with a face full of contempt. "I was so desperate for a taste of freedom, I allowed my desire to override everything else. Alejandro's not to blame. It's my fault. But I have no regrets over what I have done."

The affection and pride in Alejandro's eyes made her heart want to dance and sing. Whatever consequence she faced would be worth it. If she hadn't disobeyed, she would never have gotten to know him, kiss him and fall in love with him.

"Your stepmother worked so hard to turn you into a proper Aliestlian princess." Her father spoke with disdain. "But you have always been too much like your mother."

Jules smiled. "Thank you, Father."

His nostrils flared. "It isn't a compliment."

Her smile didn't waver. She would cherish the words no matter what fate had in store for her. "It is to me, sir."

The wrinkles on her father's forehead deepened. He stared at her with a look of bewilderment then turned his attention to King Dario. "I trusted you with my most prized possession. You promised she would be safe, yet you allowed this to happen."

"We had no idea she was sailing." King Dario sounded contrite.

"Her well-being is our number one priority," Enrique added.

Jules hated how they spoke as if she wasn't present. "I'm right here, gentlemen."

Alaric ignored her. "If that's the case, how come no one noticed she was missing from the palace? Not even her fiancé?"

"I've been busy with work and wedding plans," Enrique answered hastily.

Alaric's lips snarled. "Wedding plans are women's work."

Enrique flinched.

"My brother had no idea because he works nonstop as crown prince. He would have no reason to suspect anything was amiss because Julianna didn't allow the sailing to affect her obligations as his fiancée," Alejandro explained. "There was no harm done."

"No harm?" Her father's ruddy complexion reddened more. "Her blatant disobedience has thrown Aliestle into chaos. A small feminist movement has taken her participation in the race and run with it. They are holding rallies across the land and protesting for equal rights. It's disgusting."

No, it was progress. The kind of change Jules wanted to influence in her country. Satisfaction flowed through her.

Approval gleamed in Alejandro's eyes. He knew what this meant to her.

She smiled at him.

He smiled back.

"This situation is completely out of hand and unacceptable," Alaric announced. "I'm canceling the marriage contract."

Panic clawed into her heart. Jules didn't want to return to Aliestle. She wanted to stay on the island with Alejandro.

What now? Did she dare defy her father again?

As the king's words echoed through the room, Alejandro stared at Julianna. The distress on her face twisted his insides.

Emotions clamored in his heart, demanding to be acknowledged. Not respect or attraction or friendship. Deep feelings. Intense feelings. Ones that scared him.

Not love. He knew better than to fall in love. This had to be... something else.

Still his hand itched to reach out to take hold of Julianna. He wanted to protect her from the fallout and make everything better.

Brandt cleared his throat. "Father, please—"

"This does not concern you," Alaric said through clenched teeth.

But it concerned Alejandro. He wanted to punch King Alaric in the nose and free her from this tyranny. But that wasn't what Julianna wanted him to do. And it certainly wouldn't help her with her father. In fact, acting out the fury balling in his gut would cause more trouble for his own family.

Alejandro's frustration rose.

If she returned to Aliestle, her sense of duty would lead her to marry whatever nobleman her father picked out.

Alejandro couldn't allow that to happen. She had to stay on the island. No matter what. "Your Majesty, if I may…"

King Alaric glared at him. "Haven't you done enough already?"

"Sire." The old-fashioned word felt weird coming off Alejandro's tongue, but perhaps it would resonate with the misguided and medieval King Alaric. "Julianna needs to remain on La Isla de la Aurora."

"Why?" Scorn laced King Alaric's word.

"Because I want to stay here, Father," Julianna said.

She smiled softly at Alejandro.

His heart turned over. And that hurt like hell because to do the right thing, he had to let her go.

"The people are wild about her, sire." Alejandro had been in his brother's shadow his entire life, but this time he belonged there. Only Enrique could give Julianna the kind of life she was raised for, the kind of life she wanted. She wanted to use her position as the crown prince's wife to influence change and give her people a better future. She could accomplish all she desired and more as the future queen. "Julianna has touched their hearts with her compassion and friendliness. They've embraced her as their princess, and one day they'll love her as their queen."

"My daughter was raised to be a queen," Alaric admitted.

"Everyone can tell she has received the finest training." Alejandro fought the desire to claim her for himself. But too much was at stake. He could never give Julianna what she wanted and make her happy, even if she wished to be with him. He swallowed around the lump of emotion in his throat. He had to push aside his own desire and do what was best for her. "You say her actions have caused chaos, sire. But her countrywomen see someone they can relate to and rally around. A respected and beloved leader. As the future queen of La Isla de la Aurora, Julianna will be able to do that for women not only in Aliestle and here on the island, but all over the world."

"Please consider my youngest son's words." Appreciation gleamed in Dario's eyes. "Alejandro may not be a conventional prince, but he is wise for his age and speaks the truth."

That was the first compliment his father had ever given him. And the words couldn't have come at a better time.

"Julianna has enchanted the entire island," Enrique added. "And all of us."

Especially Alejandro. But his feelings didn't matter. Julianna would get what she wanted and by default, so would he. He wanted freedom from the monarchy, not a princess bride who dreamed of happily ever afters.

His thoughts tasted like ashes in his mouth. But he had to be realistic. He didn't want to be a prince. He avoided romantic entanglements like the plague. It would...never work.

King Alaric looked at each one of them, but his assessing gaze lingered on Alejandro. "So it seems."

"I stand by the marriage contract," Enrique announced. "I want to marry Julianna."

Her face showed no change of emotion, but his brother's words crushed into Alejandro like a left hook. He resisted the urge not to carry her off to his boat and sail away. But he was the second son, the spare. He wasn't what Julianna needed.

"I don't know." King Alaric's gaze bounced between Alejandro and Julianna. "There seems to be a strong...connection between these two."

"Friendship, sire." Enrique sidled closer to Julianna, as if to reclaim his prize. "They both enjoy sailing."

Alaric looked doubtful.

Perceptive man, Alejandro had to admit. Other than passion, there wasn't anything binding him to Julianna. There couldn't be. "We are friends, sire."

"There will be complications if Julianna has done more than sail with her friend Alejandro," Alaric said. "If there is any reason to doubt the paternity of an heir, the embarrassment to our family name..."

Julianna flushed.

Anger surged. Alejandro couldn't believe her father was

questioning her virginity. He balled his hands into fists. "I assure you, sir—"

King Alaric cut him off. He stared at his daughter as if she were a peasant, not a princess. "Is there any reason you shouldn't marry Enrique?"

The question mortified Julianna. Her heart pounded in her chest, so loudly she was certain everyone could hear it. But no one said anything. They stared, waiting for her to answer.

Her father with his dark, accusing eyes.

King Dario with compassion.

Enrique with panic.

And Alejandro with hope.

Is there any reason you shouldn't marry Enrique?

Yes, a big reason. A six-foot-two-inch-tall reason with dark hair and dark eyes.

Alejandro.

Jules loved him, but couldn't understand why he kept talking about her being a future queen. She wanted to stay on the island, but with Alejandro, not his brother.

She made a silent wish from her heart.

Claim me.

Jules wanted Alejandro to forget about everything. His family, her family and their two countries. She wanted him to declare his love and claim her for himself.

Alejandro gave her an encouraging smile filled with warmth.

Relief washed over her. Her tense muscles relaxed. He would come to her rescue once again and claim her. Everything would turn out fine.

"You can still do your duty and help your country," Alejandro insisted. "All you have to do is tell your father that marrying Enrique is what you want."

Emotion tightened her throat. Her body stiffened with shock.

No. She didn't want that. She loved Alejandro. His actions told her he had feelings for her, too.

There was something between them. Something special.

Yet he wanted her to marry his brother. Jules struggled to breathe. She stared at him.

His smile disappeared. His expression turned neutral.

Why was he doing this?

And then something clicked in her mind and she remembered...

Once you and Enrique marry and have children, I'll be free from all royal obligations. I can concentrate on business and not have to worry about any more princely duties.

The truth hit her with stark clarity. She didn't want to believe it, but nothing else made sense.

Alejandro might have feelings for her, but the feelings didn't run deep enough. He chose not to act upon them. He wasn't willing to sacrifice what he wanted. His freedom was more important than duty. Love. Her.

Julianna's heart froze, leaving her feeling cold and empty.

Despair threatened to overwhelm her, but she didn't give in to it. She needed to answer her father's question.

A million thoughts jumbled her mind. But one kept coming back to her. Her actions on the island had created the very sort of change she desired in Aliestle.

Was that enough reason to marry Enrique?

She looked at Brandt. If she didn't go through with the wedding now, the repercussions would reflect badly on her brother. He was the one who was supposed to be escorting her safely to marriage. The Council of Elders would blame him, so would the press. Their plans to help their country would never come to fruition if she returned home.

Before Alejandro and getting caught up in a fantasy, she'd had a plan—a life outside of Aliestle, helping Brandt and her country, falling in love with her husband and becoming a mother. She might not achieve all of those things now, but she could have some of them.

That would have to be enough.

Shoulders back. Chin up. Smile.

"There isn't any reason I shouldn't marry Enrique, Father." Jules sneaked a peek at Alejandro. The gold flecks in his eyes burned like flames. Somehow she would have to learn to live with Enrique as her husband and Alejandro as her brother-in-law. And be satisfied with that. She swallowed a sigh. "No reason at all."

"I am satisfied." Alaric proclaimed after a long minute. "The marriage contract will be honored, provided Julianna not sail in the Med Cup tomorrow. I'll be here to see to it that she remains in the palace all day long."

Every one of her nerve endings cried out in protest. Jules had earned the spot in the final, but she remained silent as any proper princess would.

"As will I," King Dario said.

"Me, too," Enrique agreed.

Alejandro nodded. "Julianna is a skilled helmsman, but I agree it's best she doesn't sail."

Even he was taking their side. Her heart shattered into a million pieces, each one jabbing into her at the same time. If love and passion brought this kind of pain, she would rather go back to how she lived before arriving on the island.

With what strength she had left, Jules forced all her emotions to a deep, dark place. She'd survived before by sleepwalking through life. That was how she would survive again.

The dullness in Julianna's eyes struck at Alejandro's heart. He knew she was upset at being banned from the race. Competing in the Med Cup had been important to her. At least she was getting what she wanted. She could help her brother and her country now.

But the lack of emotion on her face and her lifeless eyes bothered him. Concerned, he turned toward her. "Jul—"

"There's no reason for you to remain at the palace, Alejandro." King Dario interrupted him with a pointed glare. "Return to your villa and prepare for tomorrow's race."

Alejandro didn't want to leave. He wanted to stay near Julianna. "I don't mind staying here."

"Go." His father touched his shoulder. "Keep your distance until the wedding."

Julianna didn't glance Alejandro's way. He knew why.

She'd put her princess mask back on.

He wanted to reach out to her, to shake some sense into her, but he couldn't. He'd pushed aside his own feelings to help her be a proper princess again. A mistake, probably.

But that was what she needed. More than she needed him.

Alejandro had to let Julianna go so she could fulfill the royal duty that was so important to her. She wouldn't disappear from his life. She would disappear into being his distant sister-in-law. Thinking about it now, having her leave the island might have been easier to deal with.

"Perhaps you should stay away after the wedding, too," King Alaric said. "I'll see to it you're well compensated, Alejandro."

His temper flared. He wasn't about to allow Julianna's father to pay him off to stay away. "That isn't necessary, sir. I know my place."

"You're now free from your royal obligations, my son," Dario announced. "I know this is what you've always wanted."

Alejandro nodded. But he didn't feel any relief. No happiness. "Thank you, Father."

He'd gotten what he set out to get—his freedom. He'd never have to step back inside the palace or appear at openings, dinners or charity events. He was free to live his life as he wanted— building boats, racing and turning around the island's economy. No more royal orders. No more royal interference.

But it felt…anticlimactic. Wrong.

Julianna moved closer to Enrique.

Sharp pain sliced Alejandro. A black void seemed to engulf his heart. Seeing her so willingly embrace her future with Enrique shouldn't hurt so badly.

Alejandro shook off the feeling. He was jealous and feeling guilty for what he'd done. That was all.

Enrique had won again. No doubt his brother would punish him for going behind his back.

"Under the circumstances," Enrique said. "I do not think it wise for you to be my best man."

"I agree." Alejandro looked at Julianna. "You're the best

helmsman I've had the privilege of sailing with. You'll be missed."

"Thank you for allowing me to sail on your boat." She spoke politely as if he were some hired help.

The ice princess had returned. But he knew she wasn't cold and heartless, but warm and genuine. He wanted to rip the mask off her face so he could see the real Julianna.

"Good luck with the race tomorrow," she added.

She'd earned *La Rueca* the spot in the finals tomorrow. But she had known her father would never allow her sailing to continue once the truth was out.

"I know you want to sail, Julianna," Alejandro said. "But it's best if you resume your life and do what is best for your country and mine. I don't see any other—"

"No explanations are needed, sir." She emphasized the last word with a haughtiness that put him in his place. "I know my duty. I always have. I was using you as a means to an end, one last hurrah before settling into the life I've chosen. No hard feelings, right?"

Each of her words pierced his heart like a dagger. He had hard feelings, ones that were becoming difficult to ignore and fight.

Using him? Okay, he'd used her to do well in the race.

Alejandro hated to think what she said was true. They'd shared good times, their hopes and their dreams, and hot kisses. Maybe she didn't have feelings for him or maybe she was back to pretending. It didn't matter.

The next time he saw her, they would be required to wear polite faces and share a meaningless conversation. Everything in the past would seem like nothing more than a dream.

No hard feelings, right?

"Right." Alejandro bowed. "I wish you much happiness. All of you."

With that, he packed his bag, picked up Boots and left the palace feeling worse than he'd ever felt in his entire life.

CHAPTER THIRTEEN

THE TWO KINGS, satisfied to have the marriage between their children moving forward, retired to the library to have a brandy. Jules sat in the sitting room with Enrique. He'd wanted to talk with her alone. She didn't blame him. She figured he wanted to talk about his brother.

Alejandro.

Her heart ached.

Who was she kidding?

She felt as if her heart died when Alejandro left. The raw hurt in his eyes made it hard for her to breathe. She'd hurt him with her words. Worse, she'd done it on purpose. She'd lashed out in her own hurt because he'd been unwilling to make a commitment to her.

She wanted to scream and cry, but instead she sat showing no emotion on her face. The way she'd done her entire life, except for the time she'd spent with Alejandro. Sailing, talking, building castles in the sand.

The best time of her life.

Don't think about him. As he'd said, she had to resume her life…

"I understand how easy it must have been to get carried away with the sailing, but I must know…" Enrique rose from the damask-covered settee. He stood in front of her, towering over her while she remained seated. His mouth narrowed into a thin line. "Did you have sex with my brother?"

It wasn't as much a question as a demand. An easy one to answer, but she hesitated.

Jules knew her life on the island would be better than life in Aliestle, but not by much. Enrique would see to that. He only cared about himself. She would always be an extension of his persona to be controlled so she wouldn't embarrass him.

She stood and raised her chin. "I didn't have sex with Alejandro."

The tension on Enrique's face disappeared.

"But I'm in love with him," she admitted.

"I'm not surprised." Enrique sounded more amused than angry. "Alejandro has seduced many beautiful women and left a trail of broken hearts on this island. Someone as innocent as you never stood a chance. Do not worry. Once we're married, you'll forget him."

Surprise echoed through her. "You still want to marry me knowing I love another man?"

"Of course," Enrique said. "I thought he might have wanted sex from you. I realize he wanted to win the race so he could promote his business. But now that he received so much publicity today, winning the race, and therefore you, are no longer necessary."

His words took the wind out of her sails. "I'm a necessary part of his crew."

Enrique shrugged. "If that's true, why didn't he argue to have you race with him tomorrow?"

Feeling like she'd hit a reef and was taking on water fast, she struggled to breathe. To think. "Because of my father. And you."

"Believe that if it makes you feel better, but one day you'll realize the truth."

Jules knew the truth. Alejandro had told her it himself.

If La Rueca *places in the top five, the resulting publicity will boost my boatyard's reputation and raise the island's standing in the eyes of the yachting world. To do that I need you steering the boat.*

She narrowed her gaze. "Your brother wanted me so he could win the race. And you want me for my dowry."

Enrique grinned wryly. "Your royal bloodline doesn't hurt."

The two brothers were similar. Both men were selfish.

The realization hit her full force, the pain soul-deep.

But she couldn't entirely blame Alejandro for pursuing the freedom she was too scared to reach for herself.

She had let him go, but she couldn't let herself go. Surrendering and being obedient wasn't going to bring real change and happiness. She had to find her own path like Alejandro had done.

Effecting change meant not passively waiting and hoping, but required real, risk-taking leadership. The women's rights rallies weren't occuring because she'd been a dutiful princess, but because she'd been a defiant one who sailed in a race like her mother.

If she married Enrique, she would perpetuate the same repression her father had returned to in the wake of her mother's death. Jules wouldn't be an example for change, but of the status quo.

She'd been sleepwalking through life out of duty, but there was a higher duty: to be true to one's self.

However much we love people or have loved them, we still have to be the person we are meant to be.

Alejandro had been talking about his family when he'd spoken those words to her. Jules hadn't realized how much the words spoke to her soul until now.

Being true to one's self had more power to improve lives than she realized. Alejandro had taught her that. And she wanted to teach that to any children she had, both sons and daughters.

It was time for her to wake up for good. She needed to stand up for herself and go after what she wanted. She wanted to be the person her mother wanted her to be, the kind of person the women of Aliestle could be proud of.

She squared her shoulders. "La Isla de la Aurora might be more progressive, but you and Alejandro are as selfish as the men in Aliestle. Neither of you value women for who they are, but for what they can provide you."

"Why are you so surprised?" Enrique asked. "You agreed to

an arranged marriage. Did you think this would turn into a love match?"

"Yes. I hoped it would." Ridiculous fantasy that it was. "Like my parents' arranged marriage."

Enrique laughed. "Love is a childish notion that royalty cannot indulge in."

His words strengthened her. "I appreciate you wanting to marry me, but I can't marry you. I ask to be released from our arrangement."

His eyes flared with surprise. "Because of Alejandro."

"No. He doesn't want me." The knowledge bit into her, but she refused to give it any measure. She'd awoken to possibilities thanks to Alejandro for which she would always be grateful. "But that doesn't mean I can't find love, a real love I can count on."

"What have you done?" King Alaric looked as if one of the blood vessels in his forehead might burst. "You march back in there and tell Enrique you were mistaken."

"I'm not mistaken about this, Father." All she'd learned while on this island paradise empowered her. "Enrique only wants my dowry."

"So?"

She boldly met her father's gaze. "So I want more from a marriage than that."

"You'll see what you end up with when we return home and you marry an Aliestlian."

His words unleashed something deep inside of her, something lying dormant for too long. "I'm not returning to Aliestle," she said with a new sense of conviction. "I'm not going to be forced into a marriage I don't want."

"This is your duty."

"Perhaps once, but no longer. I believe my mother would've understood."

"I will not stand for this impertinence." He stood, his nostrils flaring. "You will obey me or I will disown you. You will lose your title, your home, your allowance. I will strip you of your passport. You will have nothing left. No money. No home. No country."

The thought of losing everything hurt, but she had to follow her own path. Her own heart. Jules didn't need to be claimed by a man or rescued. She could take care of herself. "If that is what you must do, Father, go ahead."

"You are dead to me," he screamed.

Tears stung her eyes. She felt an odd mix of sadness and joy. But she held firm. For the first time in her life, she was completely free of duty. Until now, everything in her life had been planned out, dictated by others. "Father…"

He turned his back on her.

She would have to make her own way, create a new life for herself. She was in charge now. She got to decide who she would be.

But Jules already knew.

She was like her mother, Queen Brigitta. Jules was a sailor, and a sailor sailed. She needed to get back into the Med Cup race even if Alejandro didn't want her. She needed to do it for herself, her mother and for all the women in Aliestle.

"I'll always love you, Father."

And she walked out of the room to an uncertain future.

Alejandro barely slept. Early the next morning, he wandered through his villa, unable to shake his uneasiness and loneliness. Strange, given he was back home, free to race and do as he pleased.

Boots meowed, sounding sad as if he knew Julianna and her treats were gone.

Gone.

He'd let Julianna go so she could be happy. Now he was miserable.

Alejandro dragged his hand through his hair. He missed her already. He'd done everything on his own for so long and been self-reliant, but this past week and a half, he'd been in a partnership. One, he realized now, he didn't want to end.

Everything in his life—Boots, *La Rueca* and his plans for

the island—had become built around Julianna. He cared what she thought about things. He valued her opinion. He was happier than he'd ever been when he was with her. She was happy, too.

That had to count for something.

Would it be enough?

He hoped so because he realized that he was willing to fight for it. For her.

Letting Julianna go had been the wrong decision. One he regretted with his whole heart. Somehow he had to show her happiness and love were as important as her sense of duty.

I love her.

His heart pounded a ferocious beat. Feelings he'd tried to ignore burst to the surface. He staggered back until he hit the wall.

Alejandro wasn't sure when it had happened, sailing or on the beach, but he loved Julianna. Body, heart and soul. He loved the way she could be so prim and proper, but yearn for adventure at the same time. He loved the way she sailed as if her life depended on it. He loved her smile, her laughter and her tears. He loved the way she made him want to be a better man.

He struggled to breathe.

Love might not always last, but they weren't his parents. Julianna was too important not to at least try. The life Alejandro wanted wasn't going to work unless she was a part of it.

"I've got to go after her," he said to Boots. "I have to convince her we have a future together."

Boots meowed.

Alejandro ran out the villa's front door.

The sun rose as he drove up the windy road to the palace. No red sky this morning, just golden-yellow and orange rays. The beginning of a beautiful day, he hoped.

The only other car on the road was his security detail following him. No matter what time of day, they were always right there behind him. His father must have forgotten to tell them their services were no longer required.

Inside the palace, he ran through the hallway to her room. Yvette wasn't sitting outside.

He knocked.

No one answered.

He knocked again.

"She's not here." Enrique slurred the words. He wore the same clothes as last night sans jacket and held a bottle of wine. "Julianna broke off the match. Alaric disowned her. She's gone."

Alejandro's heart soared. If Julianna called off the wedding and gave up on doing her duty, that might mean she loved him. If she didn't, he'd show her the feelings between them were real. "Where is she?"

"What is all the noise?" His father walked down the hallway in his robe and slippers. "Do you know what time it is?"

Enrique burped. "His fault."

"Where is Julianna, Father?" Alejandro asked.

"I don't know," Dario admitted. "I offered to let her stay in the palace until she sorted things out, but she said it was time for her to start doing things on her own."

"Is Klaus with her?"

"King Alaric forbid the bodyguard from going with her," Dario said. "I thought Klaus was going to cry. Brandt is with him now."

"Yvette?"

"She broke down." Dario shook his head. "Elena is with her."

"I must find Julianna, Father. I need to know she's safe." Alejandro had spent much of his life rebelling and retreating from his duty, wanting to be alone and doing everything himself. But not today. "I love her. I need to tell her that even if she doesn't feel the same way."

"She's an ice princess." Enrique swaggered down the hallway. "All that money gone. Gone. Gone."

"Alaric took away Julianna's passport so she's on the island," Dario said in earnest to Alejandro.

"It's a start." But where on the island would she go? She didn't know anyone that well.

His father placed a hand on Alejandro's shoulder. "I was

wrong trying to control everyone. That is what drove your mother away. I didn't want to lose you, too, so I wouldn't allow her to take you. But I fear I have lost you anyway, Alejandro. We don't always see eye to eye, but I hope you know I love you and am proud of the man you've become."

Alejandro choked up. That was all he'd ever wanted from his father. "I love you, too."

"We'll have to start listening to each other as a family. Perhaps you can show me your plans for the properties you've purchased."

Alejandro nodded.

His father smiled. "Good luck with Julianna, son."

"Thanks." Alejandro ran to his car. The island wasn't that big, but searching for her alone would take too much time. The crew was preparing for the race.

The race.

No, Julianna was more important.

He saw a familiar car and sprinted over to his security detail. "We must find Princess Julianna. I don't care if you have to search every single hotel on the island. Find her."

For the next two hours, Alejandro searched to no avail. He checked the tunnels, the beach, the dock and the yacht club that was sponsoring the race. The narrow streets grew crowded as the town came alive. Excitement about the Med Cup finals filled the air.

Text messages from the crew asking where he was and why he wasn't at the boat preparing for the race, grew more frantic. They also wanted to know if J.V. was coming.

Alejandro didn't want them to know Julianna was missing. He finally sent a reply he never expected to send: Go without me.

He'd regret not looking for Julianna more than he'd regret missing the race.

The race.

He'd checked the yacht club earlier, but she might go to the boat to race.

Hope glimmered, the first time all morning.

Traffic clogged the roads. Impatient, Alejandro parked on the side of the road, exited the car and jogged to the marina.

Up ahead, a woman with long, blond hair wearing the colors of his crew headed toward the yacht club.

"Julianna," he yelled.

She didn't stop. Alejandro ran after her, but was going against the crowd of people. He found himself being pushed back.

He had to reach her somehow.

Alejandro saw a narrow opening between buildings. He worked his way over, but a large hedge blocked his way.

Nothing was going to stop him from reaching her.

Looking around, he saw a crate. He dragged it over and climbed over the hedge. His team jacket caught on a thorn and tore. He didn't care. He dropped down on the other side, jumped over some small plants until he made it to a paved walkway that led to the marina.

Alejandro ran, his legs pumping as fast as they could, but he'd lost sight of her. Julianna was…gone.

A bolt of grief ripped through him. His fault. He had no one else to blame.

He stared at the marina in the distance. A familiar mast caught his attention. *La Rueca* was heading out to the course to race.

Alejandro didn't know whether to laugh or cry. He pulled out his phone instead.

Good luck, he texted.

Sam replied: We've got J.V., no luck needed.

Alejandro read the message three times before the words sunk in. Julianna *had* been on her way to *La Rueca*. She'd made it onboard in time.

But he hadn't.

He laughed.

Now he would have to wait to see how things turned out both with *La Rueca* and Julianna. But at least he knew she was safe. That was enough. For now.

He texted Sam, asking him to hand his mobile phone to Julianna.

What? she asked.

He typed, You OK?

OK. You?

Alejandro typed a message and hit Send.

That was all he could do now.

He called his security detail and his father then made his way to the yacht club. There, he could watch the race unfold. His boat was out there with the woman he loved at the helm. He didn't want to miss a single minute of it.

The race was in its final leg. Not having Alejandro aboard was strange, especially during such a tight race. *La Rueca* had made up distance since heading upwind, but couldn't catch the lead boat.

Jules clutched the wheel, the wind whipping through her ponytail. The same frustration etched on the crew's face must be on hers. "We're going to run out of course."

"We'll never catch them this way," Phillipe agreed.

"Alejandro will be satisfied with second place." She thought about the text he'd sent as they headed out.

If we lose the race, we lose. But just being here, we've already won.

She'd already won her freedom. She'd lost her family and...

No. Jules needed to focus. "But he deserves a win."

"We can still win," Phillipe said confidently. "But it's going to take the best tack of your life. You up for it?"

She grinned. "Just tell me what to do."

"Not what, when," Phillipe explained. "The rules make it hard to overtake a boat. But if we can tack below and come ahead."

"We'd have luffing rights," she said.

Phillipe winked. "Our helmsman has read the rule book."

Jules nodded. Her hands trembled with excitement and nerves. She wanted to give Alejandro and *La Rueca* the victory.

"The lead boat is tacking on starboard," Phillipe yelled. "Wait for my call."

The crew readied themselves for the final maneuver. They were on port, left of the lead boat. Instead of passing behind their competitor, they were going to tack below them and try to gain the advantage and the lead.

"Now," the tactician ordered.

"Tacking." Julianna turned the wheel. She focused on her job. She knew the other crewmembers were doing theirs, everyone in sync. The wind seemed to be on their side as well.

"Faster," Phillipe yelled.

Jules turned the wheel. Her hands and arms ached from three days of racing. She ignored the pain, thinking about Alejandro instead. This boat and race meant so much to him. Placing would give him more publicity so he could start turning the island into a sailing-centered tourist spot, but a win would be a huge boost to his boatyard.

He'd helped her. Jules wanted to do the same for him even if he didn't want her the way she wanted him.

She pressed the boat closer to the wind.

Phillipe whistled. "That's it. They're getting our dirty air now."

They edged out in front, taking both the lead and the wind.

"They're falling away," Mike called. "Looks like we can pull this off."

A few minutes later, the prow of *La Rueca* sailed between the buoys marking the finish line. They had done it. They had won the race!

Laughter overflowed along with deafening cheers. Jules wanted to celebrate along with the crew, but the victory was bittersweet.

Yes, she had proven herself. But now that the race was over, she had no idea what would happen. What would she do next?

Exhilaration shot through her. At least she was the one who got to answer that question, not anyone else.

The boat arrived at the marina. Alejandro stood on the dock with champagne bottles. A jubilant smile graced his face. Approval filled his dark eyes.

"Good race." He shook her hand, the pressure warm, secure, making her ache to have him pull her into his embrace. "World class sailing out there, Julianna. You won the race for us."

For you, she wanted to tell him. But seeing him brought a rush of emotion. Tears welled in her eyes. She didn't want to start crying because she was afraid she wouldn't be able to stop.

"Thanks." She forced a smile even though his greeting broke her heart. Not that she expected anything else, but they had won the race. A hug would be...appropriate. "And it's Jules, not Julianna."

"Thank you, Jules," he said.

A member of the yacht club led the crew to a platform surrounded by fans and press. Trophies were handed out. Through it all, Jules kept stealing glances at Alejandro. She forced her attention off him. When a bottle of champagne ended up in her hands, she took a swig.

The crew cheered.

Sam grinned. "Now that's the proper way a princess should drink, mates."

She laughed.

Alejandro pulled her aside. "We need to talk."

Her heart beat as fast as a hummingbird's wings. She followed him to *La Rueca* and climbed aboard. "I'm not going to marry Enrique."

"I know." His mouth twisted with regret. "I'm sorry, Jules. I thought you and Enrique marrying was for the best, but I was fooling myself. I'm miserable without you. I thought I had to rely only on myself. But I needed you to sail the boat. And then I realized I need you in my life. I love you."

The air rushed from her lungs. "You do?"

"Yes. I do." His tender gaze caressed her face. "I love everything about you. From the way you drive a sailboat to the way you kiss me until I can't think straight. You can go from haughty royal to sweet young thing in about three seconds flat. That made it hard to know the real Julianna or Jules, but I realize she's all of you. And that's okay."

Jules stared up at him. "I'm sorry for what I said to you. I was hurt. Angry. Wrong."

"It's okay now." He squeezed her hand. "I'm here for you.

I'll take care of you. I can be a prince if that's what you want. Though you'll never be a queen."

Joy flowed through her, filling up every space inside her. She touched his cheek. "I don't care about being a queen. I don't need you to be a prince. I love you, Alejandro. That's all that matters. But we'll have to take care of each other. Equally. I wouldn't have it any other way."

"Fine by me, Princess." He brushed his lips across hers. "You've already rescued me from being alone, from believing I was the black sheep who had to prove himself, from avoiding my problems with my family and running away from being a prince."

"We rescued each other."

"And we'll continue to do so." Alejandro dropped down on one knee. "I love you, Jules. There's no other woman I'd rather spend the rest of my life with. Will you do me the honor of being my wife?"

"Yes." She pulled him up and kissed him hard on the lips. "A hundred times, yes."

"I want you to pick out a ring you like." He pulled something out of his pocket. A thin piece of line knotted into a ring. "I hope this will do in the meantime."

Tears of love crested her lashes. "It'll do fine."

She'd been wrong. So very wrong.

Alejandro hadn't been selfish. He'd been afraid. But he was still the same dashing hero from her midnight sailing adventure. And she knew from the bottom of her heart, totally devoted to her. Love overflowed as he placed the handmade ring on her finger. A perfect fit.

Her heart sighed. "I'm ready to sail off into the sunset."

"Not yet," he said.

She looked up at him. "I thought…"

"I'm going to marry you, but first I want you to take some time to live your own life. To be on your own before we settle down. Maybe six months to a year. I want you to experience the freedom you've longed for. Travel, sail, whatever you want."

"I want to be with you."

"I want to be with you, but this is too important." He kissed each of her fingers. "Don't worry. I'm not about to let you have all that fun without me. Some things we'll do together. Others you'll do on your own. But know I'll be here to support, love and marry you when it's time."

"I'm counting the days."

"I'll have a real ring for you by then."

She stared at the rope on her finger and smiled up at him. "This ring is real. Like your kisses. Speaking of which…"

He lowered his mouth toward her. "I thought you'd never ask."

EPILOGUE

One year later...

STANDING ON THE deck of the eighty-five-foot sailboat, Jules listened to the wind against the sails. The sun shone high in the blue sky. The oiled teak gleamed. The old-fashioned schooner was something out of a dream or a pirate movie.

Contentment flowed through her. She'd spent the last year chasing her dreams. She'd sailed in numerous races, including winning a prestigious offshore race as part of an all-women's crew. She'd traveled and worked on women's rights issues. All the while Alejandro was there supporting, encouraging and waiting.

But this was the one dream she wanted to make come true.

She couldn't imagine a better place to get married. No heads of state, no strangers, no media in attendance. Only friends and family. Her father, stepmother and four brothers were here as well as Alejandro's father, mother and brother. Not quite a happy family, but Jules hoped in time differences could be... forgotten.

Alejandro squeezed her hand. He stared at her as though she were the sun and his world revolved around her. She felt the same way about him.

"I pronounce you husband and wife." The ship's captain smiled. "You may kiss the bride."

Alejandro's lips pressed against hers, making her feel cherished and loved. Jules kissed him back with her heart and her soul. She wanted him to know how much he meant to her.

Those in attendance clapped and cheered.

"I feel like I'm dreaming," she whispered.

"Wake up, Princess." He brushed his lips across hers. "Your dreams are coming true."

"A happily ever after, too?"

"Nothing less will do." Alejandro ran his finger along her jawline. The caress sent tingles shooting through her. "But we have to do one thing first."

Anticipation buzzed through her. "What?"

"Sail off into the sunset."

Jules's heart overflowed with love. "Sounds perfect."

"Just like you."

"I'm not perfect."

His smile crinkled the corners of his eyes. "Then you're the perfect not-so-perfect princess for me."

* * * * *

WEDDING AT
PELICAN BEACH

EMILY FORBES

*This book is dedication to all the Aunts in
our family, from our Mother's aunts,
to ours and to our children's.*

*Fed and Nancy, you may see a little
bit of yourselves in this one and although
the Conga-line didn't make it this time, Fel,
there's always another story to be told.*

So to all those wonderful women, thank you.

Emily Forbes is an award-winning author of
Medical Romances for Mills & Boon. She has
written over 25 books, and has twice been a finalist
in the Australian Romantic Book of the Year Award,
which she won in 2013 for her novel *Sydney
Harbour Hospital: Bella's Wishlist*. You can get in
touch with Emily at emilyforbes@internode.on.net
or visit her website at www.emily-forbesauthor.com.

CHAPTER ONE

'NOT again!' Zac Carlisle looked in the direction discreetly pointed out by his colleague, Dr Lexi Patterson.

The trail of disaster left behind by Bob Leeming, the recently 'let go' human resources manager, apparently had one more sting in its tail. A sting that was about five feet nothing and wearing little more than a cropped top and some sort of hip-scarf covered with hundreds of little gold coins, which were jangling as she leant on the nurses' counter, hips swaying to a beat only she could hear.

'A belly dancer? The hospital is falling apart, we're desperate for a nurse and he takes on a *belly dancer?*'

'Shh,' was Lexi's helpful reply. 'She'll hear you.'

And it seemed the belly dancer *had* heard. She turned around, grinning, and the wattage of her smile made him forget about the fact she was the most inappropriately attired nurse he'd ever seen. Until Lexi smothered a giggle and he came to his senses. A gypsy, that's what she was. A gypsy sent to take his already sanity-testing work life one step closer to hell.

'I've gotta run, I need to collect Mollie, but I'll call later, have fun,' she said as she left, leaving him to send the new disaster packing.

The new disaster was walking towards him, holding out her

hand, her grin lighting up her face—how could a smile that huge fit on a face that petite and fine-featured, a face like a china doll's?

'I take it you're Dr Carlisle.'

He'd thought she was English—the nurse he was expecting was coming from the UK—but beneath the rounded vowels lurked an Australian accent. She waggled her proffered hand a little, prompting him to shake it.

He did, reluctantly taking her tiny hand in his own—surprised at the firmness of her grip—then releasing it as quickly as he could. A woman who had him thinking about china dolls, gypsies and belly dancers was not a woman to be trusted.

'I'd ask your name but I'm afraid you're going to tell me it's Eva Henderson.'

'No.'

'No?' His luck had changed and Bob Leeming hadn't thrown another disasterous employee in his path?

'Actually, yes, it is, but I prefer Evie.' She laughed. 'And I wanted to see if you'd brighten up if you didn't think I was about to start working here. But I gather I *am* the problem.'

She slipped a hand onto her half-naked hip, just above the scarf-thing which he saw was tied over a barely-there skirt, and although he kept his gaze firmly on her face there was such an expanse of perfect creamy skin on show it was not without effort he resisted a peek. She was tapping her foot, but with impatience or still to the invisible beat she'd been moving to when he'd first seen her he couldn't tell.

'Bob Leeming took you on?'

'You're not going to tell me there's a problem, are you? I mean, I know he's left, but I'm here, and…well, I need the job.'

Large, dark eyes were staring up at him, framed by lashes that were indecently thick and sooty-coloured. He'd like to think the gaze was pleading but he had a bad feeling the mood was more one of confidence. She knew he couldn't send her packing.

'Funny, you don't look like you've come dressed to work.' He was aiming for sarcasm but he just sounded as exhausted as he felt.

'It's the country, I figured we could be more casual here and—' She broke off and patted him on the arm. Presumably she'd seen the look of utter panic that had swept across his face at her announcement—things *were* every bit as bad as he'd guessed. 'I'm joking. Really. I don't start until tomorrow. I just dropped in to visit someone and to finish off my paperwork. See, I am responsible. I'm a day early.'

'I didn't say you were irresponsible.'

'You didn't need to.' Her tone was as merry as his was glum. 'You might just as well have yelled it across the room. It would have fit nicely into the same sentence as "belly dancer"—I think that was the word you used.' She laughed again. 'Sorry, I'm talking too much, I must be nervous.'

'I don't know why you would be. You seem to have made yourself perfectly at home in around ten minutes flat.' Maybe in the next five minutes he'd get a handle on this meeting. Right now he was trying to ignore the thought that Eva—Evie, he corrected himself—was the most extraordinary case of walking, talking confidence he'd ever seen. And just his luck, she'd landed slap bang in the middle of his already enormous pile of problems. 'Who were you visiting? You're not from here.'

'Letitia.'

'My *patient* Letitia?'

'You're her GP?' She considered this for a moment, then looked him up and down without any attempt to be discreet and added, almost to herself, 'Yes, I guess you are.'

He nodded, words seeming less and less possible by the second.

'She's my sister-in-law and— Oh.'

'What?' He looked around for the source of her surprise. 'She's your sister-in-law and what exactly?'

'What exactly?' She took his hand in hers again and shook it with great enthusiasm as she talked. '"What exactly" is that we're going to be neighbours.'

'Neighbours?' He was reduced to repeating her last words.

'I've moved into Jake and Letitia's house so I can look after their girls when they go to the city for Lettie's surgery. She mentioned how weird it was to live next door to her GP but, as we all know, that sort of thing is par for the course in the country.'

'This is hardly the country.' He'd recovered his powers of speech at last. 'And *you* are hardly a country girl. At least, not from any country I've ever been in,' he muttered.

'Correction. I *am* a country girl. Jake and I grew up in Wagga Wagga.'

'New South Wales? I thought you were English?' But that would explain her curious accent, he could definitely hear an Aussie twang.

'Nope, just been living there.'

He was having trouble keeping up with her conversation, a situation he was unfamiliar with. Her state of dress, or undress, was offputting. And she was still grinning at him. No wonder he was having trouble concentrating. 'Are you always this cheerful?'

She nodded. 'Don't worry, it's not contagious. At least, not unless you kiss me, then you'd have a terminal case of cheer.' She laughed, apparently confident she'd silenced him for good this time, and, waggling her fingers at him in a wave, positively sashayed out of the department and along the corridor.

Leaving him very, very worried that if this was Evie when she was brand spanking new to a place, what would she be like once she'd settled in?

As he watched her almost dance down the corridor he could feel the tenuous grip he had on everything start to slip. But how could a woman who was about as big as Lexi's eight-year-old niece Mollie pose *any* sort of threat to the future of the hospital? Any more of a threat than it was already under.

Why could he still feel the imprint of her tiny hand on his palm?

The questions were coming faster than he could mentally articulate them.

Why would any woman—a soon-to-be-employee to boot—run around a hospital in a be-coined, jangling hip-scarf?

And just how long would it take him to get the image of her swaying hips, curving up to a tiny waist, out of his mind?

'Dr Carlisle!'

Zac, with one hand on his office door, felt his heart sink at the sound of his name being called. The heavens were conspiring to ensure he never got on top of the administrative nightmare his life had become of late. Thanks to an emergency last night, he hadn't even been able to check Evie's qualifications like he'd meant to. Now it was only eight a.m. and he'd already been here for two hours, delivering a baby who wasn't meant to arrive for another three weeks.

Turning, he suppressed a sigh but couldn't muster a smile. 'Yes, Doris?'

Doris tutted at him. 'You know I wouldn't bother you if it wasn't necessary.'

His smile came of its own volition. 'I know, Doris, but I haven't switched my pager on and I'm not officially here, yet you manage to track me down.' He tugged at his tie, still unfamiliar attire, but he wore it because he couldn't be sure when there'd be an impromptu visit from a certain government department hell bent on dismantling the hospital, brick by brick. First impressions counted and with a tie on, he rationalised, he had an armour. Of sorts.

'Better than a bloodhound, I know. Lisa and Bruce called through.' She named two of the local volunteer ambulance officers. 'They're bringing in a teenager with complications and they're not sure what they're dealing with. ETA five minutes.'

'Schoolies' week?'

'A fair bet, I'd think.'

'Bloody kids.' He was striding towards the emergency department. 'When are they going to learn that descending on a small seaside town intent on killing themselves isn't the smartest way to mark the end of their school lives?'

Doris was trotting at his side, making a fair attempt of keeping up without actually running. 'They're teenagers. In their minds that makes them invincible.'

He pushed open the doors to the emergency department and stopped in his tracks. Doris, not having any warning, bumped squarely into his back and let out an 'Oomph' of surprise before scooting past. He scarcely registered. He only had eyes for Evie.

Except he'd stopped short because he hadn't been sure it *was* her. Deep in conversation with another nurse, she hadn't seen him. She was dressed in a crisp white nurse's shirt, tucked into a pair of navy trousers, no coins around her waist today. Her dark hair was pulled back and secured tightly at the nape of her delicate neck into some sort of bun. The image wasn't nearly as disconcerting as the belly dancer of yesterday and he was conscious of a moment of disappointment.

Then she looked up and flashed her gypsy smile at him, letting him know his abruptness yesterday hadn't shaken her confidence. Please, he prayed silently, let her confidence be justified. An over-confident, incompetent nurse—could there be any worse fate for him?

'Good morning,' she sang out, moving towards him with lithe grace. 'I was getting the run-down from Libby—'

She broke off as the screech of a siren was heard in the distance. 'Shall we?' She motioned to the external door and they fell into step, exiting the department through the automatic doors out to the ambulance bay.

Judging by the siren, the ambulance was almost there and he had no idea what to expect from their patient, and even less from the nurse meant to be assisting him. 'Are you equipped to deal with this?'

Had she bristled? He didn't care if she had. He had a department to run and if he, as one of the senior staff members, had no time to indulge his own ego, he sure as hell wasn't about to make room for hers.

If she had bristled, she didn't take the bait, merely nodded, adding, 'Of course,' in an unflustered tone.

Evie wasn't about to start an argument with Dr Carlisle. She needed this job, and she didn't have time to cater to the ego of Mr Big Shot Country Doctor. That wasn't why she was there and she wasn't going to give him the satisfaction of pulling her up.

But if he'd been trying to needle her he let it drop. Maybe he was just checking, nothing more. Besides, she liked him. First impressions counted, although this morning he looked even more dishevelled than yesterday. She risked a sideways glance up at him, assuming he wouldn't notice as he seemed somewhat distracted. He towered over her, a shadow of a beard darkening his jaw. What time had his day started? It didn't look like he'd had time to shave. His thick brown hair was longer than conventional—was it intentional or was he overdue for a haircut? His blue-grey eyes were solemn and he reminded her of a big shaggy bear, grumpy after a long hibernation, in need of some company, perhaps in the form of a great big belly rub. And she was great at belly rubs. First, though, she'd get rid of that ridiculous tie which he obviously felt uncomfortable in, and—

The shaggy bear's voice broke into her thoughts. 'Today, Nurse Henderson.' Oops.

She didn't even bother with a reply, just hotfooted it next to him as the ambulance screeched into the bay. Zac threw open the rear doors before the driver had turned off the engine and inside the ambulance Evie could see a second officer leaning over the patient.

Zac greeted him. 'Morning, Bruce, what have we got?'

Bruce climbed out of the ambulance and Zac pulled the stretcher towards him, watching as the legs unfolded to support its weight.

'Seventeen-year-old male, complaining of chest pain and stomach cramps. Heart rate 140 and irregular, resps 50 but settling with oxygen,' Bruce replied as he took charge of the stretcher.

The patient had an oxygen mask over his mouth and nose and Evie could see a saline drip running into his arm. A portable oxygen cylinder and a drip stand were attached to the stretcher.

'Apparently he had hallucinations of some sort and became aggressive and then confused.' Bruce continued to talk as he pushed the stretcher through the hospital doors. 'We're assuming he's been drinking and has perhaps taken drugs or a mixture of drugs. We're told he vomited, but the kids aren't telling us much more so we're working blind.'

'What's wrong with these kids? Does someone have to die before they'll see sense?'

'At least one of them thought to call us, but it would help to know what we're dealing with.' Bruce's tone was calm in contrast to Zac's frustration.

Evie hurried alongside the stretcher, guiding it to a stop inside the first examination cubicle. Fortunately the emergency department was empty at this hour of the day and she didn't waste time drawing the curtains—she wanted to start treatment. The patient was in a bad way. Very bad.

'What's his name?' she asked Bruce, not bothering to introduce herself. There'd be time for that later and if he was going to fuss he could read her ID tag.

'Stewart.'

Evie leant over the boy, shaking him gently by the shoulder. 'Stewart, can you hear me? You're in the hospital.' She pulled up his eyelids as she spoke and that got his attention. He lashed out at her, knocking her arm away. She wasn't hurt but cursed herself for not reacting faster.

Stewart pulled off the oxygen mask and continued to thrash about, swearing and yelling. His pupils were dilated, his breathing shallow and rapid.

'Grab his arms, he needs restraints.' Evie caught Stewart's left arm, just before he managed to rip out his IV line. 'My money's on crystal meth,' she said as she clung to Stewart's arm with all her strength, gratefully aware that Bruce had pinned Stewart's other arm.

'Pardon?' Zac's voice came from the foot of the stretcher, where he was trying to hold Stewart's flailing legs. Stewart was doing his best to connect and, despite his size, Zac was struggling to contain him.

'Crystal meth, methamphetamine—you know, ice, speed. He's got all the right symptoms of an overdose.'

'Do you *know* that, or is it something you've seen on a TV show?'

Evie decided to ignore the jibe. It wasn't her fault she knew more than he did. 'I know you don't know me, but I know what I'm doing.' She let go of their patient's arm as Libby finally tied a restraint around his wrist, fixing him to the stretcher. Replacing the oxygen mask on Stewart's face, she continued, 'I'm from *London*. This is like a common cold there.'

He looked at her a fraction longer through narrowed eyes, his expression unsure. She didn't have time to go into further detail. She needed to take a blood sample and drawing blood from an eighty-kilogram moving target wasn't easy. Libby had fastened the other straps and fortunately Stewart gave up the struggle once he was restrained.

'What if it's not drugs? What if he's had a fit?' Zac asked.

'It's possible,' she conceded, 'but I'll bet my first pay packet it's drugs. I'll take blood and we can get it tested.'

'We can't do that here. Bloodwork gets sent to Adelaide. We're a small-town hospital, we don't have all the services you're used to in London.'

He had no idea what she was used to, she thought. She wasn't always in London and she'd worked in far more primitive conditions than Pelican Beach. But now wasn't the time to have that discussion—their patient was her priority.

'If you can do an EEG, that might give you some info but if it was a fit it's over and the treatment plan would be virtually the same.' Evie popped a tourniquet around Stewart's left biceps and slipped a needle into the vein in his elbow as she spoke. 'Until we contact his parents we've no way of knowing his medical history. He's not wearing a medic-alert so I'm with Bruce. I think we should treat it as a drug-related problem.' She was watching Zac—creased brow, blue-grey eyes—who looked torn between believing her and telling her to get out of the department.

Something lifted in his expression. Had practicality won out?

'What do we do?'

'Stabilise him, monitor him, rehydrate him. Sedate him if necessary. The effects of ice are made worse by lack of sleep and lack of food. My guess is they've been partying all night. Stewart needs to be rehydrated and sedated while the drugs wear off.'

As Evie finished speaking, a policeman entered Emergency and Zac, after nodding in her direction, which Evie took as permission to start treatment, left her side to talk to the officer.

She enlisted Libby and Bruce to transfer Stewart to a hospital bed then Bruce was free to go. Libby and Evie worked in harmony to retie the restraints, attach a new bag of saline to the gelco in Stewart's right arm and connect him to the monitors. Evie started a chart and filled out an order for a sedative, ready for a doctor's signature. She placed the chart at the end of the bed, turned around—and collided with Zac. For a tall, solidly built man he moved awfully quietly. His hands shot up and he held her arms, steadying her.

'You OK?' He dropped his hands, but not before she knew she'd have preferred it if he hadn't. 'When you've finished, Bill would like a word with us both.' Evie glanced over to where the policeman was waiting. 'It seems the kids have been buying drugs, ice included.'

So she'd been right—nice to know, at least from a professional point of view. She stopped herself from saying 'I told you so' because it was suddenly important for him to like her.

She crossed the room, holding out her hand. 'Bill, I'm Evie Henderson.'

Bill shook her hand. 'Welcome to Pelican Beach. Sorry about the circumstances.'

'Not a great start, for me or Stewart.'

'How is he? Lucky to be alive?' Bill asked.

'I think he'll be OK. You've spoken to the other kids? They were taking ice?'

'Smoking it, apparently, but they weren't too forthcoming with the information. Scared, I reckon, but I think they were more frightened by not knowing whether Stewart was dead or alive.'

'It's pretty rare for ice or speed to cause heart failure or to stop respiration.'

Zac shot her a dark look. 'Are you condoning the habit?'

'Of course not, but we all need to understand the drug and what we may have to deal with. The deaths associated with its use have usually been attributed to people inhaling their vomit and drowning. In the light of the fact you've got…how many kids descending on the town?'

'Thousands.' His tone was grim.

'I think we need to find out whether Stewart has taken the drug before. If he has and he's had a psychotic episode previously, it increases the likelihood of it recurring. But if he hasn't taken it before, or hasn't had this reaction, then you may have a problem with the quality of the drug and Stewart won't be our last customer. Someone has to tell us about Stewart's drug history and we need to get hold of the rest of the batch. Even better, find the supplier.'

'We're onto it.' Bill handed Evie a piece of paper. 'Contact details for Stewart's parents,' he said and then he left with Zac, leaving Evie to get back to day one on the job.

And back to wondering how to get a certain tousled-haired, harried-looking doctor to chill out and accept her. Just enough to be friends. Friends was what she needed. Friends, plural, but she sensed a challenge in Dr Carlisle, and she wasn't one to back away from a challenge.

She had two months, give or take, before she returned to her semi-nomadic existence. Two months was long enough for all sorts of things.

One never knew where life would take you but you could always enjoy the ride. Would Dr Carlisle be prepared to get on board?

* * *

Somehow Evie was in control of the situation.

Zac didn't know whether to be pleased, surprised or annoyed. He watched as she checked Stewart's drip and listened as she spoke quietly to her patient, even though he wasn't responding. He realised he had no grounds to be annoyed with her. She was doing her job and doing it well. Was that the problem? That she was proving him wrong in no uncertain terms?

He owed her an apology. But he didn't move, he just stood there, watching her. There was something about her, an energy, a vibrancy that demanded attention. His attention. He had dozens of other tasks waiting for him. So why couldn't he drag himself away?

Evie looked up from her patient. 'Did you want something, Zac?' An encouraging smile showed him she wasn't irritated.

'Do you need me to sign for anything?' He said the first thing that popped into his head.

'Could you sign for a sedative?' She held out the medication chart, indicating where she needed his initials. 'He really just has to sleep this off but we need to contact his parents. Would you call them?' She dug in her pocket and retrieved the piece of paper the policeman had given to her. 'I'm sure they'd prefer to speak to a doctor in the circumstances.'

Even Bill had figured Evie was in charge of the situation but Zac knew she was right. Stewart's parents would expect to hear from a doctor or the police. But he hadn't dealt with this before. What were the specifics?

'It could take a few days for the drug-related chemicals to break down so he'll have to be admitted.' Had Evie picked up his uncertainty—was she feeding him information? Or had she judged his ability, like he'd judged hers, he thought. He didn't like the idea. 'Tell them you'll speak to them in greater detail when they get here.' She glanced at the paper. 'They have an Adelaide address. I assume they'll drive down.'

She held out the paper and he automatically took it. She obviously had things under control and didn't need him. Raising a hand in farewell, he left her to it, busy with his thoughts.

So much for judging a book by its cover.

Which was what he'd done. One look at that hip-scarf and bare midriff and that's exactly what he'd done. He should be pleased—if what he'd seen so far was any indication, Evie was competent. That meant one less problem for him to sort out. He should be pleased. He *was* relieved, but the flip side was he'd been shown up. And that didn't feel so good.

'Is everything OK?' Libby's return interrupted Evie's musings.

'Yes, he's stable.'

'I heard Bill say it was drugs.' Evie nodded. 'If this is how things are going on day one of schoolies week, we could be in for a busy time.'

'You'd better tell me what to expect this week. It sounds a far cry from the quiet coastal life I was promised.'

'With a bit of luck we've seen the worst of it but you have arrived at our busiest time, luckily for us. Schoolies is a bit of an institution. Thousands of seventeen- and eighteen-year-olds "invade" us after their end-of-year exams and sometimes it seems as though all they want is the chance to run amok. There's been trouble in the past with underage drinking, sexual assaults, driving under the influence but we haven't had a drug problem before. I guess it was only a matter of time.'

'And medically speaking?'

'Mostly it's nothing out of the ordinary, just the number of people through the door increases. A task force was set up this year by Max Stoppard, our police chief, who wanted to look at ways to control the crowds. The locals have a bit of a love-hate relationship with schoolies week. It's a good money-spinner for a lot of local businesses but a nightmare for most permanent residents in terms of the kids' behaviour. Max had a mini-conference with the principals of a lot of the schools whose pupils come down here every year and also spoke to the mayor and the publicans.'

'What was the verdict?'

'For the first time there's going to be an organised party in the park on the foreshore, with bands and entry by ticket. The idea was to get the kids into one place to make it easier to supervise. Just enough supervision to let the kids know their behaviour is being monitored, which hopefully lets them celebrate safely. It's an experiment.'

'When's the party?'

'Tomorrow night.'

'I hope Bill has time to get a lid on the drugs issue otherwise we could have our hands full,' Evie said.

'I think they have some contingency plans in place, but I'm not sure if they counted on starting the weekend off with an overdose. Did Bill say what they'll do now?'

'He's going to try to get more information from the kids—we need details—and Zac's gone to ring Stewart's parents.' Evie hesitated but curiosity got the better of her. 'Tell me, is he always so sombre?'

'Zac?'

Evie nodded.

Libby shrugged. 'He's a serious type of person, I suppose. He's got a lot on his plate right now. He takes it all to heart, which is good for the hospital, probably bad for him.'

'What's he dealing with?'

'He's just joined the hospital board and I gather there's a bit of politics going on. I'm not sure why he put his hand up for the responsibility. When I work him out, I'll let you know. But as long as we're doing our jobs, and doing them well, he'll be happy.'

Libby's opinion was cut short by Zac's return.

'Were your ears burning?' Evie quipped. He looked horrified to think they'd been discussing him but didn't ask questions. How long would it take him to lighten up? She guessed he'd run a mile if he had an inkling as to where her thoughts lay.

'I've just spoken to Stewart's parents. They're on their way here and should arrive in a couple of hours.' He had his 'serious' face on again. She was positive he'd have a great smile if she could coax one out of him. 'I've given them a few details but I've left any further questions for when they get here.'

He'd addressed this to both women but then Libby excused herself and it was just the two of them. He seemed a little uncomfortable, but not in a hurry to leave.

'I owe you an apology.'

'You do?'

'The previous HR manager had a knack for putting the right people in the wrong jobs and vice versa, and employing some absolute disasters. It took me a while to sort all that out. I jumped to conclusions when I first met you and I'm sorry. I questioned your ability as a nurse. I've been put straight.' He spoke earnestly, as though it was a matter of grave importance and he anticipated a blast. 'I apologise.'

'Apology accepted,' she said graciously, although she hadn't given two hoots. 'I guess I was lucky my first patient wasn't a shark-attack victim. I don't know how impressed you would have been then. Overdoses I've had plenty of experience with, sharks—not so much,' she said, smiling, and expected a smile in return. But, once again, nothing.

Her two-month time limit suddenly seemed a bit ambitious. Zac looked like he might be a hard nut to crack.

Evie was beaming at him and he found himself completely disoriented. Her smile was like a beacon, drawing him closer.

He shook his head, trying to clear his mind, aware he was staring but unable to turn away. He tried to focus on what she'd said. Overdoses. That was it. Something about being familiar with overdoses.

'You did a good job. Stewart was lucky you were here,' he said, before he bade her goodbye and left the department, as fast as decently possible. Getting away from her distracting smile, away from thoughts of narrow waists, dark hair and large, expressive eyes. Eyes that looked as though they'd seen a lot and had liked most of it.

What had she seen? he wondered. And what had her experience with drugs been? Personal or professional? She hadn't made that clear and there was a lingering doubt in his mind. Was there more he should know?

He had to check her references and her credentials. He couldn't afford to make any mistakes, especially now. He'd judged her too quickly the first time—but he'd better make sure he wasn't leaning too far the other way, on the strength of one good performance, especially with Bob Leeming's terrible track record.

He hoped her past was clean. She'd be good to have around.

Good for the hospital, he clarified, that was what he'd meant. They could use her skills.

Unbidden, an image of Evie floated into his mind, her shimmering scarf-like skirt shifting around her thighs, jangling with gold coins as she moved with a lithe step. The image, so free, so *care*free, it mocked the beleaguered mood that had been his constant companion of late. Resentment he hadn't known he had burned inside him. She was the epitome of everything he'd *thought* he was. Only now he was finding out his life must have been a lie because, just a few weeks into his new role, he couldn't even keep up the appearance of being on top of his job.

He'd hesitated today with the drug case, and it didn't sit well. She'd sailed right in there, no hesitation, no doubts. What did that show? That he'd lost his nerve, just when he'd needed it most?

He reached his office and opened the door, marching to his desk and yanking his chair out to sit down.

No, he hadn't lost his nerve. All he needed was a few extra days in the week. And a benefactor with pots of money to get the hospital out of its predicament.

The hospital might benefit from her skills but there was nothing a belly-dancing gypsy with an incredible smile could do for him.

Nothing that didn't spell trouble, and he already had enough of that.

CHAPTER TWO

EVIE stitched and bandaged, disinfected and swabbed solidly for another two hours before Libby sent her for a break with words of encouragement ringing in her ears. She was desperate for a coffee but would there be a stash of condensed milk in the staffroom? That was the only way to drink it, two-thirds deliciously rich, totally addictive condensed milk with an inch of thick black coffee dripped on top. So thick the spoon could almost stand up by itself. Yum. Zac thought she'd been condoning drug-taking but coffee was her only vice and, as far as she was aware, it wasn't illegal. Although if she didn't get her condensed milk hit this side of lunch, she might well commit an illegal act.

'Lettie!' She shoved open her sister-in-law's hospital room door and flopped into the chair at her side. As there wouldn't be condensed milk, there was no point wasting her time with a coffee-break. 'Resting after your five-k run?'

'Sure, a brief respite then I'm off to the gym. Me and my trusty wheels.' She motioned to the wheelchair parked nearby.

'And here I thought you were faking it.'

'Don't I wish.'

'Any news about a transfer?'

Letitia shook her head, a wave of dark straight hair shifting across her shoulders. 'But now you're here I'm ready to go.' She reached out and took Evie's hands in her own. 'Thank you so much for coming back for us. You have no idea what it means to us and we know what you've had to give up—'

'Rubbish.' She cut Lettie off. She didn't need another tirade of thanks. 'It took me a second to decide and I can pick everything else up when you're back here, bossing my brother and two gorgeous nieces around again.' Which wasn't quite true. Being torn between two causes was an experience she didn't want to repeat any time soon, but there was no way she'd tell Lettie that. The whole martyr-thing wasn't her style. 'Speaking of which, I hope you know I have no intention of feeding my nieces vegetables while you and Jake are gone.'

'You love vegetables!'

Evie shook her head. 'That was just a cover until I got the gig of looking after the girls.' She'd successfully, if underhandedly, distracted Lettie by introducing one of her pet loves: discussion of her children's diets. Being married to the hospital chef and working in the kitchen herself, balanced diets were a favourite topic of conversation and seeing children with poor diets could send her right off. 'Secretly, I'm a hot chips and sauce girl. Besides, you won't be able to chase me when you're flat out doing your rehab. And, you should know, I'm intent on becoming the girls' favourite aunt while their parents are gone.'

'You're their *only* aunt.'

'All the more reason I shouldn't make them hate me by forcing them to eat their greens.' She glanced at the watch pinned to her shirt. 'Gotta run. I don't want big bad Dr Carlisle eating me alive on my first day for being late back from a break.' Lettie was making a strange noise. 'What? Are you choking? I was just joking about the veg—' Then she realised and, turning slowly towards the door, felt a laugh rise up in her throat.

Big, bad, *shaggy* Dr Carlisle was standing in the doorway. And from the look on his face, he'd heard every word she said. Oops again.

'Um, just so you know, that's Letitia's name for you, not mine.' She couldn't help it, she knew it wasn't funny, but she giggled.

'Evie!' Her sister-in-law's tone was scandalised.

'Letitia, I have some news for you.' He paused, looking pointedly at Evie.

She took the hint—it was hardly an obscure one—and stood, bending down to drop a kiss on Letitia's cheek. 'Don't give the nurses too much grief.' Heading for the door, she added, 'I'll pop back on my lunch-break.'

As she passed Zac, she heard him say softly, 'She'll be looking forward to it, no doubt.'

Was that exasperation or a hint of amusement in his voice? She slowed her steps to peer up at him but his gaze was so in-scrutable she'd need a jackhammer to get at any hidden meaning. And a ladder to get a close-up view.

'How tall are you anyway?'

'Pardon?'

She really, really hadn't meant to say that out loud. 'Nothing.' Three strikes and you're out? Was that how things worked here? She didn't stick around to find out and, speeding back to the emergency department, made a vow to come down from the high she'd been on since arriving. She hadn't realised how much she'd missed her family and although she was here because of Letitia's condition, and although she still felt sick at how she'd let down the project in Vietnam—the children!—part of her was euphoric about being here. What a pity Dr Carlisle was in such furious disagreement. If she couldn't change his mind then being rather unwelcome on that front might take the gloss off her stay a bit, and if that didn't, the reality of juggling shift work with the care of a six- and a seven-year-old could well sink in some time in the next few weeks.

She thought of the small box sitting in Letitia's kitchen. Twenty just wouldn't be enough. This was easily a fifty-tin mission. But did Pelican Beach stock enough condensed milk to see her through?

And just what would Dr Carlisle say if he got wind of her addiction? She didn't know him well—or at all, really—but she just *knew* he wasn't one to tolerate addictions. Of any sort.

Libby popped her head into the examination cubicle where Evie was checking Stewart's obs. 'Zac's here with Stewart's parents. They'd like to see him.'

'OK, just stall them for a minute while I untie these wrist restraints. I'll leave the ankle ones on, they're covered by the sheet, but I don't want them to see him tied down.'

'What if he lashes out again?' Libby sounded nervous.

'He's pretty heavily sedated, we should be OK.' Libby nodded and ducked out as Evie untied the straps. She'd just put them into the bedside drawer when Zac appeared.

'OK to come in?' Zac waited until she nodded, then drew back the curtains to admit Stewart's parents. 'Evie, this is James and Helen Cook. This is Sister Henderson, she's been looking after Stewart.'

James shook Evie's hand but Helen, after giving her a brief nod, headed directly for Stewart's bedside. She picked up his hand and began talking to him before turning to Evie, a look of concern on her face.

'Is he sleeping or is he unconscious?'

'He's had a sedative. He was quite distressed and he needs to rest.'

'Why is he still in the emergency department?'

'Stewart needs close monitoring and Evie has the most experience with these cases. He'll be transferred to a room when he's stable, but it was best to keep him with Evie,' Zac explained.

Of course, once they heard she was the expert, all questions were directed to her.

'Is he going to be all right?'

'We won't really know for a few days until the drug-related chemicals are cleared from his system but, physically, he should be fine. Emotionally it might be a different matter.'

'He's never done anything like this before. I don't understand it.'

'Truth be told,' said Stewart's father, 'we'd probably be the last to know if he has been experimenting with drugs.'

James was right but Evie wasn't about to say that out loud. Helen was shaking her head.

'No, his behaviour has been quite normal, even with the pressure of final exams. I'm sure this is just a one-off.'

'It's quite possible this was his first experience with methamphetamines. I imagine the kids are quite easily persuaded to experiment a little in a party environment like this. But one of the problems with crystal meth is that it's highly addictive. People have become addicted after one hit.' Evie paused to let that sink in. 'Stewart is going to need counselling and education and he's really going to have to be watched to make sure he stays away from drugs. You can't pretend this hasn't happened and you can't afford to think it was a one-off. I've seen how quickly people become addicted and what a mess it can make of their lives. The most dangerous thing you can do is to pretend it won't happen again.'

'What can you tell us about crystal meth—is that what it's called?'

'Yes. You've probably heard of "speed" or "ice"?' James nodded. 'Speed is the powder form of the drug and ice is the crystal form. Because the drug is illegal, there's no control over the formula and no control over the amounts kids take. They can snort it, inject it or smoke it, although I didn't see any evidence that Stewart has injected anything into his veins.'

Helen looked horrified at the image Evie described but James stayed focussed. 'What effect does it have?'

'Most take it for the feeling of euphoria and increased energy it gives. It can increase alertness, meaning kids can stay up all night. Some girls use it as an appetite suppressant. The drug and alcohol centre will give you a lot more information. The best thing to do is make an appointment for you to go as a family. They'll answer all your questions and if you do it together, you all get the same information.'

'When will I be able to talk to him?' Helen asked.

'The sedative will wear off later today but once people come down from the high they're usually exhausted and can sleep for the better part of a few days. I wouldn't expect to get much sense out of him until after the weekend. We'll move him to a room later this afternoon and you're welcome to sit with him, but don't expect too many answers. I'll leave you with him now for a few minutes. Call if you need anything.'

'We will,' they replied, and she left them, turning to acknowledge their thanks as she left the room.

Would this family be able to pull Stewart through? Would there be a happy ending? She'd seen too many cases where that hadn't happened but she didn't have long to dwell on that thought before another case came through the doors.

At least one problem he'd woken up with had been resolved.

He'd gone to sleep with some lingering reservations about Evie and had woken up knowing he had no reason to doubt her. It had just been his bruised ego whispering in his ear.

She'd proved herself and for once Bob Leeming had stumbled on a competent employee. Ironically, now that he'd fixed the mess left by Bob, the only position he had to fill before handing personnel issues back to the HR manager was the position of HR manager. He had two interviews lined up over the next few days and his fingers were firmly crossed that one of the applicants would be suitable. Then he could officially hand the whole thing back where it belonged.

He checked his desk clock. His long day was nearly over, just a board meeting to get through. It was scheduled to start in thirty minutes. Half an hour to pull a miracle out of his hat. He needed a miracle if they were going to find a solution to the funding crisis that was threatening the hospital. Zac cursed the state government for their narrow-mindedness. Why were the rural communities always being short-changed to benefit their city cousins? Zac knew why this government was proposing to decrease funding to rural health services but it didn't mean they had to accept it without a fight. There had to be a way around this, but he couldn't seem to find it.

Two heads might be better than one. He picked up the phone to dial his fellow board member and GP, Tom Edwards, not that their discussions about the hospital's future had got them anywhere so far. Married to another of his colleagues, Lexi Patterson, the couple had become his good friends since he'd moved to Pelican Beach.

Twenty-five minutes of brainstorming got them no closer to solving the crisis facing the hospital, but it almost made them late for the meeting. Two hours of frustration later they left the meeting together, both more dejected than when they'd started.

'Beer on my porch?' Zac asked, although they were already cutting across the hospital lawns towards his house, the beer a foregone conclusion. 'Has Lexi given you a leave pass?'

'Absolutely. Her favourite programme is on so she prefers it when I'm not home on a Friday. Apparently my wisecracks at the expense of the extraordinary stupidity of the characters offend her sensibilities. Can't think why.'

'Why, indeed.'

Tom pulled up short as they reached Zac's front gate. 'It's not home brew?'

'What's not to love about my home brew? But, no, I haven't had the time lately. Cooking is the only relaxation left to me.'

'Then we're still on.'

Tom took a chair on the front porch while Zac went inside and within a minute was back again with two cold bottles of beer. Flicking the caps off, he passed one to Tom before taking his seat and settling into the evening darkness, both men content to sit with their thoughts for a while after the stresses of the day.

Taking a long draught, Zac looked across the front garden towards the hospital, its windows lit up, faint noises drifting back to them on the warm, scented evening air. The hospital was less than a hundred metres away, and the staff accommodation, a few hundred-year-old row cottages, were in its grounds. Great in some respects but it meant he was never really away from his work. If the on-call doctor couldn't be tracked down, he was all too available.

Into the peace came another sound.

His new next-door neighbour.

Evie.

She'd come out of her front door—all of three metres from where they were sitting—and was seeing a visitor off. He couldn't see her over the stone wall dividing their front verandahs but her voice, surprisingly deep for someone so tiny, was soft and smooth.

He stilled, the beer halfway to his lips, as he listened.

'Bye, and thanks again. It was a great night. My place next week?'

The voice of her visitor was low and muffled, not clear like Evie's, and he couldn't hear their side of the conversation. Evie called a last farewell and he heard her door close behind her, heard her footsteps as she walked down her hallway. Had she just had a date? Annoyance, plain and simple, rose in his throat. She'd only just arrived and she seemed as settled in as he was. More so, because, despite Lexi's best efforts at match-making, he didn't date.

'Lexi?' Tom was off his seat, calling out into the semi-darkness of the path in front of the cottages.

'Tom! Don't freak me out like that.'

Both men left their chairs and walked down the front path.

'What are you doing here? I thought you were at home, watching that show.'

Zac opened the gate for her and the three of them went back to the verandah, Lexi insisting she didn't need a drink and Zac insisting she have his chair.

'I'm just as happy on the front step,' Lexi replied, before turning to Tom. 'And as for you, *that show,* as you call it, happens to be Evie's favourite, too, although she's a season ahead, coming from the UK. We thought it'd be fun to watch it together. Mum's home with the girls,' she said, referring to baby Erin, her daughter with Tom, and her orphaned niece Mollie, whose guardian she was. 'Evie's nieces are fast asleep. We've had a good night. She's lovely, very funny. Don't you think?'

She'd directed this last query at Zac. He nodded. 'I don't know her very well yet but, sure, she seems nice enough.'

Tom chuckled. 'Nice enough, he says, but he hung on her every word when she came outside just now. She even got his mind off the hospital crisis for a moment.'

'Really?' Lexi said, and Zac cursed Tom for bringing this down on him. Now he'd be under scrutiny from Lexi every time Evie's name was as much as mentioned. And, other than a basic physical attraction, there was nothing to tell. Period.

'You think you might be interested?' And there she went, straight on to the possibility of hooking him up with Evie. 'You'll have to hurry, she'll be heading back to the UK once Jake and Letitia get home.' She paused, obviously scheming. 'But if you fall madly in love, maybe she won't go.'

'What *is* that rubbish you watch on TV, honey?' Tom was laughing. Sure, he could find this amusing, the scrutiny wasn't directed at him. 'My guess is he's just relieved Evie doesn't have three heads, like some of the other staff Bob took on.'

'Thanks, mate, but it's too late to close the stable door now. Your matchmaking wife has well and truly bolted.'

'Then again,' Tom added, 'Evie is hot.' Lexi shot her foot out and kicked Tom in the shin, not too gently either. *Good shot,* thought Zac.

'She is, but you're married, you're not allowed to say that. Zac, on the other hand…' She paused dramatically, waiting for his answer.

'If I agree she's nice-looking, will you drop this?' Nice-looking! If she bought that, he was better at bluffing than he'd thought. Nice-looking didn't come close. *Hot* didn't touch it either. Neither word captured the elusive quality about her, a quality he was yet to identify.

'No, I won't. Why don't you take Evie out while she's here? It'd be good for both of you.'

'Because, right now, my life is crazy.'

'Crazy with work,' Lexi agreed, 'which is all the more reason to make time for pleasure. You should come and picnic with us outside the concert tomorrow night. It'll be fun.'

'Lex, when Zac says he doesn't have the time, believe the poor guy, OK? You know I've been flat-chat lately, double that for Zac.'

He could almost hear the cogs turning in Lexi's brain as she weighed up Tom's words. 'How is the hospital situation looking?' she asked Zac.

Being married to Tom and being an attending GP at the hospital, Lexi was one of the few people beyond the board to know the situation.

'The staffing issues are at least under control. You had me worried when you first pointed Evie out, but she's highly competent.'

'Sorry.' She grimaced. 'I'd heard from Letitia she was a great nurse but I shouldn't have teased you like that.'

'It's OK. Choice of clothing aside, she proved herself pretty quickly. But as for the funding issues, they're not going away any time soon.'

'How'd the meeting go tonight? What's going to happen?'

'At this point, we don't know,' said Tom. 'But the pressure is on to take some fairly drastic measures, beat the government to it so we can show we've taken big steps to cut overheads. And the options aren't pretty.'

'The options aren't options,' added Zac. 'We have to find other solutions.'

'Unless we have a miracle, Zac, the options are the *only* options. And top of the list is the nursing-home.'

'You'll close it?' The horror was clear in Lexi's voice.

Zac stood in one swift movement, anger at the situation pulsing through him. 'Over my dead body,' was all he said.

He could sense Lexi shooting a look at Tom, querying his reaction.

'Zac feels reasonably strongly about this.' Tom's voice was mild, making his words seem even more of an understatement.

'A decent society doesn't neglect the young, the sick, the disenfranchised or the old. We're starting with the elderly here but, guaranteed, the government will work its way down the list, cutting funding to the groups that need it and can defend themselves least.'

Lexi came over to him and wrapped him in a hug, saying all the right things to show her support.

'Thanks,' Zac said. 'It'll work out.'

'It will. We'd better head off but will you come to the concert tomorrow night? Just for a while? We can pretend we're young again and find out what's cool in the music world nowadays.'

'As long as there are no emergencies, I will.'

Lexi pulled him in close for another hug before accompanying her husband out the gate. Zac watched them leave hand in hand, two people who fate had brought together again after misunderstandings had torn them apart for years. Their laughter lingered, just like the warmth of Lexi's hug on his skin.

The touch of a friend was always welcome, but for some reason tonight it left him feeling sad. Or was it the sight of his two friends so happy together that threw into even sharper relief the loneliness that lurked beyond the frenzy of his life?

Once it had looked as though life was going to turn out differently. Three years ago he had been married and expecting his first child, now he was alone in a country town, overworked, underpaid and with no prospects of anything other than the occasional hug from a friend.

The dreams he'd shared with his wife had turned into a nightmare. His life hadn't been easy but he'd thought he'd found his perfect partner, yet their love hadn't been able to withstand the pressure they'd faced and their relationship had shattered like glass they moment it had been stressed.

People made all sorts of promises in good faith but he'd

learnt the hard way that people often weren't as brave or as strong as they'd like to be, and he included himself in that category.

Once he'd risked everything for love—he wouldn't make that mistake again.

This was his life now. Relationships were not for him.

CHAPTER THREE

THE sound of Arabic music pounding from the nursing-home common room was not what Zac expected to hear. It caught him off guard and he paused, one hand flat against the door, ready to push it open. OK, not pounding exactly, but it was hardly the normal volume for the golden oldies channel. He could take a guess at what he might find on the other side— did he need to go in and make his day worse? He hesitated, then entered. Gingerly. As if something was waiting to bite him.

'And shimmy, two three four and shimmy, basic Arabic, forward, hip lift. Left, right and back, two, three, four, shoulder shimmy, and change.'

He sidled up to Pam, the diversional therapist, and whispered, 'What's going on?'

'Evie's entertaining the troops.' She didn't take her gaze off Evie, as transfixed as the twenty residents, who hadn't even noticed him enter the room. Evie hadn't noticed him either.

'We don't have enough cardiac equipment for this. Look at them! Half of them are ready to go into arrest with the next whatever you call that hip…' His attention caught by the movement, he couldn't formulate the words. He tried again, 'That…hip…'

'Wiggle?' Pam supplied, the amusement in her voice

clear. Since Evie had arrived, there'd been far too much amusement at his expense. Which was not what he needed right now, with the future of the hospital resting partially on his shoulders.

Evie turned and her gaze landed on him, her smile broadening immediately as if challenging him to interrupt her. She shimmied her way towards the back of the room where her nieces were sitting, as mesmerised as the rest of the crowd.

'*Now* what's going on?' Zac muttered.

'You missed the best bit. She did a proper dance, now she's just been taking the residents through the routine, breaking it down into parts,' Pam replied. Evie's nieces had taken the floor now, and were shaking their non-existent hips and holding their skinny arms aloft in various poses in line with their aunt's instructions. 'This is the G-rated part of the show—Gracie and Mack are doing their thing, they're just learning. Pretty sweet, isn't it? Look, they have mini-hip-scarves just like Evie's. Dear little things.'

'Poor Letitia.' Zac shook his head. 'What will she say when she gets home to find Evie has turned her daughters into delinquent gypsies?' Except Pam was right, Gracie and Mack *were* adorable. But Evie wasn't just giving instructions, she was still dancing, too, and from the look of the crowd, while the women might be oohing and aahing over the children, the men hadn't taken their eyes off the aunt.

'Silly, that's how Evie and Letitia met up again. They'd been at school together, and a few years later Evie was back for a holiday, and they were both doing a dance class. Letitia only stopped because of her hip trouble.'

'This whole performance needs to stop. Mr Louis is going purple.' But Zac knew it was from excitement rather than exertion. Evie was having the same effect on him. Sure, the girls looked gorgeous but their aunt? Their aunt was a walking advertisement for natural Viagra. Again, exactly what he *didn't* need in a nursing-home. 'How long is this scheduled for?'

'Shh.'

'Egyptian fifth, now turning in full circle, hip lifts all the way. And pose, Egyptian sixth, and hold, two three, four—and that's it!'

'Praise the lord,' Zac muttered as Pam left his side to check on the residents and Evie headed for the CD player to switch it off.

The applause was thunderous and was accompanied by a few wolf-whistles of appreciation and at least two walking sticks being thumped enthusiastically on the floor.

As the initial noise subsided, the room was still abuzz with the over-excited chatter of twenty octogenarians. A group, he saw now, that included his great-aunt Fel and her best friend, Nancy, both of whom were always in the thick of whatever fun was to be had here. He took a step in their direction but was beaten to it—Gracie and Mack had already run to them, one girl clambering onto each lap as though it was their natural place in the world. And from the smile on the older women's faces, they agreed.

A light touch on his arm told him the delinquent gypsy was at his side. She was beaming up at him, glowing from the dancing.

'Hi there.'

'Hi.' A master of the English language he wasn't, but what did you say to someone who one minute was a nurse working with utter professionalism and the next was decked out in bright orange silky stuff, fringed all over with gold beads of some sort, shaking her booty for all it was worth? And from what he'd seen, it was worth quite a significant amount.

She was chatting away at his side. 'It's not usual, to do a lesson like that, but as I don't have a dance troupe at my beck and call, I can't put on a full-scale show. This seemed like the next best thing.'

He recovered the power of speech. 'Perhaps that's a good thing. I don't think the Pelican Beach nursing-home could withstand a full-scale show.'

'No?' She mulled this over for a moment before peering at him more closely. 'You don't have an issue with me doing this, do you? I gather things can get a bit monotonous.'

He considered her question. Did he have an issue with it? The image of twenty smiling faces swam into view. 'As long as no one has a cardiac arrest, no, I don't. Monotony *is* a problem but we don't have the resources...' His sentence tailed off. He'd been so distracted by her he'd almost forgotten why he'd ducked into the home in the first place. Monotony was insignificant compared to the other problems facing the nursing-home residents. It was just that no one knew it yet. No one except him and the board, which left him feeling more like a traitor every second—but what choice did they have? He changed the topic. 'I don't suppose you have any more sedate talents? Yodelling? Knitting?'

The shine in her eyes increased a degree. 'Put it this way, if I were a Miss Universe entrant, I wouldn't have to think too hard about filling in my special talents section on my form. This is it. I couldn't even whip up a soufflé for the judges, and as for baton-twirling, I'd be liable to knock someone out.'

He laughed and, although it sounded a little rusty, even to his own ears, the troubles of the day slipped back a little. 'If you were a Miss Universe entrant, soufflés and batons would be the least of your problems.'

'Why?'

'You'd be spending all your time avoiding being stepped on. You'd only come up to the other contestants' knee-caps.'

'That's size-ist, even if you are right.' She tried to look affronted. And failed miserably. 'I'm an uncoordinated, culinary-challenged shrimp. So I have to dance for my supper.'

'What's it called, anyway? Harem dancing?'

She rolled her eyes. 'The ancient art of Oriental dancing. Popularly known as belly dancing, a term I know you're familiar with,' she said with a grin. 'Lots of different styles fall under the name. I do some of them.'

He rubbed at his jaw, aware a sparkle had come into his own eyes in response to the light in hers. 'Like I said, harem dancing.'

She laughed. 'You're such a bloke. You all think it's for you but…' she winked at him '…it's a secret weapon.'

'How come?'

'If I told you, I'd have to kill you. Probably with a hip lift.' She gave him a demonstration, her hips moving as though they were separate to her upper body. With difficulty, he kept from staring. She was right. If she ever did that in private for a bloke—*for him*—it would finish him off.

'Those things should come with a written warning.' He shoved his hands deep into his pockets and nodded at the general region of her hips. He couldn't risk a closer look, he might never drag his eyes away. 'They're lethal.' He sounded like he was joking. He wasn't.

'You see?' She nodded vehemently, and if she knew the effect she was having on him, she was keeping an impressively straight face. 'The secret weapon. When a dancer does this…' she bunched up her hair, holding it on top of her head, all scrunched and messy with tendrils falling down over the smoothness of her shoulders '…and this…' she shimmied around in a circle, whipping her head around so she scarcely lost eye contact with him '…men can't talk.'

She stopped as suddenly as she'd started, grinning. She'd

proved her point and she knew it. 'So men think it's for them but, really, when a woman dances, a man doesn't stand a chance. And as for becoming empowered in one's femininity, there's nothing like it.' She tilted her head just a touch on one side. 'You should try it,' she encouraged. 'When you can talk again,' she added, her expression a picture of innocence.

He ignored that, even though she was more than half-right. He had to concentrate to talk. He didn't want to place a bet on what he'd go to sleep envisioning tonight. If the image would *let* him sleep. 'Can I ask you a favour?'

'Sure.'

'Please, don't *ever* do that little number in here without a cardiac unit on standby. And so you know, our public liability insurance doesn't cover death by a belly-dancing nurse.'

'Ah.' She nodded, her face straight again. 'But I was watching Mr Louis, among others, and I'm pretty sure he was thinking, "What a way to go".'

He groaned. 'Tell me you didn't just say that.'

'Say what?' She laughed. 'I'll catch you later. I'm helping Pam with morning tea.'

Didn't she ever stop? She, like his great-aunt, always seemed to be in the midst of things. He glanced towards his aunt. Gracie had left her lap and was now sprinting across the room with her sister, their little hip-scarves jangling all the way. Evie waited beside him while her nieces ran over.

'Hi, Dr Carlisle!' they chorused, and Gracie added, 'That was fan-tas-ta-losa, awesome fun, Evie. Can we do it tomorrow?' Both little girls were bouncing up and down like wind-up toys, their eyes shining bright like their aunt's.

The image struck a chord with him. *That* was what Evie reminded him of—she still had that childlike enthusiasm about her, that glow that told a thousand stories. She lived in the moment. When had he last stopped and savoured a moment?

He was usually knee-deep in all the problems of the future. The thought of how he was nowadays, contrasting so greatly with how *she* was, made him feel, oh, about a thousand and three.

From across the room, an ear-splitting whistle rang out, bringing him back to the present. He'd done it again, forgotten to be where he was, letting his mind drag him off somewhere else he didn't need to be.

'Evie, darling, promise me you'll spare an old bloke a thought and come dance again.' It was Mr Louis, one of the gentlemen who'd been particularly vocal about his appreciation during Evie's performance. 'That was as much fun as I've had since the war!'

'And you've got as much chance of dating this dancer as you had back then,' called his sparring mate, Wilf. 'Buckley's and none.'

Evie raised a hand over her head and waved, making a big show of ignoring Wilf. 'Thanks, Mr Louis. I hope you're not going to let me down for the Big Night Out concert tonight. Pick me up at seven?' she said, sending a huge wink in the old man's direction.

She was a flirt, no doubt about it, but one with such charm she could get away with it. 'Thanks a million, Evie,' Zac muttered dryly. 'You've finished him off for sure, just thinking about it.'

But what he was really thinking was how Wilf would rate Zac's own chances of asking Evie out on a date.

Blast Lexi, she'd put the idea into his head last night.

And blast Evie, too.

There was one thing he did know, having seen her dance today, he had next to no chance of erasing the image of her bejewelled hips moving in a motion all their own, hair loose and streaming down her back as she wiggled and shimmied to the frenzied beat of the music.

* * *

Evie wandered over to the refreshment table to help Pam pour the tea, but couldn't stop herself from observing Zac out of the corner of her eye. He said goodbye to the girls as they ran after her but he didn't leave immediately, as she'd expected. She watched as he crossed the room to chat briefly to the two old ladies on whose laps Gracie and Mack had made themselves so at home. He was smiling at the women and Evie marvelled at how his smile lightened his demeanour. It was a great smile, just as she'd suspected. His laugh, too, when they'd been discussing her lack of talents, had taken her by surprise, but in a good way. The serious, almost forebidding expression he normally wore had been replaced by one that implied he might once have known how to have a good time. Evie was sure he'd almost smiled at her when she'd first noticed him in the room and she was determined to get him to do it properly. It was worth it.

He bent to help the women from their seats before kissing them both on the cheek. Not normal behaviour for medical staff by Evie's reckoning, and definitely not what she'd expect from a man as reserved and in control as Zac was. Who were they?

She wasn't left wondering for long.

'Welcome Evie. I'm Felicity and this is my dear friend, Nancy,' said the taller of the two women as they approached the refreshment table. 'Two cups of tea, please, and why don't you join us when you're finished here? We love a new face.'

'Gracie and Mack, choose some morning tea and come with us,' Nancy suggested.

The girls didn't need to be asked twice, quickly piling a selection of sweet things onto a plate before trotting off to a table with the women, leaving Evie to finish pouring tea as she scouted the room for Zac. There he was, deep in conversation with Matron. They made their way out of the common room, still talking, and Evie felt a moment of disappointment when he didn't seek her out as he left. Choosing not to dwell on that thought, she headed to her nieces, put her water glass on the table—there wasn't any condensed milk so coffee was out of the question—and pulled out a chair. Grace and Mack were busy devouring their scones, which was keeping them quiet but Fel and Nancy made up for the girls' silence.

'You're here to look after the girls while Letitia's out of action?' Fel asked.

Evie nodded. 'You know her?'

'Absolutely. She's our favourite dinner lady and we all love the girls.'

'I can see they feel quite at home here.' Evie smiled.

'Any news on when Letitia will be having her operation?'

'Not yet.'

'Imagine having to have two hips replaced before you're forty,' Nancy remarked.

'I'd have thought it would be you or me, yet here we are, over one hundred and sixty years between us and still going strong.'

'And learning how to belly dance, no less. That was the most fun we've had in ages.'

'Since the time we tried to chat up that nice young physio who Zac organised to talk to us about exercise or some such.'

'Remember how horrified Zac was with us!' Nancy giggled.

'He needs to let himself go a bit, he's far too serious. Takes after my brother. And look where his serious nature got him— stress put him into a early grave.'

'Your brother?' Evie wasn't sure if she was following the conversation.

Fel nodded. 'Zac is my great-nephew, my brother's grandson.'

'I didn't realise he had family in Pelican Beach. He's not from here, is he?'

'No. He grew up in Adelaide but his family has a holiday

home here. He arrived a few years ago, he needed a change of pace.'

'A change of pace?' Evie sipped her water, trying to conceal her curiosity.

'He went through a nasty marriage break-up, although that's not common knowledge. He's kept his own counsel.'

'How is that possible in a town this size?' Evie asked.

'People won't pry when it's made clear it's not welcome. They accepted him into the community but they haven't interfered. He knows everything about everyone, he's very good at listening, but he doesn't give away much about himself.' Fel explained. 'People adore him but you ask anyone what they know about him and I bet the details will be sketchy. He plays his cards very close to his chest. He's immersed himself in work and that's become his life now. But I still think he needs a good dose of the scallywags. I bet even Zac can't remember when he last had any fun.'

'Maybe we can persuade him to join us for one of your belly-dancing sessions, Evie,' Nancy suggested.

'You will do more?' Fel didn't sound as though she was used to taking no for an answer.

Evie smiled. 'I plan to, but right now I need to get the girls home to get changed. Their dad's taking them to the beach.'

Evie ushered the girls out of the nursing-home and steered them along the footpath towards their house on the other side of the hospital. Halfway home they ran into Bill.

'Evie, I was just looking for you. Could I have a quick word?' He looked at the girls and back to the Evie. 'Alone, if possible.'

'Girls, why don't you go over to the rose garden and pick some flowers to take to Mum while I talk to Bill?'

The girls skipped off and Evie motioned Bill to a garden bench where they could talk as she kept an eye on her nieces.

'What's up?'

'I've got more information about the drug Stewart was smoking and I want to pick your brains, if you don't mind.'

'Go ahead.'

'It *was* ice. We've been able to test the batch Stewart's hit came from and apparently it was about seventy per cent pure.'

'How did you get some to test? Did the kids hand it over?'

'Not directly. Would you believe one, or more, of them contacted a lawyer and the lawyer dropped the drug off to us. Protecting their own hides, more afraid of what would happen to them if they were caught with the drug than of what would happen if they smoked it. Unbelievable. We're more concerned with where they got it from.'

'Did the lawyer tell you that?'

'Apparently the kids bought it off some guy down here.'

'Which means there's probably more about the place, sold to kids with no idea what it can do to them.' Evie frowned as she watched her nieces, skipping between the rose bushes. They were a picture of innocence but who knew what the future held for them? For any of them.

'Exactly. If they'd brought it to town with them, it might not have such an impact, but if it's being sold in Pelican Beach, we really need to track down the source. We've spoken to a couple of small-time dealers but the drug of choice down here has always been marijuana and, more recently, a bit of ecstasy. The drug squad thinks it might be someone from out of town, taking advantage of schoolies week to make a quick buck. They're sending a team down to investigate but I wanted to ask you what we should be doing in the short term. It's the big concert tonight. This is all unfamiliar territory to us and to the ambulance staff, too—they're only volunteers.'

'From a medical point of view, you'll need people who can deal with any repercussions after the drug's been taken. I spent time yesterday putting protocols in place for the emergency staff at the hospital to follow, but there's not enough time to train up the local ambos—can you get some city crews sent down for tonight, crews who'll have experience with this?'

'We should be able to organise that. I'll make sure it happens.'

'I'm sure word'll be getting around the streets about what happened to Stewart but it won't keep everyone away from drugs, especially as kids will be drinking—they'll be more likely to engage in other risk-taking behaviours. Realistically we have to be prepared for more cases like Stewart's and I think calling in experienced reinforcements is your wisest choice.'

'So the hospital team know what to do?'

Evie nodded. 'Yes. But having city paramedics on the ground here is a priority.'

'OK. I'm on it.' He stood and shook her hand, a big, serious man with a lot on his plate. Very similar to Zac in that regard, but he didn't invoke the same shivers of attraction in her that Zac did. 'Thanks, Evie.'

'No problem. Let's hope for the best.'

'And expect the worst.'

'Probably wise.'

Bill left, his worried expression still in place, but at least he had a plan.

As did she.

Look after her nieces and let Jake and Letitia head to Adelaide with no concerns.

Work hard but leave time for fun, too.

Preferably with a particular doctor who'd got under her skin when she'd not expected it.

She might have teased him with her hip lifts earlier, but she had an uncomfortable feeling it would be her, not him, lying awake tonight with a tingle of longing, aching to be satiated.

* * *

What was a man to do?

A man needed an evacuation plan in the event of situations like this.

If he could get out of his kitchen, he would, but part way through cooking dinner was an awkward time to make a run for it.

Then again, one more minute of listening to Evie's singing would do permanent damage to his ears. He'd been trying to block all thoughts of her out of his mind but was finding it impossible. And her 'singing', for lack of a better word for it, wasn't helping.

For the last half an hour, she'd been belting out hit after hit at the top of her voice, the sound carrying with ease to him from next door. But sung so appallingly that, despite his ears being assaulted, it was sort of charming. In a way. And maybe for three minutes, not thirty.

He'd seen her talking to Bill on the hospital lawns. Seen her sit with him on a garden seat, and although he knew they'd been discussing work—Bill had spoken to him next—he'd been surprised by the sensation the sight had evoked in him. He hated to admit it, it was unreasonable and he didn't do unreasonable, but he'd been jealous. Annoyed with himself, he'd tried hard to think about other things, and there were plenty of other problems to occupy his mind, problems that didn't involve a tiny, vivacious, belly dancer. But it wasn't working and now she was pushing her way into his consciousness and evoking other visions, other visions that just weren't going to happen. Couldn't happen. There was only one solution, bar deserting his meal and sprinting to the nearest restaurant.

It took all of five seconds to leave his stove, turned down to simmer, and reach her front doorstep, knocking loudly so she'd hear him above her din.

Gracie answered. 'Hi, Dr Carlisle.'

He squatted down to her level. 'Hi, there, Gracie-girl, your aunt is singing.'

The little girl with dark, dark hair, like her aunt's, nodded solemnly. 'She's making dinner. Daddy is at the hospital with Mummy.'

There went his plans for restoring peace and quiet. They were already covered for food. Which should make him happy—soon she'd be eating and there'd be no more singing. So why did he feel disappointed?

Gracie slipped into the circle of his arms and nestled against his knee. She dropped her voice to a conspiratorial whisper. 'She's not very good at it.'

'At singing? I can hear that.'

Gracie shook her head earnestly. 'At cooking. We have to tell her what to do. Mack is helping, I'm hiding, that's why I heard you.'

'Is that right?' He made a show of mulling the news over, fighting back a chuckle. 'I thought your aunt loved vegetables—doesn't she know how to cook them?'

'She has them *raw*. Yuck.' She giggled. 'She eats bunny food.' She sniffed the air. 'Your dinner smells yum.'

He snapped his fingers. 'I have a plan. Hop on.' He swung the little girl around on to his back and stood, Gracie tapping him on the shoulder to get him moving.

Cantering down the tiny passage, a mirror image of his own, the terrible singing voice increased in volume until he pulled up short in the kitchen doorway. Mack saw him and waved but Evie, in little more than her underwear, had her back to them, belting out another tune, oblivious to the fact her audience had just increased.

He was almost lost for words—she was every bit as gorgeous under her hip-scarf as he'd imagined. He did the right thing and cleared his throat to let her know she had company. She screamed at the noise, her hand flying to cover her mouth as she flung the spatula across the room and looked around wildly, presumably for the nearest thing to cover herself with.

'It's not your mouth that needs covering, Evie, it's the rest of you.' He knew he shouldn't, but the next moment he'd thrown his head back and was roaring with laughter. 'Don't you *ever* wear clothes?'

She seized a teatowel and held it spread out in front of her abdomen. 'I started out wearing clothes, but I spilt sauce on me.' She indicated a sodden pile of clothes in the corner of the kitchen. 'And I wasn't expecting visitors,' she added pointedly. 'What are you doing here, anyway?'

'I've come to extend a dinner invitation. To all three of you.'

Her eyes lit up with hope. 'Now?'

He nodded. Gracie, still clinging to his back like a little monkey, let out a whoop of excitement and Mack added, with a touch of relief, he thought, 'That's a great idea!'

'Really?' That was Evie.

'Truly.' Maybe even madly.

'Can you cook?'

He looked at the pots and pans strewn around the kitchen, none of them appearing to hold anything edible. 'Are you really in a position to ask that?'

She followed his gaze before nodding emphatically. 'You're right. When shall we come?'

'It's almost ready, you can come now if you like. Although you might be more comfortable with some clothes on.' She didn't answer so he added, 'The fabric things you drape over yourself to give the appearance of modesty.'

She grinned and jiggled the teatowel. 'What do you call this?'

'Can Mack and me go with him now?' asked Gracie.

'Mack and I,' Evie corrected her, before shrugging her shoulders, giving up on the grammar lesson. 'Sure, if it's OK with Zac.'

'No problem. We'll see you there.' He swung Gracie down to the floor and beat a hasty retreat back the way he'd come, girls in tow. He'd stopped the singing but now he was going to be tortured with sights instead of sounds. Not that the sight of Evie standing with her back to him, almost every curve of her tiny body revealed, could be called torture. But it would distract him even more than the singing. How was he going to get through the evening? How was he going to pretend he wasn't attracted to her?

Did he want to pretend?

He thought about that as he swung his front door open to let the girls in, and by the time he'd closed it behind him, he knew. It wasn't a matter of want, it was a matter of there being no other option. He didn't do unreasonable and he didn't do foolish. And thinking about kissing Evie was pure madness.

It had only taken her a minute to pull some clothes on, grab a couple of necessities, leave a note for Jake and walk the few steps down the tiny garden path, out the front gate and back up the matching path to Zac's front door. She'd done her best to appear unflustered but was 'mortified' too strong a word for her colleague seeing her almost naked?

She giggled. She wasn't mortified, not in the least. The disbelieving expression on his face had made any fleeting embarrassment worth it. She'd thought about spending a *little* more time getting ready—but what was the point of fussing over her appearance when he'd just seen her in her underwear? She raised her hand and knocked at his door. When he answered, pulling back in welcome, wiping his hands on a clean towel, she noticed there wasn't so much as a splotch on his white T-shirt or pale linen shorts. He still looked good enough to—

'Almost done.' He ushered her inside, breaking her train of thought. His gaze was on the objects she was carrying. 'What have you got there?'

'My specialty, coffee with condensed milk. I thought I'd make you one after dinner.'

'Sounds good. Come through. The girls are setting the table, you've got them well trained.'

She shook her head, stepping in behind him and following him to the kitchen. 'It's the other way around, isn't it, girls? After tonight I think they'll be begging to fend for themselves at mealtimes.'

'Much safer.' Mack giggled. 'We've set the table—can we play with your world globe?'

'Sure.' They scampered off into the adjacent living area. 'They love that thing,' he said. 'Just out of interest, how are you planning on not poisoning them while their parents are away?'

She sighed. She hadn't been joking when she'd said dancing was her only talent. Tonight was the proof. 'Jake already has the fridge and freezer well stocked, but I thought I should give it a shot while he was still here. Just in case I burnt the house down or something.'

'That bad, huh?'

She shuddered. 'You have no idea. It was *terrifying.*'

'Perhaps you should leave it to the experts.' He was lifting pot lids while he spoke, stirring, testing, pretty much behaving in the same expert manner as her brother. She'd always loved watching Jake cook—she blamed him and their mum for making it unnecessary for her to learn. But she'd never imagined she could watch anyone cook for hours and not tire of it, yet that was her first thought as she watched Zac. And it wasn't just because she and the girls were running the risk of starvation or weeks of take-aways. 'You'll need the bomb squad in just to clean up the mess you've made.'

Yup, even insulting her, he was delicious. She pulled a face at him anyway, and he laughed, lifting a steamer lid and starting to serve.

Sidling up, she took a peek at dinner, peering in through the glass lids of the pots. It looked delicious. A man who could cook—there was something very attractive about that.

He gave a little nudge with his hip to move her out the way and turned off the stove. 'When you've finished snooping, you can dish for the girls.'

'I'm impressed.'

'That I knew you were snooping?'

'That you can cook. Sometimes I think I might be the last remaining person on the planet who has no skills in the kitchen.'

Zac's smile was lopsided, full of cheek, his arms crossed loosely over his chest as he leant back on the bench, serving spoon in hand, considering her. 'I'm sure you have a plethora of skills in the kitchen, they just don't involve cooking.'

She laughed. 'Now you're getting suggestive.'

'Absolutely.' He nodded, the dark light in his eyes sending a thrill through her. Where was this conversation going? 'For instance, I can't wait to see how skilled you are at cleaning up after dinner.'

Ah. That was not the direction she'd been hoping for. He was holding the two children's plates out to her, laughing as he waited for her to take them.

'You're in the presence of genius, buddy. I can load a dish-washer like no other woman in Pelican Beach. And that's a promise.' She took the plates and banished all thoughts of things other than dish-washing happening in his kitchen. Wretched man, to put crazy images in her head then refuse to follow through! She'd banish all thoughts of Zac, too, but standing so close to him, that was impossible. He smelt delicious and he had some serious charisma going on. She shivered as she brushed against his side, his touch sparking warm, sugary responses in her.

Thank goodness for the distraction of Gracie and Mack—that was all she could think as they all made short work of the food, seated around Zac's plain kitchen table, laughing at the girls' comments and stories about school and life in general.

All too soon Evie heard her brother's voice calling from the front door. Gracie and Mack made a dash for the door, Zac close behind. Evie followed them, heard Zac offer Jake a coffee, listened to him refuse.

'It's time to get these two buttons off to bed. Thanks…' he nodded at Zac '…for feeding them. You'll keep an eye on them? Throw them the occasional crust if my sister forgets? She's passionate about the world's needy, I'm just afraid it'll be my two who *are* the needy by the time Letitia and I get back from Adelaide.'

Zac laughed, Evie poked her tongue out and Jake winked at her before scooping Gracie up onto one shoulder before she could dash off back down the hall.

'Gee up, Daddy,' Gracie said, holding on around her dad's neck as he bent again to attempt to lift Mack onto his other shoulder. 'Humph,' he said, his voice muffled as Gracie's arm slipped too high and covered his mouth. Letting go of Mack, he tugged Gracie's little arm lower.

'Yup, you're a strong boy, Daddy, but not strong enough,' Gracie said, as Evie fought a stitch in her side—she'd spent too long tonight trying not to laugh. Gracie was going to be the death of her in the next couple of months. 'Looks like we'll have to get a stronger boy here.'

'Are you going to give your aunt this much cheek when Mummy and I are away?'

Gracie considered. 'Yes.'

'That's OK, then.'

Gripping his errant youngest daughter with one arm, he managed to swing Mack into position and left cantering like a pony back next door, the girls squealing their delight and experimenting with holding onto their father's neck with only one hand.

Leaving Evie able to give in to her laughter and Zac half laughing, half watching as she doubled over in the doorway.

She was gorgeous.

And when she laughed like she'd burst, she was delectable.

Her only flaw was that she couldn't sing a note.

It was irrelevant.

He wasn't interested in finding a woman. Any woman. So it didn't matter what he thought about Evie.

She straightened up, tears in her eyes, seeking his gaze, and he returned her smile. Suitable woman or not, he was glad she was there.

'My nieces are a hoot,' she said when they were back in the kitchen and she could talk again.

'They're going to miss their dad and mum. They're lucky to have you. Letitia told me you were coming to look after the girls so we could organise her surgery, but she didn't tell me you'd be working at the hospital. Was there a reason she kept that quiet?'

'I guess she had other things to think about. I was coming, that was the main thing. The job was secondary and if I hadn't got it, I would've come anyway. We would've just needed a miracle so I could support us all as Jake won't be able to work while he's with Letitia.'

'I knew there were problems but Letitia wouldn't elaborate, just kept saying she could go when you got here.'

She considered, her head tilted a little on one side. 'Too proud to tell you, I guess. They can manage without Letitia's wage, just, but not Jake's. Jake insisted on being with her and we all think that's wise. Letitia tends to be anxious at the best of times and even more so about this situation. Plus they don't have whatever insurance covers you for being sick but not when it's not terminal.'

'Trauma or income protection?'

She nodded. 'Someone needed to go with Letitia, someone needed to stay with the girls.' She ticked off the 'someones' on her fingers. 'And someone needed to earn money to pay for it all. I'm the last two people,' she added with a flourish.

'You're not big enough for two people. Aren't there other family members who could help out?'

'There you go again, selling me short.' She sent him a wink that had him grabbing plates and scraping the contents with unnecessary vigour into the rubbish. She cleared the rest of the table, chatting as she stacked crockery into the dishwasher, oblivious to the effect she had on him. 'Mum and Dad will come as soon as they can, but they have to sell their roadhouse business first. They can't just shut it down and leave, they can't afford to do that. If I won the lottery,' she added, her voice full of cheer, 'that'd solve everything.'

'Your parents own a roadhouse? A restaurant and a garage for truckies, that sort of thing?'

'Absolutely. On the highway heading into Wagga Wagga.'

'They're selling up for Letitia?'

'They were thinking of it already, planning their semi-retirement, and Letitia needing bilateral hip replacements made their minds up. But these things take time. Once they're here, I'll head back.'

He stopped in mid-scrape, the dish at an angle over the rubbish bin.

He'd known she was here short term but hearing it from her felt like she'd thrown a bucket of cold water over him. He probably should have done that to himself every night since he'd first seen her, but it was too late now.

He risked a look in her direction and caught her gaze, dropping the pot onto the kitchen counter, scarcely mindful of his actions.

Then he knew. It was definitely too late.

It didn't matter what he'd told himself, it didn't matter that he wasn't looking for anyone, it didn't matter he had nothing to offer.

What he was about to do had been inevitable from the first moment he'd seen her shake those hips.

He was looking at her strangely.

If she hadn't known better, he was looking at her like she was kissable and he was planning on doing something about it.

Her toes curled in pleasure at the thought, fictitious though it might be.

There was only one way to sort fact from fiction. Absent-mindedly, she touched her lower lip with her tongue then caught it between her teeth, biting gently, just for a second.

If it was true, she'd be reaping her just, if short-term, rewards for putting her life on hold to come back here.

Stepping towards him, she was half-aware of a smile playing about her lips. She was aware, too, of just how absorbed he was by her mouth. His gaze hadn't left it.

He was absolutely still, watching her come to him, and she saw the darkness in his gaze deepen, his breathing quicken. Then she was standing in front of him, so close that, even without the look of desire she knew was in her eyes, there could be no question of what she wanted.

With a groan, he reached for her and pulled her swiftly into the circle of his arms, half lifting her from the floor, her tiny frame no obstacle to sweeping her closer and closer still, until she was pressed hard against his torso.

Her eyes fluttered closed in anticipation but his mouth didn't close over hers. 'Evie.' There was a catch in the depths of his voice.

'Hmm?' She peeked out through her lashes, reluctant to break the spell.

'This wasn't what I had in mind when I invited you over.'

She licked her lips again. 'Is it what you have in mind now?'

'The only thing.'

'Then there's no problem,' she whispered, raising her mouth up to his, eyes closed again. This might not have been what he'd had in mind, but there'd been a good part of her mind that had been occupied with exactly this since she'd first seen him. 'Kiss me already.'

There were no further arguments, no further attempts to do the sensible thing.

He did what they both wanted, bent his head to hers and kissed her like there was no tomorrow.

CHAPTER FOUR

HE WOULD have kept on kissing her if the front doorbell hadn't rung. Then rung again. And again.

They both pulled away, as reluctant as each other to break the magic of their kiss.

He didn't want it to end. Ending it meant he'd have to remember all the reasons he couldn't do this, when all he wanted was to keep on kissing her, for hours if possible. Could he forget the outside world, forget rational decisions for one night?

Evie was glowing. Gorgeous. How could one kiss be enough?

Couldn't he forget his resolutions? Just for a moment in time? Just while she was here? Or even just for tonight? Then his mobile began to ring, too. The outside world wasn't going to grant his wish.

Dropping a kiss on the tip of her nose, he stepped away, missing the call on his phone, and went to see who was still pressing the doorbell.

'Tom!' Damn, he'd forgotten his acceptance of their invitation to the Big Night Out.

Tom shoved his mobile back in his pocket. 'Your house isn't that big, mate. What were you doing?' He motioned to the street. 'Lexi is in the car, ready to go.'

Zac's mind was doing calculations at a rapid pace and coming up with nothing useful. How did he…?

He saw Tom look past him down the hall. 'Evie, you're coming, too. Excellent.' He winked at Zac and almost certainly would have thumped him on the back if Evie hadn't been right there.

'Where?'

'The Big Night Out. We're sitting outside in deference to our advanced ages but it'll be fun. We don't get much live entertainment down this way. Get your gear, let's go.'

'I promised I'd go with old Mr Louis, but he hasn't called.' Her face was open and happy and, except for lips that were slightly pink and swollen, there was no clue as to what had just happened. Would Tom work it out? If he did, Zac would get no peace. 'I think he was just toying with my affections,' Evie was saying about Mr Louis.

Tom hooted with laughter and five minutes later they were all in Lexi's car—she'd given him a most unsubtle wink when she'd spotted Evie—heading for the concert.

Which was one way, reflected Zac an hour later, to get his date with her. Tom and Lexi had left to wander around the perimeter of the concert, leaving him to try and work out what had happened between him and Evie, but there was no point in talking about it—the music was pounding in their ears.

The concert was being staged near the foreshore on a grassy square bounded on two sides by two of the oldest, and most popular, hotels in town. The other sides faced the sea, separated from the beach by a strip of park. They were now sitting in the park near the town's Ferris wheel.

Kids wandered in and out of the gates in the temporary fencing delineating the concert from the public areas. Were they looking for things—drugs?—they couldn't access inside or just being kids with short attention spans? For once Zac decided to let it go—tonight it wasn't his concern. There was an increased police presence, he'd noticed several teams of police with sniffer dogs patrolling the streets and plenty of ambulances about, too, including trained paramedics from Adelaide, so tonight he could relax.

One young couple sat on a bench nearby, the boy pulling the girl onto his lap where they kissed hungrily, his hand snaking inside her T-shirt. The noise of the band carried across to them, the slight ocean breeze not strong enough to whisk the music away.

'I'm too old for this,' he mouthed at Evie above the scream of base guitars and screeching vocals—was that singing? It made Evie's voice sound like an opera singer's.

'I *knew* I should've come with Mr Louis,' she mouthed back, her eyes alight with mischief—and happiness?

If she was feeling uncertain after their kiss, she didn't show it. She hadn't missed a beat, chatting naturally in the car on the way here and once they'd arrived until the roar of the music had made conversation impossible.

Whereas he was filled with mixed emotions, with questions, and few, if any, answers. He stiffened momentarily as she leant further into his side, resting her head against his chest in such a way he had to wrap his arm about her shoulders to support her there. It shouldn't feel so natural, so good, if it was wrong. But he knew she *was* wrong for him. Or he was wrong for her? Or maybe the issue was precisely that she *felt* right for him.

He thought of the reasons he didn't date. The one, non-negotiable reason. A reason not even a gorgeous belly-dancing woman with a terrible singing voice, a warm sense of humour and a wonderful natural touch with children could persuade him from.

Not even if she kissed like a passionate gypsy.

She looked up at him as if she'd sensed the direction of his thoughts, and a tiny, teasing smile played around her lips. Over the jarring sound of the music he couldn't be sure if she'd whispered the request or he'd just imagined it but, either way, he knew he'd been lying to himself. Evie was challenging his resolve and she was winning.

Couldn't he have just one night?

Reason be damned, he thought, suddenly angry he'd been forced to make a choice.

One night with Evie? One night kissing this incredible woman who'd be gone soon? Was it too much to ask?

He looked deep into her eyes, his desire mirrored there by her own. That was his undoing.

He bent his head over hers and kissed her, all sensible, reasonable, rational thoughts obliterated by the all-consuming idea of Evie.

He was kissing her in public, in the middle of town. She'd never have thought he'd do that. But there was no way she was going to stop him so she put her heart and soul into kissing him back, the sound of the concert receding into the background as she focussed on Zac.

A wolf-whistle distracted her. She opened one eye a smidgen. If the whistles were for them she'd be getting no more kisses in public. She broke away, felt his body tense as he, too, opened his eyes and glanced around. But the attention was focussed elsewhere.

Two young girls traipsed by, their long legs and perfect figures on display. In very short skirts and minuscule tops, they tottered on three-inch heels, followed closely by a few teenage boys. They looked like the college kids she remembered from her schooldays, the boys all dressed in the 'uniform' of expensive, branded board shorts and surf T-shirts with slip-on leather thongs or unlaced trainers on their feet. They held beer bottles and from the snatches of conversation Evie could hear, it sounded as though they'd had a few drinks already.

There was another whistle, followed by a suggestive comment, and both had come from a couple of boys—locals?—who were approaching from the opposite direction. Evie saw the girls hesitate, slowing their steps to let their male companions catch up. Safety in numbers?

Evie felt Zac sit up a little straighter, watching carefully, one arm still around her shoulders. The band had finished its set and there was relative quiet now. She sensed trouble.

The boys with the attitude had stopped on the path, about twenty metres from where she and Zac sat, blocking the girls' path. The girls stepped onto the grass but the boys moved across, blocking them again, making obscene gestures, laughing loudly.

Two of the college boys looked around nervously but the third, taller and bigger than the rest, kept walking, stopping an inch away from the others, shielding the girls with his body.

'Give it up, guys, they're with us.' Their voices were clearly audible over the background noise of the crowd.

'You don't know what you're missing, girls,' said one of the locals, leaving no doubt as to his meaning and accompanying his words with explicit gestures.

'In your dreams,' retorted one of the girls.

Keep quiet! Evie thought.

Zac and Evie stood at the same time, both sensing this could go either way.

'You won't have time to dream if you come with us.'

'I said, leave it.' The bigger college kid wasn't backing down.

'You gonna make us?' The kid pushed past, deliberately bumping into the college boy, shoulder to shoulder. As he went past, the college kid stuck a foot out, tripping his antagonist and sending him sprawling across the footpath.

His mate shoved the college kid backwards and Zac started moving, but the first punch had been thrown. The college boy had tossed his beer bottle away, shattering it on the ground, and he'd got the first proper punch in. The local kid who had tripped got to his feet and that seemed to mobilise the other two boys, who'd been trying to blend into the background. It was three against two, but the college boys didn't look as if they'd had much experience in street fighting. One was felled by a punch in the face and went down in a crumpled heap, blood pouring from his nose. The other was shoved and sent staggering backwards, colliding with the girls.

In slow motion, Evie watched as one girl went flying, landing heavily on the edge of the footpath. She sat up, screaming, looking at her hand. Evie could see the broken neck of the beer bottle embedded in the girl's palm and raced to assist, barely registering that Zac was now in the middle of the fight. It was two against two now but the fight would have to wait.

'Zac. I need help,' she yelled at him, as she ran towards the girl.

She saw Zac turn his head in her direction, distracted by her voice. Too late she realised what she'd done. She stopped dead and tried to yell a warning as she saw the kid take aim, but her voice deserted her. Zac was looking directly at her and must have seen something in her expression because he ducked, but not fast enough. The kid's fist hit him beside his eye, splitting the skin.

Zac was bleeding. He wouldn't thank her for that, but she couldn't afford to worry about him now. 'Stop it. All of you. I need help,' she shouted, and this time she got everyone's attention. She crouched beside the girl, who was still screaming, and saw Zac had turned his back on the fight and was heading her way. Fortunately his departure seemed to defuse the situation and the boys gave up the fight. The two local boys strutted off, still swearing, but at least they were going.

The girl had pulled the broken glass out of her hand and was squeezing her palm closed with her other hand, trying to stop the blood flow.

'I'm Evie, I'm a nurse. What's your name?'

'Sally,' the girl said between sobs, her face pale.

The other kids had crowded around, forcing Zac to push through them to reach Evie. He squatted beside her and she motioned to him. 'Zac is a doctor.' The kids gave him incredulous looks—not surprising really, he was a mess. He looked more like a shaggy bear than ever now, his hair was sticking out all over his head, his face smeared with blood, his own probably, as the cut above his eye continued to bleed.

Sally was shivering, despite the warmth of the night. One of the boys had a lightweight cotton jumper tied around his waist.

'I need your top to keep her warm, she's in shock.' He handed it over and Evie wrapped it around Sally's shoulders as she told Zac what had happened.

'Can I have a look at your hand?' Zac asked. He prised her fingers away, opening up her palm. Blood covered everything, making it difficult in the darkness to see exactly what damage had been done. 'Does anyone have any water?'

The other girl passed Zac her water bottle. He stripped off his shirt, turning it inside out, and then took the bottle and removed the lid. He poured water over the injured girl's hand, holding it at an angle so the water ran off, washing the blood away. Evie tore her gaze away from Zac's naked torso as an image of a gladiator, bloodied and bruised from battle, replaced that of a shaggy bear. She could see the gash at the base of Sally's thumb and forced herself to concentrate on that.

It was still bleeding but fortunately the glass had sliced into a vein, not an artery, and the blood flow was relatively slow.

'We'll have to wait until we get you to the hospital to have a proper look at your hand. It needs stitching at the least, and I can't do that here.' Zac tore his T-shirt into strips, packing some against the wound, tying it in place with more strips of fabric. As he worked, he spoke to Evie. 'Can you call Tom? We need a lift.'

She was about to ask for the number when she saw Tom and Lexi hurrying towards them.

'What's going on?'

'Long story, but we need a lift to the hospital.' Zac was wiping blood from his brow as he spoke. Too late, Evie remembered her scarf tied around her hips. Undoing this, she pressed it to Zac's forehead in an attempt to stem the blood flow. Zac put his hand to his eye, placing it over Evie's hand, his palm warm on her cool skin.

Tom didn't waste time with more questions. 'I'll get the car.'

'Lexi, do you mind waiting here? I'd like Evie to come with us and Sally's friend.' Zac indicated the other girl with a tilt of his head. 'I'll send Tom straight back.'

'Of course. Do you want me to get the police?'

Zac shook his head. 'I can't imagine anyone will want to make a complaint. They're all at fault and this injury was just an accident.'

Tom pulled up at the kerb and Evie and Zac bundled Sally and the other girl, Zoe, into the car. Zac turned back to the boys who were standing, dumbstruck, on the footpath beside Lexi. 'Lexi's a doctor, too. Wait here with her and Tom'll come back and drop you home.' The boys nodded, looking completely bewildered.

Tom pulled into the ambulance bay and Zac and Evie ushered the girls into the emergency department. Libby was on duty and she didn't know where to look as they walked through the doors, Zac shirtless and covered in blood, one eye hidden behind a scrap of fabric, with two teenage girls in tow.

Zac grabbed a clean gown from a trolley, throwing it on backwards, like a shirt, restoring some semblance of modesty. Evie directed Sally and Zoe to an examination cubicle before starting to fill Libby in on the situation. She sat Sally in a chair as Libby wheeled a table into place, positioning Sally's hand on the tabletop before fetching two blankets from the warming cupboard, one for each of the girls.

Evie went to wash her hands and, standing beside Zac as he wiped his hands dry, she was treated to a display of rippling chest muscles under his open gown. He had the body of an athlete and she wondered what exercise he did. She had a serious case of lust going on here. She knew so little about him but she knew she wanted more.

Libby settled next to Zac, anticipating his needs as she administered analgesia and swabbed the blood away. Evie was left to play the role of spectator, left to watch Zac.

'You've cut a vein and damaged a tendon, possibly a nerve as well. Injuries to a hand aren't something to take lightly. You need microsurgery and you'll need to be transferred to Adelaide tonight. I'll organise an ambulance but I need to speak to your parents. I assume they're your next of kin?'

Evie waited with Sally while Zac called her parents and made arrangements for an ambulance transfer. Once Sally was on her way, Evie took charge.

'Your turn,' she said to Zac.

'What for?'

'First aid. The cut on your head needs attention.'

Zac touched his fingers to his eyebrow then pulled them away to inspect them. 'It's stopped bleeding.'

Evie pushed him into a chair, not an easy task but he didn't resist her, and positioned an instrument trolley behind him as she answered. 'Only just. It still needs cleaning and a couple of steri-strips. Unless, of course, you'd prefer a scar?' It would probably suit him, add an air of mystery to his features, but it would be at odds with his reputation of being responsible and in control.

'Scars are only interesting if there's an interesting story behind them.'

'In that case, sit still and let me do my job.' She dragged a stool closer to Zac's chair and sat down, her thighs either side of his left knee. She had to be close in order to see what she was doing but the proximity was distracting. His chest, bare under the open gown, had a smattering of dark hair, leading her eyes lower. With an effort she kept her gaze directed at his forehead, avoiding his eyes, which she could feel were focussed on her. Pulling on surgical gloves over her clean hands, she swabbed Zac's wound with Betadine. He flinched at the sting but said nothing. She was sitting a fraction higher than him and each time he exhaled she could feel his warm breath brush over the base of her throat, filling the dip between her collarbones. The sensation sent a tingle through her body, making it difficult to concentrate. If she left him with a scar, he'd only have himself to blame.

Evie removed three steri-strips and placed them carefully over the cut, pulling the edges together. 'All done.'

She dropped her gaze, finally meeting his eyes. He was still watching her, his gaze so intense it made her catch her breath. He was so confident in his skin, in his masculinity. Flustered, she dropped her gaze even further, down to his bare chest, but that didn't help. Not a bit.

'Thank you.' His voice was deep and rich and resonated through her body.

'My pleasure.'

Zac stood, affording her another eyeful of his broad chest. She felt herself flush and scooted backwards on the stool, out of arm's reach, before she was tempted to stretch a hand out to touch him.

'I'd better go. I need to see about getting Zoe home. Not quite the end I had in mind to the evening.'

'It's OK. I'm beat, I just want to fall into bed.'

Zac's grin matched the mischievous glint in his eyes, but he kept quiet, still in control. The interruption to their evening had broken their connection and Evie wasn't sure what would happen next. Maybe he'd taken tonight in his stride? Relax, let it happen? Somehow she doubted it. It didn't fit his serious persona, but neither did oh, so delectable kisses under a golden moon.

He took her hand, rubbing his thumb in tiny circles over the tender skin of her wrist. 'I'd better go,' he repeated. 'We never did get that coffee. Can I take a rain-check?'

Evie nodded and watched him leave, with Zoe in tow, and wondered what tomorrow would bring.

'So we kissed. Big deal.' Evie was sitting on Letitia's bed, waiting for Jake and the girls to arrive. The retrieval team would be on their way to transfer Letitia to Adelaide and Evie had timed her lunch-break to coincide with it. 'We're both adults, why get all het up about it?' She kept her voice low since, as Letitia's doctor, Zac, would soon be there, too. She wasn't going to get caught out a second time, discussing him with her sister-in-law.

'Was it?' Letitia was in the spirit of things, despite her increasing nerves about leaving her family. Which was why Evie had introduced the topic, but now, having done so, she found she did need to talk about it for her own sake.

'Was it what?'

'A big deal?'

Evie closed her eyes and remembered, opening them again as Letitia started laughing. 'You don't need to answer that, your expression said it all.'

'What did it say?'

'It was a *very* big deal.'

Evie grinned. 'I didn't say it wasn't heart-stoppingly great, just there's no need to get het up about it.'

'I suspect he is.'

'He is what?'

'Getting het up.'

'Why?'

'He's been a dedicated bachelor ever since he arrived here and, as far as I know, he doesn't date so my guess is he'll be thinking this over.'

'Great,' Evie moaned. 'He'll probably decide he's made a big mistake and head for the hills.'

'Now who's getting het up? It was just a kiss, you said.'

Letitia was laughing and Evie knew it was at her expense. Zac's kisses had been amazing. They couldn't mean nothing! 'Maybe I need to ask Fel. I need some inside information.'

'Zac's Aunt Fel?'

'Yes. I've met her. She said you're one of her favourite staff members and I've seen for myself how much she adores the girls.'

At the mention of her girls, tears threatened to well up in Letitia's eyes. Oops, time for some more distraction. 'Have you got some good books to take with you?'

'You know I'm not much of a reader, not like you.'

'It's never too late. I wasn't always a voracious reader but when you're totally out of it for three years, like I was, you kind of have no choice.'

The door opened, admitting Zac, as Evie was speaking.

'Totally out of what?' Zac asked, his tone cautious.

Evie and Letitia both ignored his question as they stared openly at his face. The cut across his eyebrow was almost unnoticeable as it was overshadowed by the discolouration around the eye itself. His eye was purple and swollen and half-closed.

Letitia was full of sympathy. 'You look dreadful. Does it hurt?'

Zac touched it self-consciously and then grimaced. 'It's not too bad as long as I don't touch it.'

'Let me guess,' said Evie. 'We should see the other guy, right?'

'I have no idea how he looks—he ran away.' Zac matched her quip but there was a reservation in his voice that hadn't been there last night. Was that just because they weren't alone? Or was there something more? She'd thought he might pull away but hadn't thought it would be so quickly.

'I never picked you for a tough guy,' said Letitia.

'I'm not. I'm tipping the other bloke looks fine, I didn't lay a finger on him,' Zac answered Letitia but was watching Evie, and she cursed silently as she felt herself blush. She turned away, wondering how she was going to explain this, but was saved from further embarrassment when laughter from outside the room announced the arrival of Jake, Mack and Gracie.

Letitia had insisted the girls not see her leave in the ambulance or even being put on the gurney, and the girls had insisted they say goodbye. A compromise had been struck that the transfer team would take Letitia downstairs in a wheelchair and Mack and Gracie would say their goodbyes on the ward.

The transfer team, two young men, entered with the wheelchair, swelling the room past capacity but Evie knew the distractions would help Letitia cope.

She sneaked a glance at Zac. What was it about him that had so quickly made her forget her plan to befriend him, to help him lighten up? Those intentions had been overtaken by one thought only—to be kissed much, much more by him.

Unlike Evie, Letitia only had eyes for the wheelchair.

A riot of colours, it was decorated in a combination of paper streamers and hand-made cards bearing crayon-scrawled messages of 'Get well soon, Mummy, love Mack' and 'I lov yoo, Mummy, love Gracie.' A few pink balloons drifted behind for good measure. It was so heavily decorated the wheelchair itself was scarcely visible.

Letitia blinked back tears and held her arms open for her daughters, who scrambled up next to her on the bed. 'That's the most beautiful sight in the world.' She dropped a kiss on each little head and Evie knew she was talking about her girls, one cradled in each arm, not the wheelchair.

'We're going to come to see you after the operation.' Gracie's eyes were open wide, bright with excitement, oblivious to the real situation. 'And…' She dropped her voice to a loud whisper. 'We're getting a *day off school!*'

Her comment lifted general spirits for the goodbyes and Letitia managed to keep her tears at bay, at least until the lift doors had closed on the group which included Zac and Jake. Evie doubted the bravery would last much beyond the lift ride. She squatted down and scooped a niece to each side of her, kissing the tops of their heads just as their mother had done.

But the image that stayed with her was of Zac's face as the lift doors had closed. He'd kept his gaze on her. Even when she'd broken it to look at Letitia and Jake, she'd felt it. And if there'd been questions in his eyes before, there'd at least been desire. But now? For some reason, only the questions were there.

There was something else about Evie, something other than her ability to get under his defences, something that had been niggling at his peace of mind since he'd first seen her.

It's never too late, she'd been saying to Letitia as he'd entered the room. *When you're totally out of it for three years, like I was, you kind of have no choice.*

She'd known exactly what they'd been dealing with when Stewart had been brought in. Not just that it had been drugs, but which drug. She'd been spot on.

Was that why she'd been 'out of it' for three years? When?

And if she had been, what did it matter to him as long as she was no longer using and not a risk to their patients? She couldn't be into drugs if she was as good at her job as she seemed, could she? He could ask her—but would she admit she'd had a problem? And if she didn't have a history, he'd risk offending her. No, no risk, it was a certainty.

But he didn't know her at all. All he knew was she was capable of dismissing all reasonable, rational thought from his mind. He'd kissed her, damn it, on two occasions last night. He hadn't known he'd been going to do it and he never did something he hadn't planned, debated or come to a sensible decision about.

She was unlike anyone he'd ever met. He was a planner and she made him forget about plans. So, chequered past or not, she was dangerous.

The problem was, it felt good to forget.

He was in danger of wanting more.

But more of Evie meant he'd be less in control.

And there were great big questions hanging over her head. Questions he needed answered, not just for his sake but for the sake of the hospital.

Their little group was moving at a great pace through the hospital and he focussed on the couple in front of him. He needed answers, he couldn't think rationally without information. Could he ask Letitia? Jake?

What else had Evie said when they'd met with Stewart's parents? She'd agreed with Stewart's dad that if Stewart used drugs they'd be unlikely to know. Did she know that because she'd managed to keep *her* past—her present—a secret?

They reached the ambulance bay, the warmth of a summer's day easing over his skin, but he was scarcely aware of it. Letitia was saying goodbye to Jake, who'd follow the next morning to be with her in time for the surgery. Tears were running freely down her face. Jake was still being strong but he was holding his wife tight, like he didn't want to let go.

So, no, now was not the time to poke around in Evie's past.

'Thanks for everything, Zac, you've been wonderful.' Jake had released Letitia from the hug and she was wiping tears from her cheeks with one hand, holding Jake's hand with her other.

'No thanks necessary,' he said, and he meant it. 'You just concentrate on getting better and coming back to us as soon as you can. I'll come to see you after the op.'

'You don't need to do that. I know how busy you are.'

'Consider it part of the after-sales service.' Letitia managed a smile at that. 'And strictly no worrying about your girls, we'll all be looking out for them. And they've got Evie. They're in good hands.'

But as he watched Letitia being lifted into the ambulance and stood aside as husband and wife held eye contact until the doors closed, saw the trust and love between them, simple, strong and plain, he repeated his last phrase to himself.

They're in good hands.

But were they?

Jake had excused himself quickly to return to his daughters, eager to spend time with them before he left for Adelaide, leaving Zac free to do what he'd intended when he'd first met

Evie: check her personnel file. He'd meant to do it but had been sidetracked. Correction, had allowed himself to be sidetracked, had convinced himself he didn't need to know more. But he did.

One benefit of being responsible for sorting out personnel problems was that he didn't have to voice his concerns to a third party to get her file checked, he could do it himself, discreetly. Not that the file would tell him much—she'd have been unlikely to declare a drug-use history in a job application form.

Unlocking the personnel manager's office door, he scanned the filing cabinets. Locating the G–O drawer, it took only a second to find her file and retrieve it, trying to ignore the feeling he was snooping. He wasn't, he had a legitimate concern and he'd be negligent not to look into it. He'd do the same for anyone else. *But she's not anyone else,* was the whisper in his ear as he read and reread the large print of the label on the cover: MS EVA HENDERSON.

If he found out she had such a past, what then? What steps would he have to take?

He stood with the file in his hand for thirty seconds before he could open it, and when he did, he flipped it open like it could bite.

Her personal history was summarised on the first page. The plain black and white page seemed at odds with the vibrant woman who'd already got under his skin. Born, raised and schooled in rural New South Wales. Gained her nursing qualifications in the UK. He knew the school, it had a good reputation. Nothing much there. Flipping over pages with impatience, he reached the references. The first was from a consultant no less. In what universe did consultants write references for nursing staff? *Ms Henderson would be an asset in any hospital.* And another, from her locum agency by the look of it. *We wish Ms Henderson all the best for her return*

*to Australia. She leaves knowing she has a place with us at
any time in the future should she choose.*

There were more. He skimmed them, knowing they
wouldn't tell him what he needed to know, but they were telling
him what he wanted to know—Evie was a great nurse, highly
skilled, well regarded, reliable, empathic. The list of adjectives
went on.

He flipped back to her employment history. She'd started
with a permanent job at St Martin's in London and had resigned
less than six months later. Since then she'd been solely
employed in casual work. Why? There was one main reason
he could think of for a new graduate to quit a secure job in
a prestigious hospital—the pay was better doing contract
work. Which was no crime. Lord knew, nurses were gener-
ally grossly underpaid considering their responsibilities and
training. But had she had a particular reason for needing more
money? An expensive habit to support?

Glancing back up the page, the dates listed next to each entry
came into sharper focus. Each year, for the past five years, there
was a gap of three or four months her dates of employment
didn't cover. Those months simply weren't listed.

He looked up, the file gripped in one hand, glanced at his
watch and cursed. He was running late. The missing months
would have to wait.

But he knew already she hadn't spent that time in Australia.
Letitia had made it clear how excited they had all been to see
her, saying Evie had only had a few flying visits home to see
the girls, as she couldn't afford any more time off work. What
excuse had she made to her family when she'd had so much
time away from work but hadn't been able to make time for
them?

More to the point, where *had* she been and what had she
been doing?

The missing months were only part of it. If he'd overheard right, there were three other *years* to be accounted for.

He cursed. Why, when he hadn't kissed a woman since his marriage had disintegrated, did his resolve have to be so tested now?

Evie was addictive and he wanted more; despite his doubts and all the reasons not to, he wanted more.

More of her time, more of her laughter, more of her kisses.

But that path was closed to him. That was non-negotiable. He'd learnt that lesson with his ex-wife—it was the legacy he had to live with.

But there were moments of madness when Evie made him forget about his past and the constraints on his future.

How was that possible when in over three years he hadn't lost sight of his resolutions even once?

Just who was Evie Henderson?

CHAPTER FIVE

JUST who was this man who could kiss her like he'd never stop, then go cold in an instant? He'd gone cold while she'd still been bubbling away at boiling point at the mere thought of how she'd felt in his arms…

Her thoughts took their own course as she made her way to the nursing-home. Her shift was almost over but she'd been called to assist with a resident who'd fallen. She was on an early and after today she'd need to race to get the girls from school. Today her brother was still at home, so it didn't matter if she went over time but tomorrow he was leaving—and then what? How was she going to juggle everything without the huge inconvenience that had just sideswiped her? She was falling for Zac.

Damn and double damn, she didn't need that. Having family ties here made it hard enough to stay away for such long periods of time. Another temptation to sway her from her chosen path was not what she was looking for. She was already torn constantly between her two lives, always feeling guilty about not doing enough in one camp or the other.

Striding rapidly to the nursing-home, she saw Zac in the distance, eyes cast down, walking with a file gripped in his hand, his steps swift as if he was late for something. Her heart all but stopped in her chest at the sight of him, at the memory of him kissing her. And how!

Her reaction confirmed it: she was falling for him. She couldn't argue with that conclusion when a quick glimpse of him was all it took to leave her feeling as though she'd been physically knocked off her feet.

'What's up, love?' Mr Louis was sitting in the warmth of the afternoon sunshine, and his question broke into her reverie.

'Mr Louis! Hello. Sorry I can't stop, someone's had a fall.' She hoped he hadn't seen her leap as he'd spoken, so deep had she been in her thoughts.

'Probably Wilf doing acrobatics again, old fool, just won't accept his youth is over,' she heard him call out as she sped towards the entrance doors. She entered the common room to find Pam crouched next to a prostrate figure. She was holding a pad firmly over a cut on the person's head, soaking up blood, and another beside the patient's mouth.

Fel?

The situation took her thoughts straight back to Zac. She glanced around. Zac hadn't been heading this way, he might not even know. The residents who'd gathered around stepped aside to make room for her and she knelt down beside Fel.

'What happened?'

'Fel had a fall. Her knee is playing up and it went from under her. She hit her head on the side of the table.' Pam nodded at a wooden table, its edges sharp. 'She also bit her lip, she's given herself a nasty cut with her teeth. I haven't tried to move her, just in case.' Evie nodded. 'The orderlies are on their way, they were all busy in Theatre.'

'Hold the pads down as much as you can while I check her over. We really need clean cold water on her lip, but I'll check her first.'

Evie started her examination, moving her hands gently

over the old lady who had rapidly become one of her three favourite residents—Fel, Nancy and Mr Louis. She explained what she was doing to both Pam and Fel as she worked, but Fel, though conscious, wasn't answering.

The bleeding from her lip and the cut on her forehead was subsiding. 'You'll have a nasty headache and perhaps some stitches to show for this afternoon, Fel, but it looks as though you're OK otherwise. I'm sure the doctor will want a CT scan and you might be kept in hospital overnight for observation. Other than that, your knee will need looking into if you're not already seeing someone for it.'

'She's a stubborn old girl.'

At the sound of Zac's voice behind her, Evie started to get up but overbalanced, collecting Zac with the full force of her movement as she stumbled into his chest. Too close, too intimate. Was she flushed? Touching a hand to her cheek, she kept her face turned from him, bending back down to Fel.

It didn't help. He crouched down, too, and the proximity was disconcerting. Not that he seemed affected. His concentration was solely on Fel and he scarcely seemed to notice Evie was there. So one of them was in control of their emotions and, no surprises, it was him.

'You didn't need to come over,' mumbled Fel. 'I told them not to bother you, Tom will come and see me.'

'Tom won't be at the hospital for a good few hours so you get what you get, and that's me.'

The orderlies arrived and the room felt crowded. Evie felt superfluous but didn't know if she should go or stay with Fel.

Zac stood, addressing the orderlies. 'Take her to Radiology, please.' To his aunt, he said, 'I'll go ahead and get a CAT scan organised. I'm not expecting to find anything, but with a knock and a cut like that, it needs to be done. Either way, you'll stay in hospital overnight.'

He nodded at Pam and Evie and left, leaving the orderlies to transfer Fel to a stretcher and Evie to trail along with them to Radiology, confused. He wouldn't want to make it obvious he'd kissed her, wouldn't want to single her out for any special attention, but he'd scarcely made eye contact with her.

What had happened since he'd kissed her? What had changed? Or was it nothing to do with her? A bad day at work, perhaps?

The trouble was, she didn't know him well enough to guess. His kisses melted her soul, he was a fantastic cook and he seemed like a brilliant doctor—but what else did she really know about him? According to his great-aunt, he'd had a nasty relationship breakdown but what red-blooded man decided to ignore a physical attraction like theirs? Not one she'd ever known.

She refused to be ignored—she'd make him talk. But when? She'd promised to take the girls to the beach after work and Jake would be at home tonight, but from tomorrow she'd be on her own with her nieces. That would make it hard to catch Zac, especially if he didn't want to be caught. She left Fel in the care of the radiographers and went off duty, mulling over her options.

He'd catch Evie tonight, Zac decided as he slid his aunt's scan up on the light box. The radiologist had given Fel the all-clear but he wanted to see for himself. He'd make sure Fel was comfortable. And then he'd do his sleuthing. His bridge-burning.

He should be calling Evie into his office, quizzing her at work, but he'd kissed her—so how could he do that? One kiss then—bam! The next day he was forced into investigating her background, tossing up whether to accuse her of using or having used drugs. Not the best way to follow up their first date—not that he'd call it that. Tom and Lexi and fate had orchestrated it. He didn't date.

As it was, Fel was asleep so there went the first item on his list. He'd have to come back and see her later, after dinner, which meant trawling through Evie's file and then, if that didn't clear up his questions, confronting her jumped up a notch. He wasn't ready!

Tucking her file under his arm, he left the hospital and headed home, the summer light still strong. When had he last left work at this time, even though it was late enough for dinner? But staying at his desk to tackle paperwork or search for answers to the funding crisis wasn't where he wanted to be right now.

Neither was doubting Evie.

Which meant he spent the next half-hour chopping, mixing and stir-frying, creating a delicious dinner a full two hours earlier than he'd normally eat but not able to create a solution to the Evie problem. The file remained where he'd dropped it on the kitchen bench.

His meal finished and cleared away, he headed back to his bedroom to grab a T-shirt, having donned only faded old jeans when he'd arrived home. A knock at the front door waylaid him.

Evie. Her hair was wet, pulled back into a mess of a ponytail, and she smelt like the ocean. A light summer dress floated around her.

'Can I come in?'

She stepped inside, not waiting for an answer—or did he nod? She headed for the kitchen, Zac adding a belated 'Sure' as he followed her along the passage.

This meeting was premature—he had nothing to say to her yet, he hadn't finished looking at the file. But he couldn't pretend he had no issues either. Which left him—where, exactly?

Which left him playing host. 'Can I get you a drink?'

'Thanks. We've been at the beach and I've played one too many games of stuck-in-the-mud and jumped one too many waves.'

'The girls had fun?' He was at a loss for something to say but he cringed inwardly as he came out with the obvious.

She nodded and perched on a bar stool, watching him as he grabbed glasses and filled them with cold water from the fridge. Why did she have to look so at home there? So right? He'd have to come out with his questions soon or it would become impossible if he played the polite host for too long. Deep breath. Just ask about the missing months.

'Why have you got my file?'

Damn, he'd left it out in full-view, her name in bold letters across the front. The role of polite host evaporated as he tried and discarded various answers to distract her from her question.

'Are you checking up on me?' She'd got it straight away, but she didn't seem angry. 'Have I done something wrong?' She seemed worried. Was that good or bad?

'Not exactly.' Not yet. 'But you said something today that I needed to check. And I didn't have a chance at work so I brought your file home. You weren't meant to see it.'

'And now that I have? What is it you need to check?'

He glanced at the file.

'You can ask me directly if you like.' She was too distracting, perched on his stool, the worry on her face replaced by something approaching amusement—at his obvious discomfort, no doubt. 'I'm right here.'

'You are, indeed.'

'Ah. And you don't want me to be. It must be pretty bad, whatever it is you think I've done.' She sounded chatty. Who made small talk in a situation like this? Apparently she did.

'I haven't finished looking. I don't want to ask you questions that could offend you when I haven't finished reading your file. I'm sure it'll clear it up.'

'I promise not to be offended. Come on, out with it, it'll

save you time.' Head tilted to one side, she teased him with a tiny smile. 'You know you want to.'

She was too, too distracting.

He focussed, with difficulty. 'Have you ever used drugs?'

'Never. Next question?'

'You're not on drugs now?'

'I think that's covered in my first answer, but you're new at this, I can tell, so I'll humour you. No, I am one hundred per cent not on drugs now.' She drew a finger across her chest in the shape of a cross. 'Haven't even had a Panadol for weeks and weeks, and I'm happy to swear to that. Next?'

'You're taking this awfully well, if what I'm asking you is totally off base.'

'Zac, you're on the board of the hospital, I need my job, I don't think abusing you is the right response. Besides,' she added cheerfully, 'abusing people is not my style. Why drugs, just out of interest? It's not to do with Stewart, is it, or you would've asked me this earlier?'

If he didn't sit down, he'd fall down. He sat on the stool opposite her. 'You said to Letitia today you were out of it for three years.' By the twinkle in her eye, there was a joke he wasn't in on. 'And your file says you have three or four months off work every year.'

'And you think I'm off perfecting my drug-taking techniques or maybe it's harvest time and I'm farming my drug crop?'

'If I'm on the wrong track, you'll think I'm crazy, but I have to know for sure. It's—'

'Your responsibility, I know. And I'd hate to be the one to come between you and responsibility. Not when you're so good at it.' She caught the look on his face and laughed. 'Sorry, I imagine these sorts of investigations come with a strictly no-teasing-allowed tag. You'll have to forgive me, I haven't been investigated as a potential drug lord before. I'm not au fait with the procedure.'

'Evie,' he said, 'awkward or not, I'd appreciate an explanation.'

'I hate to disabuse you of the notion that I'm an underworld figure, it sounds so much more dramatic and alluring than the truth. Are you sure we can't leave it like that?'

'Quite sure.'

She pulled a face at him and hitched up her dress to rub the back of one slender, beautifully formed knee. 'Drat the mossies,' she said. 'I miss my Australian summers terribly, except for the mosquitoes. They love me, eat me alive, even on the beach. I'd put spray on, except—' she was suppressing a laugh '—I hate using the stuff, all sorts of awful toxins in them.'

'Evie.'

'Oh, all right, it was worth a try. Reason why I'm not on drugs, number one. Or rather, reason why I was out of it for three years, they're interchangeable, I imagine. I had chronic fatigue syndrome during high school and missed most of years nine through to eleven. I made it back for my final year but I was pretty behind by then, so the marks I'd always taken for granted I'd get didn't come my way.'

'Chronic fatigue syndrome?'

She screwed up her perfect nose. 'See? Not nearly as mysterious and enticing as you were thinking.'

'I'd hardly use those words to describe being a drug user.'

'You're right, of course. I just hate having to think about being sick. I made a promise to myself years ago not to think about it, just to make sure it never happened again. Which is also why I'd be the last person, ever, to use drugs. I don't even touch alcohol. Apart from being boringly dedicated to the pursuit of good health…' she raised a finger, as if considering something '…with the exception of my daily dose of coffee, there is no way

I'm befuddling my senses with substances other than natural ones. I've missed out on three years, I'm not missing any more.'

It sounded feasible. It also fitted with the fact she was a glowing picture of good health. But...

'The months off work? Let me guess, a hard-core health farm?'

'Now you're teasing, which isn't professional of you.' She hesitated and he sensed she was stalling for time—didn't she want to tell him?

'You're drug-free but you're an ex-con on the run? Some secret life no one knows about?'

She was fidgeting with the hem of her dress, showing him those legs again. As a distraction technique, it was fantastic. He could hardly remember what he'd just asked her.

'Nothing secret and nothing illegal, just a bit unusual. There's no reason you shouldn't know,' she added, seemingly more to herself than to him. 'It's there somewhere in my file anyway. Those "missing months", as you call them, I spend in Vietnam.'

Vietnam. 'Why?' As she'd said, it probably was in her file, he just hadn't had time to find the details.

'I got involved with a foundation there, just as a volunteer, a number of years back. The foundation works with disadvantaged children and it's become so much a part of my life that I deliberately choose work that pays me well enough so I can indulge my wish to be involved.'

So he had the answer to why she'd quit a permanent, prestigious job soon after graduation. She'd wanted the money casual work offered but not for any reason he'd guessed.

'So there you have it, the complete summary of my life, work and interests, all in one neat package.'

'You don't look happy when you say that.'

'Only because the package isn't so neat at the moment. I

was meant to be there now but I was needed here.' She shrugged a slender shoulder. 'Don't get me wrong, I wanted to come, Jake and Letitia didn't pressure me at all, but I still feel I'm letting everyone in Vietnam down.'

'What were you going to be doing that someone else couldn't do?'

'It's more a matter of whether there's anyone available to help. There are a lot of people committed to helping but there's never enough and if I'm not there, they're short one more. They're desperate for people with skills, especially in the health-care area.'

'You don't feel spending months there every year has been a decent enough contribution?'

'It's not just guilt—I feel an almost physical pull to be there. This is the first time in years I haven't been able to go and I'm feeling weird about it. Incomplete maybe. If that doesn't sound too pretentious.'

'Not pretentious, just saint-like.'

She laughed. 'I'm no saint. I'm talking about the personal satisfaction I get. So, really, it's all about me.' The sparkle in her eyes was back.

'What does the organisation do?'

'It was established to help street kids, children with no options, no homes, no future. It's expanded significantly to provide medical help in a number of clinics, there's a school for disadvantaged children, including those with disabilities, a vocational training programme. The list goes on. There are all sorts of people all over the world who make it possible, I only play a small part.'

'Your eyes light up when you talk about it. It means a lot to you.'

'It means the world to me to be involved.' There was the slightest pucker between her eyebrows, the only indication she was mulling something over. 'So this is why you were behaving strangely today? You thought I had some deep, dark secret? You *were* keeping your distance, weren't you?'

Her directness, her openness, her apparent ability to let his suspicions wash over her cut through his own natural instinct to keep his feelings under wraps.

'I had some doubts. We have to work together. Conflicts between work and personal life are guaranteed. And when I overheard you talking about missing three years, I panicked.'

'Didn't your mother tell you eavesdropping never brings good news? But now you know I'm squeaky clean, so there's no problem.'

Looking at her, swinging her legs as she sat on his stool, hair dried now into a riot of dark curls, she looked delicious. She looked like she belonged. But she didn't, she was passing through, this was a temporary—and maybe not entirely welcome—hiatus from her usual life.

He knew he'd been looking for excuses when he'd grabbed her file. Hoping to find something in there to help get her out of his head. But it hadn't worked. She'd done nothing wrong. Nothing except stir his libido.

But that was a no-go area. How could he stick to his resolve if she was there, forcing him to confront the fact there was a whole part of his life he couldn't share?

No problem, she'd said.

But he had big problems. And the biggest was that every time she swung her leg or flicked her hair over her shoulder or looked at him with her enormous brown eyes, it got more and more difficult to remember why he should stay away. Far away.

'Evie?'

'Yes?'

She'd never imagined, when she'd knocked on his door that night, that he'd be reaching for her like he was aching for her.

It was exactly what she wanted. And needed.

So there was no question of saying no, of reminding him he was saying one thing and doing another. That was his problem, not hers! She opened herself to his touch, sliding off the stool into his arms, moulding her body to the strong lines of his as she let herself melt into his kiss.

He tasted of the sea spray and salt she knew was on her own lips. Now it was his taste.

Her hands rested on his chest—the chest that had been distracting her from the moment he'd opened the door so she had no power against it now—fingers spread over the warmth of his skin, eyes closed, the world spinning slowly, so slowly it left only the two of them, with everything else ebbing away from her consciousness.

She could have stayed here for ever. In his arms, his lips on hers.

But she didn't have for ever.

And the time she had here was stolen time, stolen from a life she'd already committed to.

Casual flirtation was fine.

But what she was feeling now wasn't that. What she was feeling now was far from casual. What she was feeling now had 'danger' written all over it.

Danger? She should be running screaming in the opposite direction.

Instead, she leant in further and he deepened his kiss in response.

She had a crush—a schoolgirl crush. That's what it was. She'd missed out on so much in her adolescent years, it was only natural she'd regress at some point.

So she'd regress and enjoy it and take some memories with her when she left.

How long did crushes last?

CHAPTER SIX

CRUSHES were all very well but Evie had a sneaking suspicion hers was getting out of hand. She was working in Emergency, monitoring the oxygen sats on a teenager in the midst of a severe asthma attack, an easy job compared to some and one that left ample time for daydreaming. She'd never had fantasies about a dream wedding, not like some of her school friends. Her teenage fantasies had been about what she'd do when she got well—settling down had never crossed her mind, she was going to be a doctor or a lawyer or a physiotherapist. And then that hadn't worked out so, angry and disillusioned, she'd grabbed her backpack and fled overseas.

But if she'd had those dreams, it wasn't impossible to imagine Zac waiting for her at the end of the aisle. Thoughts of Zac had her skipping over the wedding and landing in the honeymoon, which was when she was interrupted by Libby.

'Evie, do you remember Stewart, the boy who was rushed in the other night?' Evie nodded. That sort of introduction to a job wouldn't slip her mind. 'He's here with his parents. They'd like a word if you have a minute.'

Evie handed over her monitoring to Libby and ducked out of the cubicle to find Stewart and his parents waiting for her.

'We didn't want to leave without saying thank you,' James said as he shook her hand enthusiastically.

'Glad to help.' She retrieved her hand and massaged her crushed fingers before turning her attention to Stewart. 'How are you feeling?'

He shrugged, maintaining a stubborn silence. Was he embarrassed? Dreading going home with his parents and being under what Evie knew would be his mother's vigilant monitoring? Or still feeling the effects of the ice?

'He's still tired, but you said to expect that.' Helen was filling in the awkward silence Stewart had created. 'I'll be glad to get home, that's for sure.'

'Did you see the news this morning?' James asked.

Evie shook her head.

'The police in Adelaide have arrested two men on drug charges. Pulled them over for traffic offences and found plastic containers of amphetamine paste, 20,000 hits worth. The police think they were heading for Pelican Beach.'

'I'm glad that's not going to make it to us.' Evie turned to Stewart, on the off chance he was receptive.

'Please, look after yourself, you only get one chance and that's particularly true where this drug is concerned.' Would he heed her warning? Who knew? She could only hope his parents would take what had happened seriously. Regardless, she'd done her job and now it was up to them as a family.

Her priority was to look after her own family and tomorrow she was taking the girls to visit Letitia. Zac was driving them and she let her mind drift back to her daydreaming as she returned to monitor her asthmatic patient.

If Evie had been dreaming of idyllic honeymoons while she'd worked, the drive to Adelaide put things into perspective. Gracie and Mack talked the whole way, leaving Evie no chance to talk to Zac, let alone daydream, and her powers of concentration were fading as they reached the hospital.

The lift doors opened, depositing their group onto the orthopaedic ward where they'd come to see Letitia. Evie scanned the corridor, looking for the nurses' station. Letitia was in Room Eight but Evie had no idea in which direction to head. Zac didn't hesitate and Evie and the girls fell in behind him.

Zac introduced himself to the ward clerk, who directed them to Letitia. The girls raced off, not concerned at all about the unfamiliar surroundings.

'Remember, girls, no jumping onto the bed, your mum will be sore,' Evie called after them.

'I want to speak to Letitia's surgeon if he's around the place,' Zac said to her. 'I'll join you in a moment.'

She met Mack and Grace at the door. 'In you go. Mum will be so excited to see you.' She pushed the door, holding it open as the girls sprinted in to their mother.

Letitia's smile lit up her face and she held her arms wide to embrace her daughters as they flung themselves at her, one on each side.

'Hello, my darlings,' she said, showering them with kisses. 'How are you?'

'Good. We brought you more pictures.' Gracie and Mack allowed their dad to sneak a kiss in before they dug into their bags, pulling out their paintings. Sticking these to every available vertical surface around Letitia's bed served to keep them both occupied while Evie chatted with her brother and his wife.

'You look brighter than I expected.'

'I'm feeling good. The constant, deep pain in my hips has gone. My muscles are sore from the surgery and the exercises but I know those aches are only temporary.'

'You're even sitting out of bed.'

'This is fantastic.' Letitia indicated the armchair, its extendable legs raising it higher than a normal chair. 'I don't have to bend my hips too much to use it.'

'We'll need to hire one for home, I guess,' Jake said.

'And a few other things, but that's easy to organise, I'll sort it out with the rehab staff,' Evie replied.

'Thanks.'

'No problem. How long have you been sitting out for?'

'About ten minutes. I'm waiting for the physio to come to do my exercises with me.'

'Whose is this?' Gracie had found Letitia's walking frame and was swinging on it like a little monkey.

'That's mine.'

'It's like the ones in the nursing-home! Are you old now?'

Letitia laughed. 'Not very old, darling. I just need it while my muscles get strong.'

The door swung open, admitting Zac. Evie's heart leapt at the sight of him and her reaction surprised her. Twenty-eight years old and responding to a man like a hormone-riddled teenager? The smile Zac sent her way made her pulse race faster still as he crossed the room to shake Jake's hand and greet Letitia. 'I've just spoken to Mr Forrest. He seems very pleased with the surgery.'

'Now it's up to me to get through the rehab.' She grimaced.

'And to remember to take things slowly. You've got a long recovery ahead of you.'

'I know. I'm so relieved to have the surgery behind me, I'm not going to risk compromising the surgeon's efforts.'

'Glad to hear it. Evie's doing a great job with the girls, you've got nothing to worry about other than getting yourself better,' Zac said.

Letitia turned to her sister-in-law. 'Does that mean the girls have been getting some vegetables?'

'Not exactly, but I have remembered to take them to school and to make them lunches. That has to count for something.'

'It counts for a lot. I appreciate everything you're doing. You've put your life on hold for us.'

'I wouldn't have it any other way.'

'I'll do my best to make a quick recovery so you can return to your old life.'

'It will still be there whenever my services are no longer required here.'

Evie saw the questioning look Zac gave her but the arrival of the physio put paid to any further discussion.

'OK girls, why don't I take you to the zoo while Mum does her exercises?'

'Can we have an ice cream, Auntie Evie?'

'Gracie! Where are your manners?' Jake said.

'Can we have an ice-cream, *please?*'

'I meant, don't ask for treats!'

'It's OK,' Evie smiled. 'Yes, you can have an ice cream.'

'Are you coming too, Zac?'

'I'd love to, Mackenzie, but I have a meeting in forty minutes,' he said as he glanced at his watch.

'That's OK, we can wait.' Mack sat down on Letitia's bed, her arms folded, and Jake chuckled at the sight of her.

'She looks just like you do, Evie, when you want something. She has that same stubborn expression.'

'Go, girl,' Evie said to Mack, high-fiving her. 'But we can't wait here because your mum needs to do her exercises and there's not enough room for all of us.'

'Please?' Mack was not giving up. Evie looked at Zac. Did he really want to go with them?

'I'll give you a call when my meeting is over and see if it's worth catching up with you.'

'Yippee!' said the girls. 'We'll see you later, Mum. Bye.' The girls kissed their parents and ran out of the room.

Evie followed and Zac caught her by the hand as they entered the corridor. 'If you walk through the botanical gardens, I'll wager you the girls will take at least half an hour following secret paths and whatnot. And then I shouldn't be too far behind you by the time you reach the zoo.'

'Sounds lovely.'

'It's signposted at the front of the hospital, it's all close. What time do you need to have the girls back to Jake?'

'Around five. He's going to take them out once Letitia settles down for the night. Why?'

'I'd like to take you out to dinner before we head home.'

This wasn't likely to be a spur-of-the-moment invitation. She was sure he didn't do those. Which meant he'd thought this through and had still asked her out. On a date. Woo-hoo!

'Sounds great.' She fought to remain cool, calm and controlled. If he knew how excited she was, he'd probably run a mile.

Zac squeezed her hand, pulling her close and kissing her on the lips. 'See you soon.'

'Hello again.'

Evie had just paid for her nieces' ice creams and was putting her purse away when she heard Zac's voice. She looked up into his smiling face and greeted him with a smile in return.

'Hello yourself. How did the meeting go?'

'It's still going on.'

'Do you have to go back?'

'No. Greg Evans, the hospital CEO, is there. They don't need me.'

'It was a hospital meeting?'

'Plotting the future direction of the hospital. Very dull.' Zac squatted down to the level of Gracie and Mack and changed the topic. 'What have you seen?'

'The baby zebra,' said Mack.

'The ice creams,' said Gracie.

Zac laughed. 'You haven't seen the lions yet? They're my favourite.'

'We can go there now if you want,' Gracie said, holding out her little hand.

Mack checked the map. 'This way, past the flamingos.' Mack and Grace ran off, assuming the adults would follow.

Evie and Zac trailed behind, past the flamingos, the siamang monkeys and the sun bears, before finally reaching the lions' enclosure where the girls were delighting in the antics of the four cubs and their mother.

'Where are the daddy lions?' Gracie asked.

'I think they have to separate them from the cubs. I guess they'd be in another enclosure,' Evie replied. To Zac, she said, 'What is it you like about the daddy lions, to use Gracie's terminology?'

'What's not to like? What a great life, lazing about waiting to mate, lazing about some more while the lionesses make the kill. All without lifting a paw.'

Evie punched him lightly on the arm. 'I never pegged you for a chauvinist, Zac Carlisle!'

'That's quite a right hook,' he protested, rubbing his arm. 'If it's the politically correct answer you're after, then I grew up in a house just across the parklands and at night, lying in bed, I could hear the lions roar. I used to imagine I was on safari in Africa.' He stood for a moment, watching a cub who was stalking and pouncing on the twitching tail of one of the lionesses as she rested. 'One day,' he said, seemingly to himself, 'I'll get there.'

If he was going to divulge any more he was interrupted by

the ringing of his mobile phone. 'Hello… Speaking… Where did you hear this information?'

He moved away but Evie wasn't out of earshot. She hadn't intended to eavesdrop but his tone suggested a problem and it didn't sound personal. Meaning she didn't try very hard not to listen.

'Yes, I was at the meeting… I can't confirm that. No decision has been made… I'm out of town at the moment. Can you hold the story until I get back? I'd be happy to give you a statement when I'm back in Pelican Beach… Thank you.'

Zac came back to her and leant on the fencing around the big cat enclosure, drumming his fingers on the top rail. He didn't resume their conversation. The phone call had obviously unsettled him.

'What's going on?'

She half expected him to deflect her query but he answered her. 'It was one of the journos from the local paper, chasing a rumour that the nursing-home is being closed.'

'Our nursing-home?'

Zac nodded.

'Is it?'

'The government's cut our budget and we're having to look at options but no decision's been made.'

'You can't close it!'

'We might have to.'

'What about the residents?'

'Do you think we haven't thought of them? Nothing's final yet but what I didn't want was for people to go off half-cocked, which is exactly what will happen if this story gets out. I'll have to get back this afternoon to do some damage control.'

He was looking into the distance, his mind clearly already in Pelican Beach, ticking over, weighing up the situation.

'We'll drop the girls back with Jake and head off.'

He gave her a blank look, almost as if he'd forgotten she was there. 'You don't need to come. There's nothing you can do.'

'Except I need a lift home. I'm working tomorrow and Jake's not bringing the girls back until the evening. If you don't take me, I'm stuck.'

'OK, but we'll need to head off soon if I want a chance to set things straight. The paper comes out tomorrow.'

'Girls.' Evie called them over to her. 'It's time to head back to Dad. Race you to the meerkats on the way out?'

The girls led the way without argument and forty minutes later Evie and Zac were in the car, heading south. The radio was on and when one of her favourite songs was played Evie couldn't resist joining in.

'I love this song,' she said, singing along. Halfway through the first chorus she saw the look Zac gave her and he didn't seem captivated by her performance. 'Don't you like it?'

'I have no objection to the song…' Zac let his words trail off, implying his thoughts, too polite to voice his opinion.

Evie laughed. 'I know, I should only sing in the shower. But some songs just can't be ignored. How about I stop singing and you tell me about the meeting?'

It was clear Zac was battling with the options but, in the end, talking won over her vocals.

'What do you want to know?'

'You said you were plotting the future direction of the hospital. What does that mean?'

'We're trying to determine which services the hospital can and should offer. No final decision has been made. At least, it hadn't when I left the meeting today.'

'What were you discussing?'

Zac hesitated and Evie started humming softly, playing her trump card. When Zac smiled she said, 'You may as well tell me. Sounds like I'll be able to read about it in the paper tomorrow anyway.'

'But which version? That's what worries me.'

'What did the journo say?'

'He says his contact at Parliament House told him the nursing-home was being closed.'

'And is it?'

'I rang the CEO while you were dropping the girls back with Jake and the journo's source has got it wrong.'

'But you said yourself you were looking at options.'

'The government says they're cutting the health budget because they need the funds to meet their election promises for education. Today's meeting was about trying to convince the government not to reduce our budget.'

'Aren't governments always promising money for education *and* health?'

'Sure, but most of the people in our electorate vote for the opposition and the government isn't interested in catering for people who don't vote for them.'

'That's appalling.'

'It's a fact. Our bargaining power lies in organising unfavourable media coverage of their actions. That's why I need to put the lid on this story before it runs because although it could paint the government in an unfavourable light, it's just as likely the journo will put the negative spin on the hospital board. Whatever makes a story sensational.'

'Why were you at the meeting?'

'To give the medical view and to explain why we need those specific services and the funds to provide them.'

'What's going to happen?'

They were beyond the city limits now, driving past acres of vineyards as they wound their way through the start of the hills. Over Zac's shoulder, beyond the soft green of vineyards, Evie could see the sparkling waters of the Gulf of St Vincent, but the scenery went almost unnoticed as she concentrated on Zac's story.

'If our funding is reduced, we'll have to cut services. I was trying to show them that everything we currently provide is necessary. They wouldn't give us any straight answers and kept intimating we could do without the nursing-home. They can't actually make that decision but they must have voiced that thought if the journo heard about it. It's the only way I can see that this story has even got off the ground.'

'When do the proposed budget cuts come into effect?'

'In six weeks. And parliament doesn't resume until after that so it'll be difficult to get a result by then. We're hoping lobbying and media attention will work in our favour, but we haven't had time to put things into motion. We've been too busy sorting out staffing problems and looking at the finances.'

'What services are under threat?'

'The nursing-home, Day Surgery, Emergency or selling off the hospital housing.'

'Closing down the other departments?'

'Worst-case scenario.'

'You can't close Emergency!'

'We know. We could sell off the housing but that would only be a short-term solution to cash flow, and because the tenants do pay rent, it's a source of income for the hospital, albeit small.'

They'd reached the top of the hill and the road continued to wind down the other side, passing herds of dairy cows now rather than vineyards. Zac slowed down and steered his car towards the dirt verge as a teenage driver in a hotted-up utility, complete with spotlights and several radio antennae, overtook them, crossing a double white line in his attempt to get around them before the next corner. Evie watched him as he raced off down the hill, taking the corner far too wide and too fast.

'Bloody idiot,' Zac commented. 'That's why we need an ED. Too many drivers doing stupid things on the road.'

Evie's mind was still on the crisis. 'What about Day Surgery?'

'That almost pays for itself so we wouldn't save much here. The nursing-home is heavily subsidised so it's an obvious one to privatize, but the board is reluctant.'

'You're not thinking of closing it?'

'No, but selling it off might happen.'

'Tough call.'

'Yeah, I know.'

As Zac negotiated the final bend in the road Evie noticed two black skid marks sliding off the road to their right. 'Someone didn't take the corner too well,' she said, as her eyes followed the line of the tyres. 'Oh, my God, Zac, pull over.'

Zac slammed on the brakes, pulling the car off the bitumen and onto the dirt verge. Checking for traffic, he swung the car in a U-turn before stopping beside a white roadside marker which had been snapped in two, presumably when it had been hit by the car, which was now resting, badly damaged, in a paddock beyond the road.

'Call triple-O, ask for the CFS, as well as the ambulance. Priority one. Tell them we're at the bottom of Willunga Hill, south side, where the road straightens out.'

She'd already reached for her phone and punched in the three zeros while Zac reached under his seat and pulled out a fire extinguisher. Climbing from the car, she checked the registration number for the operator so the emergency services could pinpoint their location. Zac had retrieved what Evie assumed to be a first-aid kit from the boot of his car and she quickly made her way to the wreck as soon as she had completed the call.

She looked at the vehicle's caved-in roof, its shattered windscreen, damaged when it must have rolled over, and the smashed spotlights. 'This looks like the car that passed us coming down the hill.'

Zac nodded. 'I reckon it is.' He'd walked around the ute and was still hanging onto the fire extinguisher and the first aid kit. The paddock was quiet. The car's engine must have cut out in the accident, and there was no sound from within the utility's cab.

Zac wasn't trying to get to the driver. Why?

'Petrol tank doesn't seem to be leaking.' Zac put down the things he was holding and Evie realised he'd been checking for danger first. She knew the procedure—DR ABC. Danger, response, airway, breathing, circulation.

She didn't wait any longer. She was at the driver's door banging on the window and calling out as she tried to open the door. Even as she pulled on the handle she knew she was wasting her energy—the roof was so badly dented there was no way the door would be able to open.

'We'll have to go through a window,' Zac said. The glass was crumpled, lines like a spider's web spreading across its entire surface, but it was still in place. Through it they could see the young driver, head slumped forward on his chest, unresponsive. 'I'll break the passenger window, but you'll have to slide in—I won't fit.' Zac didn't ask her if that was OK. They both knew she'd do it.

He handed her a pair of disposable gloves before picking up a rock and smashing the window, spraying the passenger seat with little squares of broken glass. Still not a flicker of movement from the driver. Evie tucked the gloves into her pocket and glanced at Zac. This didn't look good.

'Please, don't let him be dead,' Evie whispered.

Zac knocked out the last bits of glass clinging to the window-frame and she scrambled inside, heedless of the glass strewn across the car.

'Check the steering-wheel, make sure there's no airbag.'

Evie hadn't given that a moment's thought but she'd heard stories of airbags going off after the event and the damage they could do. 'Doesn't seem to have one.'

She licked her fingers and stretched her hand out, holding her fingers under the boy's nose, waiting to feel him exhale. Was that a tiny puff of air? She couldn't see his chest rise and fall and she held her fingers under his nose for longer, wanting to make sure. Yes.

'He's still breathing.' So he still had a pulse, too. 'Hello. Can you hear me? You've been in an accident.'

Still nothing.

'We're not going to be able to get him out until the fire truck gets here. What injuries can you find?' Zac asked.

She pulled on the gloves and checked the boy out. 'He's got a swelling the size of a mango on his forehead. Broken wrist, right thigh is bleeding quite heavily. I think the door must have cut into him.'

'I'll pass you a torch. Check his pupils.'

Evie reached back to take the torch. She crouched in the seat, looking up at the boy, not wanting to move his head at all. She lifted one eyelid, shone the torch into his eye and watched the pupil constrict, then repeated the process on the other side. 'Right pupil is sluggish,' she reported. The possibility of a closed head injury didn't surprise either of them. The boy's loss of consciousness was showing no signs of lessening.

'Can you get a BP cuff on him?'

'Should be able to. His left arm seems OK.'

Zac dug out the blood-pressure cuff from his kit and passed it through the window. Evie wound it around the kid's arm, holding her breath as she waited for the reading.

'Eighty over fifty.'

'He needs to get to hospital. Where's the bloody CFS?'

They couldn't move him without the help of the Country Fire Service, but she could check if he was trapped anywhere else while they waited. She lay across the seats, running her hand down his legs. His feet were free and, apart from the wound on his right thigh, his legs seemed OK. But his stomach was quite distended—was abdominal bleeding the cause of his low blood pressure?

'His legs aren't trapped but he must have some internal bleeding. His stomach is tight.' He had to be bleeding from somewhere, she just couldn't find it.

'I can hear sirens,' Zac said.

'Did you hear?' she said to the boy. 'The ambulance is coming. We'll get you out and take you to hospital. You just have to hang in there.' Talking to him was all she could do for now. Maybe it wouldn't help but she had to try.

The ambulance and the fire truck arrived together and Zac pulled Evie out of the wreck once the officers made it to the car. The adrenaline that had flooded through her while she'd been in the car left her abruptly, leaving her legs like jelly. Unable to support her weight, she fell against Zac. He caught her and lowered her gently to the ground.

An ambulance officer wrapped a space blanket around her shoulders. 'Are you hurt?'

Evie shook her head, waving him away to help the boy while she sat, unneeded now, and watched the retrieval effort.

The CFS crew removed the smashed windscreen and peeled back the roof of the ute with the 'jaws of life,' leaving the car looking like a opened tin can. Evie could see Zac's lips moving but she couldn't hear anything over the noise of the rescue process. Someone was in the car where she had been, talking to the boy, wrapping a hard cervical collar around his neck.

The boy was lifted out of the car on a Jordan frame, an oxygen mask over his face, and carried to the ambulance. He was still alive but didn't appear to have regained consciousness.

'I'm going in the ambulance—they need me.' Evie jumped at the sound of Zac's voice. She hadn't noticed him walk over. He squatted next to her. 'One of the CFS volunteers will drive you home in my car. Will you be OK?'

She nodded silently. Of course he'd go in the ambulance. He was a doctor after all, more qualified than anyone else there. Which left her with nothing to do. She wasn't needed any more. She struggled to her feet before Zac could help her. She was OK. She was fine.

A few minutes later, Evie was sitting in Zac's car, a stranger next to her in the driver's seat, watching the ambulance speed away, lights flashing, siren screaming, as she thought about the boy in the back. The boy who was so close to death. So young and his life in the balance.

Would he make it?

Evie couldn't settle. She lay on the couch and tried to read but her mind kept wandering. The house was too quiet, with Jake and the girls away in Adelaide, too empty. She'd spoken to Letitia on the phone and everything was well with her but Evie felt restless, frustrated.

She'd felt like that since the ambulance had driven away, taking Zac and the injured boy.

She'd wanted to be the one in the ambulance, to be useful, and the fact she hadn't been grated on her nerves. How was the boy going? No one would tell her anything over the phone but all she had to do was walk over to the hospital and she'd know. Instead, she was wandering around the house, feeling irritated.

She'd persuaded herself she should stay home as she'd showered and was in her pyjamas but it didn't take much effort to throw a pair of trousers on over a singlet top and boxer shorts. Finally deciding that being at home on her own wasn't the answer, she went to grab some other clothes. She had one leg in her cargo pants when there was a knock on the door. She pulled them on then went to answer the door.

'Zac.' He was on her doorstep. He looked exhausted, his face was pale, the shadow of his stubble a contrast to the pallor of his skin, his thick hair more dishevelled than usual, and he wasn't smiling.

'He didn't make it.'

The boy in the ute. Gone. No more dreams. No more plans. Dead. Just like that.

She tugged at Zac's hand, pulling him inside and into her arms. He accepted her embrace and enveloped her in his arms in return. They stood, joined together, silent, comforting each other.

'Sometimes I hate my job.' Zac spoke first, breaking the moment, breaking the embrace.

'Come with me.' Evie led him through the house to the lounge. For the first time that night she was grateful she had the house to herself. She led him to the couch, making him sit, her earlier unsettled wanderings forgotten now she had a purpose.

She went to the kitchen and searched Jake's pantry until she found a bottle of brandy. She had no idea what it was like, Jake probably only used it for cooking but it didn't matter. Zac needed a drink of something. She screwed up her nose at the smell as the golden liquid splashed into the tumbler.

She carried it to Zac, who glanced at it briefly before swallowing it in one gulp.

'What happened?'

Zac put his glass on the coffee-table and rubbed his hands over his face. Hard.

'Mark had a collapsed lung. We got to that, but he had massive internal injuries, haemorrhaging everywhere. It was too much. His heart gave out. We just watched him die.'

Evie held one of his hands in hers. 'I'm sure you did everything you could. It's not your fault.'

'Just because it wasn't my fault doesn't make it easier to deal with.'

'You weren't making him drive so recklessly and you certainly didn't make him roll his car. You did everything you could to help.'

'But it wasn't enough.'

'From the sound of it, no one would have been able to do any more. At least he didn't die alone in his car in some paddock.'

'I wish he hadn't died at all.'

'Death is part of life, Zac, and part of medicine. What's bothering you? Is there something different about Mark's death?'

Zac was leaning forward, shoulders slumped, his hands buried in his thick hair. 'He was the same age as Clare was when she died. Almost exactly the same age.'

His words were muffled by his posture and Evie wasn't sure if she'd heard correctly. 'Clare?'

'My sister.'

Evie hesitated and then asked her question, tentatively, in case her concern wasn't welcome. 'What happened?'

'She had cystic fibrosis and she died when I was sixteen. She missed her eighteenth birthday by ten days. Mark would have turned eighteen in a week's time.'

The pain in Zac's voice was raw. She squeezed his hand but said nothing. Saying she was sorry, the only words she had, would be useless to him.

'I miss her. She fought as hard as she could, she was unfailingly brave, but there was nothing we could do.' Zac took a deep breath before clenching his jaw. Evie took him into her arms. 'She was too young to die.'

Evie kissed his forehead gently, pressing her lips to his skin, using her touch to soothe him, offering comfort. What other way was there when words were useless?

CHAPTER SEVEN

EVIE was skittish the following morning, her emotions in turmoil. The happiness she'd experienced when she'd been in Zac's arms had been dampened by the overwhelming sadness she'd felt as she'd listened to him talk about his sister. She was walking through the hospital in a world of her own and only looked into the staffroom by chance, her attention drawn by virtue of the extraordinary amount of noise emanating from the room. Judging by the throng around the coffee-machine, something was afoot.

'What's up?' Evie joined the group.

'You haven't seen the local rag?' Evie shook her head in response to the question from Claudia, another RN. 'The rumours were spreading like wildfire yesterday that the nursing-home was being closed. Tom did his best to stamp them out but it's all here in black and white.' She waved the paper she was holding before passing it to Evie, who stepped away to read the article.

It wasn't hard to find—it was the feature headline on page one. *Nursing-Home Shock.* Followed in slightly smaller print with *City doctor leaves own aunt homeless.*

What she read confused and infuriated her.

Zac Carlisle, GP and board member of Pelican Beach Hospital, yesterday offered 'No comment' in response to news of the imminent closure of the nursing-home where his frail and elderly aunt has been a resident for a number of years.

Our sources confirmed the home will be closed, leaving dozens of elderly residents stranded. With no other facility in the local area, residents will be forced to relocate long distances away, putting them out of contact with friends and family—and with their friends within the home. Our investigation yesterday confirmed long waiting lists at all of the State's nursing-homes contacted, with some even refusing to take any more applications.

The paper dropped out of her hand onto the coffee-table, landing with a flutter that echoed her unsteady heartbeat.

What was she meant to make of that?

She tuned back into a conversation on the other side of the room. There seemed to be a split, with two of the staff arguing that the report was definitely true and fitted stories they'd heard of the extra time Zac had been seen in the nursing-home admin area—what had he been doing there if the paper wasn't right? A third person argued they couldn't know one way or another until the board had made a formal announcement.

Evie slipped away. It was nearly time for her shift to start. It might be hours until she had a break so she'd have to wait to find answers to her questions. She needed Zac—or did she? She'd asked him for answers yesterday and he'd told her there had been no decision. Had he lied? Or had the journalist got the facts wrong? And how did she work out whom to believe?

The emergency department was busy, as it often was at seven in the morning, before the medical clinics opened their doors and took some of the pressure off the hospital. But the emergencies hardly qualified as such—a greenstick fracture of an arm that needed a cast, a baby with a very high temperature and vomiting who needed fluids and intravenous anti-nausea medication and an elderly gentleman with chest pains who responded to GTN spray.

Unfortunately the straightforward nursing care allowed Evie plenty of time to run though all the different scenarios for the story in the paper. The moment her morning teabreak started she headed for the nursing-home, determined to see for herself just what the situation was.

The first person she bumped into outside the nursing-home was Lexi.

'Evie! I'm glad I ran into you. Are we still on tonight?'

'Tonight?' Evie paused, her mind was so completely occupied with the rumours she couldn't even think what day of the week it was. Friday, their TV show. 'I'll have to let you know, but do you have a minute now?'

'About the nursing-home?'

'How did you guess?'

'It's all anyone's talking about, and as Tom is my husband, and he's on the board, people think I'm in the loop.'

'Are you?'

'I think it's best I stay out of it, actually, but I'll tell you this. As far as I'm aware, no decision has been made about the nursing-home.'

'Then the article?'

Lexi shrugged. 'Who knows where that came from. But it's caused a lot of anxiety. I'm here now because I had to give Mrs Kale a sedative to calm her down.'

'Why isn't the board saying anything?'

'Zac and Tom have both been here, trying to allay the residents' fears, and I know they're both pretty stressed. Their priority is speaking to the residents, not to the public. The

CEO is in Adelaide and not due back until tomorrow. I think the paper contacted him but his reaction isn't as newsworthy as Zac's, because of Fel's involvement. I'm afraid the focus has fallen on Zac and he's doing his best, Evie. That's all I know. I have to run. Call me later, OK?'

'Sure.' Evie headed in the opposite direction, walking quickly. She knew where she was going, she just didn't know what she was going to find.

The last thing she expected to see was a small brawl between the residents over who would be interviewed by the journalists who were apparently due to descend at any moment. Despite the arguing, the mood was one of excitement.

Zac was nowhere to be seen. Pam, the diversional therapist, was attempting to restore order amidst the rising pitch of the discussions, and in the midst of the chaos, Fel and Nancy sat calmly, looking like they knew a great big secret.

She knew who to speak to. 'What are you up to?'

They chuckled. 'I know I'm "frail and elderly",' Fel quoted the article, 'but I have a few tricks up my sleeve yet.'

'Did one of you speak to that journalist yesterday?'

'Absolutely not,' said Nancy.

'Then how did he know about the connection between Fel and Zac?'

The glint in Fel's eye caught Evie's attention and she fixed the elderly woman with a look. 'I might have had a few words when he came calling,' Fel admitted.

'You never!' Nancy was horrified.

'It's for the best, you old worry wart. How are we going to get what we want if we don't give them a whiff of scandal? The papers won't be interested unless they have a hook, and without coverage we're not going to get the publicity we need to turn this nursing-home fiasco around.'

'But he's your nephew!' Nancy said, clearly scandalised but, Evie suspected, enjoying herself immensely.

'Great-nephew,' corrected Fel, 'and what he doesn't know won't hurt him.'

'But, but…' Evie was lost for words. She stopped and took stock of the situation. 'Is this nursing-home closing or not?'

'Zac assures us nothing's definite but we also hadn't been told anything for sure until yesterday when the journalist started fishing around. So I took a punt that where there's smoke there's fire and did some damage control.'

'More like fanning the flames, Fel,' said Evie, her voice dry.

At least she knew where the link to Zac had come from. But where had the story started in the first place? And was it true? She still didn't know.

'What are they all arguing about TV crews for?' Evie indicated the other residents nearby.

'You're tenacious, young lady,' said Fel with approval. 'You'll be a good match for Zac.'

Evie sniffed. 'I don't want someone who throws people out of their homes.'

'Ha! So you want him if this story isn't true! Excellent,' said Nancy, rubbing her hands.

She felt a blush creep across her throat but she wasn't admitting to anything. Besides, if Zac had lied to her, that would be it. It would be over before it had started. She forced her attention back to the nursing-home drama. 'Can we focus on the issue?' She wasn't sure which of them she was admonishing. 'TV crews?'

'The reporter from the weeknight current affairs programme in Adelaide is coming down in a few hours to get some interviews. Everyone wants to be on the telly.'

'And? Why aren't you over there, staking your claim?'

'We've already got it stitched up.'

'How?' Should she be disapproving of this? All she felt was amusement, which was increasing by the second.

'The reporter phoned me direct as I was named in the paper this morning. He's interviewing Zac first, then me. Zac doesn't know about my part yet. I've promised Nancy I'll share my screen time with her.'

Nancy patted her short curls into place. 'It's our fifteen minutes, we're going to make the most of it.'

'Come and watch—we'll page you,' Fel invited.

'I finish at three. I'll come by then and see what you're up to. Jake is bringing the girls back today and staying overnight so I'll have a bit of time straight after work.'

'You should be using you free time to enslave Zac.'

'I'm officially ignoring you. Is there any point in telling you two to stay out of trouble?'

'None at all,' said Fel, her face wreathed in smiles.

'Only if it makes you feel better,' added Nancy. 'But it won't do much else.'

Would it make her feel better? she wondered as she left the two women to go back to work.

She doubted it, but not because of any sense of disapproval over their antics.

From the little curl of excitement in the pit of her belly, she had a sneaking suspicion that if only she found out Zac hadn't lied, she was actually enjoying the drama as much Fel and Nancy.

At three-thirty Evie was back at the nursing-home. The common room looked like a movie set. Silver reflective light shades were angled down at two couches which had been repositioned, Evie assumed, to suit the programme's director. Zac was seated at one end of a couch, immaculate in a grey pinstriped suit, white shirt and a blue-grey tie knotted perfectly at his throat. Even the yellowing bruise around his eye had been disguised with make-up and the contrast to his normal rumpled appearance was astonishing. At the other end of the couch sat a woman who was dressed in a black suit, her hair coiffed and perfect, her mouth a slash of red lipstick. The sound equipment was being held aloft over her head, the camera was rolling and the woman was chattering away nineteen to the dozen while a man Evie took to be the interviewer was seated off camera, apparently waiting to speak. Evie watched for a minute, waiting to hear Zac's comments before realising he'd be lucky to get a word in. The woman clearly loved the limelight.

'We are appalled at the government's plans to radically slash funding to our rural areas, forcing hospitals to close, turning out elderly residents from nursing-homes,' the woman was saying. Evie tuned out, her attention focussed on Zac, who didn't appear to have seen her yet. That was not the face of a man who did unkind things was all she could think. 'This flies in the face of their election promises and shows once again why this government is not to be trusted.'

Evie noticed Nancy and Fel sitting in one corner of the common room, also watching proceedings. They were being so uncharacteristically quiet she hadn't spotted them immediately. They motioned her over, both of them beaming with pleasure. 'It's a political bun fight we've landed in—isn't it wonderful!' Fel whispered, drawing a glare and a shake of the head from the sound technician.

They fell silent, listening to the interview, although Evie was sure they were stifling giggles at having been told off like schoolgirls.

'Thank you for being with us today, Ms Knapman.' The woman added her thanks and the focus swung to the reporter. 'Shadow Minister for Health, Ms Victoria Knapman, at the Pelican Beach Nursing-Home.'

Ah, so that's why Fel had mentioned politics.

'And also with us is Dr Carlisle.' He went on to describe Zac's position at the hospital. 'Dr Carlisle, with the board of the hospital, has been blamed by the local residents for closing the nursing-home without community consultation. Your response, Doctor?'

'The government has hit the hospital with a raft of unpalatable funding cuts and is still undertaking a lengthy inspection process aimed at enforcing even more cuts.' His voice was calm and deep and thrilled Evie with its quiet assurance. Zac was commanding. 'I will reiterate that the board has not made a final decision on what steps will be taken to accommodate those shortfalls in funding. Closure of the nursing-home is an option but one that will be taken only as a last resort.'

'Do you have any response to claims you issued a statement of "No comment" yesterday to the *Pelican Beach Weekly*?'

'I was phoned when I was out of town, which I explained, and said I would contact the reporter later that day when I returned. Unfortunately I was waylaid by a medical emergency and by the time I was free, the story had already been filed.'

'And what of the reports claiming your aunt is in the home?'

'She is indeed. Another reason why, contrary to rumour, I will do everything in my power to ensure the home remains in operation, for her sake and for the sake of all the residents.'

Filming stopped. Zac's interview was finished and attention turned to Fel and Nancy who, within minutes, were being seated on the couch, obviously trying to decide whether to ham up the frail and elderly angle or put their best camera faces on. The shadow minister hovered, looking for more minutes of camera time, but Zac seemed eager to get out of there.

He was crossing the room at a rapid pace and Evie thought for a moment he wasn't going to stop to talk to her—hadn't he seen her?

'Zac,' she called out to him, and he looked startled, almost guilty. Had he been intending to walk straight past her?

'Evie.' His voice alone was enough to send shivers of excitement through her. Deep and rich, it was the perfect voice for a big man.

'So the paper did get it wrong?'

'The background was right but their conclusions weren't accurate, which was what I was worried about. With the accident, I didn't get to the journalist, if he deserves the title, until too late.' He paused, checking his watch. 'I have to get over to the surgery, I've got a clinic starting in a few minutes, but could you come over tonight, about eight? I need to see you.'

'Eight it is.' She watched Fel and Nancy's interview but wouldn't have been able to tell anyone what they said, she was too caught up in making plans for the evening. Everything was okay. Last night she'd been afraid he'd use Clare's death to pull away again. And today, she'd been confronted with the fact that he might have lied to her about the nursing-home. Her fears had been put to rest on both points. There was every reason for tonight to be perfect.

Zac stripped his shirt off as he walked through his front door. Five past eight already. Did he have time for a quick shower? He threw his shirt into the laundry and was bending down to untie his shoelaces when he heard a knock at the door. Evie.

'It's open,' he called, slipping his shoes off, throwing his socks into the laundry basket and padding in bare feet out to the kitchen. He froze in the doorway. Evie was standing in the kitchen, her back to him, obviously wondering where he was.

She wore a skirt that sat low on her hips and swirled about her legs in a riot of bright colours and her feet were clad in soft red shoes that wrapped about her ankles. A large expanse of smooth creamy skin was on display beneath a tiny top.

Shiny bangles adorned her arms and glittered in the light as she flicked her dark hair over her shoulders, sending it tumbling down her slender back. She turned slightly and he caught a glimpse of her face in profile. Her cheeks were flushed, her eyes huge and dark. She was gorgeous and he felt his body's unbidden response to her presence. He fought his desire to gather her into his arms.

For a man who'd sworn off relationships he'd spent an awful lot of time thinking about this woman. This woman standing before him, an arm's length away, half-dressed while he was half-naked. It took all his self-control to remain in the doorway.

'Evie.' His voice was hoarse, choked with raw emotion.

She turned to face him and he saw her register his bare chest, watched her gaze travel down over his hips and back to his face. Saw her swallow and blush. Again he fought the desire to close the distance between them and take her in his arms. But Evie didn't hesitate. She took that step, stopping an inch from him, raising one hand and placing it over his heart. He closed his eyes, focussing on the pressure of her fingers on his skin, lost in the shivers he felt coursing through his body.

He couldn't afford to lose control, but this was too much. He couldn't resist her, couldn't fight it.

The world didn't exist except for Evie.

Nothing else mattered.

There was nothing else. Nothing except wanting her.

He gave in to his desire, pulling her close, and together they dived into a world where nothing else existed except their mutual need.

'That was amazing.' And it had been. Deliciously, mind-blow-ingly, incredibly amazing.

Zac looked dazed. She knew the feeling but—was it more than that? He seemed disorientated.

She sat up and grabbed for the sheet that was tangled at the foot of the bed, suddenly feeling vulnerable. Zac raised himself up, too, on one arm, his biceps straining under the weight of his upper body. The distance between them widened.

'What's wrong?' Did she want to know? But she had to ask, she couldn't bear the strained silence that had sprung up between them.

'That shouldn't have happened, Evie. I knew it but I wanted you so badly I let myself forget.'

'Then you can keep forgetting.'

Zac shook his head. 'This can't happen.'

'It just did.' Evie scrunched the corner of the sheet up in her hand. Her heart was pounding, nervousness taking over.

'But it can't happen again. I'm not looking for a relationship, commitment.'

'Who said anything about commitment?' Evie wasn't certain she was following this. How could he share that experience with her and then say it wouldn't happen again? 'We have unbelievable chemistry, we can explore that without having to make a major commitment.'

Zac shook his head. 'I can't do that.'

Evie reached out to him but he shied away from her touch. 'Let go a bit, Zac, live in the moment. You miss so much if you don't.'

'It's not about the moment. It's about the future.'

'The future will take care of itself. Don't miss out on what you've got right now by worrying about the future.'

'You don't understand, Evie. If we go down that path, if we explore this chemistry, then before you know it we'll be in a relationship and you'll want commitment.'

'Even if you're right, what's so wrong with that?' The sheet, pulled up to her shoulders, was down low on Zac's side, leaving too much of his tempting abdomen on display.

'Commitment means marriage and babies—I'm not doing that again.'

'What do you mean, "again"?'

'I've been married before. We didn't have the happy ever after I was hoping for.'

'And babies?'

Zac's voice faltered. 'A daughter.'

'You have a daughter?'

Zac shook his head.

'I'm not following you.' She waited for Zac to explain.

Would he? She doubted it, but she needed to know. And after last night she was entitled to an explanation, she was entitled to know why he was pulling away.

He hesitated, then started to talk, the words rushing out as though a dam had burst. 'We started out so sure of ourselves, convinced our love would get us through anything, but when everything was thrown at us, it was more than our marriage could handle.'

'I think you'd better start at the beginning.'

'The beginning is Clare.'

'Your sister?'

Zac nodded. 'Clare had cystic fibrosis but I'm a carrier.'

'One CF gene and one normal?'

Zac nodded. 'When Gabby and I got married, we knew we wanted a family. We talked about all the possibilities we faced, given I was a carrier of CF. I wanted Gabby to be tested as well, but she refused. Our families had known each other all our lives. Gabby knew as much about CF as I did and she said it wouldn't matter—no parents would be better able to cope than us. I went along with her, against my better instincts, because I loved her.'

'Gabby fell pregnant and then she started to panic. I tried to calm her, reminded her of our promises to each other, but she couldn't cope with the thought of a child with special needs. She had chorionic villus sampling and the baby, a girl, tested positive for CF.'

'Gabby wanted an abortion. To me, that wasn't an option. She was beside herself but agreed to see a genetic counsellor with me. In the end, she didn't wait. She went ahead with the termination. I only knew about it afterwards.'

He was hunched over now, his arms wrapped around his knees, closed to her and, oh, so changed from just a few hours ago. 'In different ways I lost my sister, my daughter and my wife to cystic fibrosis. Our marriage disintegrated, we couldn't hold it together after that.' He exhaled a harsh breath, closing his eyes for a moment and rubbing at them vigorously with the back of his hand, blinking hard when he opened them again. 'I don't blame Gabby. I should have insisted she get tested before we tried for a baby. One in twenty-two people carry the gene for CF and it wasn't unreasonable to think she might. I didn't insist on testing but now I know better.'

'You were both carriers so you each have one faulty, or CF, gene and one normal, right?' Evie asked. Zac nodded. 'So even if you knew you were both carriers, then that wouldn't automatically mean a baby, any baby, you had would have the disease, would it? They might just be a carrier or not even a carrier.'

'But if we were both carriers, there would have been a one in four chance a child would inherit a faulty gene from both of us and have CF. Bad odds. I know you're trying to understand, but what you really need to understand is why I can't commit again. People make all sorts of promises in good faith. Gabby and I both did. We promised to love each other through good and bad, in sickness and in health but when reality hit, we couldn't do it.'

She put a tentative hand on his arm and he didn't shrug it off. Which was better than nothing but not as good as what she really wanted—a repeat of last night and not to be having this conversation into which he was putting all his effort to convince her they couldn't be together. 'I'm really sorry, Zac, for your losses.' She hesitated—was she pushing too far? Probably, but she didn't want to accept he was ending this. It was still too much to believe he could consider it, after last night. 'But you and Gabby are only two people—that doesn't make it true for everyone. Some people make it through the tough times.'

If he'd heard her, he didn't let on, hell-bent on drumming his reality into her head. 'We weren't able to keep those promises under pressure and it's unrealistic to think anyone does. So now I don't ask people to make promises to me and I don't make promises. We don't know how strong we are until we're put under pressure. The one thing I do know is I'm not strong enough to cope with any more loss.

'My daughter would have been almost three now, running around, talking, throwing her arms about me, driving me crazy with her mess. I can't go there again. So the best solution for me, the only solution, is not to get involved in the first place.'

Evie started to speak but Zac placed a finger across her lips. 'I know what you're going to say but, please, understand, I've been through every scenario myself, many times. I've made a decision. I'm sticking by it.'

He climbed from the bed and crossed the room, stark naked. Evie heard the shower and briefly entertained the idea of joining him, but she knew any attempt to dissuade him at this point would be futile. She waited. And waited. The water kept running. He was staying in there until he was sure she'd gone. There was only one thing to do. Take the hint and leave before he came out of the bathroom.

CHAPTER EIGHT

HE DIDN'T do commitment.

He didn't want it and even if he did, it wasn't a possibility, not with his background.

He'd made that decision three years ago and hadn't had any trouble sticking with it. Until he'd met Evie. Now he was having trouble thinking about anything else.

He hadn't told anyone, other than his family, about what had happened to his marriage. He'd needed to tell Evie. Had to make sure she understood, that she'd respect his need to keep his distance.

But, try as he may he was having trouble blocking Evie out of his mind and his mother, who was spending the weekend at her holiday house, wasn't helping.

'So, who is this Evie I keep hearing about from Fel?'

'She's a nurse at the hospital, she lives next door.' If he kept her neatly compartmentalised—colleague, neighbour—maybe he'd manage. If he could keep the lid on the compartment labelled 'intoxicating, belly-dancing gypsy,' maybe he'd survive.

'Fel seems to have taken quite a shine to her.'

His mother had a gift for making her questions sound like statements. He thought about ignoring her but knew he wouldn't get away with it.

'Evie and Fel are like peas in a pod, outspoken and impetuous.'

'Not your type, then?' His mother was watching him carefully and he wondered just what Fel had said. 'When do I get to meet her?'

'You don't.' Any further comments he felt like making about his mother's insatiable curiosity were put on hold by the appearance of a pair of smiling little girls at his back door.

As he stood up to open the door he said, 'But you can meet the next best things.' Gracie and Mack scampered in, pulling up short when they saw his mother. 'Gracie, Mack, this is my mum, Mrs Carlisle. Mum, these two young ladies are my next-door neighbours.' He paused for effect. 'Evie is their aunt.'

His mum was all smiles, standing up to shake their hands as she greeted them, which apparently earned her immediate approval from the girls. 'And what brings you here today?'

'It was a 'mergency,' said Gracie.

'An emergency,' clarified Mack.

Gracie nodded, her little face, so like her aunt's, set earnestly.

'Evie is going to cook,' added Mack.

'Ah,' said Zac. 'Say no more.'

'And that means she's about to start singing, too.'

'You're right, there was nothing for it but to escape.'

A knock at the front door had Gracie and Mack in a panic. 'She's found us!' squealed Gracie, as she ducked under the kitchen table, dragging Mack with her. Both were giggling furiously, finding it all a huge joke.

'Seems like I came by at an opportune moment,' said his mum. 'Are you going to invite them to join us for lunch?'

Squeals of 'Yay!' from the girls followed him up the hallway. Lunch was a popular idea.

Evie stood on the doorstep, fidgeting with the hem of her T-shirt, and he was sure she was avoiding his gaze just as he was trying to do the same. 'Did the girls come?' She broke off, raising her eyes heavenwards as she heard the giggling.

'Come in. They're in the kitchen.'

Evie followed him down the passageway, coming to an abrupt halt when she saw his mother.

'Sorry, I didn't realise you had company.'

His mother laughed and stood up to introduce herself. 'I'm hardly company, I'm Zac's mum, Lydia. You must be Evie. I'm very pleased to meet you.'

Evie shook Lydia's hand, looking a little puzzled.

'She's just met the girls,' Zac said, trying to explain how his mother knew of her.

'Are you going to join us for lunch?' Zac could have throttled his mother. After the past thirty-six hours he and Evie had had, he didn't need the added complication of the two of them getting chummy. Having Fel in Evie's corner was bad enough; he knew his mother would like her, too. Everybody did.

'I can't do that.' Good. Evie didn't want the complication either.

'Yes, you can. I insist.' Evie didn't look too thrilled about the idea, but as the girls weren't coming out from underneath the table and it was obvious his mother wasn't going to take no for an answer, she didn't have much choice.

Within five minutes Evie clearly had his mother's approval and after half an hour Zac was wondering if they'd even notice if he left the table so engrossed were they in their conversation. They'd scarcely looked at their lunch as they'd eaten and Evie hadn't given any clue that she was even aware of Zac, much less upset or angry with him. Good at pretending? Or was this what she'd meant by living in the moment—and at this moment she was talking with his mum?

Gracie and Mack had run off to play with the world globe, leaving him to sit and listen as the two women held an intense discussion on various aspects of fundraising. His mum was passionate about the topic and had been heavily involved in fundraising for the Cystic Fibrosis Council for years—but Evie?

It didn't take long for him to find the connection.

'Lydia, what do you think about the prospects of pulling together a fundraising event for the nursing-home? Not a black-tie sort of affair like you hold, more like a community fête on as large a scale as possible.' Her eyes were alight with interest, she was leaning in towards Lydia, engrossed in their conversation, alive and sparkling. In a nutshell, captivating.

'Anything is possible if you want it enough,' Lydia said with a glance in Zac's direction. What was that about? 'When are you thinking?'

'A week? Two?'

His mum had to be baulking at the idea of such a short time-frame but she didn't miss a beat, just nodded and continued talking. He knew Evie was spontaneous but there was no way she could pull off an event like that in that time. She wasn't even from here, she had no contacts.

'I don't think my son agrees with me, though, judging from the frown on his face.'

He'd been sprung. 'I don't want to rain on your parade, but what's your aim?' Coming up with objections wasn't a smart move after everything that had happened, but he had to be honest. 'If the home is privatised, this is all academic, and you can't raise enough to cover the ongoing costs and enable us to keep it as part of the hospital.'

'There's no point waiting to see how it all pans out, it's too late by then,' Evie countered, speaking directly to him for the first time since she'd sat down. 'Why not show the community is behind the home and we're all willing to make sure it stays? Won't that give you more ammunition to go to the media with, to embarrass the government into doing the right thing?'

His mother was on Evie's side. 'You were right, Zac. Evie is a lot like Fel, brimful of ideas and not afraid to make them happen.'

'You said that about me?' He nodded as she looked at him consideringly, but she said nothing further.

'Shall we go next door and make some plans?' Lydia suggested to Evie, and without waiting for Zac's reaction they rose from the table. 'Zac, you'll look after the girls while Evie and I get the ball rolling?'

He wasn't going to be left at the table by himself without putting his two cents in. 'Evie, are you seriously telling me that in the last hour you've committed to the idea of a fund-raiser, just like that? And, Mum, you see no problems with it?'

'Nothing that can't be surmounted.'

Evie responded at the same time. 'Not just like that. I've been mulling over solutions to the hospital's financial problems and then I meet your mum and it turns out she's an expert in the art of fundraising. Besides, I don't want to be accused of being too spontaneous.' She tossed her dark waves of hair back from her shoulders, the gesture almost inviting him to challenge her. 'So I'm thinking it'll be today fortnight, rather than in a week.'

'A huge concession,' he said, smiling at last. This was exactly like Evie after all, and it was what he liked about her. And, as unbelievable as it all sounded, he'd wager she'd pull the whole thing off.

She was an incredible woman.

Just not for him.

Evie glanced around at the crowd in the nursing-home common room. It had been a crazy evening. The babysitter had been running late, Gracie had had a stomachache and hadn't wanted Evie to leave, she'd heard Zac in his garden, talking on the phone, and had delayed leaving until he'd gone inside. All in all, it had been an effort to arrive on time for the meeting and to arrive calm and unflustered.

She'd liaised with the television crew, who'd returned for more footage, keen on the 'community' aspect to the story, and was now waiting for the final few people to find their seats. The general turnout looked promising and the mood was energised.

The extra commitment of spearheading the fundraising project had turned out to be a blessing, filling in the last spare moments of time she had in her busy schedule and stopping her from dwelling on Zac. The initial success made her feel a little less of a failure for messing up so badly.

Young and old had turned out to help and there was enough enthusiasm in the room to make her believe anything was possible. Even the mayor had promised to arrange the relevant council permits to enable the fair to take place on the town's foreshore. Amazing what the presence of a camera could do.

After welcoming everybody, Evie divided people into what she hoped were workable committees, groups of people who'd get along and get on with the job, then she gave a short interview to the television crew, doing her best to deliver sound bites that would encapsulate their cause in short, snappy statements.

Two hours later all the groups seemed well on the way to having firm plans for the event and Evie had a main committee organised to oversee the general set-up.

'I think I've delegated all my responsibilities,' she said to Fel as the last few people left the room.

'Then you're a natural leader.'

'Let's wait and see how it all turns out. I should get to work and you must be exhausted.'

'I slept all afternoon in preparation. We haven't had so

much fun here in ages and if they're going to close us down,
we're going out with a bang.'

'It's not going to happen,' Evie said, trying to sound upbeat
and positive. 'I've even got the shadow minister's secretary
saying she'll be here for the fête. I know she doesn't give a
damn about this—she's after the publicity and she'd attend the
opening of an envelope—but it's a good issue for the opposition and guarantees us more coverage.'

'And more coverage is more leverage. You keep working
that charm and you'll have us all safe in our beds yet.'

Safe in her bed wasn't what she wanted. It was Zac in her
bed that would make her happy. But according to him, it
wasn't going to happen again. Ever.

Ever was a long time to wait for the best sex she'd ever had
to be repeated.

Ever wasn't going to cut it.

Night shift at Pelican Beach Hospital was often busy during
summer, Evie had been told, as it was peak tourist season. Two
hours into her stint, when she'd only seen one patient, she
feared it wasn't going to be one of those nights. And she
needed to keep busy. She couldn't make miracles happen at
work, and it was a miracle she needed to put things right
between her and Zac. So she needed to keep her mind off
Zac—or his bed to be precise.

She checked the doctor's roster, just in case she needed to
call for assistance. She should have expected as much—Zac
was on call. She should be grateful it was so quiet she didn't
need to work with him tonight. But the empty department left
her with too much time to think. Which meant, of course, she
thought about Zac.

At one-thirty in the morning Evie saw her second patient
for the shift, a twenty-four-year-old woman who was con-

vinced she had appendicitis. Fortunately, on examination, the woman's stomach pain turned out to be nothing more than abdominal cramps that eased with muscle relaxants. Evie breathed a sigh of relief. She'd handled it on her own and there'd been no need to call Zac.

Her relief was short-lived. An hour later she took a panicked phone call.

'My wife's in labour. What do I do?'

'How many weeks is she?'

'Thirty-six.'

'Is it her first baby?'

'Yes.' Evie relaxed. The pains could very well turn out to be Braxton-Hicks' contractions and, if not, she should have time to call Zac and direct the couple to the birthing suite in the hospital.

'How far apart are her contractions?'

'Not very.' Not the most helpful of answers. 'My wife says she wants to push!'

Damn. It sounded like the real thing, she wasn't going to be able to divert them. 'How far away are you?'

'Five minutes.'

'Tell your wife to pant, little breaths. Get here as quickly as you can. I'll meet you in front of Emergency.'

Evie hung up the phone and concentrated on what she needed to organise, all the issues with Zac pushed to one side. She called the medical wards and confirmed they had extra staff on night shift and could bring her a humidicrib. They would also alert the helicopter retrieval team in Adelaide to be on standby and call Zac, leaving her free to check the size of the suction tubing on hand, connecting the smallest diameter one she had available, sized for a neonate. Oxygen was no problem. She just hoped she'd be able to get the expectant mother into the emergency department. She didn't fancy delivering a baby in a car.

Slipping on a fresh gown, she grabbed two pairs of surgical gloves and pushed a barouche out to the ambulance bay, scanning the street for the headlights of the car. She was ready.

A figure emerged from the darkness, jogging towards her. Zac. Even in the darkness she recognised him, and her body recognised him, too. Her heart rate escalated, her breaths came more rapidly and she felt the familiar tingle run through her. He was in casual clothes, a cobalt-blue polo shirt and cotton trousers, his hair tousled from sleep. The tingle intensified. She stamped on it, firmly, and got in touch with her wounded pride. It wasn't hard.

'Evie!' He sounded surprised to see her. She'd forgotten it hadn't been her who'd paged him. He stopped beside her and she breathed in his scent of warm bed, fresh sheets and mint. She didn't want to think of warm beds!

'What have we got?'

He was all business. She could be, too. 'Primigravida at thirty-six weeks. She's ready to push. No other information. They should be here any minute.' She pulled on her gloves, handing him the second pair. He pulled them on, covering his long fingers, evoking sensations she didn't want to remember. She turned away, pretending to be absorbed in watching the driveway.

Headlights. Excellent. She could get her mind back on the job.

A car screeched to a halt in front of the emergency entrance. A distressed young man almost fell out of the driver's seat in his haste to get out of the car. Lying on the back seat, knees flexed, her hair soaked in sweat, was his pregnant wife. Evie quickly introduced herself and Zac to the couple, Steve and Caroline, before Zac started his examination. The external lights of the hospital gave out enough power to light the back seat.

'I can see the baby's head.'

Thank God it wasn't breech.

Zac gave her a thumbs-up. 'The cord's clear.'

'You're doing really well, Caroline. We're going to transfer you to a bed and get you inside, then you can push,' Evie said.

'I'll lift her out. Can you take her legs?'

Evie pulled the barouche alongside the car and nodded. Zac got his hands under Caroline's armpits and waited for a contraction to ease off. Evie squeezed in next to him, conscious of the heat radiating from his body. Zac started moving Caroline, pulling her out of the car. Evie reached for her legs, lifting her behind the knees and moving her onto the barouche. Together they whizzed Caroline into the hospital, Steve trailing behind them.

'OK, let's meet your baby. You can push with the next contraction,' Zac instructed Caroline once they were inside. 'That's it. Here comes the head. You're doing a great job. Rest for a minute, you'll need to push again when I tell you, to deliver the shoulders.' Zac's hands were ready to turn the baby's shoulders to guide it into the world. Evie felt a lump form in her throat at the sight of Zac waiting, ready to deliver a new life. He insisted a family wasn't an option for him but if he felt what she did, wouldn't he want to work through that?

Didn't he feel what she felt? She thought of their lovemaking. He'd felt the magic, that was one thing she didn't doubt.

'Now, Caroline, last push. Here we go.' There was a collective exhale as the tiny baby slid into Zac's waiting hands. 'You have a daughter, a perfect little girl.'

Evie was ready with the suction tubing and busied herself cleaning out the baby's airway. She couldn't bear to look at Zac. She could only imagine how difficult it must be to deliver other people's babies. Other people's daughters. Evie kept her focus on the newborn. She was tiny and wrinkled—being four weeks early, she hadn't had time to lay down fatty reserves. But Zac was right, she seemed perfect.

Evie stopped suctioning and the baby started to wail. Zac clamped and cut the cord. 'We need to warm your baby up, Caroline, while I deliver your placenta.' Evie hung the suction tube up, ready to take the baby, but as she turned around she was aware of another pair of hands waiting. Another nurse had arrived.

'I'm Susan,' she said, her voice cheery and reassuring. 'I've brought down a heat lamp and the humidicrib. There's a Vitamin K injection ready to go as well.' Susan took the baby in a warmed blanket, placing her under the heat lamp and running through the Apgar test. 'Seven out of ten,' she reported. 'Two point six one kilograms, thirty-four centimetres.'

'Your baby's fine, Caroline.' Zac kept talking as he delivered the placenta. Evie stood beside him as he checked it and Susan relayed information about the baby.

'Five minute Apgar score, nine out of ten.'

'Can I hold my baby now?' Caroline asked.

Zac nodded. 'Yes, of course.'

Susan brought the baby back to her parents. Evie stepped back and observed the new family. Caroline was on the bed, cuddling her daughter. Steve stood beside his wife, stroking her hair, a look of absolute amazement on his face. The baby nuzzled in, searching for her mother's breast.

Evie blinked back a tear. Newborn babies never failed to make her cry. She chanced a glance at Zac—how did he do this? She listened to him as he congratulated Caroline and Steve. He was saying all the right things but his expression was solemn.

It had to be hard. He congratulated the new family again and then turned away abruptly. The loss of his own daughter would be heavy in his heart but was he also thinking about his vow to lead a solitary life? It was obvious to her he wasn't made for that. He had love to give. Was he really going to deny himself that?

'Susan, let's take the family up to a maternity bed.' He gave Evie the briefest of acknowledgements before he left the department. 'Good result, everyone. Well done.'

And they were all gone, leaving Evie alone to clean up, Zac's heartache foremost on her mind.

She'd sell her soul if it would buy Zac peace.

The realisation she'd do anything for him, anything at all, stopped her in her tracks.

She was in love. In love with Zac.

She sank down onto a chair and tested the phrase again. It was true. She loved him.

When had it happened? She didn't know but there wasn't a doubt in her mind. She loved him with everything she had and she was going to fight for him. He was carrying a lot of pain, deep, raw pain, but there was still love to give, she knew it. Anyone who had loved before could love again. If he could move beyond the all-consuming belief that love hurt too much and promises were worthless.

How was she to convince him of that? To convince him to take a chance on her?

By the time she'd finished straightening up the department, she knew how, or at least where to start. The first chance she got she was going to see Lexi.

Fate seemed to be on her side. Lexi had had a free appointment that same morning so she'd had her blood test, no questions asked and Lexi had promised to rush the results if she could.

It had been two days now, two days in which Evie had seen Zac only in passing. She'd acted as if everything was right with her world, letting him think he'd won her over with his arguments. He seemed preoccupied—but, then, he would be, with the nursing-home issue still hanging over his head.

Evie was at work when Lexi walked into the emergency department.

'What brings you here?'

Lexi had an envelope in her hand and she held it out to Evie as she spoke. 'Your results are back. I thought I'd bring them to you.'

Evie took the envelope. 'What do they say?'

'Don't you want to read them yourself?'

Evie hesitated, suddenly nervous despite her confidence it would be fine. 'No. You tell me.'

'You tested positive. You're a carrier.'

Surprise battled with disbelief. Disbelief won. 'There must be a mistake.' She couldn't be a carrier for CF.

She'd been assuming she'd be negative and she'd planned to use the results to convince Zac to give them a chance. But where did this result leave her now? It would be the final nail in the coffin of their relationship.

'They're definitely your results. I didn't ask before, but I can see it's upsetting news, so can I ask why you wanted to know? Does this have something to do with Zac's sister?'

'Can we treat this as part of the consult? Patient confidentiality and all that?'

'Of course.'

Revealing Zac's secrets about his marriage wasn't an option. Instead, she said, 'It is related to his sister. From what I can gather, Zac is terrified of having a child with CF and he won't get involved in case it gets serious.' An understatement if ever there was one, but how could she break Zac's confidence on the real reason for the break-up of the marriage? The termination of his baby's life behind his back.

'But you're already involved, aren't you?'

'I care for him, really care for him, like nothing I've ever felt. And I was hoping, assuming really, I'd test negative and be able to lay his fears about taking a chance with me to rest. But it's not going to happen like that, is it?'

'I guess not but—' Lexi stopped in mid-sentence. 'Listen, it's Zac you need to talk to. If you care about him, you have to let him know. What have you got to lose?'

'My self-respect when he turns me down? Again?'

'If you care about him enough, I'd imagine that's a chance you'll take. Just like if he cares about you enough, he'll set aside his notions that he can't get involved just in case something bad happens. You've tested positive—big deal.' She emphasised her words with a shrug. But she didn't know the full story.

'There endeth the lesson?'

'Tom always says I go on too much but, that said, I'm here if you need to talk about this.'

'Thanks. I appreciate the offer.'

More talking would have to wait as a string of emergencies came through the door almost the moment Lexi left. A child with a nasty burn on his forearm after upending a cup of coffee over himself, a suspected case of meningitis that needed admission, a suspicious lump in a groin, which had been noticed weeks before but left until the pain had been excruciating, followed by a split chin from a fall in the bath.

But thinking didn't have to be postponed totally, and between the lump in the groin and the split chin, the solution presented itself.

If she was right—and maybe it was a big if—but if there was a chance he could feel the same way about her, then they wouldn't have children. That was the barrier between them.

They wouldn't have children.

Or they'd adopt.

She saw her last patient out and retreated to a cubicle to finish her thoughts between cases.

Why hadn't this occurred to her before? She'd been pouring out all her love to the children in the home in Vietnam, never thinking beyond it. She hadn't fallen in love before, not like this, so she'd never seriously thought about having children, had just assumed they were waiting somewhere in her future.

Of course they'd adopt.

It made perfect sense. Surely that's why fate had led her to Vietnam in the first place, to show her love didn't only come in one form.

They'd adopt from Vietnam if Australia had a programme established—hadn't she heard it was under negotiation? And if it wasn't, they'd adopt from another country they could both fall in love with, another country that could become a part of their life together. Vietnam had shown her the heart—her heart—didn't have a prescription for love. Love could be found in all sorts of places. The only thing that mattered was that when you found it, you celebrated it for the gift it was.

But how did she convince Zac that it was a gift, and not a curse?

CHAPTER NINE

'*CODE black. Code black. Medical staff to Emergency. Code Black.*'

Zac sprinted along the corridor, pulse racing, ready for any eventuality. But he wasn't prepared for the chaos that greeted him as he skidded into the emergency department.

There were bodies piled up in the middle of the floor, people yelling, orderlies running past him towards the writhing mass on the floor. It took him a few moments to comprehend the scene in front of him. It was difficult to tell where one person stopped and another started, but by the movement he assumed that most, if not all, were still breathing. There were two people in ambulance uniforms and another two in hospital uniforms all lying on top of a fifth person, who was yelling and thrashing about like a man possessed.

Zac stood, rooted to the spot, until one of the ambos spied him and called out. 'Hey, Doc, come and give us a hand. This guy's gone crazy.'

Zac realised what was happening—they were trying to restrain the man at the bottom of the pile, who was having some kind of seizure. Zac moved, ready now to lend his weight to the effort. From the corner of his eye he saw Evie, tiny Evie, approaching the heaving pile. She held a syringe in her hand.

'Hold his arm,' she shouted.

Zac moved towards the man but one of the ambos moved faster, pinning the man's arm to the floor. But the change in his position had left one of the man's legs free, he kicked out, connecting with Evie and sending her crashing into a chair, her left arm taking the full force of her weight. Zac dived for the man's leg before he could do any more damage.

'Are you OK?'

Evie nodded as she picked herself up from the floor and came back to the patient. She still had hold of the syringe and this time she was able to get the needle into a vein. She depressed the plunger. 'Don't let him go.'

'What is that?' Zac asked.

'Midazolam. He's psychotic, another ice user.'

Evie emptied the contents of the syringe into the patient and then disposed of the needle while the rest of them continued to pin the patient down, waiting for the sedative to take effect. She rubbed her upper arm, where she'd collided with the chair. Once the sedative took effect Evie issued instructions as a spinal board was assembled under the patient.

'He needs to go to ICU. He's had enough midazolam to stop a charging bull. They'll need to monitor him on an ECG and make sure his heart doesn't stop.'

The patient was lifted onto a barouche and wheeled to ICU, accompanied by one of the other nurses. Zac knew he should go but Evie was hurt. She was hugging her left arm against her body, rubbing it with her right hand.

'Let me look at that—you landed pretty heavily.'

'It's nothing,' she said, but she didn't resist when he led her to a cubicle and sat her in a chair. She looked exhausted and thinner than he remembered, even though it had only been a few days since he'd seen her properly.

He turned back the sleeve of her shirt, exposing the smooth, fair skin of her upper arm. Already there was a purple stain spreading across her skin. He ran his fingers lightly over the bruise and wasn't surprised to feel a large haematoma under the skin. Evie flinched at his touch, her face pale.

'I'm sorry, I know it hurts but I need to see what we're dealing with.'

'I'm OK.'

'Sure you are. Can you make a fist and bend your elbow?'

'Nothing's broken. It's just a knock,' she said, following his instructions. 'I'll put an ice-pack on it, it'll be fine.'

'And you? Are you OK?'

'A little the worse for wear.'

'Don't blame yourself. You weren't to know he'd kick out like that. If anyone's to blame, it's me. I was too slow off the mark.'

'I'm not talking about the patient, I'm talking about you and me.'

'Now isn't the time.'

'I have a feeling it's never the time, from your point of view. But I need to say this.' Her voice faltered a little. 'I care about you, Zac, and I can't pretend otherwise. I tried not to think about you, about us, but I couldn't do it. And then I thought I had the answer, I thought I'd be able to convince you to take a chance with me, so I asked Lexi for a blood test. I asked her to test for the CF gene.'

'Damn it, Evie. Why couldn't you just let it lie?' The wind had been knocked out of him. His legs gave way and he sat down heavily on the bed beside her chair.

'I couldn't because I can't live like that, ignoring the chance to have something wonderful. And I didn't promise you I would.'

'I've told you I can't get involved. You wanted to know why so I told you what I haven't told anyone other than my family. I did that because I thought you would understand. Can't you respect that?'

'I'm a carrier.' She blurted it out and he had a brief thought that this was not the way she'd planned on telling him before he really heard what she'd said.

She'd tested positive?

It didn't matter. It made no difference either way. 'Why can't you understand? Even if you weren't a carrier, we, you and I, couldn't go anywhere. I'm not getting involved.'

'So even if I was negative, you'd still be saying no?'

'Yes.'

'Does it make any difference if I tell you—?' She stopped and chewed at her bottom lip and he really, really didn't think he wanted to hear what she was about to say. 'I'm falling in love with you. I want to be with you. You. I don't care about getting pregnant, I don't need to have my own babies. I just want you.'

He was right. That was the one thing he didn't want to hear, the one thing above all others because, as much as he cared, he couldn't give her what she wanted. And he'd never meant it to end with pain for either of them, but of course pain was the one inevitable thing in life. Pain and death. He'd argue his way out of it, show her all the additional reasons why it could never be. He had to make her see sense.

'And Vietnam? London? Your work? Your life? The children waiting for you to return? What are you planning on doing about all that?'

'I'd give it all up if it means I can have you.'

'And children—you'd give up on having children, too?' He was incredulous. 'That's not a decision to make lightly.'

'I didn't say I didn't want children, I said I don't need to have biological children. We can adopt.'

She looked confident but had she given any thought to what she was announcing? As if she'd give up Vietnam! And not have children? Or adopt? Who came up with such life-changing ideas in a spilt second? Apparently Evie Henderson did. She rallied again, her confidence growing, and he didn't know what worried him most. 'None of it's as important as you.'

She was confused, she had to be confused to even think of suggesting such plans. Worst thing was, he knew how she felt, like the world had gone crazy. The difference was he knew enough to ignore it. You didn't change your path in life just because emotions swamped you when you weren't expecting it. Because it didn't last.

'Evie, we scarcely know each other.' His tone was harsh, angry, and he hated himself for it, but he had to make her understand, had to push her away, for her sake as much as his. He saw her blink back tears, fighting to control her emotions, but he was struggling to control his, too. Too many emotions were fighting for room inside his head. 'It's ludicrous to jump from discussing why we can't date to talking about options for a future together. We can't have this conversation. You decided to get tested despite me making it clear what my intentions were. We don't have a future.'

'You're telling me you won't give us a chance under any circumstances.'

'That's what I've consistently told you. And you say you'd stay, say you won't bear children, but they're spur-of-the-moment decisions, promises even, you'd never keep.' He held up a hand to silence her objection. 'You think you will now, but that'll change.'

'You think you know what I want more than I do?' Her voice was quieter now. Angry or hurt? He thought of what he'd just said to her and knew it was both, but he had to make her understand.

'I know promises made with the best of intentions are still liable to be broken.'

'You know me so well? I know you, too. And you care for me, too, I know it. When we ma—' She broke off, flustered, and waved her hand instead. 'The other night, I saw it, felt it. You cared. I've never begged someone to be with me. So if the truth is you don't like me enough to be with me, even short term, just tell me.'

'It was only ever a fling.' How could he do this to her? 'We both knew that.' How could he not?

'It was more than that, and you know it.' Two red blotches appeared on her cheeks as she vented her anger at him. 'So tell me straight, what's the real story? I'm not good enough? No one is ever going to be good enough?'

'Maybe you're right.' The pain it cost him to say those words very nearly tipped him over the edge, very nearly had him pulling her to him, kissing away all the hurt and confusion and promising her the world. But he'd only break that promise later, tomorrow or next month—it made no difference—but break it he would. One of them would. It was better to have the pain now.

She looked close to tears. Frustration, disbelief and anguish were burning behind those dark eyes, which were impossibly liquid in their expressiveness. He'd be tortured for nights at the look of bewildered hurt he saw before she turned away, before she turned her back on him. Now it was only her narrow shoulders peeking through a tumble of dark curls—curls he'd tangled his fingers in only days ago, lost in the exquisite rapture of her—he could see.

He didn't know how to respond—he couldn't undo the hurt, he couldn't offer what she wanted. So he stayed quiet. An option he should have exercised earlier.

She'd raised her head now but still faced away from him and, heel that he knew himself to be, he was glad because he didn't have to confront the accusation of betrayal he knew was still burning brightly in her eyes. 'If that's what it really is, that I'm not good enough to make you risk feeling again, loving again, then…then…' She stopped, took a great gulp of air and said, 'Then you deserve to be alone.'

She stood up from the chair in one smooth movement, threw back her shoulders, tossed her head and stalked to the door. Her hand on the handle, she turned around to add, 'Just so there's no doubt, we're over. For good.'

If it were only a matter of him believing she wasn't good enough, he thought as he left the hospital, then he would deserve to be alone, just as she'd said. Very alone. For ever.

He'd left her thinking she wasn't good enough.

In three years, he hadn't been tempted to spend an hour with a woman other than as friends. Then Evie had come along and he'd fallen under her spell at lightning speed, so fast he hadn't even known it had been happening until he'd pulled her into his arms that first time and kissed her as if life itself depended on it. Then they'd made love and the world had shifted. And the shock of what they'd discovered together finally kicked a desperate self-preservation into gear, shattering the illusion he'd allowed to shroud their time together. Shattered it into a thousand pieces and held a nightmarish mirror up to his eyes to remind him of what loss felt like.

How had he forgotten, even for a second? But he had, and now he'd caused them both pain and a new cruel ache had lodged in his heart. He hadn't thought there was room for more pain but he hadn't even touched the surface. But if he didn't end it now, there'd be worse to come later.

So he had no choice.

She wasn't thinking straight. He'd give anything to throw himself into that heady senselessness with her, but one of them had to think for both of them.

Because she'd never stay.

And he'd never give himself like she deserved. He'd never be free of ties to the past, free to love her as she wanted.

He couldn't love like that.

He didn't do love and he didn't do tears, not since his daughter.

It didn't matter about the genetics. It didn't matter if they could or couldn't have children together.

What mattered was that he was never putting himself in the way of the pain that had ripped him apart when his child had died.

And letting Evie convince him with her passion and her crazy plans for having a life together would only ever end in pain. He'd just proved that point.

She'd promised she'd stay, promised she didn't care about being pregnant. Sooner or later, her promises would crumble and turn to dust. He was certain of that.

His wife had made similar promises in good faith. She'd vowed to love him for ever, sworn it wouldn't matter if their child had CF. She hadn't been a bad person, quite the contrary. But she'd broken her promises just the same.

And he didn't blame her. For all the promises in the world, no one ever knew how they'd react when life played one of her cruel tricks.

Which was why he didn't do love.

And why he'd rather break both their hearts now. Because if it was inevitable, he'd rather get it over with. Better than waiting until she became so much a part of his life that having it end would hurt more than he could bear.

Evie returned to work despite her bruised and aching arm but spent every moment praying to whichever gods were listening for a miracle, to wind back the clock and erase the last hours from her life. Give her another version. Give her Zac.

The girls were going to a friend's house for the night, straight from school, so she was free—but it was the last thing she wanted. It meant having time to deal with what had just happened.

What had just happened was that her heart had been ripped from her chest. Her earlier concern that her pride would be bruised didn't even rate a mention compared to the pain of being rejected in no uncertain terms. She'd never thought it would really happen like that.

But it had.

And worst of all, Zac had been trying to extricate himself from her right from the start. She'd read it all wrong and made an idiot of herself in the process. Had she really just told him she didn't care if they didn't have children, that she'd stay here and give up her life, her dreams, her passions? Heat flooded her face and she could scarcely stand to stay in her skin, so acute was the humiliation pumping through her. She'd thrown herself at him, made all sorts of rash promises—and he didn't want her! She needed to run and run and escape until she'd left only her shadow behind to deal with the mortification. But it didn't work that way.

There was nothing but time to ease the wrenching anguish slicing through her chest, carving her in two.

So by the time her shift ended, she was intent on fuelling her anger so she didn't have to feel the pain.

Distraction and denial were great strategies—how long could she rely on them?

For ever?

She dawdled when it eventually came time to go, hoping for divine intervention to keep her at the hospital. Her prayers were answered. A message came from Pam, asking her to go to the nursing-home.

Fundraising business, she thought. Just what she needed to

keep her busy. She made it there in record time and the common room was buzzing with excitement when she entered.

She saw Pam and headed over.

'Evie! Fantastic news!' Pam's face was glowing with excitement, oblivious to Evie's strained demeanour. 'The government isn't going to cut the funding. The nursing-home won't be closed.'

'That's fantastic. When did you hear?' Her voice sounded tinny and forced even though this was what she'd been praying for. Distraction. She seized it, not just with both hands but with every molecule in her body.

'The CEO announced it after a board meeting ten minutes ago, then we got a call from that nice Victoria Knapman—she was so excited for us.'

Ms Knapman's excitement probably had more to do with the positive media coverage she'd receive, but Evie kept her own counsel.

'The CEO was going to tell you but as we have you to thank for this in large part, I asked if I could speak to you first so you could share the news with the residents.'

What would Zac think about her being credited like this? 'That's very kind but my part would have been minimal. The board has done the hard yards and I think Fel and Nancy might have had major roles, being the media's sweethearts.'

Pam didn't look convinced but let the subject slide. 'The residents have been asking if the fair will still go ahead. It would be a shame to cancel it, everyone's worked so hard.'

She was right, the fair was no longer necessary for financial or publicity reasons. But it had done so much to occupy the time and minds of the residents, how could they cancel it?

And she needed it as much as the residents. Distraction, distraction, distraction. She'd deal with her rejection and her pain later.

Like next year.

Next year, when she'd finally made it back to Vietnam and could make a new start. Next year, when she was back where what she had to give meant something, where she could cuddle and kiss love into the hearts of children, nurture them, teach them to trust again when life had been so hard and cruel. She wasn't what Zac wanted so she'd go where she was wanted, where she was needed. She was good enough and she wouldn't be told otherwise.

She'd deal with the raw pain inside her later and until that time she'd pretend it didn't exist. Maybe it would go away all by itself if she pretended hard enough.

'Of course we'll go ahead with the fair,' she said, her voice full of confidence. Pretending like a professional already.

'I told you she'd forge ahead, Nancy.' Evie heard Fel's voice behind her.

'Thank goodness, or we'll be resting our coffee-cups on mounds of calendars for years to come.'

'What calendars?' she asked.

'These.' Fel held up a calendar with tear-off pages, one per month, and to cries of '*Playboy,* eat your heart out' and 'Ta da!' the cover was flipped over to reveal a black and white photograph of a beach on which half a dozen naked 'elderly citizens' were walking off into the sunset on their walking sticks and walking frames, the assorted shapes and sizes of their backsides forming a glorious central focus for the photo.

'Oh, my!' Evie started laughing, despite herself. 'You didn't?'

'We most certainly did. If it's good enough for those English women, it's good enough for us.' Fel's eyes sparkled green with mischief. 'Can you pick who is who? Mind, there's been no digital enhancement, so we can take full credit for our beauty.'

'I think I can.' Evie bent to take a closer look. 'Tell me you didn't both adorn your backsides with tattoos for this?'

'Unfortunately they're only temporary,' said Nancy. 'And all the store had was skulls or roses.'

'The tattoo parlour won't touch you if you're the wrong side of seventy,' added Fel, her voice filled with exaggerated offence.

Evie peered closer. 'So you went with the skulls option. Charming.' She shook her head at them. If she pretended hard enough, maybe the pretence that everything was right with her world would work its magic and become real. Fat chance.

'Zac won't like it one little bit,' said Fel, with no small measure of satisfaction.

Had Fel looked closely at her again as she'd said that? Evie kept her face impassive and changed the topic. She couldn't go there. Too raw, too painful, too humiliating. 'How did you manage to get the calendar done so quickly?'

'Digital technology,' said Fel. 'Shuffling about naked on the beach was easy, we were only nervous about being stuck with the stock if the fair was cancelled.'

'Then you'd be left sweet-talking the current affairs crew into buying them,' said Nancy to Fel and Evie.

'You know they won't be back now the nursing-home story is no longer news?' Evie said.

'I hadn't thought that far,' said Fel.

'I'll buy one for everyone I know if I need to, but the fair is on and I suspect you'll sell out in an hour.'

'Zac's made the same promise.'

Zac and promises were not what she wanted to talk about. She made a show of checking her watch. 'Is that the time? I have to run. I've got people to see if this fair is going to be a success.'

Her attempt to deflect Fel's question failed. 'Have you two had a falling-out?'

Evie shrugged in response.

'Don't let what is meant to be slip away without a fight.'

Did Fel know what had happened? 'Sometimes our fate
is in our hands. Other times, it's not. I'm learning to know the
difference.'

It was just a pity she hadn't worked it out before she'd made
such a spectacular fool of herself.

Evie was used to being surrounded by people at work but she'd
always been content with her own company, too. Probably a
result of the years she spent battling chronic fatigue syndrome.
But since her fallout with Zac she found herself longing for
a friendly face and a warm hug so it was with great relief she
prepared to welcome Letita home. She pushed open the
hospital door, eager to see her sister-in-law and find out how
she'd survived the transfer back to Pelican Beach Hospital.
She wasn't greeted with the enthusiasm she'd expected.

'Evie! You look terrible.'

'Thanks very much. You're the one recovering from major
surgery, not me.'

'I know, which makes it even worse. What's happened?'

'Nothing's happened.'

Letitia fixed Evie with a hard stare. Evie sighed and elabo-
rated. 'OK. To be more precise, nothing I want has happened.
Zac has told me, in no uncertain terms, he doesn't want me.'
She filled Letitia in on the details, pretending it didn't hurt half
as much as it did. She'd been pinning her hopes on the pretence-
become-reality wish for hour upon hour now. Wishes came true
sometimes, didn't they? 'End result is, he told me point blank
the real reason we couldn't be together was because he doesn't
care about me like that.' She blinked away memories. Too
much painful detail. 'He'd been trying to let me down gently,
I guess, until I made that impossible. At the end of the day, the
question of children aside, I'm not the woman he wants.'

'Why did he get involved with you in the first place if he didn't like you?'

'Seven-year itch? Or, in his case, the three-year itch. Convenience? Opportunity? It doesn't matter why, the problem is I'm not good enough to change his mind. Maybe if the right woman came along and blew rationality out of the water, hauled him beyond his safety net of detachment, he'd have to take the chance. But I'm not that woman.'

'And now?'

'Now I have a plan and I intend to stick to it.'

'A plan?'

'I'm going back to Vietnam. I was thinking I'd start over when I got back there, thinking that was going to be a long time to wait, and then I realised I didn't have to wait.'

'Just like that?'

Why were people always saying that to her? What other way was there to make decisions?

Letitia hadn't finished. 'You're leaving? Just when your mum is coming?'

Evie's parents had called the previous night to confirm the business had been sold and her mother would be arriving soon, leaving her father to make the final arrangements. Her mum would be here for Jake and the girls. She'd spoken to HR and had been assured they could, miraculously enough, replace her quite easily. She could go.

'How can I stay? I have to preserve some measure of self-respect. I need to go back to where what I do matters.' Taking a steadying breath, she said, 'I'm going to miss you all like crazy, especially the girls, but I need to do this. I'm going where I can make a difference.'

Letitia thought it over. 'But how will you afford that? You've always worked in the UK to support your time in Vietnam.'

'I'm hazy on the details, but it'll sort itself out. With the astoundingly huge exception of Zac, fate usually sets things straight.'

'I couldn't live like that, not planning, not knowing.'

'You live by your heart, Letitita, you do what feels right inside. That's all I do, too, it's just that what's right for you isn't right for me. I thought briefly it might be, settling down and all the rest, but I've been left in no doubt that's not the case. I have other things I need to be doing. So I am.' Her smile was wry, but at least after their chat she could smile again. 'Broken heart and all.'

She stood and leant to kiss Letitia goodbye.

'You won't talk—?'

Evie held up a hand to silence her plea. 'I have my limits when it comes to being rejected. I made a mistake, Letitia. He's not the man I thought I was falling for. I thought he cared. I'm not saying he's horrible, I'm saying he read me wrong and that's my fault, in part. He tried to let me down gently and I was too distracted by attraction to take the hint.'

Leaving Letitia, she headed for the foreshore, to walk through the area that by tomorrow night would be a hive of activity as those involved in the fair arrived to set up for the next day. Her heart was heavy in her chest as she passed the bench where she'd sat with Zac. The bench where he'd kissed her.

She'd walk, and she'd think, and she'd plan. People kept saying, 'Just like that?' when she spoke of her plans. What they didn't know was that she did think things through, she just didn't fight her gut instinct about things, she went with her intuition and that was nearly always the right way to go. Nearly. Except, as she'd told her sister-in-law, with the momentous exception of Zac.

She might be spontaneous, she might know how to silence a room with a twist of her hips, and people might judge her for that, but she wasn't stupid. Displaying the raw pain she felt inside was not an option. Neither was sticking around, hoping Zac would change his mind.

She was done with begging.

She was through with humiliation.

Whatever Zac and she had shared had been a fiction.

And waiting around for him to realise he'd written a dud ending wasn't going to happen.

Two more days—three at the most—and she'd be in Vietnam with the people who had stolen her heart a long time before Zac Carlisle had come into her life.

People who didn't doubt she was worth something, who knew she had something to offer.

Children who needed her.

And if the children's home would have her, if she could find some way of making a living while she volunteered there, if she was lucky, the move would be permanent.

It took all of thirty minutes for the news to reach Zac.

Evie was leaving.

HR had already given her the OK to go. With all her support for the fair, it seemed people were happy to do her favours. And she was happy to take them.

How long had her resolve to stay lasted? A blink in time and she'd changed her mind.

He dismissed the thought she was leaving because he'd made it impossible for her to stay. Her family was here. Apparently her mother, who she hadn't seen in well over two years, was arriving any day. If love and family meant so much to her, she'd be staying. She'd promised to look after her nieces. She was bailing out at the first opportunity.

Love and family didn't mean so much after all.

She was just like everyone else. A promise was a promise

only as long as it suited. After that, it was just an inconvenience to be circumvented as imaginatively as possible.

Taking the first plane out of the country was one way.

And if he'd let himself believe her promises, she'd be taking his heart with her, too. Thank goodness he'd resisted. At least this way his heart was intact.

Just.

CHAPTER TEN

'GRANNY!'

'She's here, she's here!'

From their vantage point at the front window, Gracie and Mack's squeals announced Jake's arrival from the Adelaide airport with their grandmother.

Evie raced up the passage, opened the door and narrowly avoided being bowled over by her nieces, who were beside themselves with excitement.

'You've got so big, Gracie!' June wrapped her granddaughters in arms that were always ready to hug. 'You're almost as tall as Auntie Evie, Mack. Evie, have you been eating? There's nothing of you.'

'Come in and give me a proper hello before you start nagging me, Mum.' Evie, stepped into her mum's arms, biting back tears that were always ready to fall, no matter how old she was, when life wasn't going well, and June gave her a hug. Blinking hard, she covered up her distress. 'I have to head over to the fairground in a moment to help set up. If you're not too tired, you should come with me.'

'I'm a retiree now, honey. I've got energy for everything.'

So twenty minutes later all five of them left for the fairground, although what contribution the little ones would make, Evie wasn't sure.

The fairground, set up on the wide strip of grass along the foreshore, was already looking festive, dotted with hired tents and trailers and an odd assortment of other, more makeshift shelters. The old Ferris wheel had been garlanded with lights, the organising committee had booked a jumping castle, rock-climbing wall and mini-golf, the food stalls were decked out with signs advertising their wares and a stage for entertainment was being erected. People hurried to and fro and the atmosphere was already one of excitement as they prepared for the next day's fair.

'A Shetland pony ride!' Mack and Gracie saw the sign and dragged Jake off to find the ponies.

'They'll be looking for a while. I doubt the ponies will be here before tomorrow,' Evie commented.

'What can I do to help?' June asked.

'Let's go to the Country Women's Association tent and see if they can do with a hand. I know most of the people there, they've been feeding us while Jake's been away.'

Within minutes June had been welcomed into the fold like a long-lost sister and, with her sleeves rolled up, was busy folding serviettes and arranging tables ready for the Devonshire teas the CWA would be serving.

'You're in your element, Mum. You're going to love living here.'

'I can't wait to have a social life and people to help now we're out of the truck stop.'

Evie had a light-bulb moment—was there one more thing she could put into place before she left? 'If being busy and meeting lots of people is what you want, I might have something just perfect for you. You'll have to give me a few hours to mull it over.'

'You and your dreaming, Evie. You've always had something going on, even as a child.' June gave her a kiss and resumed the conversation she'd been having with Mrs Lees about flourless chocolate cake, working all the while. Her mother was made for the CWA, for living in a community where people got involved and helped one another. Her mother was made to live in Pelican Beach among people like Mrs Lees and Fel and Nancy.

Leaving the tent, Evie spied Greg Evans, the CEO of the hospital, being shown the PA system on the stage, ready to open the fair tomorrow with the mayor. Just the man she wanted. Providence was letting her know her plan had been approved. He saw her when he left the stage and came straight over, pumping her hand with gratitude.

'This is due to you, Evie, and although there were various reasons why the government backtracked, the pressure you put on them by showing the community was committed and ready to fight played its part. Thank you.'

'It was my pleasure.' He'd thanked her before, she didn't need more thanks. It wasn't why she'd got involved.

'Isn't there anything we can do to persuade you to stay? You've breathed new life into the nursing-home, it's a shame to see you go.'

'That's what I wanted to talk to you about. I can't stay but I have an idea. Do you have a few minutes?'

They bent their heads together and Evie gave him her pitch, the best she could manage given the idea had occurred to her less than ten minutes ago. Zac would never jump in like this, she thought as she spoke with enthusiasm to cover the rough patches in her plans.

Not that she cared two hoots what Zac would and wouldn't do.

But, she deliberated, as she looked at the stage and thought of one of the planned events, there was one more parting gift she could give Pelican Beach. One she didn't need the CEO's approval for.

* * *

'I can't believe I'm doing this,' Zac muttered to himself as he stood in the stall selling calendars emblazoned with photos of his naked, elderly aunt. Hundreds of people were browsing through the stalls in the warm summer sunshine or sitting on the grass in front of the stage, watching a succession of local performers, some excellent, some woeful. The smell of hot dogs and hot chips wafted on the air. None of it was putting him in the festive mood.

'Relax and enjoy. You're now an official accomplice in our dark deeds,' said Fel as she took money from an older gentleman in the queue and handed him his calendar. He winked at her and held out his calendar for her to sign.

'Which one are you?' the customer asked Zac.

Zac forced a smile. 'They knocked me back. I wasn't centrefold material.'

'No, but you're bachelor-of-the-year material,' said a lady in the line. 'My money's on you. For my daughter,' she added when her friend nudged her in the ribs.

Zac handed her a calendar—what on earth was she talking about?

The fair had been officially opened by the mayor, who was now introducing Greg. Zac turned to the next customer while he listened with half an ear to the CEO.

He should have paid more attention. Before he knew it, he heard his name called and the line of people in front of the calendar stall became a swarm with the express purpose of propelling him onto the stage before he could refuse. Perhaps he'd resisted, but he was taken by surprise and then there he was, looking out at the crowd, which had now swelled to ridiculous numbers, standing in line with another five or six bewildered locals about his age. The butcher, the owner of the news agency, the local radio announcer, a high-school teacher and a dairy farmer. The only thing they had in common, as far as he could work out, was—

'Oh, no,' he groaned. They were all single.

'Oh, yes, they're doing things the traditional country way,' said the butcher, 'and having a beauty contest.'

'And we're the judges?'

That drew a wry laugh. 'The contestants.'

He glanced left and right—what were his chances of making a run for it?

'Don't even think of it. I've got first dibs on a quick escape and I'll tackle you for it.' Paul the butcher, laughed. 'Come on, mate, relax. Get into the spirit.'

What spirit? Did grumpy old men have spirit? That's how he was feeling. Grumpy. Old. Miserable.

Greg was hamming it up in his introduction, most of which Zac had now missed, so he had no idea what was happening when six women came onto the stage and deposited cooking utensils on a table.

Evie.

The world stopped.

Evie was one of the women.

The women approached the men and led them to the tables set out with bowls and eggs and egg beaters.

Evie smiled as though she didn't have a care in the world. She also didn't seem to have a thought for him, refusing eye contact with him and making straight for Paul, taking him by the arm. Anyone would think Paul had just won a sausage-stuffing competition he was grinning so much, but what man wouldn't be happy to have Evie standing slap-bang in front of him, in cut-off denim shorts and a brightly patterned vest top, hair loose, dark eyes shining? Dark eyes that weren't looking in his direction.

'Egg beaters at the ready. First one to crack six eggs, separate them, beat the whites and hold the bowl upside down over their heads without any spillage, is the winner of this round. Automatic elimination for the last to finish.'

If he finished last, he'd get out of there.

If he finished last, he'd lose in front of Evie.

The whistle blew and Zac had his first egg cracked and i[n] the bowl while the butcher was still making eyes at Evie. H[e] wasn't a doctor for nothing. If it was concentration he neede[d] that was what he had. Six egg whites were in the bowl and h[e] was beating the white liquid into frothy peaks. The news agency guy was one step ahead, lifting his bowl—could h[e] overtake him? He assessed the eggs. No, not quite there. A fe[w] more flicks of the wrist... The crowd roared with laughter an[d] clapped and Zac took a quick look to see the news agent's hea[d] covered in still runny egg whites—too quick off the mark.

He was done. He lifted his bowl, said a quick prayer an[d] held it upside down over his head. The crowd roared—and th[e] eggs stayed put.

Zac spun his bowl back down as the next contestant, the[n] the next, held bowls aloft with varying degrees of success.

Paul came last. 'Deliberate, buddy. The early bird catche[s] the worm and I'm going to introduce myself to the little lady[.]

Zac's stomach muscles clenched and they both turned t[o] find Evie but she was already in deep conversation with con[-] testant number two who'd been hot on Zac's heels. Had sh[e] even seen him win?

Now there were five bachelors left. Pie-eating came nex[t] after which Evie disappeared—with Paul? Zac was so dis[-] tracted by that thought he made a mess of the knit-a-line com[-] petition and only just managed to scrape through. He blitzed th[e] fillet-a-fish task, thankful the butcher had gone before that on[e] That left two of them—him and the news-agency guy, Tony.

Then he heard it.

Arabic music.

He closed his eyes and prayed, hoping it wouldn't mea[n] what he thought.

The gods weren't listening.

Greg announced the competition and the crowd roared their approval just as Zac's world froze at the news. A dance-off. What was Greg saying? The last task was to have been a sleeping-bag race around the stage, but a late offer from Pelican Beach's most eligible woman had upped the stakes. Evie would teach the two finalists how to shimmy and shake, and the loudest applause from the crowd would decide the winner.

As Evie ran lightly onto the stage, the crowd went wild.

Clothed in a bright pink skirt that swished around her calves and sat low on her hips—those hips!—a heavily beaded bra top, showing every enticing curve, her eyes highlighted with dark eyeliner, her cheeks flushed, she took her place in the centre of the stage, rousing the crowd to join in, apparently enjoying the catcalls and whistles and clapping.

If he'd humiliated her with his rejection, he knew he was about to pay for it now.

He resigned himself to the fate he deserved.

She was in front of them, giving them instructions, laughing as his competition, Tony, made a joke.

'Are you ready, boys?' Even her voice was in character, every part of her the seductress. She could have been his. For a while, she could have been his. But it would never have been for ever.

Did for ever matter?

He thought of his baby, the one he'd never know, and thought of the pain that remained in his heart still. Pain that would be with him for ever. For ever did matter.

'Ready,' said Tony, earning himself a gorgeous smile from Evie.

If for ever mattered, then the opinion Evie would take with her of him mattered, too.

He sought her eyes, finding a blank gaze. No smile for him.

'I take no prisoners,' was all she said, adding a teasing smile for Tony's benefit. The smile died on her lips as his eyes met hers. He knew her words had been a challenge to him.

He'd match it, rise to the occasion. 'Ready,' he announced, giving his hips a half-decent twist, to thunderous applause from the crowd.

That earned him his first smile from Evie, but it was thin. It said she'd match his challenge.

And they were off.

First, learning to bend from the knees, not the hips, the secret of belly dancing. The crowd joined in the tempo of the music kicked up a notch, the beat irresistible. She was irresistible. The movements came thick and fast, rocking the hips, lifting the hips, shimmying the arms, twisting the wrists. Men's wrists weren't made to bend like that! His hips weren't separate from his torso! But he'd bend and twist and rock and shimmy if it did him permanent injury. He had no doubt he'd never looked so ridiculous but at least there were two of them—and the crowd was coming along for the ride, too.

And the one thing he knew was he wasn't quitting, even if his hips never moved again. But Tony wasn't quitting either.

The music ended and the crowd cheered. Their laughter and applause was deafening, and they cheered louder when Greg came on stage to thank Evie before announcing that Pelican Beach's most eligible bachelor was, by a whisker, Tony the news agent.

It was over. He'd gone along with it in the spirit of the fair and had come second. As he left the stage, he reminded himself he was happy not to have won—Tony would be fielding offers from women all day now, even if only in jest, and he didn't want to deal with that.

What he wanted was to find Evie.

She was leaving Pelican Beach. He had to try and put things straight. She'd be coming back to visit her family and he needed to make sure they could be civil when she did. That was why he needed to see her. It had nothing to do with the feelings she'd roused in him when he'd seen her on stage, watched her dance, seen the life and joy in her face as she'd moved. The shadows in her eyes when she'd first appeared on stage had disappeared as she'd danced, oblivious to her audience, at one with the beat and the rhythm of the music, in her own world, where everything was magic.

It had nothing to do with feeling his heart expand with bitter-sweet joy as he'd watched her, combined with the pain of knowing she was leaving.

It had nothing at all to do with how he felt. He only needed to make amends in some small way.

He was just doing the right thing. Again.

So why did the right thing leave him feeling so damn rotten?

He found her by the Ferris wheel, talking with Tony and Paul, laughing with them. He put his question to her. 'I hate to interrupt, but could I speak to you for a moment? It's about the hospital.'

Medicine was never questioned as an excuse. The other men left them to it but not before promising to seek her out later.

'You don't need me for work. I'm not on call and neither are you.'

She'd changed her clothes now, no longer the dancing gypsy, but her eyes were still highlighted with dark liner, her cheeks still flushed, her hair tumbling down over her shoulders. She was still lovely. And still as little disposed to be near him, judging by the distant expression in her eyes.

'No, but I wanted to talk to you. I heard you're leaving.'

She looked away, didn't confirm or deny, just looked away.

Then she said, a bite in her voice, 'And it took seeing other men being interested to make you care about that?'

'That's not why I'm here, but I can accept you might think that.'

The Ferris wheel came to a halt and the people shuffled off. 'Ride with me?' He put out a hand to take hers but she shrugged it away. Still, she joined the line and waited while a cage was opened for them, sitting herself as far over to her side as she could manage.

'Evie, there are things I need to say before you go. I know I've hurt you, and I'm sorry. It was never my intention.'

She shrugged and looked out over the fairground, away from him.

He opened his mouth to apologise again but instead asked the question that had been on his mind ever since he'd heard her news. 'Why are you leaving? Your mum has just arrived back, you haven't seen your dad yet, and Letitia is still in hospital.'

He had to know whether her promises to stay, to make a life together, had amounted to nothing, or whether there was some all-compelling reason she had to leave. He had no right, but he couldn't restrain himself.

She turned to face him, anger blazing in her eyes. 'You're seriously asking me to explain myself?'

'You said you'd stay if we were together. You were offended when I said I thought you'd leave one day.'

'I would have stayed for you. But you're not asking me to.' She was angry and agitated and hurt, clearly hurt. 'Are you?'

The Ferris wheel jerked to a halt, their cage swinging mid-air, suspended in no-man's-land. Just like him. She was waiting for his answer. He couldn't give her the one she wanted.

'I never meant to hurt you but I couldn't start something I know has to end.'

'Really?' Her tone was dry but he could feel the fury underneath it. The Ferris wheel creaked to a start again and she grabbed at the side rail. 'The way I see it, you already did.'

She was right. He had. She had every reason to despise him and from the way she was glaring at him now, it seemed she'd thought of them all.

The cage swung down towards the ground—they'd almost completed one revolution. He'd brought her here to let her know he was sorry, but somehow he'd managed to imply she'd lied to him and she'd never have stayed anyway. He'd made her hate him in the time it had taken to complete one full circle on the Ferris wheel.

Their cage reached the ground and the wheel slowed down but didn't stop. Evie pulled the pin and unlocked the door, scrambling out while the wheel continued to turn. She stumbled in the process but Tony was waiting there for her and scooped her up, half lifting her away from the wheel.

The wheel rose again, leaving him to watch as the woman he'd managed to drive away was held close to the chest of another man. Pelican Beach's most eligible bachelor no less.

They disappeared from sight.

The wheel rose higher as his heart plummeted in the opposite direction.

CHAPTER ELEVEN

To: Evie@emailme.com
From: letitiaandjake@pelicanmail.com.au
Subject: the coffee might be good but so is an email once in a while
We haven't heard from you for weeks (at least three). What's news in Ho Chi Minh City? Thanks to your sweet-talking of the CEO, your mum is having a ball organising fundraising and social events in the nursing-home as the new Activities Queen—she's even on the payroll—and your dad is now busy fixing things around the hospital (he's not yet on the payroll, I'll keep you posted. What is it with your family and helping out?). On another note, you won't ask so I'm telling you, Zac looks like he's been told he's got three weeks to live, i.e. not great. He restrains himself to only ask after you in a polite way but I can see he's aching to know every little thing. I know he hurt you but are you sure there's no hope? Won't stick my oar in any more. We love you, stay safe and drop us a line.

To: letitiaandjake@pelicanmail.com.au
From:Evie@emailme.com
Subject: all is well…
But email access is not easy, hence lack of them. I'm working

in the medical care programme with children up to age eighteen, heart-breaking but uplifting. One little guy, Tran (but he prefers Jonno) has stolen my heart. He is HIV positive, abandoned by his family, too poor to provide for him. Don't know what the future holds, we're doing all we can. My dream is to spend a few months at least in the foundation's rural medical station in Mekong Delta if the anti-malarials hold out. Please don't tell me about Zac, it's too hard to hear since there is no hope. I'm still hurt beyond words but the truth is, if there was a way I could have been a bigger fool, I can't think of it. Pray for Jonno. Love you, miss you all, Evie

To: Evie@emailme.com
From: letitiaandjake@pelicanmail.com.au
Subject: Good news!!
I coaxed your anti-technology mum into looking at the website for where you are and she's now knee-deep in raising the funds to give you your three months at the rural centre and sponsor a child—we're hoping it will be Jonno. Will keep you posted, but I now know where you get your 'can do' attitude! Pelican Beach is right behind her (so is Zac—you wouldn't believe how he's thrown himself into the project). Love L

To: letitaandjake@pelicanmail.com.au
From:Evie@emailme.com
Jonno died two days ago. Very sudden. He got pneumonia and his immune system just collapsed. Six days ago I told you he was doing well, and he was. Now his wasted little body is all that's left. Is there anything after death? How can I not believe that a child's spirit lives on, even if it's only in our love for them? Pray for him. We bury him tomorrow. This is where I'm meant to be for now, and I

know one day there will be another child who is meant to have me for a mother. Love hurts but I'm going to keep on doing it. Love to all of you, Evie.

'Letitia, you're in danger of becoming permanently attached to that thing.' Zac entered Letitia's hospital room and waved a hand at her laptop, lying, where it always was, on her lap in her bed.

'It's amazing how addictive the internet is and, of course, I never know when I'm going to hear from Evie.' She pursed her lips and considered him for a moment, her blue eyes thoughtful. 'Which I just have. I know you never ask to read her emails but I'm also pretty sure I'm getting a few more visits from you than is strictly necessary just in case I have any news. I told you about the little boy, Jonno?'

He nodded. He'd had recurring visions of Evie with a dark-haired child, holding him, laughing with him, showing him someone cared. Showing him he was loved.

'But this one,' Letitia went on, 'I think you should read for yourself.'

He hesitated—was that trespassing? But Letitia hadn't offered before so she must have thought it through. It was only because of Letitia that he knew anything about Evie's life in the last two months. He knew what he was doing, knew where his future lay, but hearing about her let him feel it was possible she'd be part of his life again one day.

He took the laptop and read. It was like hearing her voice again. She wrote the way she spoke and the emotion rang out in her words.

Jonno had died? The email was dated yesterday—was she burying him now, while he read? He gritted his teeth and swore under his breath. He should have been with her, should have moved things along more quickly—but there were things to do. He had to get it right if he had any chance of setting things straight with her.

'I can see you still care, Zac, despite what you told her.'

He handed the laptop back to her, not trusting himself to meet her eyes without losing control. 'I do still care. I just didn't realise how much until I'd made a complete hash of it all and she'd gone.'

'I'll only say one thing, then. Don't let too much time pass by if you intend to set things straight.'

He'd held himself back. He'd needed to know he was doing the right thing. He didn't want to act on a whim and end up hurting them both even more. But Letitia was right. He hoped he hadn't left it too late.

The noise and chaos was unbelievable. Even from the vantage point of the taxi window, wound down to let some breeze in to combat the stifling humidity, it was hard to take in. The smells of the street stalls and the fumes from the traffic, the roar of vehicles, the multitude of sights, the mass of people, the stalls and shops, the architecture, all so unfamiliar, combined to assault his senses.

Mopeds and motorbikes packed the roads, the drivers appearing oblivious to the need to stick to one side of the road, weaving around other vehicles at crazy angles, multiple passengers piled up on the bike more often than not. He'd counted three children, two adults and a large basket of shopping on one—how did they stay on? But they did. The road was large enough for two lanes in each direction, but the drivers seemed to have decided at least seven lanes would be better and used the road accordingly. Car horns honked, and among it all pedestrians simply walked out onto the roads, apparently trusting the traffic would swerve around them. It was like nothing Zac had ever seen before but it seemed to work.

His taxi cut across the path of a van, a truck and a motor-bike, pulled sharply round a corner into a side street and screeched to a halt in front of a long, low brick building. He wasn't a religious man but he'd been dishing up prayers for most of the trip. The driver turned around and beamed at him, waiting for payment for a job well done. Was it? Zac peered out the window and spotted a large brass sign, lettered in black, announcing this was, indeed, the foundation. Counting out the unfamiliar notes until he reached the price they'd agreed on, he added a bit extra to thank the gods he'd made it there in one piece. The driver nodded his head fervently and insisted on helping Zac get his luggage out of the boot.

And then he was alone, on the doorstep, the chaos of the main street receding in the distance, the foundation in front of him.

Would he find what he was looking for?

Or was he too late?

Evie dashed around the corner to the local internet café—dawdled, more like, in the damp heat, and went online to check her emails.

She scanned the list and pretended she wasn't hoping to see one from Zac. She was lousy at pretending. Letitia had written again, though, and from the subject heading, she had good news. Good news had been in short supply in the few weeks since Jonno's death.

'Yes!' Evie cheered. Bingo games, raffle tickets, sell-out slap-up dinners for families and friends in the nursing-home common room—including one for Nancy's 85th birthday—had exceeded expectations. Her legend of a mother, with the help of a loyal band—Zac among them, although she'd try and ignore that inclusion—had raised the funds to allow her to stay on for at least another three months. Letitia was at pains to stress it wasn't charity for Evie—Pelican Beach had rallied around the cause as a way to thank her for saving the nursing-home.

There was more, and by now she was grinning so hard she was in danger of straining something. So much had been raised that a sizeable one-off donation was also to come. Finally, an email campaign—that had to have been Letitia's doing as she didn't credit anyone in particular—circulating details of the foundation and calling for people to band together to sponsor children had resulted in pledges to sponsor at least five children.

Hitting 'Print,' she waited with impatience before heading back to the foundation. This time she went at a run, straight to Alla, the indefatigable woman whose massive task it was to oversee all fundraising and sponsorship, and vetting and placement of volunteers. She was as thrilled as Evie with the news, and enveloped her in a hug against her matronly bosom.

'I'm hearing the words "Pelican Beach" a lot nowadays. I've been trying to catch you to mention Zac Carlisle.'

'Zac? How have you heard his name?'

'More than heard his name, honey. I shook his hand not more than two hours ago. He's here and he made it clear we have you to thank for leading him to us.'

Evie sat down in the chair opposite Alla, the whir of the ceiling fan hardly audible over the ringing in her ears. She hadn't heard right—

'I was at my wits' end, trying to find a doctor for the new centre up north. I was almost at the point where we'd have to pull one of the staff from the Mekong clinic. Now you've fixed the problem and brought us Zac.'

'There must be a mistake.'

Zac couldn't be here. How could she face him? The memories of what she'd done, and said, came flooding back in full Technicolor glory. If she could have crawled under Alla's desk and howled with the excruciating agony of it all, she would have. With thousands of miles, wave upon wave of sea between them, she was getting through her days. Just. Pretence hadn't become reality but it was better. Now reality was crashing through and declaring itself present. Present and about to be accounted for.

'No mistake. He's been in, signed on and headed for his hotel. He's probably back here by now to have a look around. We'll train him up for a few weeks before shipping him up north, so to speak.' Alla was now sorting papers on her desk, talking and working simultaneously coming naturally to a woman who eked more hours out of her day than humanly possible. 'He's fine-looking. Is there nothing to tell? We need a nurse up north, too. It's an easy matter to assign you there instead.' She plopped a pile of papers on her desk and pinned Evie with a look.

'I—' Zac was here? It didn't make sense.

'I'll leave you to think about it. I haven't processed your placement yet, I was holding off until you heard about funds. I can hold off a day or two more.'

'Thanks but—'

Alla waved away what she probably thought was an expression of appreciation. It wasn't—she'd been going to say she didn't need even a minute to know she wanted to be at the opposite end of the country from Zac. He didn't even like her!

'You let me know when you're ready. I have to run, I've a meeting with the government department about visas.' Alla bustled around her desk and swept Evie along with her out the door, leaving her with a wave. Evie simply stood there with no idea what she was meant to do next.

She couldn't see him—and if he had any feelings for her at all, he'd never have come here. Steeling herself against the inevitable meeting, she returned to the medical centre, instructing herself to put one foot in front of the other and act like everything was OK. There was no room for her personal issues here, not when there was real need behind the brave faces of each one of their children.

But there he was.

She stopped as if she'd been stunned by a mallet.

She *had* been stunned.

It was definitely him. Straight back, broad shoulders, dark hair cut shorter than when she'd last seen him, but definitely him. If she wanted to believe her eyes were lying, her treacherous body wasn't letting her buy that for a minute. After everything that had happened, after every hurtful word, after recalling every morning that he didn't want her, her body hadn't learned a thing. She still wanted him.

As much as she ever had.

More?

She hung back, to watch, to see what tricks fate had in store for her. He was speaking to Carrie, the psychologist from Canada, and Shane, the GP from Melbourne. He was looking… happy? In long, lightweight trousers, a crisp white shirt that would be a nightmare to keep clean and uncreased, and leather sandals on his feet, he looked at ease. In profile, he looked thinner—or was it just the loose fit of the clothes? With the exception of the shirt—madness!—he looked like he belonged.

Which meant—what?

A doctor was always more in demand than a nurse here, harder to recruit and harder to keep. He'd trump her presence any day.

So where did that leave her?

Carrie was shaking him by the hand, Shane slapping him on the back in welcome before they went their separate ways, leaving Zac to look about.

Leaving Zac to turn straight to her, as if he'd sensed her there. Which was ridiculous.

The relaxed confidence surrounding him a moment ago ebbed almost visibly away and he hesitated before coming to her.

'Evie.' He reached out to touch her then dropped his hand when she took a step back.

'What are you doing here?' Ridiculous question. She knew what he was doing here. What she needed to know was why he had come. How could the fantastic news about the fund-raising efforts be so quickly tainted with this? Why did fate have to flaunt the one thing she wanted and couldn't have in front of her like this?

He'd looked pleased to see her for a moment but the apparent joy had quickly been replaced by a smile that was less certain. She didn't know which was more confusing.

'Can we talk?' He was earnest, his voice modulated, low.

'Just tell me what you're doing here.'

'Let's grab one of those coffees you're hooked on and I'll explain.'

She didn't want to share her coffee with him.

She didn't want to share any of this with him.

This was supposed to be her safe haven but now it…wasn't safe?

Or wasn't hers?

Zac lifted his hands, imploring her to listen. 'You don't have to talk but if you'd be prepared to listen, I've got things I'd like to say. Need to say.'

'I have…' she glanced at her watch '…an hour, no more.' Once she'd had all eternity to give—but she'd offered that and he'd turned her down and left her with no doubt that the single night they'd shared had been more than enough.

Heat burned through her at the memory. If she lived to be a thousand, she'd never forget the feeling of being rejected. By this man, the one, the only man she'd ever loved.

'An hour, no more.' If she repeated it enough she'd remember her mantra—no more. No more hurt, no more wishing, no more daydreams about a future that was never going to happen.

No more Zac Carlisle.

He'd started with an hour but the minutes were already dwindling. They'd spent five minutes walking here, to a street stall, ordered their coffee and now they were perching on two bright red plastic chairs on the potholed pavement next to the road that, considering it was a side street, was still carrying its fair share of traffic.

Watching the dark coffee drip through its aluminium filter onto the inch-thick layer of condensed milk in the glass below was like watching an egg-timer marking off the minutes until Evie blew the whistle and said, 'Game over.'

Her hair was pulled back, a light sheen on her flushed skin the only sign that she was at all affected by the dense heat of the late afternoon. She looked well, but she was tense, had been from the moment he'd seen her today, and she was watching him with wary eyes like he was a venomous creature and she was the prey.

Sitting opposite her, their glasses positioned between them like a miniature wall, he floundered, and the words he'd thought would come so easily dried up in the face of her clear wish to be somewhere else, anywhere else other than here with him. Where to start? With what she'd asked him before.

'You asked me why I'm here.' She jumped as his voice broke the silence that had fallen between them. He was trying to make eye contact but she was staring resolutely at her glass, seemingly mesmerised by the drip, drip, drip of the coffee onto condensed milk. He could have sworn she was mouthing something under her breath, over and over again, 'No more' maybe? He was conscious of the fascination the stall owners had with the spectacle taking place in front of them. What were they predicting? She'd hurl her coffee over him any moment? Judging by the frown set in place on her usually happy face, it was a front runner in the list of possible outcomes.

He gave up on the eye contact.

And he gave up on trying for the perfect formula, the perfect speech. He'd wing it. Go with what he felt.

'There's no right place to start, there's so much I want to say to you. So much I need to say. I offended you in every possible way but I didn't realise until I had hour upon hour of emptiness after you'd gone to relive every daft word I'd said, every daft thing I'd done.'

If he hadn't seen her swallow, hard, like she was fighting back her emotions, he'd have sworn she hadn't heard him. She picked up her little metal spoon and started to stir her coffee into the sweet white layer below.

'I knew within a day I had to come after you, had to apologise, even if you never wanted to see me again afterwards, but really what I wanted was to bring you home, start over. But I didn't know where you were. I ended up asking your mum and one thing led to another and there I was, involved in the fundraising, doing the exact opposite of what I wanted: raising funds to keep you here. But the more I got involved, the more I understood what it meant to you, being here.'

She snapped her head up at that, defiance in her eyes. 'If you really meant that, you wouldn't have come.' The bite in her voice was covering the hurt, but only just. How could he have so carelessly trampled over her heart then added a few extra stamps for good measure? 'Being here is everything to me but you waltz in and…' Her words were left hanging.

What was he doing here?

There was a note of desperation in her voice, in the taut

carriage of her body that made him doubt, for a flicker of a moment, his right to simply launch himself into her life, this life, when he'd told her in such cruel terms to get out of his.

'I owe you an explanation. I made a lot of assumptions and they were all wrong. It's no excuse, but I was confused. Afraid. Plain stupid.'

She didn't argue the point. 'You did make a lot of assumptions but it doesn't matter now. You don't have to come and smooth things over. You wanted me out of your life, I went. So why have you come into my life here? Now?'

He could hear confusion mixed with anger in her words. Her mum, Fel, Letitia, the whole damn town had been cheering him on in his quest to come and find her once he'd announced his plans, wishing him well, reaffirming at every point he was making the right choice. The only choice. Had he glossed over how much he'd messed up?

'Please, hear me out, then if you never want to see me again, I'll respect that.'

Her nod was as grudging as it could be.

He took what he could get and pressed on. 'I've come here for two reasons. The more I got involved in the fundraising, the more I knew there was a new path I was meant to take, whether or not you ever spoke to me again. I applied for the position up north so if you didn't want a bar of me, you wouldn't have to even know I was here.'

The stall owner chose that moment to slip their glasses away, and spoke to Evie, perhaps asking her if they wanted more. She hesitated then replied. He hadn't heard her speak Vietnamese before. She'd insisted she spoke it poorly but they seemed to be having a rapid exchange of words and a moment later the man had handed them each a baguette liberally slathered with cheese.

A baguette she showed no interest in and he knew she'd ordered them only to do the right thing by the stall owner. Yet he'd hurled it in her face that they didn't even know one another. How could he have got it all so badly wrong?

His momentum broken, he toyed with the unwanted baguette, buying time until he'd picked up his train of thought. 'If you tell me you never want to see me again, I'll go north and I promise I'll leave you be.'

Her concentration as she tore her baguette into tiny pieces was impressive but was there a flicker of indecision in her brow? A crack in her armour of self-control and containment? He wouldn't know until he'd risked as much as she had when she'd offered him everything and he'd given her nothing.

It couldn't hurt more than it already did.

'The other reason I came is this: I love you.'

Now he had not only eye contact, he had her gaping at him, incredulity clear on her face. Adrenalin surged through him—could she hear the mad pounding of his heart? 'I've loved you since the first moment I saw you shake those hips of yours.' Was that a slight, ever so slight upward twitch of that perfect mouth of hers? 'Maybe since the first moment I saw you. I fought it, God knows, and hurt you in the process. I was trying to protect myself but I've ended up hurting myself more than ever. And, worse, I've hurt you. So whether or not you give a damn, that's the second, or the first, really, the main reason I'm here. I love you and I want to be with you. For ever. And I want to share your journey here. All of it.'

She stared at him. He waited for her to speak.

Finally, she broke the silence. 'You don't like me. I'm not what you want, not who you want. I'm not good enough.' She listed all the versions of the awful words he'd said to her all those weeks ago. The list rolled off her tongue. He knew in that moment, in a blinding flash of insight, that she'd lain awake at night hearing those hurtful, horrible words over and over in her head.

There was more.

'And you thought I was selfish, coming back here. You didn't say so, but I could see it in your eyes, in the way you behaved. You thought I was selfish to leave when Letitia was still recovering, when my mum had just arrived.'

'It was all a fiction, Evie. I thought I had to push you away, for both our sakes.' He broke into her flood of words, desperate to stem their flow and make her see how wrong he'd been. 'I'd tried explaining my reasons, reasons I thought would make you run for the hills. But you didn't. You stayed. And got tested for CF.' He shook his head at the wonder of it all. He still couldn't believe this incredible woman had done that for him. She'd risked her heart and he'd been afraid to meet her even an inch down the path, let alone halfway. 'You were brave. Wonderfully so. You made promises I just didn't, couldn't, believe were real. I was a fool.'

She'd swept the crumbs of her baguette aside and was no longer fidgeting. She was looking back at him as if he was speaking a language of which she had only a limited grasp, making comprehension a struggle. But she was listening.

'And as for why you left, I know I helped drive you away. I can't put into words all the mistakes I've made. I've spent the last two and a half months listing them all and it seemed to me that every minute we spent together, I hurt you in some way. There's no reason in the world why you should believe I love you, but I've quit my job, packed up the house and I'm here. For at least a year. And after that, who knows? But if I get what I want, whatever I'm doing, it'll be with you, wherever you want to be.'

The mask of control had been thrown aside now, replaced by the same panic and confusion he'd seen on her face when he'd spurned her love all those weeks ago. 'You don't work like that. You're not spontaneous. Sooner or later, you'll realise you don't mean any of this and then you'll go back to your old life. The one you didn't want me to be a part of.'

'Now you sound like me, fighting what's so damn obvious.' He reached out to lift her hand and she didn't resist—he couldn't even be sure she knew he'd done it. 'And you're right, I'm not spontaneous. Which is why, when loving you happened so suddenly, it terrified me. You crashed through all the barriers I'd built, turned all my reasons not to love upside down. I panicked. I did the only thing I knew how. I put up more barriers, and drove you away in the process.' He paused, brushing his hair off his forehead, unused to the sticky heat, his discomfort compounded by the desperate need he had to explain, to convince her. 'I lost my sister when she'd only just begun to be the woman she should have lived to be. I lost my daughter before she ever had a chance to live. There was nothing I could do for either of them. What was I meant to think except that love hurts like hell and promises are worthless?'

'And there you were.' He dropped his voice, the love he felt for her evident in his tone. 'Making the most incredible promises.' He pressed her fingers between his own, willing his convictions to filter through to her, to persuade her. 'I wanted so badly to believe, so very badly, but I didn't know how. So I pushed you away. But I'm here now. I'm here and I'm hoping that sometimes miracles do happen.'

His voice caught on his words and she went to tear another piece from her baguette and found her hand was in his— when had that happened? She tugged at the contact, but it was half-hearted. She wanted desperately to accept he was really here for her. But if she gave an inch, she'd end up lost in his world again. She couldn't afford to be swayed by him tugging at her heartstrings, but his sincerity was urging her better self to return his honesty.

'You're right,' she said, drawing the words out as she thought it over. 'I made all sorts of rash promises. You were right not to believe them, right to question them. I sounded insane, and I knew that by the time I arrived here. Coming back here calmed me, cleared my mind, and although I tried hard, I could no longer deny that I hadn't thought any of it through.' She hadn't met his eyes. The mortification of how she'd thrown herself at him was still too strong for that. 'I would have run a mile, too, if someone had proposed a life together and babies and moving countries to be together in the way I did.'

She felt his hand cup her face and turn it up gently. 'It sounded rash, Evie, but eventually I realised you believed what you were saying. You knew what your heart held and I was a stranger to mine. I was afraid to love because I knew it would end in more pain. I was wrong. Loving you didn't hurt, letting you go did. And letting you go, believing I didn't care, believing I didn't want you, has been indescribably terrible. I've spent the best part of the last two months hating myself and throwing myself into the fundraising as a way to stay close to you, to keep your dreams alive. And I found my new path. I've done what I could do in Pelican Beach, at least for now, but here I can make a difference. Here I can give love and care to a multitude of children, give all the things I wanted to give my daughter. And do it while being with you, loving you, sharing your dreams.'

'But your life is in Pelican Beach, your work. You're saying you'll sacrifice all that to be where I am?'

'It's not a sacrifice, it's an adventure, but it's one I've thought through. I'm not asking for an answer now. I'm asking you to give me a chance. You showed me there are many paths to love and if you're lucky enough to stumble on your true path, you seize it. This is our path, our adventure. Take this path with me, Evie. Trust me. Love me, like I love you.'

Frantically, she searched her mind for all remaining obstacles. There was one, but when he was looking at her like that it was all she could do not to give in.

They should go. They should walk. Walking would clear her head. Walking would mean he couldn't look at her like that, as if she was his world. Because that was exactly what she wanted to be.

And there was one more obstacle that couldn't be easily swept aside. One more hurdle that might still be too high.

He'd thought she was about to close the distance between them and when she stood, his heart expanded to fill every corner of his chest. But she lifted her little red chair out the way and said, 'Can we walk? Please?'

He followed suit with his chair and thanked the stall owner, using the few words he'd learnt from his language book, and walked beside her along the street. Her posture was rigid. Something was still bothering her.

'What's wrong?'

'Children,' was all she said, her voice a whisper. 'You were right. I want—need—to know children are in my future.'

'We can't have children. I can't take the risk of a child having CF.'

She turned away. He touched her arm, turning her to him, and his heart caught in his throat at the expression of pain on her face.

'You spoke about adoption. Is that still what you would do, what is really in your heart?'

She nodded.

'That was the final dream of yours I had to be certain I could share with as much conviction and passion and love as you.'

'And can you?'

'Yes.'

Hope and joy flared in her eyes for a brief moment before clouds came into her expression again. 'Do you really know that's right for you? It's a long, intrusive, demanding path to travel. You have no idea how much prodding and poking you have to endure from officials, how much assessment and paperwork and red tape you'd face. And it's necessary, to ensure everything is aboveboard and the child who'll eventually become your son or daughter has no options in their birth country other than growing up in an institution, often in immense poverty. I couldn't go down this path with you if it's all going to come crashing down when reality hits.'

'This isn't a spur-of-the-moment decision, it's another reason why I had to wait to come to you. I wanted no doubts between us. I've spent every possible minute looking into this. I needed to be sure it was what I wanted before I came sailing back into your life on a raft of promises I couldn't keep. I've been to information nights and seminars and group workshops and trawled the internet and libraries for information. My friends and family think I've joined some secret men's club in Adelaide because I've disappeared so often.'

Her eyes were huge, their expression hovering somewhere between incredulity and excitement, her lips parted, hanging on his every word.

'I've met wonderful families and seen the love they have for their children. They've formed their families via another path but the love is the same. This is not only what I want but where I'm meant to be.'

'You did all that for me? For us?'

'It's the tip of the iceberg. There's nothing I wouldn't do to have the future I dream of with you. You're my future, Evie. Let me love you, let me show you what you mean to me.'

A sob tore from her throat and he resisted the urge to gather her to him, comfort her when she might still pull away. He needed to convince her. There were still things left to say.

'And one day there will be a child who was meant to have you for his mother, whose chubby little arms were meant to wrap tight around you, whose dimpled baby hands were made to stroke your face.' A single tear slid down her cheek but she made no effort to brush it away, if she even felt it. 'He, or she, is real, Evie. I can almost feel our child, and one day it will happen.'

He was done. He'd said what he'd needed to say. He took her in his arms and for the first time since he'd arrived she let him hold her. They stood there, body to body, heart to heart. And he let himself hope.

He'd seen almost every emotion under the sun in her face today and he'd thought, hoped he'd seen love among them.

'Come with me to the northern clinic—there are places for both of us. Give me the chance to show you how I feel, give us the chance to start again.'

She shook her head. 'No.'

His world stopped. 'No?'

She raised her face to look into his eyes and her gaze was at odds with her words. 'No chances. You don't need a chance.' Her smile was radiant. It was all for him. 'I believe you,' she added simply as if that was enough.

Maybe it was.

'You believe me,' he said. 'Enough to trust me? Enough to let me love you?'

'Enough for all of that and more. Enough to love you back. I've never stopped, I've wished I could, many, many times, because that would have ended the pain, but love doesn't work like that.'

'Thank God for me.' He lifted her up then and kissed her, kissed her with every ounce of love he had, and the kiss was everything he'd ever hoped, everything that had kept him tossing and turning through endless sleepless nights these past two months.

All his love and dreams and passion were in that kiss.

And in his arms, kissing him back as though they were the only two people on the planet, was the woman he loved more than life itself.

When they drew apart, minutes later, she whispered, 'I thought wild horses wouldn't drag this out of me after how it went down last time, but I love you, Zac Carlisle. And I will love you every minute of every day for the rest of my life.'

'Only the days? What about the nights?'

'Especially the nights.' She reached up for him again, kissing him once more, more gently this time but with just as much passion. 'And that's a promise.'

A promise.

How could he ever have thought promises brought trouble?

Promises had brought him Evie.

Which left him in no doubt at all that some promises were, in fact, for ever.

'Mistress,' Nikolai slotted in cool as ice.

Shock had welded Ella's tongue to the roof of her mouth because
he was sexually propositioning her and nothing could have prepared
her for that. She wasn't drop-dead gorgeous... *he* was! Male heads
didn't swivel when Ella walked down the street because she had
neither the length of leg nor the curves usually deemed necessary
to attract such attention. Why on earth could he be making *her* such
an offer?

'But we don't even know each other,' she framed dazedly. 'You're
a stranger...'

'If you live with me I won't be a stranger for long,' Nikolai pointed out with monumental calm. And the very sound of that inhuman calm and cool forced her to flip round and settle distraught eyes on his lean darkly handsome face.

'You can't be serious about this!'

'I assure you that I am deadly serious. Move in and I'll forget your family's debts.'

'But it's a *crazy* idea!' she gasped.

'It's not crazy to me,' Nikolai asserted. 'When I want anything, go after it hard and fast.'

Her lashes dipped. Did he want her like that? Enough to track her down, buy up her father's debts, and try and buy rights to her and her body along with those debts? The very idea of that made her dizzy and plunged her brain into even greater turmoil. 'It's immoral... it's blackmail.'

'It's definitely *not* blackmail. I'm giving you the benefit of a choice you didn't have before I came through that door,' Nikolai Drakos fielded with a glittering cool. 'That choice is yours to make.'

'Like hell it is!' Ella fired back. 'It's a complete cheat of a supposed offer!'

Nikolai sent her a gleaming sideways glance. 'No the real cheat was you kissing me the way you did last year and then saying no and acting as if I had grossly insulted you,' he murmured with lethal quietness.

'You *did* insult me!' Ella flung back, her cheeks hot as fire while she wondered if her refusal that night had started off his whole chain reaction. What else could possibly be driving him?

Nikolai straightened lazily as he opened the door. 'If you take offence that easily, maybe it's just as well that the answer is no.'

Visit **www.millsandboon.co.uk/lynnegraham**
to order yours!

MILLS & BOON

MILLS & BOON®

Mills & Boon have been at the heart of romance since 1908... and while the fashions may have changed, one thing remains the same: from pulse-pounding passion to the gentlest caress, we're always known how to bring romance alive.

Now, we're delighted to present you with these irresistible illustrations, inspired by the vintage glamour of our covers. So indulge your wildest dreams and unleash your imagination as we present the most iconic Mills & Boon moments of the last century.

Visit **www.millsandboon.co.uk/ArtofRomance** to order yours!

MILLS & BOON®

Why shop at millsandboon.co.uk?

Each year, thousands of romance readers find their perfect read at millsandboon.co.uk. That's because we're passionate about bringing you the very best romantic fiction. Here are some of the advantages of shopping at www.millsandboon.co.uk:

* **Get new books first**—you'll be able to buy your favourite books one month before they hit the shops

* **Get exclusive discounts**—you'll also be able to buy our specially created monthly collections, with up to 50% off the RRP

* **Find your favourite authors**—latest news, interviews and new releases for all your favourite authors and series on our website, plus ideas for what to try next

* **Join in**—once you've bought your favourite books, don't forget to register with us to rate, review and join in the discussions

Visit **www.millsandboon.co.uk**
for all this and more today!